Praise for
Hand of Prophecy

"Expands the vision of its predecessor, delving deep
into the hearts of people whose brutal mores and
ambitions shield their all-too-human vulnerabilities."

Publishers Weekly (starred review)

"Strong fully-rounded characters
and strikingly garish images
of this far future life of slavery."

Locus

"The novel walks the fine line between passion
and melodrama, but the story is more than saved
by its tenacious honesty and triumphs
by its unflinching determination to illuminate
the vulnerabilities of even the most brutal characters."

Middlesex News

"A multi-layered novel. At the very core is fear
and love and hate, and each layer above it is different."

The SF Site

"Harsh and powerful,
HAND OF PROPHECY is a cracking good yarn,
full of color and incident."

S.M. Stirling

Other Avon Books by
Severna Park

SPEAKING DREAMS

Hand of Prophecy

Severna Park

AVON · EOS

AVON BOOKS, INC.
1350 Avenue of the Americas
New York, New York 10019

Copyright © 1998 by Severna Park
Visit our website at www.AvonBooks.com/Eos
Library of Congress Catalog Card Number: 97-27459
ISBN: 0-380-79158-7

First Avon Eos Paperback Printing: February 1999
First Avon Eos Hardcover Printing: March 1998

AVON EOS TRADEMARK REG. U.S. PAT. OFF. AND IN OTHER COUNTRIES, MARCA REGISTRADA, HECHO EN U.S.A.

Printed in the U.S.A.

WCD 10 9 8 7 6 5 4 3 2 1

—————————O—————————

FOR VICKI,
who reads every page,
over and over again;

FOR AVA,
who will always be with us;

and for Jo Clayton.

ACKNOWLEDGMENTS

This book would never have come to see the light of day without the help of the following people: Catherine Asaro, Juleen Brantingham, ElizaBeth Gilligan, Lois Gresh, and Brook & Julia West.

Many, many thanks to Margaret Dowell, who gave me the gift of more time.

Any acknowledgment would be glaringly incomplete without a huge, huge, HUGE thank-you to Richard Curtis and Jennifer Brehl for making this particular dream come true.

ONE

"We don't want trouble."

Freezing midnight wind rushed past my bare feet, through my thin clothes, scattering snow into Renee's bar. The sound of the weather muffled the crunch of Olney's boots behind me. It moaned over the voice of the Faraqui slaver, whose image flickered in the holoree's grainy projection by the counter.

"Rumors of Faraqui aggression in the Emirate Frontier are simply untrue. . . ."

"Shut the door, girl." Olney pushed into the dim, narrow room, shoved his Emirate Extension Service veterinary bag at me, and stamped and slapped himself against the Nayan winter.

"Frenna?" Renee straightened up by the counter, knee-deep in wrinkled gray sheets of foam packing wrap. The bar was empty except for the three of us and the holo projection. I looked around for Martine, who was always here. Tonight she wasn't. I knew why.

1

"Shut the damn *door*," said Olney.

"Yes, D'sha," I said, and turned to shut out the wind and cold for the deeper chill inside.

"We were foolish enough to fight the Emirate a hundred years ago . . ."

This was the same interview clip I'd seen a hundred times today on the Emirate Report. In the dimness of the bar, the slaver's white robes seemed to glow with the light of truth and honesty. The effect was a flaw in the old holoree's projection units, but it took the greed out of the slaver's face and made him seem less dangerous. His voice was a soft, insinuating whisper in the cool air.

"History speaks for itself. It would be suicide for us to resort to violence. The Emirate's new intrusion into the Faraque, our ancestral territory, leaves us philosophical, not angry. Troah, as we say."

The slaver smiled without any humor, creasing the broad stripe of blue paint across his eyes—the mark of his family's tribe.

Olney snorted next to me. "Lying son of a bitch," he said. "By next week we'll be fighting those bastards in the streets. What's a 'troah' anyway?" He turned his lean face toward me. "Shouldn't you know that, girl?"

I shrugged. It was an old word, a Faraqui word, and it left a bitter, metallic taste under my tongue. *Troah*. Great Grandmother H'alath had clucked it to herself as she'd cleaned up the dishes on my eighteenth birthday, my last year at home. My mother, born long after the Emirate invasion had freed my ancestors from their Faraqui masters, had wrung her hands, sobbing the word as the Emirate officials took me away—payment for government services on our conquered world. When things went out of control, and nothing could be done, it was a word the Faraqui had left with us to express a bottomless pessimism. *Troah*. It was the bad luck that had dropped me here on Bellea-Naya as

Olney Mallau's property. It was the fateful hand that would guide the Faraqui back to planets like this one.

"Frenna." Renee motioned me over to the counter. She'd started packing weeks ago—even before we'd heard the rumors of the Faraqui arming themselves, and long before the Emirate news turned so suspiciously reassuring. She had passage offworld and would be gone by morning.

Foam wrap squeezed flat and rubbery under my bare feet. "Where's Martine?"

Renee angled a thumb at the stairs that led to her apartment in the loft, but she had her eyes on the holoree, not me.

Olney shook off his coat, watching the projection. The slaver's face faded into the color-coded political map—the boundaries of known space—which had followed these dubious assurances all day long.

"They don't want trouble," said Olney, mocking the slaver, "but good manners sure as hell won't get their old worlds back." He threw his coat over a chair and sat. "And where are we?" He pointed at the yellow strip in the projection where the Frontier fell between the Emirate and the Faraque. "Between a rock a damn hard place."

Renee gave me a whiskey bottle and a water glass. "Pour your man a drink, Frenna."

I poured the glass full and set it on the countertop. The lack of real news couldn't quash the rumors about Faraqui attacks on a handful of Frontier border worlds, not so far from where we were, here on Bellea-Naya. It couldn't keep Emirate Extension workers, like Olney, from being trapped here if the Faraqui really did invade. And the numbing repetition of false information did nothing for the hundreds of native Nayans we'd seen at the ground station, shoving each other for offworld tickets.

But the lies on the news didn't matter to me.

"D'sha," I said to Renee. "How's Martine?"

3

Renee smoothed wisps of dark hair from her dark face. "I've told you, she'll be fine. You have to believe that."

I looked away from her, down at my dull reflection in the chipped varnish of the counter. Brown eyes in my own brown Jatahn face stared up. Slick black hair past my shoulders, covering the glint of the chain around my neck. The immediate future was no brighter than the shadows along the ceiling. The responsibility for Martine's quick and painless death was going to be mine, and then Renee would leave. By morning, I would be left with Olney and an impending war. I wrapped my hands together, afraid some genetic reflex might make them flutter with hopelessness, like my mother's.

"I know what Martine means to you," said Renee quietly. "You have to understand that I only want to do what's best for her. I need you to keep an open mind when she starts Failing."

"An open mind?" I said. "She's dying."

"You know the Faraqui word, *troah*, don't you? They've been saying it on the news all day."

I shrugged.

"Tell me what it means."

"It doesn't have anything to do with Failure," I said. "A *troah* is something you can't plan for."

Across the room, Olney slapped the table. "What do I have to do to get a drink around here?"

Renee lowered her voice. "*Troah* is a fundamental change, but it doesn't have to be a terrible thing. This isn't the kind of Failure you've ever seen before."

"She's dying, Renee. I'll get a needle. I'll make sure it's fast."

"You're not listening." She pointed at the veterinary bag. "You've got a scanner in there?" I nodded and she picked up the glass of whiskey. "I'll take care of Olney. Go upstairs and talk to her, but don't you dare do anything until I get there. Understand?"

I bit the inside of my lip. "Yes, D'sha."

*　　*　　*

Upstairs in the small apartment, Martine was asleep on the disheveled bed. She was a fragile-looking girl anyway, fair-haired and pale, but the slow, feverish beginnings of Failure were draining her. Sweat beaded along her neck, under her chain collar.

I set the veterinary bag on the floor. Around me, the last two years of Renee's life had been pared away from the walls and shelves to fit into a couple of packing cases. The kitchen was stripped to the sink and stove. Thin blue rugs were stacked in rolls under the only window. Nothing of Renee was left in the sparse apartment but the bedclothes.

And Martine.

I sat on the edge of the mattress and she opened her eyes.

"You're here," she said. "What time is it?"

"After midnight."

"What are they saying on the news?"

"Same old thing."

She rubbed her eyes with the heels of her hands. "The Faraqui could be in the middle of town before we hear about it on the 'ree." She sat up and saw the veterinary bag. "What's that for?"

I bent down to pull Olney's medical scanner out of the bag's frayed inside pocket.

Martine hugged her knees against her chest and shivered in the warm air. Her sleeveless nightshirt didn't cover the slave ID number that had been burned into her left shoulder twenty years ago, a deep, hard-edged scar in the scatter of freckles. Three summers ago, when we'd made tenuous, furtive love in the meadow behind the bar, it was her brands that seemed so out of place. On Martine, they seemed like temporary marks that might vanish if she ignored them long enough, or if she could dress in something other than her worn white slave uniform.

Martine dabbed at the sweat on her neck. "Hell of a

5

way to end things." She took my hand and squeezed it. "Will you miss me when I'm gone?"

She really believed she was going to be all right. She sounded as sure of it as Renee. "What do you think?" I whispered.

She ran her fingers over my knuckles. "I don't know, Fren. When you first got here, we had something going on, but I was never sure if that was because you felt something for me, or you just needed a friend."

"What difference does it make now?"

"Now that I'm Failing, you mean?" She glanced at the scanner's palm-sized screen as I changed the calibration, from animal to human. "I think you've always been too afraid of that. When you found out what kind of time I had left, it scared all the feeling out of you. One day you were glad to be with me and out of Olney's way. The next day, you were different."

"You were sleeping with Renee," I said. "I didn't think you were interested."

"I don't mean the sex." Her damp hand tightened on mine. "I mean you changed. You . . . you retreated. You gave up something. Like a change of heart."

"You mean I stopped fighting Olney."

She nodded slowly. "I'll never forget the first day Olney dragged you into the bar. He was so sure he'd gotten a great deal when he bought you. He was positive that you were going to scrape and smile and do for him. And he kept bragging about how you were a virgin, when he'd obviously been at you for hours."

"Stop it, Martine."

"The girl from Ahmedi-Jatah," she said. "It sounds so much more exotic than where I'm from. What did you say 'Jatahn' meant in Faraqui-speak?"

"Favored Ones," I said. "Martine, let's talk about something else."

"Like what?" she asked. "My future? Or yours?" She tapped the scanner. "Tell me what it says."

"You know what it says." I turned the screen so she could see the graph of her own lagging cell-growth.

Her soft mouth went a little thinner, a bit more pale. "So," she said. "That's how Failure looks."

What she could see on the scanner was an emotionless shadow of the damage underway inside her. Two decades ago, Martine had been marched out of her village on Bey-Kinjain, another liberated, ex-Faraqui world in the Emirate Frontier, the same as Bellea-Naya or Ahmedi-Jatah. Her parents, neighbors, relatives, had all waved sad, brave good-byes as Martine and a hundred other Kinjains, no older than twenty-two, no younger than eighteen, were lined up and injected by Emirate officials with what was commonly known on the Faraqui worlds as the Drug.

It wasn't really a drug. It was a virus. But except for three years of incidental learning at Olney's indifferent knee, I wouldn't have known that.

Martine traced the edge of the yellow graph on the scanner's black screen. Inside the right angle of numbered increments, a red line and a green line quivered together, traveling downwards at a long, slow angle.

"Which one's the Virus?" she asked.

"Red is for life signs," I said. "Green is the Drug."

"The Virus," she said again. "Don't patronize me, Frenna. I know it's not medicine."

I didn't understand why she cared. "What you see is the reaction of the antibodies," I said. "You can't see the Virus. You can only see what it does." Or what it wasn't doing. In Martine's case, the Virus wasn't creating antibodies at an inhumanly rapid rate. It wasn't healing and protecting her from her own natural aging process. It wasn't keeping her young anymore—healthy, strong and sterile as a mule—the way it had for the last twenty years. The symbiosis in her body, which the Faraqui had engineered centuries ago for their gene pool of slaves, was finished. The Virus had drained her, mutated, and now it was dying, leaving her to Fail.

There was only one thing I knew of from three long years of veterinary servitude with Olney that would help her.

I turned the scanner off. "I brought you something," I mumbled to the dark screen.

She leaned closer. "You came to kill me."

I nodded, fighting down pointless tears.

Her pale face went tense and serious. "Is Failure just another *troah* for you, Fren? Bad luck, fateful hand, and all that? Is that how you'll think about it when it's time for you to die?" She waited for me to say something. "Is it going to be different for you because your people were special to the Faraqui a hundred years ago? Is Failure easier for a Favored One?"

I stared at her. "We're *not*. We've *paid* for that."

Martine shrugged. "You're still paying. The Emirate's kept your entire planet restricted ever since the invasion because your people were collaborators. Now with the news the way it is, they're afraid you'll go back to your old masters."

"We're not traitors," I said hotly.

"You're the one who keeps telling me that loyalty is genetic." She twined her arm through mine. The heat of her fever made her skin seem blister-thin. "What keeps us in collar isn't loyalty, or genes." She touched the chain around her pale throat. "You're the insurance policy for your whole family. If you run off, the Emirate goons'll go after your brother and sisters." She studied my face. "How does it feel to be a hostage?"

I stared past her. "It's traditional for the oldest to go into service for the Emirate. It's payment for what they've done for us."

She almost laughed. "You *are* a hostage. We *both* are,

but at least I'm not stuck in your *troah* denial. What if you didn't have to worry about your family?" She leaned closer, hot in my ear. "Olney's nothing but a bastard. Why don't you leave?"

"That's a stupid question," I said. "I can't."

"Can't you?" She twisted around so she could look into my face. "There's a war coming, Fren. Jatah's no farther from Faraqui space than we are right now. If the Faraqui take Jatah, and your family hasn't gotten offworld, they fall right into collar again. No one'll care about your sacrifices for Olney. You could leave."

"If it's so easy, why don't you leave Renee?"

"For one thing," said Martine, "she doesn't get plastered and rape me."

"So I should just run," I said. "That's what you're saying? After tonight, I should just get out of here, run for the ground station and see how far I get?"

"No," she said, started to say more, but I cut her off.

"Should I find a way into Olney's accounts for money?" I demanded. "What if someone calls him from the ground station to see if I'm supposed to be buying an offworld pass? I could steal some clothes and a pair of shoes—I could look just like a free woman, but what happens if the police get suspicious and scan me? When they figure out I'm a runaway, who's going to help me when they break my legs?"

"Fren—"

"And what happens if I do get away?" I asked. "What if I get all the way to Emirate space. Who do I know there? Where do I go? How do I get a job without an ID?" I took a shaky breath. "I've thought about it, Martine. I quit thinking about it, because there aren't any good answers."

Her blue eyes were dark and serious. "There are." She squeezed my arm, very hard. "I know you're not going to believe this," she said, "but my Fail's not going to kill me.

I'll be alive tomorrow. I'm leaving with Renee. I want you to come with us."

There was no doubt in her voice, not a tremor of it.

"Renee told you that?" I whispered. "You know it isn't true. She's just making it harder." I reached for the veterinary bag. "I can make it—"

"Quick and painless?" Sweat beaded under her lower lip and she shook her head. "She told me I'd have to fight. I'm ready. She did it. I can do it."

"What do you mean, *she* did it?"

Martine ran her fingers over her brands. "Renee's marked like we are, Frenna."

I blinked in disbelief. "Marked? You mean *branded*?"

Martine nodded.

"Then she's a runaway. She's changed clothes, she's—"

"She's not a runaway slave," said Martine. "She's too old."

She was right. The Virus was designed to affect an age group between eighteen and twenty-two, holding us in that youthful stasis until the day we Failed. Renee was in her late twenties. "I've seen free people with brands, Martine," I hissed. "Back on Jatah I saw—"

"You told me," she said. "You saw a free guy with a brand on his ass, and it was some kind of sex thing he did with his slaves. That's not what she is. She was a slave. She belonged to a woman in the Diplomatic Corps. She ran away and she survived her Failure. Now she's going to help me get through it."

Her expression made my chest ache. "How can you believe that? How can you *think* about believing that?"

"Suppose it's true, Frenna. Suppose you could be free of the Virus, and not drop dead at the end of—what do you have left? Seventeen years?"

"It isn't possible, Martine."

"I think it is. I've checked everything she's told me. I found her in the Slave Registry. She should have Failed and died six years ago, but she didn't." Martine put her fingertips against my cheek. "Even if the laws were different, even if we had all the money we could spend, none of us can escape what's inside of us. You're a slave until the day you die because of the Virus. Olney counts on it. All the free people count on it." She let her fingers drop to my shoulder. "What would you do if you were free?"

I bit down on my tongue, hard enough to taste blood.

She let out a disappointed hiss. "Is this what three years of being with Olney's done to you? You're afraid to use your imagination? Or are you afraid he wouldn't like it?"

"I don't care what he likes."

She nodded. "You can handle him. He's only a bastard when he drinks too much. If you thought you could be free, it might make the next seventeen years with him unbearable. All you can think about is how fast you can put me out of my misery. Like I was an animal."

Raw heat in my throat crept up to sting behind my eyes. "I'm trying to help." If the fever didn't kill her, the cell-damage would. She would thrash out the last seconds of her life, her body wound up tight with pain, while she hung onto the fantasy Renee had built for her.

Martine smoothed strands of bright hair. "Maybe I'm just wrong about you. You're Jatahn, Favored to the core. It's been a hundred years, and you still can't shake off the Faraqui."

I got off the bed, trembling.

She watched me, pale as paper. "Everything could change, Frenna. Once Failure isn't the end of us, we're free. We're all free."

I turned toward the stairs, but she caught my arm.

"Don't leave," she said. "Please. If I'm wrong, then you can bury me tomorrow. If I'm right—" She shivered and hunched over her knees. "Get Renee," she said. "Hurry."

I swung around, into the dark, narrow passage that led down to the bar. Renee, the offworld stranger who'd surprised us both with her kindness, was nothing but a liar. Martine, grounded in good sense for as long as I'd known her, had fallen for every word. I stumbled down the cold stone stairs, too tight in my throat to breathe, eyes full of scalding tears. Fairy-tale promises had no place in a twenty-year sentence. Not in Martine's, and not in mine.

Renee was at the bottom of the stairs, standing there, full of false concern.

"Is she . . . ?" She stopped. "She told you."

This betrayal was so deep, it could have split the floor. It was so obvious, I should have seen it the day she'd walked in. My fury scorched the ceiling and roared around the room. It swung my fist out in a cold, tight ball to connect with Renee's chin. Bone cracked on bone and her head jerked. My hand hurt. My arm hurt. Renee stumbled backwards, covering her face, but not the shock in her eyes.

The heat beside me was Olney. His animal bellow soured the air with the stink of whiskey and manure. The hammer of his fist hit me hard, like a bad, recurring dream.

Outside the bar, in the middle of Kagda's deserted main street, Olney shook me until the pinpoint stars blurred overhead.

"What the hell's wrong with you?" The words boiled out in a cloud of steam, echoing off stone walls of close-packed houses. "For the last two years that woman's fed you, and coddled you and looked the other way when you diddled her girl." He shook me harder, and the side of my head throbbed. "That's how you pay her back? Where's your goddamn gratitude?"

He shoved me away. I reeled sideways, barefoot over sharp ruts in the frozen, unpaved mud, tripping over the front steps of some other lightless building. My knees banged down on frozen dirt, and I huddled in the dark. The dull glow from Renee's upstairs window swam above me in the indigo shadows, a disappointed yellow eye.

Cold wind cut between me and Olney. He pulled his bulky coat closer, stiff with manure, stained with animal blood. "Serve you right if I left you here when they evacuate us." He swayed in the freezing night. "How'd you like that, girl? You want to be the welcoming committee for those Faraqui bastards? Think they'd be glad to see you, Favored One?"

He staggered over and bent down, breathing the night's worth of liquor into my face. He wound icy fingers under the warm chain around my neck and grabbed my chin. "You know what I say about this war? Let 'em have their damn planets. Let 'em breed their slaves. Then people like me'll get what they pay for instead of Faraqui-bred looks that don't mean anything. Ahmedi-*Jatah*."

He yanked me up and I twisted to look back at the bar. Two silhouettes stood in the upstairs window. Renee put her arm over Martine's thin shoulders. Martine put her palm against the glass, a gesture to hold me where I was, or to wave good-bye.

Olney lurched down the main street, heading for the Emirate compound on the outskirts of town. I plodded behind him, and the shadows vanished into the black corners of tile roofs. My feet scraped frozen mud, counterpoint to the crunch of Olney's boots, arguing with each step. *What if? Never. What if? Never.*

Troah. The word was a metallic taste in my mouth.

At the far end of the main street, a white wall blocked the view of the Extension Residences. The wall was low enough to climb, but high enough to separate the Emirate compound from the rest of town. The steel security gate was wide open, as usual. I stood inside, staring at the glitter of frost on the concrete while Olney wrestled the gate shut.

Predicting the exact minute of a slave's Failure wasn't possible, but at the end of twenty years, there were a couple of weeks on either side of the two-decade mark when it was bound to happen. Renee had started packing weeks ago. I twisted my fingers together, numb enough to ask myself the next question.

Had she bought offworld passage for Martine, even though she knew Martine would Fail?

And if Martine was so insistent about me leaving with them tomorrow, was there a ticket for me too?

Behind me, a door creaked and I turned to see a shaft of yellow light spilling out from the first-floor common room of the Agricultural residence. One of the Emirate environmentalists waved from inside.

"Hey, doc," she shouted at Olney. "Seen Kabe?"

"Haven't seen shit." Olney gave the gate a final yank and started in my direction.

I hurried ahead of him, but the woman stopped me at the door.

"Have you seen my boy, Frenna?"

I shook my head. Her slave had disappeared before dawn this morning, panicking at the nonexistent news. He might get as far as the ground station at Kagdel'aba, but certainly no further. If thousands of free people couldn't find a way to escape their own planet, there was no hope for Kabe.

"Face it, Leta," said Olney. "Your boy's gone. He's long gone, and the next call you get'll be from the cops when they pick him up at Kagdel'aba with the rest of the runaways."

Leta smoothed her dark hair with both hands, a gesture that reminded me of Renee. I slid past her, into the warmth of the commons.

Tonight, like last night, all the chairs in the room were packed around the holoree in the corner. The Emirate Report announcer floated at eye-level, muttering the news, while Extension Service staffers sat together, watching the same thing over and over, waiting for some new grain of information.

One of the men, a mechanical engineer from Newhall, looked up as we came in. "Seen Kabe?" he asked Olney.

Olney slung his coat over a chair. "Hell, no."

"Kabe's got more brains than any of us," said the woman next to the engineer, a poultry specialist from New DeKastri. "At least he's trying to get out. We'll just sit until the Faraqui come pounding on the gate."

"Don't worry." Olney sat heavily. "I locked it."

The engineer let out a nervous laugh.

On the holoree, the Faraqui slaver smiled guilelessly. *"We don't want trouble . . ."*

"Why do they keep showing that?" demanded the poultry specialist. "Are we supposed to feel safer every time we see it?"

"Don't you feel reassured?" Olney's voice grated in the warm air. He waved his arms in a wide, cynical gesture. "The government wouldn't lie to us about something this important, would it? God knows, they told us the truth about this place."

The clip of the slaver faded into a close-up of two huge, vaguely transparent animals. Holos from some arena. The slaves inside the two projections were just visible. One was a tall, muscular girl, barechested except for an emerald-green sash across her shoulders. The shot froze and bright green lettering appeared, announcing the dates and times of the next competition.

Olney snorted. "I wouldn't mind the war so much if they'd just run the sports news. I haven't seen a score in days."

The poultry specialist gave him a distracted grin. "At least it's a real war, Olney. Those fights are fake. Everyone knows that."

"Sure they're real," said Olney. "They wouldn't run 'em if they weren't *real*."

As tanked as he was, Olney would probably be up until dawn. His rooms were on the second floor, private for the moment, and quiet. I needed time to think, and I had work to do for him before tomorrow. I started across the room to the stairs, and realized I didn't have the veterinary bag.

I looked around and didn't see it—not by the door or by Olney's muddy boots, slumped one over the other by his chair. Had I brought it down from Renee's apartment? No. The bag was still by Renee's bed, right where I'd left it.

"We don't want trouble . . ."

Around the holoree, the Extension workers shushed each other and leaned in to listen to the beginning of the news loop again.

When I was sure none of them were watching, I let myself out into the cold night.

Outside, the stars were bright as spotlights, competing with Naya's half-dozen asteroid moons. I hurried across the courtyard and scrambled over the wall, leaving curls of vapor where my body touched the icy concrete.

I didn't need to be anywhere near Martine to know that her Failure was well underway. It might be short, so severe, it would be over in a few hours. Or it could go on for days, cycling through convulsions, radical changes in body temperature, pummeling her internally until her organs gave out, one by one.

One thing would cut Failure short. In the bottom of Olney's medical bag was a bottle of Thanas, a toxin so deadly, a few drops in the bloodstream would kill anything, anyone, instantly.

I started to run.

The bar was unlocked. I banged the door open and stumbled in, noisy as hell, but Renee was upstairs, and the bar was empty. The holoree was still on. The interview clip with the Faraqui slaver glimmered in the dimness, a muttering white face under its blue stripe.

Renee heard me coming up the stairs and looked up

from where she was hunched over Martine. "About time," she said.

Martine's coppery hair tangled over the pillows. Sheets twisted around her ankles in knots. I could hear her struggling for breath. My heart crowded so high in my throat, I thought I would choke. The medical bag sat next to the bed, just where I'd left it, but now it was wide open. Olney's medical scanner lay next to the pillow.

Renee held the scanner out at me, like a lure. "I can't get an accurate reading on this thing."

I took it, not meeting Renee's eyes, turned it off, and shoved it into my pocket. Martine's eyes followed me, dull blue chips in a waxy, colorless mask. I squatted next to the medical bag, groping in its dirty corners. I found a plastic case of hypoderms under the steri-packs and suture kits. On the bottom, gritty with barn dirt, I found the palm-sized, hexagonal shape of the Thanas bottle.

I pulled out the bottle and the hypos. Renee saw the Thanas. She made a grab for it, but I jerked away.

Renee stood up. "Is that why you came back?" she asked. "To kill your friend?"

Martine groaned, eyes squeezed shut.

Angry words caught in my mouth. I fumbled with the pack of hypoderms and managed to get one out. The rest of the needles spilled onto the floor, pattering and rustling in their sterile sleeves. My hands were too quivery to hold onto the empty box. It fell and the sound of hollow plastic echoed off the bare walls. The cap on the Thanas bottle was crusted shut, black liquid crystallized along the edges. I wrenched the cap open.

Renee eased toward me. "Martine's told you what I am."

"She said you were a freed slave." I backed up until my elbow touched the stone wall. "I don't know what you are." I peeled the sterile sleeve off the hypo with my teeth and sweaty fingers. I punched the needle through the top

17

of the Thanas bottle. Oil-black liquid shivered into the cartridge.

Renee came closer, less than an arm's length. She pulled her shirt down over her left shoulder. A brand shadowed deep in her flesh. I took a good look.

Her identification number was much lower than mine or Martine's. If it was real, Renee's time in collar would have started close to thirty years ago. But it didn't prove anything. I pulled the needle out of the Thanas bottle. My hands were trembling like an old woman's.

Renee watched my face carefully. "Do you ever think about what you'd be doing if you were free?"

I shook my head, a spasm of denial.

"Favored One." She pulled her shirt closed.

"Better," I whispered, "than whatever you are."

Without warning, her hand shot out, fast as an eyeblink. I jerked back, but the wall was behind me. She wrenched the hypo out of my sweaty grip and held it up in the air, well out of reach.

"Now you listen to me," she snapped. "You want to be a good little Jatahn girl and take your lumps for the next seventeen years? It's your business, but Martine and I are leaving in the morning." She hurled the needle across the room. It clinked against the stone wall, and clattered on the floor. Renee held her hand out for the Thanas bottle, hot as a coal in my other fist. "You can stay and see how this is done, or you can go home to Olney. I don't care what you do, but I will tell you this." She pulled me close enough to feel the angry heat in her face. "If you leave now, you'll spend the rest of your life wondering what the hell happened in here tonight."

Martine quivered on the bed. The frame rattled where it touched the wall. Renee shook me. "Well?"

I couldn't leave. No matter what kind of craziness I was about to witness, I knew I couldn't leave. I put the bottle in her palm, and her dark face relaxed, just a fraction.

"Come over here," she said. "Give me a reading."

I followed her to the bed, half nauseated, and took the scanner out of my pocket.

Red for life signs, green for the Virus. Both indicators were dropping. On a free person, there would be no green line, no morbid echo of antibodies on the screen. Diagnostics and interventions would flash in the margins. For Martine there was no hope of survival, and so, no medical options. All the scanner would do was record her death, one downward degree at a time.

The green line fluttered on the graph and Martine jerked. Her back arched. Her mouth stretched wide in a silent gasp. Renee grabbed her shoulders, holding her down. Martine's body shuddered, harder and harder, until her arms and legs shook loose of the bed, flopping like a doll's.

I covered my mouth and watched the seconds pass on the scanner, unable to make myself watch Martine. Ten. Twenty. Forty. The two lines steadied, and Martine shivered, breathless on the soaked sheets.

"Give me a reading," said Renee.

I turned the scanner so she could see the screen. The two indicators were less than a finger's width from the bottom of the graph. When the Viral indicator touched bottom, it would be over.

Renee reached under the bed and pulled out a small metal box, silverish, with cheap, stamped decorations. She opened it to show me a half-dozen plastic packets, each the size of a thumbnail. "You know what these are?"

"Slapneedles," I said. They were the smallest of the palm-hypoderms, designed for a quick, premeasured injection. There was a case of them in Olney's medical bag, each loaded with tranquilizers.

She turned a packet over to show me the pharmaceutical name of the contents. *Virasi lymphoma: appropriatus.*

"The common name is Virevir," said Renee. "Ever heard of it?"

I shook my head.

Renee smoothed the coppery curls from Martine's damp forehead. "Do you know what the problem is with the Faraqui Virus?"

"What?" I whispered.

"Free people have always been jealous of their slaves." She took one of the slapneedles out of the silver box and held it in her palm. "Your slave stays young, pretty, practically invulnerable, while you spend twenty years getting older. When the Faraqui first started selling infected slaves, centuries and centuries ago, the Emir devoted a huge amount of research to curing them. All they could find was that the cures were more deadly than the disease." She dropped the packet, the Virevir, into my palm. "Except for this."

Virasi lymphoma: appropriatus.

"Think about it," said Renee. "You've got some basic medical knowledge. You pay attention to what Olney's doing. What's *Virasi*?"

Next to me, Martine shuddered. Her fingers spasmed, grabbing at the sheets. "*Virasi* is a virus," I said.

"And *appropriatus*?"

"It's a colonizing virus," I said.

Renee nodded. "The Faraqui Virus is a colonizer. *Appropriati* reproduce like parasites—very difficult to kill. Now. What's *lymphoma*?"

I had no idea. On the scanner, Martine's readings quivered at the brink of another plunge. "Renee—"

"Lymphoma," said Renee quietly, "is a cancer. This *appropriatus* is a tailored, colonizing, viral cancer which takes over the immune system. It reproduces fast enough to replace what the Faraqui Virus has destroyed, and it rehosts."

Martine shook harder. Her teeth chattered and ground.

"It does what?" I said.

"Rehosts," said Renee. "It repairs and revives."

"It can't," I said. "Cancers don't work that way."

"This one does," said Renee. "It was designed by the Emir's own doctors."

"What?"

"I told you," said Renee, "they've been working on it for centuries. Not for their slaves. For themselves." She pointed at the packet I was holding. "That's the end of society as we know it."

I stared at her. "It couldn't work. When the Virus dies, the cell damage is done. She'll die no matter what's in her system."

Renee touched her own shoulder, her hidden brands. "Failure's only half of why we die, Frenna. The other half is that we're doing what we're required to do. Twenty years of submission is what kills us. Our survival—*your* survival—depends on what you believe is possible."

"You can't tell me that all it takes is a positive attitude—"

The scanner's display screen flickered. Martine gasped, stiff-armed, eyes suddenly wide. The thin color in her face evaporated.

Renee crouched over her. "What's the scanner say?"

"She's dying," I whispered.

Renee glared at me. "Give me a *reading*."

I looked down at the plunging indicators. "Six percent of normal levels."

Martine gave a strangled wail. Her life signs arced downward while she struggled against Renee's weight. Her breathing turned to sobs. The convulsion pummeled her until she lay panting in a tangle of her clothes, lips peeled away from her teeth.

"Tell me what her levels are."

I clenched my teeth hard enough make my jaw ache. "Four percent."

"When she's at one percent, you'll inject her."

21

"Me?" I said. "Why me? You've done this before."

"You need to learn, Jatahn."

The silver box of Virevir glinted in the dim light—false, tempting jewels. I ripped the plastic away from the slapneedle. *What if?* hissed the top half of the sterile strip. *Never*, whispered the bottom.

The scanner pulsed and Martine choked, her face straining, mouth open. The indicators vanished and reappeared even lower, red and green lines, wound together.

"Where is she now?" demanded Renee.

"Two percent." The two lines angled toward the bottom of the graph, wavering under hot tears that ran down my nose, onto the screen. Martine let out a feeble shriek. The seizure flung her back and forth and gave way suddenly. Her muscles loosened. She sprawled on the bed, arms and legs at awkward, gangling angles.

Renee pushed me down onto the corner of the mattress, perching me beside Martine's death-mask face. She grabbed the scanner. "You can't wait too long." For the first time, she looked worried, even scared. "There's a point where the Faraqui Virus gives out, but the cell damage isn't complete. That's when the Virevir gets its best hold. Recovery is faster."

The slapneedle was standard—heat-activated adhesive held it to my palm. The point stuck out like a thorn. Grab and squeeze. I hesitated. What kind of injection? Intravenous? Subcutaneous?

Renee wrapped her long damp fingers over mine and forced my hand against Martine's throat. Arterial. I felt Martine's thin, hot skin give way under the needle. A drop of blood slicked my palm. For a second, her carotid pounded against my fingers—then nothing.

I listened for her breathing. All I could hear was myself trying not to cry. Martine was dead, limp with death, still warm with it.

"Stay alive," hissed Renee. "Martine, you stay with me, you hear? Don't you dare die on me."

"She's dead," I whispered, but Renee pushed me away. "Martine? Martine, stay with me, girl."

I peeled the empty slapneedle off my palm while tears rolled down my face. Renee had made Martine suffer. She'd made me a part of the torture. Even if Martine had agreed to every awful second, Martine was a slave. She couldn't refuse. Renee would leave in the morning, abandoning me to Olney, with no explanation for staying out all night. Visions of being alone with him for the next seventeen years burned my eyes.

Renee straightened. "Take a reading, Frenna." Her voice was different. Sad? What in the world had she expected?

I wiped my eyes and looked down at the scanner.

Diagnostics blinked in emergency reds—low blood pressure, weak pulse. They were readings for a free woman going into shock.

For a long, strange second, I was positive that the scanner was reading Renee.

Martine took a breath. Her chest quivered.

Renee took her hand. "Tell me what you see."

I stared at the readings. "She's alive," I said. "She's alive. She's. . . ." Free. I couldn't make the word come out.

But she was. In the lower left corner of the screen, the cancer was metastasizing through her lymphatic system at a geometric rate. Something that would never have shown for a slave infected with the Faraqui Virus.

Renee tucked a blanket around Martine's shoulders. She turned to me and for a moment, I could see all twenty of her years in collar, hidden behind her eyes, buried beneath her apparent age.

I cleared the screen and aimed the scanner at Renee. Everything was normal. No Faraqui Virus. No cancer. "You don't have it," I said.

"Virevir is a temporary solution," said Renee. "Like I said, the cure can be worse than the disease."

"But how did you get rid of it?"

"I know a good doctor," said Renee. She leaned forward, elbows on her knees. "She started out a lot like you. She's the one who told me about these." Renee tapped the metal box. "And she introduced me to some of the others."

"Others?" I echoed.

"I'm certainly not the only one," said Renee. "It isn't difficult, but things do go wrong. Not everyone survives." She rubbed her temples. "I've seen people die from all sorts of things after they've been freed. With your background, you could be very useful."

My mouth went dry. "What about Olney? Or the police?"

"I don't think the police are as interested in runaways as they are in keeping order around the ground stations. Believe me, Frenna. I wouldn't make the offer if I didn't think it was worth the risk."

"I can't just leave. I have family . . ."

Renee shook her head. "The Faraqui are already inside the Frontier. Even if it's not on the news, everyone knows it. The Faraqui want a strong foothold, and they'll go to their collaborators first. They may already be on Jatah. They may even be welcome." She touched my arm. "Staying with Olney won't protect anyone."

Martine stirred on the bed and opened her eyes. "Don't argue," she whispered. "Just come."

TWO

Through the apartment's single window, red running lights glinted in the dawn sky. A skimmer's blunt shadow lowered into the street outside. Even through the stone walls, the static bristle of antigravs made the back of my neck crawl.

"It's a skimmer," I said. "Olney—"

"It's a shuttle from the ground station," said Renee. "I called them last night. They're here to pick us up."

Downstairs, someone pounded on the door.

"It's your decision, Frenna."

Favored One. I would be a runaway, a fugitive. And one day, a long time from now, I would be free. A thousand years of Faraqui breeding made my breath come slow and hard.

"I'll go," I whispered.

Renee nodded, relieved. "Let them in downstairs. We'll be ready in a minute."

The weight off my shoulders made my head feel like it

had been detached from my body. I floated down the stairs, into the graying darkness of the bar. The holo was still on, repeating the ersatz news. The Faraqui slaver glared at me, his voice hushed in the stale air.

"Troah, *as we say* . . ."

I opened the door and found myself face-to-face with Olney.

His dirty coat hung open over his rumpled coverall. He hadn't shaved or washed, and the dull morning light picked out the roughness in his face. He knotted his fist in the front of my shirt and jerked me up on my toes.

"Who said you could leave the compound?"

My breath smoked between us, vanishing into the cold. Things I had tried never to notice about him came abruptly into sharp focus. A broken net of purple capillaries wove under his wide pores. The skin around his mouth was an unhealthy gray. He was an ugly man. A hateful, ignorant bastard. He was a man to sneak away from in the dead of night, because he was the kind of man who would never let go of the things he thought he had a right to.

Behind me, the click of boots on stone was Renee, helping Martine down the stairs.

"Olney?"

He let go of me and frowned at Martine. "What's the matter with her?" His expression changed to hungover comprehension. "She's Failing?"

Renee eased Martine into a chair and came over to stand next to me. She glanced at Olney's blue Extension Service skimmer—what she'd mistaken for the ground station shuttle.

"You could make some quick money, Olney," she said.

"Yeah?" Olney snorted. "How?"

She put her arm around me. "I'll give you six hundred for her."

Olney laughed. "How much company do you need, Renee?"

Renee dug in her pocket and pulled out a cash memcard. She tried to give it to him, but he just shrugged.

"I can't sell her," he said. "She's government property."

"Take the money," said Renee. "Make up a story. Tell your friends she ran away."

Olney shrugged again. "Can't," he said. "Anyway, I need her."

Static lifted the hair along my arms, like an animal hackle. Another shadow in the dawn sky became the ground station shuttle—larger than Olney's skimmer and the color of copper. It settled into the street beside Olney's skimmer with a soft, hydraulic hiss.

Olney fastened his coat. "I've got work to do," he said, and made an impatient, irritated motion at me. "Let's go."

Renee's arm tightened over my shoulders. Her expectations were a thickness in the air.

"No," I said.

Olney raised an eyebrow. "Huh?"

"No," I said again.

"She's coming with me," said Renee. "You can take the money, or you can take a loss."

Across the street, the ground station shuttle opened its doors, and the pilot peered out.

Olney gave me a sour, dangerous glare. "Don't you have a few other people to consider, Favored One? Try not to make a stupid decision."

"I'm not," I said, but I could hear my own doubts.

"The Faraqui are in the Frontier by now," said Renee flatly. "Anyone can see that just by watching the news."

"I dunno," drawled Olney, "all I hear is that they don't want trouble."

"You know better than that, Olney," said Renee. "They've crossed the border. They're on their way to get their old territory back, and they probably went to Ahmedi-Jatah first. There are no more hostages."

"So now she can do whatever she wants?" Olney squinted at

27

me. He pushed up one sleeve, clenched and unclenched his fist.

"You're not going to knock her around," snapped Renee, "not with me standing here."

Olney grabbed my shirt. He yanked me out from under her arm, snaked his hand under my collar, twisted the chain tight enough to choke. I yelped and Renee lunged. Olney caught her in the stomach with one thick fist. Her mouth flew open in shocked, breathless surprise. Her eyes went wide and bulging and her free-woman's face disappeared for a second, like a mask coming off. Underneath was the slave she'd been—frightened, beaten—and to see that, still in her, was like watching my own face—fear that would never vanish, no matter how free I looked.

Renee staggered backwards. "Why can't you let her go?" she panted. "You'll be evacuated any day now. What difference does it make if she gets lost somewhere in transit?"

"It makes a difference to me," said Olney.

Renee smoothed her hair. She wiped her hands on her pants, slowly catching her breath, and she looked at me. "Don't forget your bag," she said. "It's upstairs." And she turned back to Martine.

I stared at the sky, thinking that my hot, helpless tears would freeze if I cried, but Olney's grip on my collar made my throat too tight for that. Had Renee left the *virasi lymphoma* for me? Was I supposed to take it as a parting gift and wait out my time with Olney in spite of everything? Was that the best any of us could do?

Olney stepped out of their way as Renee helped Martine out the door, across the street to the shuttle. Martine took one more look at me, her face ash-white. Renee didn't turn.

Olney let go of me. "Get my bag," he said, "you lazy piece of shit."

"Yes, D'sha," I said, and fled up the stairs.

In Renee's empty apartment, the bed was a rumple of

blankets and sheets. The medical bag was by the window. I dug into it, past the suture kits, the scatter of sleeved hypoderms, until I found a sealed plastic envelope—three slapneedles inside—hidden near the bottom and a mem-card ticket.

An offworld pass. My escape. I shoved the envelope into my pocket and got to my feet as the ground station shuttle lifted past the window.

From inside the shuttle, a pale hand pressed against dark glass. From downstairs, Olney was shouting my name.

I sat in the torn pilot's chair behind the skimmer's controls. Olney thumbed the square of black plastic that was the Authority key, and the antigravs vibrated through the dirty rubber matting on the floor.

He dropped into the backseat and I sat still, concentrating on keeping my face blank, watching his reflection inside the curved pane of the front window.

"What were you doing all night?" he said.

I thought about killing him, with Thanas and a needle. Would Renee have done that if she'd had a chance? Her frightened face flashed behind my eyes, and I pushed the idea aside.

"Well?"

"Nothing, D'sha." I wanted him to shut up. Above us, the ground station skimmer was nearly out of sight.

His reflection waved vaguely in the other direction. "Take us north," he said. "To Mosteph's."

I tapped the controls, and the skimmer lumbered upward.

From above, the blocky white government buildings in the Emirate compound were just as stark and out of place as they were on the ground. Icy pools of rainwater gleamed in the rutted dirt roads that led out of Kagda to nowhere in particular. Far ahead, the ground station shuttle dwindled to a glint in the pewter sky.

Mosteph's farm was thirty klicks west of the Kagdel'aba

ground station, twenty minutes by air. Or hours on foot. When did Renee's ship leave? I hadn't looked at the mem-card to see.

"She was Failing all night?" said Olney. "You had my bag. There's plenty of Thanas. Why didn't you kill her?"

The suspicion in his voice came out as saccharin interest. I blinked at the rush of ground below, avoiding his reflected eyes. We picked up speed. Harvested fields thinned rapidly to bracken, giving way to open plains. Dry yellows and russet browns stretched to the curve of the horizon.

"Well?" he said.

"Renee didn't want me to."

"I always figured she was too sentimental." He grunted. "Only Renee would buy offworld passage for a corpse."

Ahead, squat buildings gleamed dully, not the local white stone, but dark red alizarite, imported centuries ago from quarries in the Faraque. Our shadow rushed over the old slave village—once a breeding pen for human beings, now an official Emirate town. Emirate citizens, probably just as green-eyed and pale as their pure-blooded ancestors, formed a ragged column in the dry grass, making their way toward Kagdel'aba on foot.

Olney let his breath out through his teeth. "Look at 'em run." The seat creaked as he shifted, watching the straggle of refugees. "They've lived here for generations, but the first little hint that the Faraqui might show up again, and they take off. Anybody else'd stand their ground and fight." He kicked at my chair. "Why's that, Jatahn?"

"They're afraid," I said, "D'sha."

"Hell," said Olney, "I'm afraid. The damn Extension Service might just abandon us to make it look like it's safe to stay, Faraqui invasion or not. That scares me shitless. But if the Faraqui come, I'll fight." He threw a punch at the air. "Fight, you bastards," he muttered to the people on the ground.

This might have been the first time that Olney'd found

himself in a place that he wasn't free to leave, and maybe it gave him an inkling of what it felt like to be property—free one minute and trapped the next. But Olney had never been powerless.

Run, you bastards, I thought.

"They think they can get offworld, but they can't," said Olney. "Like Kabe. They'll never make it."

"Kabe?" I said. "They found him?"

Olney nodded. "The police called Leta this morning. They said he was dressed as a free man. You know how they figured out he was a runaway?"

The plastic envelope was a sharp edge in my pocket, digging into my thigh. I shook my head.

Olney's reflection bent toward me. "He tried to buy a ticket. He didn't have any identification to verify the voucher. It was a lot of money, and they started asking questions."

I pushed my tongue against the roof of my mouth. Renee and Martine. Two free women at the ground station, arm in arm, chains cut off their necks, their brands hidden under heavy coats. The image in my mind didn't seem quite so clear now, more like something in the distance, caught in glimpses through dense trees.

I tried to tell myself that the Virevir in my pocket was only an option. If I couldn't leave today, I could use it later.

Much later.

Mosteph's acreage started at the top of a steep white cliff that marked the end of the plains. The cliff shoved upwards, softening at the top to become a meandering bluff, obscured here and there by drifts of gray mist.

The rolling hills beyond the cliffs were just high enough to be considered mountains, soft-shouldered peaks with boulder-strewn valleys, and Mosteph owned them all. His Takinoshi horses, brown-bodied, with their distinct black dorsal stripe, scattered in the lower fields. Domestic reshie, heavier and less graceful than their wild, deerlike cousins, plodded up worn pathways to the feedlots behind long stone barns.

Our shadow flickered over harvested gardens and immaculate outbuildings. Below, slaves tended stock, raked down paths, swept away dead leaves. Upwind from the barn, ancient trees spread bare branches over the high walls of the Faraqui mansion where Mosteph had set up housekeeping.

Whenever we came here, Mosteph would look me over and tell Olney how much he admired the Faraqui breeding programs, their bloodlines and strict discipline. In fact, I suspected that the only reason Mosteph had any social contact with Olney was because of me. Mosteph's interest in the slavers' culture was too deep to be a hobby. He was as firmly established on Naya as the Faraqui had ever been, and all of his slaves were pure-blooded, straight from the Faraque.

Unlike the houses on the plains, his mansion had been built centuries ago as a living quarters for the slavers themselves. Mosteph maintained it as though he were head of the Faraqui clan, not the minor Emirate entrepreneur that he was. Slender alizarite towers spiraled up from each corner of the house. Solariums filled with greenery covered the balconies. Inside the walls, pathways wound through thickets of pruned trees, and fountains ran until they iced over in the winter. On Jatah, there were buildings like this, abandoned, but solid as temples. Even though the Faraqui had fled the Emirate invasion a century ago, their predatory souls had stayed; here on Naya, home on Jatah, all through the conquered Frontier. Long after settlers like Olney and Mosteph were gone, this mansion would remain. If the Faraqui found a way to reclaim their planets, their comforts would be waiting for them.

Mosteph's head houseboy waved us down between two other skimmers on the gravel pad outside the mansion's walls. One was a new model, imported at every expense from

Emirate space, no doubt, and that was Mosteph's. The other was a carryall, a small orbital shuttle, dented, patched and scratched from years of use.

Olney peered at the carryall as we settled on the ground. "Traders?" he muttered. "Or slavers?"

I popped the skimmer's cowling, and the houseboy leaned in. He was tall, with straight black hair, sapphire eyes and flawless, creamy skin.

He averted his gaze for Olney. "Good morning, D'sha." His voice was mannered, lilting, the way he'd been taught to speak in the School where the Faraqui had sent him, and where Mosteph had bought him.

"Where's your boss?" asked Olney.

The boy made a demure gesture toward the house.

Olney clambered out of the skimmer and stood in the frosty, overcast morning, scratching his neck. He nodded at the carryall. "Who's this?"

"One of D'Mosteph's acquaintances, D'sha," said the boy. "They're waiting for you inside."

Olney pointed past the skimmers to the slaves by the barn. "Looks pretty calm around here, what with the news, and all."

"D'sha?" asked the boy.

"Haven't you heard?" said Olney. "The Faraqui are on their way. They're coming to kick the Emirate out and take over their old worlds."

Of course the news was saying nothing of the kind. The Emirate Report was doing everything it could to squash these kinds of rumors.

"Doesn't that worry you?" asked Olney.

The boy shook his head, no emotion in his face.

Olney glanced at me, still hunched over the skimmer's controls. He reached over and ground his thumb against the Authority key until every light on the board went out.

"Bring my bag," he said.

*   *   *

Gray morning light filtered through one high window of Mosteph's parlor. There was a roaring fire in the hearth, but instead of being cozy, the room was smotheringly dark. Mosteph sat by the fireplace, a heavy-jawed black dog at his feet. Half a dozen of his slaves ducked around the edges of the parlor, weighted down with silver serving trays.

A free woman stretched out on the sofa on the opposite side of the small room, probably the owner of the carryall. Her dirty boots slumped on the carpet while she rested bare feet on an embroidered pillow. Her boy was scrawny, shirtless, standing right in front of the fire, sweating while he watched the flames in oblivious fascination.

Mosteph opened soft white hands at Olney. "So glad you could make it, Doctor. Meet Adrinne Martuk. Adrinne is my . . ." He pulled pale lips away from small teeth. "My representative in the less civilized parts of the Frontier."

"Pleasure," said Olney.

"Yeah," said Adrinne.

Olney dropped into a deep leather chair, his back to me. I never knew what I was supposed to do in Mosteph's house. Probably be as deaf and silent as the furniture until Olney wanted something.

One of Mosteph's girls slid a low stool under Olney's feet and gave him a glass of liqueur. She disappeared into the swells of brocade and handmade silk hung on the walls where some hidden passage swallowed her. When I looked around again, all Mosteph's servants were gone. The only slave left in the room was Adrinne's preoccupied boy. And me.

I stepped into the shadows by the door, where Olney could see me if he wanted to. I slid my hands into my pockets and found the plastic envelope Renee had left for me. Through the smooth plastic, the flat, square wads were the three slapneedle packets. The memcard ticket was rectangular. I ran my fingers over its corners. I could almost feel the name of the ship, the time of departure. The temptation to leave washed over me like hot water.

"We were just discussing the news," said Mosteph.

Olney swallowed his liqueur in a gulp. "I'm surprised you're still here," he said, and eyed Adrinne. "I saw your carryall. You've got a ship in orbit. You're taking passengers?"

"I could," said Adrinne, "but I'm not leaving."

Olney's face twitched.

Mosteph smoothed the dog's head. "Is it true that the Extension Service has no plans to evacuate its employees, regardless of what comes out of the Faraque?"

Olney shrugged, tight in his shoulders, trying not to look worried.

"That puts you in a great deal of danger, I would think," said Mosteph.

"Yeah," said Olney. "Well. Nothing's been decided, you know, from on-high. Everybody at the compound keeps talking about an evacuation, but . . ." He peered down into the liqueur glass, as though his answers were somewhere on the bottom.

Mosteph shifted in his chair. The dog shifted with him, its head dark as ebony in the firelight. "You and I have known each other long enough to appreciate each other's interests, Doctor. I understand your trepidation about being abandoned on Naya by the government. But as a student of Faraqui thought and culture, and as a friend, I feel my duty is to warn you that it might be more dangerous for you to leave."

"Are you *kidding*?" said Olney.

Mosteph raised an eyebrow. "Run your holo, Adrinne."

"You still owe me money for it," she said.

"And I'll pay you," he said. "Run your holo."

Adrinne snapped her fingers at the boy by the fire. "Breeni?"

The boy reached into his pockets. He gave her a folded

portable holoree from one and a memcard from the other. Adrinne twisted the holoree into its boxy shape and slid the card in. The air above the 'ree went opaque.

"The image isn't great." She fidgeted with the controls until the projection solidified over her lap: a grainy gibbous moon on velvet black, big as a serving platter. "We were running our jammers at capacity. Caused a lot of interference. But you can see what's going on." She stuck her finger through the image. "This is Aldi, in the F'shai System, just inside the Frontier. And these . . ." Her finger hovered over two white ships at the dark edge of the moon. "These belong to the Emirate. They're both part of a destroyer group, but they got too far away from the rest. Too nosy for their own good."

A bulky ship slid past the moon—a Faraqui transport with their tribal mark on the side—a simple, hieroglyphic eye. Conduits and power cables wormed underneath, leading to a smaller craft—a barge, which hung below the bigger ship.

I held still in the crush of musty brocade, watching as the cables snaked away from the barge, releasing it from the transport. The barge drifted downwards, streaked the moon's thin atmosphere and vanished. The transport picked up speed and disappeared off the edge of the holo.

"Okay," said Olney. "So what? They ditched a barge."

"Just watch, Doctor," said Mosteph.

The surface of the moon began to glow—red, then orange, then white hot. Heat billowed up from the surface toward the two orbiting white flecks. The flash of heat caught them like insects in fire. Both Emirate ships flared and vanished.

Olney chewed the end of his thumb. "What the hell was that?"

"A kind of thermal weapon," said Mosteph. "Reacts with a volcanic core, perhaps. Whatever it is, it looks to be a match for anything the Emirate can throw at it."

Adrinne leaned back on the sofa. "Whatever else you want to say about the Faraqui, they're patient bastards. It only took them a hundred years to figure out how to out-gun the Emirate."

"When was this?" asked Olney.

"Four days ago," said Adrinne.

Which meant the slavers were well within the Frontier, already swarming over the surface of my homeworld. I clutched at the envelope in my pocket, wondering if any-one in my family had managed to leave.

"They're coming this way?" Olney blinked nervously at Mosteph. "And you're still here?"

Mosteph nodded. "Which worlds do the Faraqui want most?"

"Everything they lost in the war." Olney waved vaguely at the dark room. "They'll want this too."

"Of course," said Mosteph, "but running to Emirate space is the worst thing you can do right now. If the Fara-qui can take on the Emirate fleet and win, the Emir himself won't be safe."

"All they've done is blow up a planet and a couple of ships," said Olney. "That's a long way from winning a war."

"Not that far," said Adrinne. "They're prepared. They'll blast everything in Emirate space, from Traja to Ankea."

"But they'll do their best not to damage their own terri-tories." Mosteph nodded at Olney. "A clever man would realize that his future is right here."

Olney dabbed sweat under his chin. "You sound like you've had a couple of conversations with these guys."

Mosteph laid his hands in his lap, one over the other. "The Faraqui are a proud, self-possessed people. They sur-vived the last invasion because they *believed* they could sur-vive. We need to show the proper respect for their traditions. Their tolerance hinges on our ability to make an offering of good faith."

"We?" barked Olney. "Good faith? You're living in their house. What kind of good faith is that? I don't care about their damn traditions—when the evacuation starts, I'll be first in line."

"If there is an evacuation," said Adrinne.

Mosteph nodded. "If there isn't, you should at least be aware of your options."

"My option is to get my ass out of here," said Olney.

"On a private ship?" said Adrinne. "Or a freighter? You better have a heap of cash, buddy."

There was a long silence, and I understood why Mosteph had called us and what he really wanted.

So did Olney. He sat up straight in his chair. "You want my girl. She's going to be your good-faith offering."

"I'll give you a good price," said Mosteph. "Enough to get a long way from the war."

Olney hesitated, probably wondering if he could get more out of Mosteph than Renee's offer of six hundred. He glanced around the room and saw me standing in the gloom by the door. "She's government property," he said. "I'd be in serious trouble if I sold her."

Mosteph smiled. "Now, Doctor," he said. "Would I let you down if you did me a favor?"

"I wouldn't pay too much," said Adrinne. "She doesn't look all that pure-blooded to me. I think she'd run first chance she got."

Mosteph raised a finger at Adrinne. "The Jatahn were the Faraqui's original breeding population, a thousand years ago. They were slaves, but they were also mythically important in Faraqui history. When the Faraqui lost Ahmedi-Jatah to the Emirate in the war, it was one of the things that sealed their defeat."

"That was a hundred years ago," said Olney doubtfully. "Jatah's been free, more or less, ever since. You think they're going to fall in line, just because the Faraqui show up?"

Mosteph smoothed the dog's black head, fondled its ears. "Do you know what this animal was bred for, Doctor?"

Olney blinked. "He's an Eamon Black. He's a hunting dog."

"And an excellent one," said Mosteph. "If I bred him with a retriever, do you think the offspring would be as fast, and as sure on the scent?"

"Well . . ." Olney shrugged. "Depending on the genetic recessives, they might be better retrievers. Maybe they'd hunt just as well, but it'd be a shame to mix that bloodline, considering his lineage. . . ."

"Consider your girl's lineage," said Mosteph. "On Ahmedi-Jatah, the recessives have come to the surface. The Faraqui have already touched ground there, and from what I understand, they were welcomed with open arms." He gathered the dog's black nape in his fist. "This dog can't help what it is, or what it does. Neither can the Jatahn."

I eased myself deeper into the drapery behind the door. He was wrong. We weren't animals, full of predictable instincts and bred-in behaviors. *I* was not an animal.

Olney rubbed his knees. "All right. But she'll cost you. A lot."

Mosteph got to his feet, and the dog rose up with him. "You'll have enough to buy your own ship. Come with me."

They left. They walked right past me. Their footsteps faded on the thick carpet in the hall, leaving Adrinne and her boy, and me.

Thirty klicks to the ground station. In a skimmer, I could be there in half an hour at the most. On foot, by late afternoon. I had no idea when Renee and Martine were booked to leave, or even if I was scheduled to go on the same ship.

Adrinne folded the holoree flat and tossed it on the sofa. She rubbed her eyes and yawned. "Make sure Mosteph

39

pays for the memcard, Breeni." She stretched out on her stomach. "Don't bother me."

"Yes, D'sha." He leaned over the couch for the card and the 'ree, and turned back to the fire, scratching his ass.

I took a step out from behind the door. Brocade rustled, loud as an alarm. Another step. Cooler air washed past my face from the hallway. I bent into it, around the doorjamb. In the corner of my eye, I saw Adrinne's boy turn from the fire, his light hair outlined in yellow flame.

"Hey," he said.

I slid out the door, out of sight.

"Shut up," said Adrinne.

A draft eddied down from the corridor's high ceiling, carrying the dry smell of winter air, dead leaves, the promise of freezing rain. I hurried along under alizarite arches, around a curve in the hallway and stopped. The front door was just ahead, slightly open, a vertical steak of light in the dim foyer. Two of Mosteph's boys crouched in the entryway, polishing wood and brass.

There was a back way out of the mansion, but I had no idea how to find it. If anyone asked, I could say Olney wanted something from the skimmer. Certainly that was legitimate.

The boys slicked their white cloths and wax through nooks and crannies in the brasswork, scrubbing at every carved detail in the dark wood. The wax was a flat, chemical taste in the air.

I walked toward the door, trying to be casual. The wiry bristle of the carpet under my feet became an intricate reed mat over the foyer's mosaic floor. One of the boys looked up—porcelain-skinned, with jet-black hair, almost a twin to the head houseboy. He blinked at me, frankly staring. His helper glanced up, and stopped in midstroke across the gleaming filigree.

"Jatahn?"

He pushed himself to his feet, his dark eyes wide with surprise.

The first boy elbowed him and they both locked their eyes on the floor.

"Let me out," I whispered, dry in the mouth.

The second boy pulled the door open, shuffling backwards, eyeing me sidewise, embarrassed or suspicious. I squeezed past him, out of the dark warmth of Mosteph's borrowed house.

Their eyes followed me as I stumbled down the wide red stone stairs, and out the gate. *Jatahn*. Like an accusation? I shuddered, neck to heels. *Favored One* was what he'd meant, as though the Faraqui had already arrived.

Olney's skimmer hunched in its patch of gravel by the barn, the cowling wide open. Beyond the barn, Mosteph's pastures swept down the mountain, breaking over rocky ground, tumbling into the patches of trees that edged the high cliff. Morning mist softened the stretch of plains in the distance. On a clear day, the city of Kagdel'aba was probably visible.

I clambered into the skimmer. The sky seemed lower through the scratched cowling, threatening, and close. I shoved the cushion off the backseat, uncovering the storage box where Olney kept his coverall and muck-boots. His filthy clothes would cover my collar, my brands, maybe even turn out to be big enough to hide how scared I was. I crouched under the low end of the cowling, knotting the coverall around my waist. The boots went over my shoulder, slung by their laces.

Thirty klicks to the ground station. I slid my fingers over the control board and the black plastic Authority key, but of course the skimmer didn't respond. Without Olney's thumbprint, there was no way to fly off this mountain, and as long as Olney could travel faster than I could, thirty klicks might as well be light-years.

Outside, Mosteph's busy slaves swept and raked, carried

41

and shoveled, minding their own business, never looking my way. I pulled the boots off my shoulder and ran a thumb over one muddy heel. The boots were steel-toed, reinforced leather. One drunken evening, Olney'd kicked the apartment door to pieces with them. I could disable the skimmer. It would be simple.

I got a good grip on one boot, both hands, one on the shank, one wrapped around the heel, and pointed the steel toe at the Authority.

Everything I'd done until now was reversible. I could put Olney's clothes away, walk into the mansion again, and wait for him to sell me off. Running wasn't safe or certain. What if the police found me like they'd found Kabe? What if Renee and Martine were already gone when I got there? I could wait. I could use the next seventeen years to come up with a more solid plan. Faraqui invasion or no Faraqui invasion, I would still Fail, and still survive. And in the meantime, I would scrape and crawl, like I had for the last three years, for Olney, or for Mosteph. Or for someone even worse.

I slammed the steel toe down on the Authority and the plastic dented into a dull black web of fractures. I bashed until it was nothing but a jagged hole in the control panel. I got out of the skimmer, wobbly from the knees on down. I opened Adrinne's battered carryall, crawled in, found the Authority and smashed it. I destroyed Mosteph's, too, breaking the smoky plastic to bits inside the tastefully tinted cowling. I slung the boots over my shoulder and headed for the feedlot behind the nearest barn.

In the shadow of the feedlot wall, I crouched in knee-deep, freezing slop. A dozen reshie stared at me with stupid brown eyes, while two girls spread hay for them in a wide wooden manger. One of the girls gave a shrill cry and the reshie turned like big fish, losing interest in me. I crouched lower in the muck, deep in the stink of urine, visible if either of the girls happened to look my way. One of them came to the edge of the feedlot, scattering straw into the mud, pressing it down with her bare feet so she could walk out without sinking. She brushed her hands over her hips, and she looked right at me.

I stared back, too frozen to move. Her soft brown eyes were just as liquid and senseless as the reshie. Maybe she saw me, or maybe she thought I was just another shadow. She wiped her hands again, turned, and disappeared into the barn.

I oozed across the feedlot, slid over the gate in the far side of the wall, and started to run.

The boots banged against my chest and my shoulders, kicking me as I bolted downhill, through the pasture, toward the woods. The field dropped away into a long, uneven slope, but I was going so fast, I was almost weightless. I crashed through stands of frail yellow saplings, flew over hummocks of coarse grass. The pasture became a tumble of stones, slowing me down. I clambered over bigger and bigger boulders. The woods were just visible at the low end of the field, huge trees growing at an unnatural angle on the steep mountainside. Overhead, the sky had turned into a bowl of steel gray, and now there was a sound that went with it—a bugling kind of bellow. My feet touched even ground. The woods were close enough to see into, trees crowded between streaks of daylight. I heard the sound again, but this time I knew what it was.

Mosteph's hunting dog.

I dove into the woods with big, breathless strides. Gray morning shuddered away into patchy dusk. Brittle leaves and deadfall caught in my clothes, and in the bootlaces and the coverall. Behind me, the dog plunged noisily into the bracken as I wrestled my way from one briar patch to the next. The dog came closer, invisible in the shadows and high brush. I twisted around, trying to decide where it was, how much of a lead I still had, and could see its breath, an odd trail of gauzy fog, hanging in the still air. The briars gave way to a sudden drop, a dirty wall of white stone that stretched off into the forest in either direction. The surface was rough enough for handholds, too high for any sensible creature to jump from. I scrambled over the edge, banging knees and elbows, cutting my feet. This short rockface was just practice for the monumental cliffs that bordered the plains. I reached the bottom and looked up to see the dog watching me, tongue out, panting puffs of steam. It disappeared and I heard it running along the top of the wall, searching for a way down. The sound of breaking twigs faded in the distance.

In the lower forest, tall conifers shaded out the thorn bushes, the bracken, and covered everything else with a thick layer of needles. I rushed through the silent woods, half running, half sliding, dodging around immense old trees.

I listened for the dog, but all I heard was my heart and lungs. I was so loud, Olney could have heard me back at Mosteph's farm. I was the loudest thing for a hundred kilometers. In no time at all, I would explode out of the forest at the top of the white cliffs. I kept running. My feet flew over the needles. Trees rushed past on their own, endless and huge. I couldn't have stopped if I'd tried. My deafening breathing set the rhythm, like fast music, a tune I couldn't quite make out.

The woods ended in a tangle of roots and a scatter of white stones. Beyond the stones—empty air. I threw myself down on the loose shale at the top of the cliffs, sliding and scrabbling, shedding skin. I stopped at the edge and lay in the sharp gravel, gasping while the sky spun. I turned over, hanging onto the ground, and crawled to the crumbling end of the world. A hundred meters down, gray stones rumpled the cover of light brown grass. In the far distance, the glint of white buildings was Kagdel'aba.

I pushed myself up on my elbows, and managed to sit.

How stupid. How *stupid*.

How was I going to get down?

Something rushed under the trees. Not wind. I got to my feet, trembly, freezing, scared. I turned around as the dog roared into the open, mouth wide, every tooth showing, its red tongue flying like a bloody flag. It hit me with all its weight. Its teeth flashed by my face. The sky widened as I fell backwards, the cliff shooting up into it, taller and taller. The dog twisted in the air beside me, scrambling, all legs, jaws and white eyes.

I remember grabbing at stones and stunted trees, cutting my hands on anything that stuck out of the white cliff face. I remember the dog dropping away from me, as though it carried the weight of Mosteph's sins and abuses.

After that, I don't remember anything.

THREE

Now it was night, or night again.

Fog hung low and flat in the dark. Faint light from the skein of asteroid moons made the plain into a surreal lake. In the distance, Kagdel'aba was a smear of rust-colored haze.

Olney. Mosteph.

Renee and Martine.

My legs were tangled in something. I reached down, aching slow, and found Olney's coverall.

Virevir.

Offworld ticket.

Troah.

Of course Renee and Martine were long gone.

My left leg throbbed. My pants were torn, stiff with blood, clumped with dirt and dry grass. The leg felt swollen, bruised to the bone, but I could move it. I bent my fingers, my toes, grateful for every little pain. I wasn't Failing. I was hurt, but my own Viral infection was already healing me. In a little while I could get up and walk.

My pockets were ripped open. The one that should have had the envelope was empty. I groped in the sharp gravel until I found it—dirty but intact.

I sat up and unfolded the envelope. Three packs of Virevir jammed into the bottom corner and the memcard ticket. I squinted at it in the darkness. The departure time and the name of the ship should have been stamped on the front. Instead, the print across the top read, *Open Passage: Seating Subject to Availability.*

I read it again. If this was the only kind of ticket they could get, Renee and Martine might still be in Kagdel'aba, waiting for available seats. Even if they had left, open passage meant I could still follow. If I hurried.

I got up and struggled into the coverall, and slung the boots over my shoulder. I took a wobbly step into the low mist and finally saw the dog—a rumpled black heap in a scatter of nearby stones. Wind ruffled its fur. I started walking.

Where was Olney? Probably already at Kagdel'aba, scouring the markets and alleys, looking for me with Mosteph. The city was the furthest thing from a safe haven, but the only alternative I could think of was to hide in the hills until Olney, or the Faraqui, tracked me down.

"Troah." The word came out of my mouth louder than I'd expected. Not an acquiescent croak, but a blurt of hot defiance in the freezing night. If this was a mistake, then let it be a big, dramatic mistake. Let Olney find me in his stinking clothes. Let the police expose me at the ground station. If I could run once, I could run again. Let the powers-that-be fight it out between the old borders. By the time they were finished, I would be gone without a trace.

On the outskirts of the city, Kagdel'aba's sodium-orange streetlights sifted through the fog, haloing the low stone

47

buildings, flattening the skyline. The crimson spike of the alizarite ground station needled into the night, the highest point in town, visible from a long way off.

I sat on a dark hillside and pulled up handfuls of winter grass, stuffing Olney's boots so they would fit. His coverall hung on me, clinging with mist and my own sweat.

At the bottom of the hill, a dirt road wound between tractor sheds, angled around a cluster of skimmers, and disappeared into an alley between two buildings. Awkward black bundles clustered along the sides of the road, and it took me a while to realize that the bundles were people. Maybe even the same terrified Nayans I'd seen from the air, with Olney, yesterday. Now here they were, swaddled in clothes and blankets, asleep by the road, waiting for offworld passage.

I smoothed my hair, brushed dirt off my face. For all I knew, this was the tail end of a line of refugees that reached all the way to the ground station. My best bet might be to curl up next to them and let the rest of the planet's population collect behind me.

I tugged the coverall over the chain around my neck, fastening the cloth collar until it was tight enough to choke off my doubts. If I stopped moving, green Nayan eyes would take in my dark skin and black hair, and then the questions would start.

Not from around here, are you?

No, D'sha.

The boots flopped around my knees as I wallowed down the hill, through the long grass. The grass gave way to icy puddles. The mist thinned to nothing. I scuffed through frozen dirt until I came to the road.

Black bundles steamed like Mosteph's reshie, faces covered with blankets, bunched together for warmth. I hunched my shoulders and walked, *tap, tap,* bootheels on hard dirt, the sound a free woman made, not the silent pad of bare slave feet. The black bundles slept on, too cold to notice something as unremarkable as me. I walked a little faster. Not one of them looked up.

The dirt road turned to broken pavement, angled between two blank-walled buildings, and turned into an empty alleyway. Offworld settlers had whitewashed the Faraqui stonework, but in the orange-lit night, the alizarite showed through.

Overhead, the slice of night sky changed from rust to a dull red. Not morning, but brighter lights, closer to the middle of town. A persistent wail from further ahead got louder, keening off the high, narrow walls. The alley made a sharp turn, and I peered around the corner.

Two women and a half dozen kids squatted at the end of the alley where it met a main street. The wail became a hopeless, angry squall—one of the women bounced the baby on her knee, mechanically, without comfort. More children milled in the street, and behind them, a mob of shoving, intent Nayans, all bundled in black coats and dark blankets.

I froze where I was. Kagdel'aba was jammed. A standby ticket was worthless if there were no spare seats. Even cargo space would be worth fighting for.

One of the women glanced into the alley and saw me. My stomach knotted. Could she see my collar? Could she tell what I was? I touched the coverall's fastenings with icy hands, cloth over the chain around my neck, trying to be casual. She kept staring. I couldn't just stand here. If seats were in such short supply, maybe Renee and Martine were still waiting. I took a step, and the matted grass in Olney's boots wound between my toes like a snare. I clumped toward the woman and her squalling baby, not meeting her eyes. She moved out of my way, indifferent. The children stared after me. Except for them, I could have been invisible.

In the crush of the main street, no one had the time to care if I was escaped property. Two tall men argued in the middle of the street, thick accents, thicker beards. Behind them, a woman hunched on a packing crate, a holoree beside her, blaring the news—not the Emirate Report this time, but a local, independent station.

". . . *Emirate sources will not confirm reports of the destruction of the two Emirate warships on the Frontier-Faraque border. . . . Strong evidence suggests that the Faraqui have new weapons, superior to Emirate capabilities . . .*"

Adrinne's news. It rang off whitewashed walls, distorting with static. I pushed through a line of slaves, fastened together with a coffle chain. I'd been here dozens of times with Olney. This narrow street would widen into a market plaza. From there, it wasn't far to the ground station.

I slid around a huddle of men in patched leather coats—Nayan farmers, smelling of soil and sweat. One had a datafeed clipped on his ear. The others bent toward him, their faces as creased as plowed fields, listening as he muttered the news.

"Emirate personnel are being evacuated from the following Frontier systems because of . . . funding cuts?" He scowled, covering his other ear against the noise. "Perkenji, F'shai, Treist Cluster . . ." The farmer glanced at his companions. "And Bellea. That's us." He glared past them, at me, cloaked in Olney's Extension coverall. "That's them."

I hurried away. Here was the evacuation Olney'd been hoping for. Did that mean he was gone?

At the end of the street, red-tinted walls opened into a crowded plaza. On my side, every shop was closed, display windows papered over with police warnings about vandalism in three different languages. On the other side, though, the food stalls were doing a booming business. White lights silhouetted hands and fists of a hundred people, holding up their money. Hawking blared into the maroon shadows where offworlder families huddled with their baggage, dazed, or half asleep, swaddled in layers of too-thin clothing, waiting for a connecting ship.

"Reshie fresh! Reshie hot!"

I blundered through the crowd, searching for familiar faces. No Renee. No Martine. And mercifully, no Olney or Mosteph.

Someone shoved me. Someone else stepped on my too-loose boots—if I tried to pull away, they would come right off. A suitcase banged my back. I lost my balance and almost fell. A cold hand caught my arm, and I looked up into the pinched face of a slave boy.

"Watch yourself, D'sha."

He steadied me, smiling nervously. He held up a skewer of reshie meat, half-wrapped in greasy paper. "Excuse me, D'sha . . . D'Emirate."

He didn't know what I really was—no comprehension in his face. All he saw was the coverall and boots. But he had the air of escape all around him.

"My people are, ah, you know, waiting." He waved the skewer in the direction of the ground station. "I can't find them. You look hungry. . . ." He held out the meat. Fat had congealed on the paper in yellow globs. The meat had been cold for hours. Silent questions glittered behind his eyes. Was I leaving? Did I have a way to take him with me? Would I take this food, and whatever else I wanted from him, as payment?

As if I had nothing to lose.

"No," I whispered. "No."

He blinked and turned, and vanished.

I went the other way, pushing through the line in front of the reshie stand until I found the street that led out of the far side of the market. Between low roofs, the ground station's red needle loomed in the beginnings of a heatless dawn.

At the end of the street, I stopped in the dull shadows at the edge of the ground station plaza. I was the only one standing in a quiet, steaming mass of huddled people. From the edges of the plaza to the walls of the station building, luggage and dark clothes heaped up in silent drifts, like black snow. A thousand refugees curled in blankets, their luggage stacked against the wind. There were more human beings than I had ever seen in one place. Piles of them, with their crates and suitcases, children, slaves, and furniture—all crushed together, waiting for what I needed. A simple escape.

The only motion was a police skimmer, heading in my direction. I edged into deeper shadows. There were police by the ground station doors. More cruised over the crowd in skimmers. Others watched from the rooftops.

The police skimmer came closer and came to a stop. The hair on my neck bristled, from the antigrav static, the cold, and plain fear. The skimmer's loudspeaker crackled.

"All passengers holding passes for the Independent Freight transport, Elyjeh, *may now enter the boarding area. Have your passes ready for inspection. Repeat, have your passes ready . . ."*

All around me, the frozen silence broke into grunts and yells. Outworlders and Nayans surged to their feet. Beside me, a woman hitched her two bawling toddlers under her arms, kicked away her battered suitcase and raced into the plaza.

The rest of the mob swarmed behind me. Two men rushed past, arms full of awkward boxes. One caught me in the shoulder. I swung around in the rush of arms and legs, crates and cases. Olney's boots hobbled me as I tried to get out of the way. His coverall flapped, loose as an extra skin, catching on luggage, children and elbows. I stumbled, flailing for balance, turned into the current, and found myself swept into it.

A long stone's throw from the station doors, we jammed into a corridor of waist-high railings, like livestock in a loading chute. The railings led into a cordoned-off apron around the station entrance. Police skimmers hovered overhead, herding us forward, while guards up ahead held us back.

"Form a single line, for your own safety, form a single line. . . ."

Now I was squashed between a thin man wearing two coats—his dark blue Extension uniform visible through the tears in the sleeves of the other—and a tall, ivory-colored woman behind me, with a bursting satchel clutched against her chest. One sharp corner of the satchel dug into my shoulder. I turned sideways, straining to see what was going on down the line. A long way off, a pair of Nayan police conferred over a handheld reader, sliding someone's ticket through it, back and forth, back and forth, tapping the reader and peering at it.

"We'll never get out," muttered the woman behind me. "The Faraqui'll be here and gone before any of us get out."

The man in the torn coats leaned over to whisper in my ear. "Take off the uniform if you know what's good for you. All you need's your ID." He motioned toward the ground station guards. "They'll let us on first. But if the rabble figures that out . . ." He glanced around nervously.

Only the railing divided us from the crush around the station. A stone's throw away, two slave boys picked their way through the press of free people, each with a bristling bouquet of skewered reshie. The motion in the crowd, I realized, was white clothes among the dark coats—slaves, fetching food from the market, then rushing back to make sure they hadn't been abandoned. I felt eyes behind me and glanced around, half-expecting to see the runaway boy from the market. Instead, I saw a girl.

Her skin was a lustrous indigo, so black it seemed blue. A long braid of white-blond hair fell to the middle of her back. Her eyes slanted in her small, precise face. She was like an exotic island in this desperate sea of refugees, and there was no mistaking the over-honed look of a pure, Faraqui-bred bloodline. She stared at me in frank surprise.

"Jatahn?" she said.

The cold dawn turned stifling.

She studied me, pinned in the act of escaping. "... D'*sha* ...?"

If she'd screamed *"runaway,"* at the top of her lungs, she couldn't have scared me as much.

The man in torn coats twisted to see the girl. "Yours?" He raised an eyebrow at my coverall. "On your salary?"

"Have your passes ready for inspection, repeat, have your passes ready."

The guards were closer now, picking out Extension employees from the line and hustling them forward. At the ground station entrance, a handful of people huddled by the doors. I squinted and recognized Leta, from the compound back at Kagda. And the poultry specialist from New DeKastri, and the engineer from Newhall.

Last was Olney, standing apart from the rest of the Extension workers, searching the crowd, arms crossed, his narrow face pinched into an expression of cold determination. Beside him, in a long, ruffled coat, was Mosteph.

Nayan police shouldered between the railings, squeezing through where there was no room, shouting over protesting civilians. I sank behind the man in the torn coat as he pulled his Extension ID out of his pocket.

"Take off that damn coverall," he whispered to me. "What're you waiting for?"

Olney shaded his eyes, searching the line. He couldn't see me. I knew he couldn't see me. But he would when the police dragged me out. I crammed myself backwards until my hip touched the railing. Two green-eyed children stared up from a blanket on the other side. Their father dozed against a pile of battered gray boxes. I looked around for the white-haired girl, but she was nowhere in sight.

I swung one leg over the railing. The man in the torn coat craned around. "What're you ...?"

I swung the other leg over and saw the understanding in his face.

"Hey," he said. "You're a— she's a—"

I flung myself past the Nayan children, their startled father and his pile of boxes. I gallumped across the plaza, shoving between black-clad strangers. When I looked back, the *Elyjeh*'s passengers were waddling into the station.

No sign of pursuit. Not yet.

Icy wind cut through my clothes. I sank down, too shivery to stand, squatting in the midst of a thousand other people who didn't have a chance in hell of getting away. I was too far from the blockhouse to tell if Olney and Mosteph were still standing by the doors. Even if they hadn't seen me, it was a safe enough bet that one of them would be there every time a ship was boarding.

Half a dozen women stared at me across their meager pile of bags. I fumbled with the coverall's cloth collar, checking to see if it was still fastened tight over my chain one. It was, but they stared anyhow. I got up and stumbled off, wondering how long it would be before I ended up with a skewer of cold reshie and some hungry stranger.

At the edge of the plaza, I found a boarded-over doorway out of the main flow of the mob. I pressed myself against splinters and sharp nails, my heart banging around, trying not to gasp for breath as people hurried by.

How had slave-Renee run away from her owner? I tried to imagine her in collar, disguised in a free woman's clothes, and couldn't. There was nothing submissive about Renee, no genetics to hamstring her, no questions when she raised her head and looked you in the eye. However she'd escaped, she hadn't had a Faraqui invasion to plan around. Martine had told me Renee'd belonged to someone in the Diplomatic Corps. If that was true, she would have been traveling constantly. She could have chosen her exit. She might have had help.

She hadn't been drowning in this river of desperate Nayans and thinly dressed offworlders.

Now that the *Elyjeh* had boarded, the flow was slowing,

or was it? I looked around, thinking that the crowd was pushing and shoving as hard as ever, but making less progress. Two people were standing in everyone's way. It took a moment for me to register the dark skin. Indigo skin and long white hair.

The Faraqui-bred girl eyed me for a long moment, then turned in the press of bundled shoulders, and nodded to a tall man behind her.

He was pale, with light eyes and dark clothes, like the Nayans, but his hair was blond, not red. Long hair, tucked into his coat. He was incredibly familiar, but I couldn't place him. One of Olney's drinking buddies? He was certainly no Nayan. But if he was some Emirate worker, wouldn't I have met his girl before?

He stared at me and I stared back. In the furtive rush around him, his motions were languid, cool, predatory. It wasn't his face that was familiar, I realized. It was what he did for a living.

He was a slaver—some kind of privateer—or a tracker who collected bounty on runaways. In the middle of this huge, ungainly exodus, was he looking for Nayans desperate enough to offer themselves in exchange for escape?

Or was I the one he wanted?

"Jatahn?" his girl had said.

I shoved into the crowd, scared now.

"All passengers with passes for the Independent Freighter, Havalok, *may now enter the boarding area. . . ."*

I squeezed between elbows, boxes, luggage, trying to keep the two of them in sight, but lost them both as the next mob barged into the plaza. Close-pressed bodies trapped me against a whitewashed shopfront. Somewhere nearby, a woman was screaming in thick dialect.

"Emirate bastard! They're giving him *my* seat! *My* seat!"

A police skimmer darted overhead, barking static.

"Stand back—for your own safety—stand back—"

A tall man stepped backwards, found my foot under his

and peered over his shoulder. His eyes slid over the filthy coverall and the winged emblem of the Emir's Extension Service. "Why don't you get on a goddamn ship?" he demanded. "They're saving our seats for you."

A woman with a cut over one eye twisted in front me. "Take her uniform," she hissed. "Take her ID."

The man hesitated. "The police?"

"Forget the damn police!"

I ducked, dove sideways, tripped against his legs. The woman's fingers closed around my wrist, hot and tight as wires. I yanked harder than she could. For a second there were no hands on me. I fell between feet and luggage.

"Stand back—for your own safety—stand back—"

The mob shifted again. I crawled, palms and knees over sharp gravel, stopped, and glanced up into a dozen angry faces.

". . . with passes for the Independent Freighter, Havalok . . ."

Time to shed Olney's skin, but no place to do it. And if I was a slave girl again, then what? Reshie on a stick?

Another notch of empty space in front of another closed shop. A broken wooden awning cast a shadow over its display window, filled with Nayan souvenirs. Carved reshie in red stone, dried blue flowers in crumbling wreaths. A dozen silver boxes, exactly the same as the one Renee kept her Virevir in. I hunched in front of the window, my breath clouding the glass, thinning, and clouding again.

My reflection stared out, chalky-scared, smeared with dirt and blood. The reflected crowd seethed under the distant red weal of the ground station's spike. Martine's freedom seemed like an improbable dream; my fall down the cliff, utterly unreal. I pushed my hands in my pockets and found Renee's plastic envelope—a gritty slice of proof.

I panted against the glass. What if Olney was the only one who could save me? What if I peeled off his clothes and slunk back to him? With enough alcohol, enough sex, enough talk, I might convince him that it was smarter to hang onto me, instead of selling me off to Mosteph. He could get us both away, and I would have some other chance to escape. But that was wrong. Olney was too greedy. Mosteph would wave the money in his face, and that would be the end of it. I stared past my reflection to the station. And saw the white-haired girl again.

Her man was with her, a head taller than any Nayan. I turned around. He shaded his eyes against the morning glare, close enough for me to see the rings on his fingers.

She pointed at me. His light-colored eyes found mine.

Recognition was the sour tang, prickling under my tongue, tightening across my chest. Tall, long hair, a broad, foreign face. *Where* had I seen him? Here on Naya? Or back home? Years ago? Last week?

I started into the crowd again, not watching where I was going. I stumbled over a suitcase and fell against a woman, bundled up in black.

"There's a *line* here," she shrieked, chapped lips stretched over her teeth. "Bitch! Emirate bitch!" Hands caught me from behind, grabbing, yanking at the coverall. Another woman's furious face shoved into mine.

"You won't be getting our seats!"

Hands on my wrists, someone kicking my legs. I fell, hard, knees on the pavement, my shoulder banging the corner of a crate.

The coverall tore. The rip of fabric was even louder than the screaming around me. The fastenings split and my body heat puffed out. The stink of old manure and dry blood engulfed me. Someone grabbed my arm and the sleeve came away like wet paper. They saw my dirty white slave clothes and for a second, everything stopped.

"Runaway," panted someone. "Just another runaway."

"Call the cops," said someone else.

"It's all right," said a man's voice. "She's mine."

Not Olney. Not Mosteph.

The slaver. His girl slid past him, pulling me to my feet.

The cold air around me was suddenly warm. It was her. I could smell her. Vanilla. Another scent . . . sharper, like curry. The combination was dizzying. In the wintry gray plaza, a thousand light-years from home, all I could think of was my mother's kitchen.

"Huh," said one of the women to the slaver. "You let her run around in *those* clothes?"

"I'd beat the shit out of her," said someone else.

The girl turned me toward her man, but I couldn't bring myself to look into his face. Her air of spice and cooking was thinner on him, mixed with the scent of his coat— familiar, reassuring, fragrant damp wool. How did I *know* him?

The girl took my arm, guiding me back to the relative emptiness in front of the souvenir shop. He followed, stopping just behind her.

"Is she hurt?" he asked.

She touched my cheek. "Are you hurt, *alatah*?"

I shuddered. *Alatah. Sister,* in the old Faraqui language, but on Jatah, it had evolved into an expression of profound stupidity. *Alatah, you've boiled the soup away.* I managed to shake my head.

"Jatahn." His voice was soft, unthreatening.

I couldn't say anything. I needed to know who he was, but I didn't have the courage to stare. I turned from the girl's tentative fingers, and saw the three of us reflected in the glass display window.

She was a shadow, half-striped with light falling through the broken awning. He was pale, distinct, a wisp of his long hair blowing against a patch of blue sky. The color moved across his face in a thin stripe, like a mask.

My breath drifted in a motionless cloud. My fingers went ice-cold.

He was Faraqui.

No stripe, no white Faraqui cloak, no covering for his

head. Nothing to identify him, except my glacial recognition.

My knees went numb, my hands, the length of my spine. I would have dropped to the ground in terror, except for the torrent of emotion in the middle of my chest. It was relief so profound, so wild and joyous, I thought I would burst into tears.

He saw it in my face. He touched my arm.

"Favored One," he said. "You'll come with me."

FOUR

He gave me my own room.

Table, chair, bed. Three pieces of furniture and clean clothes. What luxury. A bed with sheets, blankets and a pillow, not the sofa in Olney's apartment.

The chair by the window was deep, comfortable, with a silk throw over the back. Decadently soft carpets layered the floor, woven with patterns of hunting scenes, coiling cobalt flowers and birds over ivory.

The bathroom had a door that locked, and a shower.

It was warm.

Outside, I could see one flank of the ship. Communications hardware and maintenance pods dotted the hull. Beyond that, pinpoint stars.

Bellea-Naya's silver crescent rose over the ship's stern, distorting as the ship moved into light speed. The stars turned to a jumble of colored strings on dense black. Naya shrank like a deflated balloon and vanished in the tangle.

Someone knocked on my door. I glanced at the bed where the Virevir was hidden under the mattress.

"Yes?"

It was Jamilla, the girl with the blue-black skin and white hair. I was sure she knew my name by now, but she insisted on *Alatah*. From her, it sounded soberingly formal, not a joke at all.

"*Alatah*," she said, eyes on the rug. "D'Rasha will see you."

As though I had asked for an audience. As though he had to request what he wanted from me. "Thank you," I said.

Rasha. Rasha the Faraqui slaver, with a family surname too long to remember. D'Rasha.

His shuttle had been waiting on the outskirts of Kagde-l'aba—a plain suborbital skimmer, without Faraqui markings, or dire devices attached to it. Rising away from Naya, I watched the ground station's spike shrink to a thin red needle. For all I knew Olney would still be down there, waiting for me, when the Faraqui arrived in force. It was problematic, I supposed, how well he and Mosteph would manage without me as their peace offering.

I didn't care what happened to them. This place, this room, felt safer than anywhere I'd been in the last three years.

Something about it felt right. As natural as coming home.

Now Jamilla directed me through silent, carpeted corridors. I had no clear impression of the size of the ship, and it didn't seem proper to ask. What I could see from the window in my room made me think this was a transport. I wondered if there was a barge slung underneath.

Rasha's quarters seemed modest: a wide, low-ceilinged room with a row of windows and two draped doorways. Embroidered cushions were arranged around a low brass table. Tapestries hung along one wall—more hunting scenes, in cobalt and indigo. It was warm and comfortable, thick with the rich scent of curry, but I didn't see Rasha.

"He's not here?"

"He will be." She made a deferential motion toward the cushions around the table, never meeting my eyes, but watching somehow anyway. I hesitated. Was I supposed to sit—or wait? Standing? Or kneeling? Here was an entire culture of protocol I knew nothing about—stripped from my collaborating ancestors, and forgotten by three subsequent generations. The cushions, the table, her invitation, were an obstacle course. What did it mean if I sat down?

"I don't know what to do," I muttered.

"Sit, Jatahn." Rasha pushed the drape away from one of the doors, and nodded to Jamilla. "Get her something to eat."

He was too young to be the slaver on the holoree—*We don't want trouble*—but aside from his age, there was hardly any difference. The sky-blue stripe cut across his face, cheekbones to eyebrows, covering even his eyelids. Instead of the dark wool coat, now he wore a loose, bone-colored robe that fell to the floor. His head and his hair were covered with a length of soft white fabric, knotted in the back, edged with blue embroidery. He settled on the cushions on the far side of the low brass table. I stared until I realized I was staring, and looked away, at the tapestry behind him, the rug, my own feet.

"Sit down, Jatahn."

I dropped onto the nearest pillow and bumped the table with my knee. The brass shuddered, too heavy to damage. I grabbed the edge of it anyhow, hanging on with sweaty fingers.

He waited until I let go. I wrapped my hands in my lap, not sure if I should sit, or kneel, or throw myself prostrate on the floor.

"Tell me your name," he said.

"Frenna, D'sha."

"And your family name?"

"Yaeylie, D'sha."

"Yaeylie?" He studied me. "How long in collar?"

"Three years, D'sha."

"On Naya? With the Emirate veterinarian?"

"Yes, D'sha." If he knew that, he'd looked up my ID number in the registry. He knew the answers to these questions already.

"You're the oldest in your family. You were sent as the . . . the payment for Emirate services on your world?"

"Yes, D'sha."

He was silent for a moment. "Barbaric."

I didn't say anything.

"We've taken Jatah," he said.

I wasn't shocked, or stunned. I only wondered if what Mosteph had said was true, that the slavers had been welcomed with open arms. It was frighteningly easy to imagine my family—my entire neighborhood—in the street, shouting, cheering, swept up in the same rush of emotion as me, when I'd realized what this man was.

"Jatah is very important to us," said Rasha. "A hundred years is a long time, though. We weren't sure what sort of reaction we would find, or what your people might remember after four generations." He smoothed his robe across his knees. "Yaeylie Frenna," he said. "Do you know much Jatahn history?"

"What they teach in school, D'sha." Emirate Extension schools taught us that our ancestors had sided with the Faraqui because of an unforgivable combination of bred-in malice, and plain stupidity. Traitors could only work their way up the ladder of Emirate goodwill. The lowest rungs were part of our heritage, we were told, and never far away.

"What about the old language?" he asked. "Is it spoken at all?"

Troah, I thought. *Alatah*. "Not much, D'sha."

"The stories and fables?" he asked. "Those are gone, too?"

"Some lullabies," I said. "A few fairy tales, but I think they've been . . . altered a little."

"You know the story of Rexidi?"

"Rexidi?" I said in surprise. "The song about the prince?"

He smiled, boyishly pleased, creasing the blue stripe at the corners of his eyes. "Sing it for me."

" 'Behold, the . . . the . . . prince in white . . .' " It was a lullaby I hadn't heard since my youngest sister was in diapers. The tune, frankly, eluded me.

Behind me, bare feet brushed across the rug. Jamilla bent over the table with a tray of cut fruit and fresh, fragrant bread.

"Jamil," said Rasha. "The song of Rexidi."

She set the tray down and knelt in the scatter of cushions.

> *"See there, the wayward prince in white,*
> *bare of foot and bare of head.*
> *Threw off the hunting dogs tonight,*
> *but run to ground where demons tread."*

She kept her eyes on the tapestry on the wall behind him while she sang. I looked too.

Cobalt on ivory. A young man with a crown on his head raced into a deep forest. In the background, lean blue dogs and men on horseback broke through a tangle of blue flowers. Far ahead of the running prince, deformed creatures crouched in the shadows, waiting for him.

Rasha nodded and waved her away. He picked up a slice of fruit and peeled it. "What were you doing in the market? Why were you dressed in a free man's clothes?"

I wasn't sure what to say. The story of Rexidi was just a lullaby. It didn't have anything to do with me running from Olney, or being chased by Mosteph's dog. Except now I felt as though I'd committed some incredible crime. And there it was, on the wall for everyone to see. Genuine guilt was a slow, weighty expansion in my chest. I wanted to explain, or apologize, or confess all the things I'd ever done wrong—even all the nasty things I'd ever said about Olney.

"You ran away."

"Yes, D'sha."

He dropped the rind on the table and laid the fruit on a silver plate. "True Jatahn would never run. Certainly not anyone with Yaeylie lineage." He waited for me to say something, and began peeling another piece. "Tell me about your family."

I had no idea what he wanted to know. Or how much I should tell him.

"Where are your parents?" he asked.

"In Victory City." Unless the Emirate governors had allowed them to leave. If the Jatahn evacuation had been anything like the one on Naya, there wasn't much hope of that.

"Victory City is nothing but an Emirate housing complex," said Rasha. "What region did your people come from? Or do you know?"

"No, D'sha."

"What about your grandparents?"

"Victory City," I said. "We've always lived there."

"The Yaeylie came from the H'alath Mountains," said Rasha. "Very beautiful, very rugged and remote. Have you heard of it?"

H'alath was my grandmother's name. "I think they call it Highland now," I said. "It's a holiday resort."

His prickle of anger was tangible. "Tell me," he said, his voice quiet but more strained, "is it true that after the invasion, Jatahn children were separated from their parents, to make sure that they would grow up without any knowledge of our culture?"

"I don't know, D'sha."

"Is it true that there were organized abductions of young girls, and castration of the boys?"

I'd never heard of any of these things. "I don't know."

He let out his breath. "You don't even know what the Emirate took from you. They'll call us evil and do their best to make you believe it, but all they want is the best of what we bred for ourselves." He laid the second piece of fruit by the first. His hands were trembling. "Do you believe that we're evil, Yaeylie Frenna?"

In this warm room, in the middle of this civilized conversation, answering questions that clearly pained him—after three years of Olney—there was only one honest answer. "No, D'sha."

He picked up the plate of sliced fruit and held it out to me. "Take it," he said, "and I'll tell you about your family."

The fruit dissolved in my mouth, turning to sugary syrup while he talked. My great-grandmother had given birth to three children by the time she was twenty, and so her contribution to the Faraqui gene pool was complete. She'd volunteered to be infected with the slavers' Virus, to become a proper servant, not just a breeder. Her children, a boy and two girls, vanished into the Emirate invasion while she helped load barges to save at least some of the Favored Ones. She was killed in the crossfire, when she tried to pilot the barge across Emirate lines, into what was left of the Faraque.

Rasha stared at the top of the brass table. I swallowed, too loudly in the silent room.

"She came from a long line of courageous, talented people," said Rasha. "She belonged to my great-grandfather. He wouldn't have expected any less of her." His gray eyes met mine. "At least her children were allowed to keep their family name." He reached for my hand, warm fingers in my cold palm. "Favored One," he said. "It was good that you ran."

Table, chair, bed.

I sat on the floor by my window, staring at my reflection in the glass. The hot supper that Jamilla had left on the small table steamed behind me. I didn't have to turn around to know what it was.

Starchy white kimarra, fried in curry. Reshie meat, cut in strips, spiced and baked, and ladled over with sweet red sauce. Sliced pink celani fruit in a ceramic bowl, garnished with blue flowers.

On my eighteenth birthday, Grandmother H'alath had come from her apartment across town to show me how to mix a proper curry—an old tradition for girls coming of age, she'd said. My mother—her daughter—stood in silence across the kitchen with a cup of cold tea and a tight expression on her face as Grandmother H'alath pulled one little jar of powder after another from her purse.

"At least close the curtains," my mother had said. "The neighbors can see right in."

"Let them look," said Grandmother H'alath. "She's the oldest. She'll need to know these things one day."

My mother yanked the curtains shut. "She can buy curry paste at any store, Mother. She doesn't have to mix it herself."

"Offworld stores won't have it," said Grandmother H'alath. "Emirate Extension stores never do."

"That's because only the Faraqui like the taste," my mother snapped, "and she's not going to them."

"Maybe not," said Grandmother H'alath, "but she'll always be Jatahn, and she needs to know how to cook for herself."

The spices stung under my nails as we kneaded the powder into paste, and stank in the hot oil until the color and texture changed. White slices of kimarra turned red, then brown, then crisp. The rest of my birthday dinner was just as traditional. The curry, spiced reshie with red sauce, and celani for dessert.

A coming-of-age meal, getting cold on the table behind me.

A heritage of oppression, passed from mother to daughter through a thousand generations in the privacy of our own kitchens. What else had the Emirate been unable to obliterate? The song of Rexidi, and other harmless lullabies that ingrained me and my brother and sisters with the futility of escape. I was the same as the Faraqui's' abandoned mansions on a hundred conquered worlds, empty but standing, waiting for my former occupants. A part of me belonged in Rasha's room, at his table. If I stayed long enough, I could forget about Renee, and Martine, the Virevir hidden under my mattress.

Martine. Sweating and disheveled, convulsing on the bed. How unlikely that a slave could ever be free of the Virus. Was that really what had happened?

Perhaps she'd died.

My reflection stared in from the dark window. Brown Jatahn eyes, attentive and guileless. Favored One. In seventeen years, I wouldn't have any secrets from Rasha. I would fit in precisely, as close to him as Jamilla, a stitch in an embroidered scene.

Behind me, the door opened. Jamilla took a step inside.

"Are you finished with your dishes, Alatah?"

Whenever she said *Alatah*, she could just as easily have been saying *D'sha*. It was unnerving. She came closer until she could see that I hadn't touched the food. Her dark face was a study in concern. "You're not used to the spicing? I can make it milder."

"It's all right," I said. "I'm not hungry." Which was a lie. I could hardly remember the last time I'd eaten.

She leaned over the table, her long hair sliding across her shoulders. "You should try the celani at least, Alatah. It's very good." She picked up the bowl of cut fruit and brought it to where I was, on the floor by the window. She sat back on her heels, nudged the plate into my hands. "D'Rasha sliced it himself. For you."

"Thank him for me," I said.

"Alatah, I will."

She let her slender fingers rest in her lap, waiting for me to do something. I put the celani in my mouth, let the juice seep under my tongue, between my teeth, and swallowed it.

Jamilla got up and brought the next plate—the fried, spiced reshie. She set it on the floor and began cutting the meat. For a second I thought she was going to feed me, like a child.

"I can do that," I said.

She put the knife and fork down.

She wasn't going to leave. I had a sudden, awful fear that Rasha was watching all of this, and that he had sent Jamilla to feed me, then prepare me, somehow, for sex.

I picked up the fork in damp fingers. Was I so changed that I would welcome that? Or would it be the same agonizing duty it'd been for the last three years with Olney? I stabbed at a bit of meat, missed, stabbed again.

"Alatah," said Jamilla. "What are you afraid of?"

"I'm not afraid."

"You are," she said. "It's obvious. And you have every reason to be. You're not what he thinks you are."

I tried to put the fork down before it slid out of my fingers. It clattered on the silver plate. Sweet red sauce splashed on the rug.

"What do you mean?" I asked.

"You should have told him that your Yaeylie ancestors have been fighting the Emirate ever since the Faraqui were driven away. You should have told him that the children of his great-grandfather's slave had survived to produce heroes against the Emirate occupation."

"But that isn't true," I said.

"It should have been true."

"It was an invasion," I said. "What could they do against an army?"

She made an impatient gesture.

"What would you have done?" I said. "Stood up to the invaders? Held them off with sticks and stones?"

"It isn't a question about me, Alatah, or my people. We're not Jatahn. You're different from us. Your breeding was deeper. Or it was supposed to be."

"I know," I said. "We were the Favored Ones."

"More than that," said Jamilla. "In the old days, the Jatahn were the sword, and the Faraqui were the armor." She narrowed her eyes. "Is all of that really gone after four generations of Emirate tampering?"

I thought of my mother, arguing over my curry lesson with Grandmother H'alath. Whatever the Faraqui had bred into my long-dead ancestors, the thing had skipped down the generations, manifesting in my grandmother's insistence on tradition, and then landed inside of me. Rasha. I could feel him, a hook in my throat.

"Yes," I said, "it's gone."

"That's unfortunate, Alatah," and this time, there was less respect in her voice. "When I was a child, we were told stories about the Jatahn so we would know what to strive for. We could never be Jatahn, but it was enough to be like Jatahn. It's strange to see you so frightened of D'Rasha. We were told the relationship was symbiotic."

"Symbiotic?"

She nodded. "Your people weren't bred for cosmetic preferences, like other slaves. You were supposed to be companions and advisors. You were treated like family."

71

"We were property," I said.

She shifted on her knees. "You're not willing to give yourself to him. You think it's only a matter of time until he rapes you."

I wound my hands together. "Isn't it?"

"He'll send for you tonight."

"What if," I said, and had to take a breath. "What if I refuse?"

"He'd be surprised," said Jamilla. "All he understands is what he sees, and he sees Jatahn. That's how he expects you to behave."

"But what would he do if I refused?"

"He wouldn't let you stay on the ship." Jamilla nodded at the flat blackness beyond the window. "We're heading for Traja. He has a contact there. That's probably where he'd leave you."

"Traja?"

"The old border world. It used to be part of the Faraque before the Emirate invasion. I'm sure you've heard of it."

I had. In the old days, Traja had been a shared planet between Emirate space and Faraqui territory, a stopover for merchants and traders from both sides. Now it was a gateway to the conquered Frontier from the bastion of Emirate space. "We're going to an *Emirate* world? In a Faraqui ship? We'll be blown to pieces—"

"The ship is disguised, Alatah. Emirate scans identify us as a small frieghter."

"But what are we doing in Emirate space?"

"Reconnoitering," said Jamilla. "Like we were on Bellea-Naya." She smiled. "We're spies."

"I thought we were going to—"

"You thought we were on our way to Ahmedi-Jatah. We're not."

I glanced out the window, into the darkness beyond. Traja. If nothing else I would be light-years closer to Renee. "D'Rasha has a contact there?" I asked.

She nodded. "His name is Otis Tarda. He's been a Faraqui ally for years."

"Tarda is a slaver?"

"Oh, no," she said. "He runs his own business."

"What kind of business?"

"Gaming," said Jamilla. "Gambling. That sort of thing."

Some part of this wasn't true. Apprehension glimmered in her dark eyes. Her placid, delicate face was strained around her mouth, tight down to her shoulders. It was suddenly clear to me what she would lose if I stayed. Her status, such as it was, her rank, her standing in Rasha's household would all disappear. I was Jatahn. I would usurp her whether I wanted to or not.

"How long have you been with D'Rasha?" I asked.

"Twelve years, Jatahn."

Me and Rasha, sword and armor. Or a quiet escape, playing by Faraqui rules instead of running headlong, like the doomed prince in the fairy tale.

"What if I stay?" I asked.

Her expression didn't change. "He has expectations," she said. "You'll have to fulfill them. That's all."

"Troah," said Rasha. "Do you know the translation?"

The drape to the next room was pulled to one side. From the low brass dining table, I could see the mattress, on the floor instead of in a frame, thick with pillows and quilts. Jamilla moved silently through the bedroom, in and out of sight, adjusting cushions, setting out trays of finger food and glasses for wine.

"Tell me what it means," said Rasha.

I looked down, away from his eyes. If part of my seduction was a lesson in Faraqui history, then we were already well into it. On the floor, Prince Rexidi stared up in terror from the carpet. "Bad luck, D'sha."

Rasha shook his head. "Strange how language distorts

over a hundred years. It means 'Hand of Fate,' or 'Prophecy.' *Troah* isn't bad, or good. It just can't be avoided." He leaned forward, gray eyes intent behind the blue stripe. "The Emirate invasion of our Faraque was a *troah*. Our *Middayin*—our Priestesses—predicted it, generations ago. We knew it was coming, but we were complacent. We didn't start making plans to fight until it was too late. My father used to say that the Emirate invasion galvanized us as a people. But that was before my youngest sister was born. And long before she joined the Middayin." He rested his elbows on his knees. "Jamil's told you we're heading for Emirate space."

The way he said it, I had no doubt that Jamilla had repeated our entire conversation, word for word. "Yes, D'sha."

"You'll need to know certain things about my family, Yaeylie Frenna. When we get back to the Faraque, it won't be long before everyone knows your heritage. You're the great-granddaughter of my ancestor's favorite, and that carries a great deal of weight. But . . . there are things I need to tell you." He studied me for a moment. "Ten years ago, my family was on the verge of being exiled from our own tribe."

He wanted me to ask. I would have to ask. This conversation would be the beginning of my refusal. I took a breath. "Why, D'sha?"

"Because of my youngest sister."

"The Middayin sister?"

He nodded. "The women on my mother's side have always been high in the holy caste. They're respectable women, unshakable, faithful women." He let his hands fall into his lap After the invasion, my ancestors were left with a fraction of their former territory and the Emirate across their threshold. The Middayin tried to find some kind of positive sign for the future of our people. There was a glut of positive augurs. With hindsight, anyone can see that very few of them were authentic visions, but we believed them. We had to. Our survival hinges on belief. Without that, we're nothing." He glanced at me. "Does it sound naïve to fall for encouraging lies?"

All I could think of was Renee. *Survival depends on what you believe.* "No, D'sha."

"When I was thirteen, part of my initiation was an auguring. It was very theatric. Frightening really, for a child. My grandmother put on her paint and her jewels and shouted prayers to the gods until she fainted. The only thing she foresaw was the birth of my sister. My father always said when grandmother died, it was that birth that killed her."

The birth of the Middayin sister, I assumed. Rasha traced the hammered patterns in the brass and went on.

"When my sister was eighteen, she joined the Middayin. This was ten years ago, and at that time there were rumors of another Emirate expansion. There was a great deal of tension between our own tribes as we decided how to respond. My sister knew what the Midayyin wanted to hear, and she told them she'd had a dream—a very detailed dream—which was really a battle plan to defeat the Emirate. Even if she wasn't actually guided by the gods, she had a talent for strategy. The Middayin didn't care whether it was a genuine vision or not. They were so impressed, they hailed her as a prophet—what we call a Hand of Fate. For a while she was the most important thing that had ever happened to us. She was the living Hand."

"What happened to her?"

Jamilla moved in the doorway, brushing against the drape—just enough motion to catch Rasha's eye. "Perhaps you're tired, D'sha?"

He smiled. "Jamil likes to think she's my conscience. And she's right. These are things I wouldn't normally discuss, especially with a stranger. But you're Yaeylie. You and I have a common past, and there are things you'll need to know. You and I have enemies, Jatahn. If we lose this war, the Emirate will hunt us down and do their best to exterminate my people—but probably not before we start the job ourselves. You can imagine what might happen to a scapegoat. Or a family of scapegoats. Sometimes blood can make everything clean."

"I don't understand," I said.

He rearranged his robe around his knees. "Because of my sister, my people had a vision to follow. My family was related by blood to the living Hand, and we were respected as leaders. As a people we had finally pulled ourselves together, and we were euphoric." He paused. "Then my sister had another vision. On the eve of battle, when the Middayin led her out in front of the tribes—assuming that she would give one final rallying speech—she gave them a new prophecy instead." He hesitated, as though this was the confession of his life. "She said if we fought the Emirate it would be the end of us. We would lose our way of life, our heritage. And   " His jaw tightened. "And our slaves would go free."

"What happened?"

"The invasion was postponed," said Rasha, "until the Middayin could decide if my sister's vision had any foundation. Of course it did. They'd known it all along. My great-grandmother had known it before the girl was born. The only way the Middayin could redeem themselves was by getting rid of her "

"They killed her?" I said.

Rasha shook his head. "I told them that since our family's honor was at stake, we should be the ones to dispose of her."

I couldn't help it. "*You* killed her?"

He gave me a pained look. "I took her to Traja, and left her with a friend. I told the Middayin she was dead. I thought that was all I needed to do to keep her safe. She was supposed to stay on Traja, but she tried to come home. . . ." He glanced at Jamilla. "I did what I had to do."

"You had no choice, D'sha," said Jamilla.

"What did you do?" I asked.

"D'sha," said Jamilla. "There's no reason for her to know. It's better for her not to know."

"You're right. What's done can't be undone." He sat in silence for a while. "We're on our way to Traja right now. I have to see my sister before the fighting starts." He rubbed his forehead. "When we get back to the Faraque, you may be questioned by the Middayin. You won't mention this conversation to them, or anyone else. You won't tell them that we've been to Traja, or that my sister is still alive. Is that clear?"

"Yes, D'sha."

He reached across the table to take my hand.

In the bedroom doorway, Jamilla tensed.

"Yaeylie Frenna," said Rasha. "Your people were a comfort to mine for centuries. Not just as slaves. You must know, it's deeper than that. It's as deep as blood."

He squeezed my fingers. My heart began to pound.

"It's a *troah* that I found you on Naya," he said. "We'll be as close as my great-grandfather and your great-grandam."

Jamilla vanished behind the drape, silently offended.

"D'sha . . ." I said.

He came around the table and settled next to me in a soft rustle of cloth. He filled the warm room, dense as burnt curry, rippling heat in the narrow space between us.

"I know what you feel," he whispered. "I feel it." His expression was gentle, understanding, as though he was to blame for every trauma in my life. He touched the base of his throat, above the ridge of his collarbone, then put his warm finger lightly against mine. A gentle motion, just enough to find the barbed point of his hook in my body. I could see myself reflected in his gray eyes. He would pull me under, drowning me in my own desire, deep and visceral, to obey.

His arms came around my waist. He leaned forward and brushed his lips against my cheek. He kissed my chin, under one ear and down my neck.

Three years of Olney's invasions should have choked me, but this was different. Different from my clandestine nights with Martine, as well. I shut my eyes.

Thin cloth over hot skin, over muscle, over bone. My hands were on his shoulders, down a length of spine. The hook went even deeper and the air turned viscous. He pulled me close and my heart hammered against his. Soft ear cartilage under lips, breath like velvet, dark hair soft as worn silk. There was something more he wanted—or that he wanted to give me—an emotion, or a desire I had never heard of.

His hair fell across my face. The insides of his thighs pressed my knees. He straddled me and his erection pressed my belly. He wouldn't slide himself into me until I was ready. How did I know that?

Pale fingers caressing her brown skin, blond strands tangling with her dark. The barb-point of unnamed desire twisted his throat. His nipple through soft cloth. The swell of a breast that fit my hand. Her tension, her fear, surprised me.

No.

It surprised *him*.

I opened my eyes. I pulled back, and his hand came off my breast.

The room blurred like I'd held my breath for far too long, but it wasn't from lack of air. It was from being inside him.

He held my shoulders. "You felt it?" He was sweating through his robe and let go long enough to shrug it off. It fell to his hips in a waft of strong spice. He reached for me again and I jerked away. The edge of the brass table banged the small of my back. He froze where he was, on his knees in front of me, disappointment splashed across his face.

"Didn't you feel anything?" he whispered. "Jatahn?"

Armor and sword? I had touched my own body through his hands, and he had touched his through mine.

"Feel what?" I gasped.

"Don't be afraid of it." His voice shook. "Don't be afraid."

He gathered his robe up by fistfuls and started toward me, one knee, and then the other. I slid against the wall and he stopped.

He sat on his heels and wiped his face. "You couldn't feel it." He sounded agonized, crushed.

I'd felt *everything*. "Feel *what*?"

Rasha took an unsteady breath. "You should have—" He touched his throat, where the hook had twisted, a sharp, barbed connection between us. "Here. It's a small gland. It produces pheromones. It increases your—sensitivity to anyone else with the same physiology. Your people have always been special to us, but . . ." He swallowed. "In the past we weren't strict enough about interbreeding. Some of us have the gland, too. We were born with it. Like the Jatahn."

I touched my own throat and found chain links. "We're your cousins? And your slaves?"

"Partners." He moved closer. "Companions. Favored Ones." I pressed myself against the wall and he stopped. "Yaeylie Frenna, couldn't you feel anything?"

In the middle of my chest, the wild joy I'd felt at the sight of him on Naya had contracted into a defensive wad. The closer he came, the stronger the sense of false comfort—deeper, and more engulfing than any kind of sex. The more he touched me, the less I would remember about what Renee and Martine had showed me. I would dissolve into him, salivating and pliant when he met my eye. My will would shrink to nothing. I would never leave this ship, or his bed, and in the end, I would Fail and die.

"No," I said—not to his face, but to the floor, to the ship itself, and to all his relatives, light-years away. "No," I said. "No."

FIVE

Beyond the Trajan ground station's open doors, rain sluiced into the dark plaza. It beat on the canopy outside the station's entryway, heavy as a waterfall, rushing, flooding, pooling in the humid night.

I put my hand in my pocket. The Virevir packets were taped to my leg, a rough place under a layer of fabric.

"Can't we wait for it to stop?" I said.

"It doesn't stop." Rasha adjusted the hood of his slicker and stepped into the downpour.

My own slicker came down to my knees—a shapeless, clear plastic thing, like a hooded storage bag, with slits for my hands. I pulled the hood up and followed Rasha, ankle-deep in warm water.

The Trajan plaza was the same kind of wide expanse as the one on Naya, but here the space was crammed with dirty white tents and flimsy shacks, side by side. Streams of water spilled off the shacks, gushing onto the nearby tents.

The tents slumped under the weight of the rain, grimy and soaked.

"People live here?" I asked.

"This is the slave market," said Rasha. "It's the biggest in the Frontier. Quite famous." Rain glittered under his eyes, like tears. "You've never heard of it?"

"No, D'sha."

He shrugged.

Yesterday he would have been glad to fill in every gap for me. His disappointment made the warm rain seem clammy. It made the magenta streetlights tiny and bleak, overwhelmed by the saturated night. I dogged along in the wake of his boots, rain pummeling my back and shoulders.

At least I had a plan. I would stay with this Otis Tarda person until I could contact Renee. If she had enough money, she could just buy me. If Tarda wasn't interested in selling, or if Rasha had told him not to, certainly Renee was an expert at well-timed escapes. I sloshed over the black paving stones, octagonal and precisely set, softened at the edges by eons of rain. The weight of experience was a comforting feeling. If I came away from Naya and Olney with nothing else, at least I had learned that it was possible to get out of a bad situation. My time in Rasha's custody would be a small, strange chapter in the rest of a better life.

Rasha slowed down. "Jatahn."

He'd stopped calling me *Yaeylie*, as if I didn't deserve my own family name anymore. The weight of experience turned into a mass of guilt. I jogged up next him. "D'sha?"

"Traja was the first world my people settled on," he said. "We had two thousand years of history here, before the Emirate drove us out."

I glanced around. Coils of mist drifted under the lights, like displaced spirits. The half-flooded plaza had narrowed into a walled street—a roofless corridor of high black walls on either side of us.

Rasha opened his hand, palm up to the rain. "We were

shipbound communities before we came to Traja. There was nothing in our culture about farming or construction. Your ancestors were our helpmates. The Jatahn were with us from the very beginning." He flicked water from his fingers.

What did that mean? I wondered. Had his people stolen us from our homeworld, then let themselves be talked into becoming grounded by articulate slaves who missed the dirt under their feet? What had we used to persuade Rasha's ancestors? Our minds? Our bodies? Our hidden pheromonal talents?

The stone walls gleamed in the darkness around us. Not familiar red alizarite, but the same weathered ebony as the octagonal slabs in the plaza. At street level, the walls were broken now and then by passageways, each closed off from the street by a gate. One of the passages was lit. I caught a glimpse of a door at the far end with a pot of blue flowers next to it. The wall along the street, I realized, was an enormous enclosure, the same as the walls around Mosteph's acquired mansion. The Faraqui had been barricading themselves behind stone for a long time, I thought, but this was different from the Faraqui mansions on Naya and Jatah. Those had been designed with an air of grand separation, lofty souls living in a better world than the slaves who were bred around them. Here on Traja, the houses were windowless, with a single entrance, and the distinct impression of hidden exits.

At the far end of the street, one edge of the sky had changed from black to a torrid crimson. Not sunrise. As we came to the next wide plaza, what I'd thought might be dawn turned out to be a low oval of weirdly lit clouds.

"Can you see it?" asked Rasha.

"D'sha?"

"The arena," said Rasha. "The Beryl. Can you see it?"

All I could see was the red island of cloud in the dark sky. Underneath, the plaza was densely invisible, as though it was raining even harder, but soundlessly, only a few meters in front of me. The night took on a close, breathless feel. The flat black paving stones seemed to blend into it. I put my hand out, half expecting another wall.

"Not here," said Rasha. "There. Ahead of you."

Then I saw it.

A sheer cliff of oil-colored stone came straight up out of the ground. The top was silhouetted against the red-lit haze, but the stone itself seemed to absorb any stray light.

Rain spilled down my face. "What's the red?"

"A weather shield," said Rasha. "It covers the entire building. Keeps the sand inside dry."

I'd seen this arena on the holo, but never from this angle. More than anything else, the wall reminded me of the white cliffs on Naya. A long, long fall, from those red clouds to this black street.

Rasha guided me through the puddles at the base until we came to a gate in a glowering archway. Rusting filigree coiled around the gate's metal bars: two fantastic animals, locked in combat. Beyond that, the ring was a dismal pit of sand, stained red by the light of the weather shields.

Warm air brushed my face, carrying the unmistakable slaughterhouse tang of blood.

Rasha stared through the bars. "Do you ever watch the fights?"

"My man did," I said. "On Naya. He was a big fan."

"Were you?"

"No, D'sha."

He was silent for a while. "This is my fault. I made too many assumptions when I first saw you. I could never have left you for that mob, though. That would have been a betrayal."

It was almost as though he was talking to someone else. I peered through the bars, but there was no one inside.

He ran his fingers along the bars until he found a palm-lock. He pressed it and the gate swung open.

"We're going in—there?" I blinked past the rain and the gate and the blood-smelling dark.

Rasha frowned. "Jamil told you," he said.

"Told me what?"

"This is where you'll be staying."

"What?" I started to back away, but he caught my arm. "She said . . . she said you were taking me to a friend of yours—Tarda—a—a gambler."

Rasha nodded. "Otis Tarda. He owns this ring, and this team. There's no lack of betting here." He cocked his head. "What did Jamil tell you?"

Just enough to reassure me, I could see that now. If she'd said a word about an arena, I'd have stayed on the ship without a second thought. I'd have sunk as deep in Rasha's bed as I could, making the best of a bad situation—and squeezing into every cranny that Jamil meant to keep for herself.

I pulled against his grip and felt it tighten. "You can't leave me here."

"If I keep you on the ship, you'll try to escape."

"I won't," I said. "I won't. I promise."

He shook his head. "I think you will."

"I've seen the fights on the holo," I whispered. "They'll tear me apart."

"You won't be fighting," said Rasha.

"They'll make me a—a whore—a passaround—"

"They won't," he said gently, as though this pained him more that I could imagine. "They need a new medic. The last one left unexpectedly. That's what you'll be doing until the war's over."

"Medic?" I said. "I'm not a medic."

"You have all the experience you'll need," said Rasha. He made an overly polite gesture through the gate, but he didn't let go of my arm. "After you, Yaeylie."

I went in.

Arid silence muffled the steady rush of rain. Black pillars

surrounded the ring in a grim single-file procession. Between the columns and the arena wall was a passage—what I would have called a breezeway—except there was no breeze. Box seats and bleachers rose in rows high above the pit, closing in the sky, where the weather shields rippled like the surface of a bloody pool.

Metal rasped on metal as Rasha closed the gate behind us. The lock was a final, electronic *snap*.

"Don't you have a war to fight?"

A female voice. I turned as she moved in and out of the shadows, a bulky silhouette against the ruddy sand. Her hair strayed out in wisps, tinged red, like the air.

Rasha straightened. "Still here, I see."

She let out an angry choke of a laugh. "Did you think I might leave?"

Was this his sister? Was this where he left the all the things he didn't want? A Middayin prophetess, and now me?

Rasha undid the fastenings of his slicker slowly, with too much attention. "How are you?" he asked.

"Is that why you came?" she said. "To see how I'm doing?"

"Actually, I came to see Otis."

She pointed across the ring to a blot of yellow light in the far wall. "He's in his office."

"Aren't you going to tell him I'm here?"

"I can't. I'm waiting for someone."

"Are you?" Like he didn't believe a word. "Who?"

She moved closer. Her bulkiness softened into over-large clothes. She was pale, not very tall, big eyes in a small face, full lips over a pointed chin, generous breasts and hips. She gave me the same uncannily familiar feeling as Rasha, as though I knew her from somewhere else, but that was only natural. She was Faraqui. I blinked down at the dark wet stones. Maybe Otis was too. The arena was probably a nest of them.

"I'm waiting for the police," she said, "if you really want to know."

"Why would the police be coming here?"

"Maybe they knew you were on your way." She showed her teeth. "I did." She turned and saw me. "What's this?" She frowned, and even the dimness couldn't hide her surprise. "Jatahn?"

"Tell me about the police," said Rasha.

She shrugged. "The Chief Inspector has a new toy. He's coming to play. Now. Tell me how you got a Jatahn girl."

"Listen to the news," said Rasha. "Figure it out for yourself." He started for the ring, but she stepped in front of him.

"You got tired of Jamilla? Or is she a present for Otis?"

"Ask her yourself," said Rasha.

She turned her cool eyes on me. "Well?"

"D'sha," I said. "I'm a . . . medic."

Instead of looking doubtful, she glared at me.

Rasha nudged me. "Look again, Jatah."

Red light from the weather shields glinted on something around her neck.

A chain. A slave collar.

Faraqui? In *collar*? My jaw must have dropped halfway to the wet stones. Another detail Jamilla had kept Rasha from mentioning. He'd made his own flesh and blood into a *slave*. So *this* was how he kept his renegade sister from coming home. I stared long enough to be sure of who she was. The unsettling familiarity was in her wide cheekbones and gray eyes—and the sharp sensation of metal in my throat. Her barbed, pheromonal hook, the same as Rasha's, and just as deep.

"We don't need a medic, Rasha."

"You do," he said. "Doctor Frei's gone. I know all about that."

"You don't know anything," she snapped. "Otis already

has a replacement for Frei. A hospital technician. A free man. I'm waiting for him right now."

"I thought you were waiting for the police."

She sneered at him. "I'm waiting for all sorts of things, *D'sha*."

"Mind your manners," he said. "And don't lie to me, Troah."

It took me a second to connect *her* to the word. *Troah?* "That's your *name?*" I blurted.

The girl eyed me. "Take your Jatahn slut somewhere else."

"There is nowhere else," said Rasha.

From the far side of the sand pit, a long way off, I heard laughter.

"That's Otis," said the Troah girl. "I can tell you right now, he's got plans for the evening."

"Then I won't keep him waiting." Rasha took my elbow, pulling harder than he needed to. My feet came off the worn stones, into the gritty warmth of sand. I looked back between the columns, but the Troah girl—whatever she was—wasn't following.

"That's your sister?" I demanded. "That's your *sister?* You did *that* to her?"

Rasha's wet slicker flapped against my legs. He coughed, or choked, or cleared his throat. "Stay away from her," he said.

The office was a dimly lit recess in the far wall. From about halfway across the ring, I could see two desks and a pile of broken crates. Between the office and the edge of the pit, three chairs faced into the ring.

Someone moved in the sand nearby. I felt Rasha jerk. He turned, and I expected the Troah girl, but this time it was a free woman—wiry, white-skinned, with black hair cropped in a straight line around her forehead.

"Althea," said Rasha, relieved. "Good to see you."

Trainer-D'Orso was printed in blocky letters over the

breast pocket of her gray-green coverall. She crossed her arms. "What the hell are you doing here?"

"I'm looking for Otis," said Rasha.

She made an uninviting gesture towards the light. "He's busy."

Rasha glanced at the empty office. "Troah said he'd hired a replacement for Frei."

The woman shrugged. "Troah's full of shit, as usual."

"He hasn't hired anyone?"

"He's interviewing some guy who lost his job at the hospital." She shrugged again. "He'll work cheap. That's all I know."

"Cheaper than Frei?"

She snorted. "Only slaves'll work for less than Frei."

Rasha put an arm over my shoulders. "Tell Otis I've brought him a medic."

The woman gave me an appraising look. "I'll tell him you've brought us another pass."

"She's not a pass," said Rasha. "She worked in a trauma clinic in the Frontier for the last three years."

Althea came closer and patted my cheek, too hard to be mistaken for friendly. "Another piece of Faraqui garbage? How long're we supposed to keep this one?"

"You'll waste her as a whore," said Rasha.

Althea laughed. "Does she have any experience in the ring?"

"A trauma clinic is comparable to any kind of arena work," said Rasha.

"The hell it is," said Althea. She poked me. "Where did you work in the Frontier?"

"Bellea-Naya," I whispered.

"Bellea-*Naya*," repeated Althea. "How very far away. Why'd the trauma clinic get rid of you?"

"Budget cutbacks in the Frontier," said Rasha. "Haven't you been listening to the news?"

Movement in the sand behind me. The Troah girl and

89

another slave were standing just close enough to hear the conversation. The other slave was tall and shirtless, broad-shouldered—a fighter, darker than Troah, but lighter than me.

The fighter ran a hand over metallic blond hair shaved to a gleaming fuzz. A feminine motion.

"Althea?" A man's deep voice drifted in the dry air, coming from somewhere near the office.

Althea cupped her hands around her mouth and shouted back. "Rasha's here, Otis. Want me to kick him out?"

Silence from the office. Althea started toward the light. Rasha took my elbow, and we followed. Behind us, I could hear the soft scrape of bare feet in sand.

The man sitting at the desk was older, balding, fleshy in the face and neck. His skin was smooth and dark as water-polished stone. Diamonds flashed in the curve of his ear. Thin lines of gold gleamed above his eyebrows.

Rasha pulled at my slicker, tugging it off. He pushed me forward. "For you, Otis."

Althea crossed her arms. "Mind your manners, girl."

I dropped awkwardly to my knees, eyes down.

"You say she's a medic?" asked Otis.

"To replace Frei," said Rasha.

"Frei." Otis leaned heavily on the desk. "You work with a man for years and you think you know him. He killed that boy of his—the clinic assistant. Did I tell you that?" He turned to Althea. "What was the boy's name?"

"Tony," said Althea.

"The problem was," said Otis, "Frei didn't just kill Tony. He let him Fail for five days."

Althea nodded and pulled her mouth into a thinner line. "Five days of screaming. Drove us all nuts."

"Five days?" There was more curiosity than sympathy in Rasha's voice. "Why not kill the boy with Thanas? Was it a punishment?"

Althea snorted. "You know Frei didn't believe in punishment."

"Frei was too fond of the boy," said Otis. "He would have been better off having a relationship with a free man. I didn't care what he did on his own time, but I couldn't have him experimenting on the slaves."

"Experimenting?" said Rasha.

Otis rolled his shoulders in an elaborate, uncomfortable shrug. "Frei had peculiar ideas. We all knew that. He wanted to practice his 'good works,' and this is no place for humanitarians."

"It wasn't that complicated," said Althea. "Frei was in love with Tony, and couldn't bear to see the little fucker die. He dragged out Tony's Failure to keep him alive. That's all it was."

"Keep him alive?' asked Rasha. "For another hour or two?"

"Oh no," said Althea. "Days. Weeks. Hell, maybe he thought he could squeeze Tony for another twenty years."

Rasha blinked. "Interesting."

"It wasn't interesting," said Althea. "It was fucking insane."

I was afraid to look up. Renee had said there were *others*, but I couldn't believe they would be in a place like this.

"He was a fine doctor," said Otis. "The fighters trusted him." He glanced down at me. "You say she's a medic?"

"A good one," said Rasha. "You won't have any problems."

"I won't have a slave running the clinic," said Althea. "I want someone who's thinking about earning money and keeping a job."

"How much do you want for her, Rasha?" asked Otis.

"Come on, boss," said Althea. "We've got enough of Rasha's trouble already."

Otis tapped the desk. "What's your training, girl?"

Maybe Rasha's lies would save me. If not, I could tell

the truth later. There might even be a way out once Rasha was gone. "Trauma clinic," I said, eyes on the ground. "Bellea-Naya."

"Three years of solid medical experience," said Rasha. "You can't do better."

"Why don't you talk to the hospital tech?" asked Althea. "See how much better you can do."

"Hospital tech?" Otis thought for a moment. "Oh yes, I remember. The one who was fired. He called this morning. I told him I didn't like his tone."

Althea groaned. "We're not hiring for bedside manner."

"Of course not," said Otis. "We're hiring for maximum profit."

Althea flushed from her neck up to her pale cheeks. She jabbed a finger at me. "This reject's probably stolen. I'll bet she's never seen the inside of a trauma clinic, much less an arena. I don't want to find out what she doesn't know in the middle of the fights."

"You're too suspicious, Althea," said Otis. "We've had plenty of good stock from Rasha."

"Like Troah? He told you she was a pass-girl. You know what she does?"

"She cooks," said Otis.

Althea curled her lip. "You don't know half of it, boss. Downstairs they call her Hand of Death."

"What about Rasse?" asked Otis. "He fights like an animal, never loses."

"Rasse is out of his mind," said Althea. "That's why he fights like an animal."

"Really," said Otis. "I thought it was your training."

Althea flushed even more.

Otis turned to Rasha. "I have no complaints. Name your price."

"A gift," said Rasha. "For a friend and ally."

Otis smiled. "You're too kind."

"*Too* kind," muttered Althea.

"Excuse me, D'Tarda." The Troah girl appeared at the edge of the ring and ducked her head at Otis. "The Inspector's just arrived."

Otis nodded. "Show him in." He flicked his fingers at me and I was dismissed.

I backed out of the office into the darkness of the breezeway, searching for the wall with one hand, groping for unseen obstacles with the other. Another step. To my left, the phalanx of columns around the pit were flat shadows in the oily night air, which became denser and even more soundless as I moved away from the office. My fingers brushed the wet wall—my foot came down on someone else's. Warm hands caught my shoulders.

I twisted around. It was the fighter. A girl, a head and a half taller than I was. Blue eyes in a light brown face. Small breasts with large nipples. A constellation of moles ran along her left side, up the rill of muscle and rib. Thick scars wormed across her belly.

"Welcome to the goddamn arena," she said.

A floodlight came on over the ring, wiping away the red glow of the weather shields. Out in the middle of the pit, a man in an overcoat waved at Otis. Behind him, a slave boy trudged through the sand, soaked to the skin.

Otis waved back. "I thought you might not make it, Inspector."

"You thought wrong." The man pulled off his coat and slung it over one of the chairs at the edge of the pit. He had a uniform on underneath—sharp-cut gray, striped gold on the outside of his sleeves. Gold insignia closed the collar of his jacket.

I felt a movement behind me. I knew without looking that it was Rasha's sister.

The fighter hissed at her. "What the hell's going on, Troah? What happened to the guy from the hospital?"

Troah came out of the dark. "Shut up, Hallie."

Hallie—the fighter—grabbed my arm. "Who the hell is this?"

"She's nothing. She's Rasha's."

"But Otis is going to put her in charge of the clinic."

Troah glanced at the men in the office, too absorbed in their own conversations and too far away to hear us. "Relax, Hallie."

Hallie's grip on my arm hardened instead. "You said you had everything under control."

"I do." Troah pointed into the office, at the slave boy who'd come in with the Inspector. He was wide-shouldered, big, with a thick face and nervous eyes. "Remember him?"

"It's Arbitt," said Hallie. "From the DeKastri ring. So?"

"Did you know DeKastri got rid of him?"

"No," said Hallie. "But he hasn't had a win all season."

"You'll be fighting him tonight."

Hallie's face went tight with sudden anger. "I already beat the shit out of him. What do I have to do? Kill him?"

Troah touched her hand. "Take some advice, Hallie. Let him hurt you."

Hallie glared at her, and then me. "So this thing can screw up? I stay clean in the pit for the entire season, and now you think I should get chopped on purpose?"

"I can help," said Troah. "Frei showed me everything."

Hallie jerked away from her. "Don't bother."

In the office, Otis and the Inspector seemed to be sizing up the DeKastri boy, who stood like a statue. Only his eyes moved, and they flickered around the dim office.

"He's looking for you, Troah," said Hallie.

"He doesn't remember me," said Troah. "He's looking for you."

From the office, the Inspector's voice echoed under the breezeway as he patted the boy's shoulder. "Ten straight wins last year. Some bad luck late in the season, but I think the time off did him good."

"Where did you say you found him?" asked Rasha.

"I can tell you," said Althea. "DeKastri sent his worthless ass to the Mines." She slapped the boy's rear end. "Right, Arbitt?"

The boy just lowered his head.

"It's surprising what people throw out." The Inspector crossed his arms. "A skull fracture and some damage to his spine. Look at him. You can't even tell."

Althea laughed. "What team did you fight for last year, Arbitt? Can you remember?"

The boy stared at the ground.

"Is this the anchor for your own team, Inspector?" asked Otis. "You'll start with him and expand?"

Otis' sarcasm carried clearly to where we were standing, but the Inspector nodded as if it was a serious question. "We'll see how he does tonight."

Otis smiled. "Bring out one of those middle-set boys for him to fight, Althea."

"Don't insult me, Otis," said the Inspector. "Match him with Hallie again. See how he does this time."

Otis raised a gold-lined eyebrow.

Althea squinted into the shadows where Hallie and I and Troah were. "We've got the Silver team coming the day after tomorrow. I don't want any accidents."

"Then you *do* think he's still a contender," said the Inspector.

"I think he's a piece of crap," said Althea, "and I think Hallie has better heads to break."

"Be a good sport, Althea," said Rasha.

Otis turned and beckoned in our direction. "Hallie-girl. Out here."

Hallie made a soft, disgusted grunt. She walked across the sand into the light of the office and dropped to her knees in front of Otis. Even so, her head came up level with his.

"How's your season coming along, girl?"

"Good, D'sha," she mumbled.

"You remember this boy?" He waved at the Inspector's fighter.

"Hello, Arbitt," said Hallie.

The boy stared at her. The color slowly went out of his face, and his mouth seemed to shrivel around his teeth. "The Rock," he said. "Hallie the Rock."

"He remembers the fight?" asked Althea doubtfully. "He left most of his brains out in the ring."

"Saw it on holo," whispered the boy.

I could see him tremble. In a minute, I thought his teeth would start chattering.

Warm air moved next to me. The Troah girl breathed into my ear. "I don't think you're much of a fan."

I turned to face her. In the harsh light from the ring, her eyes were deep, dangerous holes. Her narrow chin seemed sharp enough to cut.

"Jatahn," she said in a whisper. "You should be on Rasha's ship, at his right hand. Why are you here?"

What she was, I couldn't begin to say. The reek of Rasha's tantalizing, gene-deep attraction hung on her. I could understand *that*, I might even be able to walk away from that, but the sensation she left under my heart was different from Rasha. Her closeness was unidentifiably intense. She made me colder or hotter, lighter, or heavier. I backed into the seeping wall until I was pressed against it. My feet slid in puddles of gritty mud. She came even closer. I lurched sideways and she put out her hand—I thought she meant to steady me—instead she held it out, palm up.

In the middle of her palm was a tattoo, dark as blood.

A hand. A hand within her hand, and it filled the night with heat.

"Troah," she hissed. "You know what it means, Jatahn."

She drew her Hand back, fast and sharp. I knew she was going to hit me. There was too much of her to get away from. The Hand came at me with the same rushing suck of air as when fires start. She slashed my cheek, each finger luridly hot, nails hard and sharp as an animal's bite. I let out a yell and dropped into the muck I was standing in.

"Favored One," she hissed. "You're not welcome in this place."

I covered my face, expecting a disfiguring burn, but there was nothing. When I opened my eyes, she was gone.

"Are you all right?"

Hairy ankles moved in front of me. A boy squatted down, shaved even closer than Hallie, down to the shine on his scalp. At first I thought he had a shirt on, but it was another tattoo. It lapped up his jaw and covered his chest, ending like a long sleeve at either wrist.

"Are you all right?" he asked again.

I pushed myself up, panting, looked around for Troah and didn't see her. I could taste her, though. Metal, under my tongue.

"What is the matter?" The boy enunciated each word, watching my face for comprehension, as though I was from somewhere so foreign, he wasn't sure I could understand anything he said.

"Her—" I pointed shakily after Troah.

"Oh," He nodded and patted me awkwardly. "It is o-kay. She'd scare anybody." He rocked on his heels, arms across his knees. "You're a new pass?"

"No," I stammered. "I'm the new medic." It sounded like wishful thinking. Not welcome in this place.

"Oh. Oh well." He stuck a hand out. "I'm Leiban." He cocked his head in the direction of the office. "I'm Althea's."

His tattoos were exotically intricate, so detailed it was hard not to stare. The design seemed engraved on him, as though it had always been part of his skin. A blue face peered out from under one nipple, wide-eyed in fright. It took a minute for me to see the dogs, the horses, and the men in pursuit.

Rexidi.

In the office, chains rattled against wood. I took my eyes off Leiban long enough to see Otis, rummaging through one of the desks. Hallie was at the edge of the ring, ankle-deep in the sand, fists on her hips. Rasha sat in one of the chairs, legs crossed like a spectator.

Otis pulled out a set of shackles and tossed them to Althea.

She caught one end of the chain and adjusted her grip on Arbitt's collar. "You want them to kill each other with their bare hands, Otis?"

"Knives," said the Inspector.

Otis searched the desk until he found one long blade.

"What's going on?" I whispered to Leiban.

"That boy's called Arbitt," said Leiban. "Hallie beat him at the beginning of last season. She hurt him so bad he couldn't fight anymore and his ring sold him off." He tapped behind his left ear. "Hallie bashed Arbitt's brains all over the ring. She got great press for it. She's the Rock, you know."

Some of this was familiar from Olney's late-night holo-watching marathons at the bar. "Her ring name?" I said. "The Rock?"

He nodded, encouraged that I was neither all that stupid nor all that foreign. "She's team anchor," said Leiban. "There's Hallie, me and Rasse." He thumped his chest. "Althea's Assassins. First place in this season's semifinals." He smiled at my lack of comprehension. "Too bad you're not a fan. If you get thrown in here, you might as well have an appreciation for the sport."

Out in the pit, Althea had locked Arbitt into a single ankle cuff at the end of the shackle. She shaded her eyes against the floodlights, squinting at Otis. "What do you want them to do?"

The Inspector tossed the blade past her into the sand and pointed into dark. "Put the knife out there."

Althea made an exasperated noise. She picked the blade

up by its tip and walked toward the center of the ring, where the light began to fade.

From the breezeway, I had a clear view of Arbitt. He swayed in his shackle, ashy-faced, wiping his hands on his shirt, over and over. Hallie sauntered across the sand until she was close enough to touch him. She took the other end of the chain and snapped it around her own ankle. The boy glanced around the ring like a terrified cat.

"Won't she just beat him again?" I said.

"If they leave him alone," said Leiban, "but they won't."

"What do you mean?"

Leiban raised an eyebrow. "If you're going to be our new doctor, you better know about Enhancers."

"Enhancers?"

"Transdermal augmentors," said Leiban. "They react with the Virus and make you open to suggestion. Once you're 'hanced, you do whatever you're told, no matter how impossible it sounds." He nodded toward Arbitt, sweating under the cold light of the floods. "They're not legal in competition, but there's not much else that'll make this kind of fight interesting."

At the edge of the ring, Otis put his arm over the Inspector's shoulders. "Let's set a wager, friend Inspector. I say your boy breaks in thirty seconds flat."

Rasha laughed. "That's no bet."

"He'll fight," said the Inspector, but he didn't seem as confident about Arbitt as he had.

"I think not," said Otis. "Not without some assistance." He motioned to Althea.

She shaded her eyes against the glare of the floodlight. "What now?"

"The boy needs a little help to get started," said Otis.

"What he needs is his goddamn missing brain cells," said Althea. "Or maybe not. Now he's got the sense to be scared."

Otis groped in his pockets and pulled out a small drawstring bag. He tossed it onto the sand at Althea's feet. " 'Hance the boy," said Otis.

"Yes, *sir*. Whatever you say, *sir*." Althea picked a handful of yellow capsules out of the bag. She opened Arbitt's shirt and pressed them along the underside of his arm, leaving an oily yellow sheen. Arbitt staggered and blinked like someone who'd just woken up. The fear in his face evaporated. Hallie backed off warily to the limit of the chain.

Althea pulled Arbitt's shirt closed, fastened it, and went over to Otis. "We fight the Silver team day after tomorrow," she said to him in a low, tense voice. "I don't want my girl cut up tonight."

"She's mine," said Otis, "not yours. And she'll keep herself together for this." Otis tilted his head at Hallie. "Won't you?"

Hallie gave a jerk of a nod.

Otis smiled at the Inspector. "Ready when you are."

The Inspector pointed at Arbitt. "On my signal, you'll fight to win. Understood?"

"Yes, D'sha," said the boy.

Hallie lowered her head, shoulders tensed. Arbitt crouched, eyes locked on the Inspector.

The Inspector raised one finger. "Ready?" His hand wavered for a second in the warm air, then slashed down.

Hallie dodged to one side as Arbitt charged. She banged both fists against the side of his head, and he pitched into the sand. She grabbed the slack in the shackle and yanked the boy's leg out from under him as he tried to scramble up. She swung at him, punching him in the face, under his ribs, until he fell backwards, crabbing away from her on elbows and heels.

Leiban shifted and crossed his arms as though he was judging style. "If she knocks him out, she'll have to drag him halfway across the ring to kill him."

"You think she needs a knife?" I asked.

Leiban nodded. "Otis wants blood."

There was already plenty of blood. It was streaming from Arbitt's nose and mouth. Hallie's hands were covered with it. She edged sideways toward the knife, which glittered in the floodlight, a needle in the sand.

Arbitt waited until she took her eyes off him to find the blade, and hurled himself across the length of the chain. Hallie grabbed for the knife and missed as he tackled her. For a moment there was nothing but a wild thrashing of limbs while the two of them hammered each other. Someone shrieked, but it was impossible to tell who it was.

Beside me, Leiban put his knuckles in his mouth and began to chew on them.

The Inspector turned to Otis. "So much for your Rock."

Arbitt reared up on his knees, found the knife and snatched it out of the sand. Hallie rolled out from under him, blood down the side her neck like streaks of black paint. She flung herself away as Arbitt slashed air. He launched himself with a wild yell, grabbed her, clamping one hand around her jaw, plunging the knife into her side. He pulled the blade out and swung again. He cut her twice. She socked him in the stomach. He staggered, fell, got to his feet, and tripped in the chain. Hallie threw herself on top of him, throttling him, groping for the knife. Arbitt writhed and choked as Hallie wrenched the knife out of his fist. She pressed the tip into his throat and, without the slightest hesitation, drove it straight down, straight through.

I expected him to spasm, then stiffen, the way animals die when their necks are broken. Instead, Arbitt's body arched as his Failure rushed over him.

"Kill him, Hallie," muttered Leiban. "Hurry up, hurry up."

She pushed her face against his ear as he thrashed. Her whisper was lost in the hiss of sand and his breathless cries. Abruptly all the tension went out of Arbitt's body. His arms flopped to his sides, his legs shuddered and went limp. Leiban let a long breath out through his teeth.

"He's dead?" I whispered. "He Failed that fast?"

"He was 'hanced," said Leiban. "She told him to die and he did what he was told."

Hallie pushed herself to her knees, holding her bloody side.

"You'd better get out there," said Leiban.

I took one step into the sand. This was crazy. It wouldn't take long for Althea to figure out that I'd never been near a trauma clinic. Rasha might try to cover for me, but when he was gone, how was I supposed to explain myself? Troah might be tolerated because she could cook, but what would happen to me?

Althea crouched next to Hallie. "Where's that medic, Rasha?" she bellowed. "Where's your goddamn medic?"

"Go on," hissed Leiban.

I took another step. On the far side of the breezeway, something moved in the darkness.

Troah.

Half lit, half black. Eyes on me, lethal as some poisonous reptile. My throat went tight. My feet froze. Her hostility fell on me like veils, layer on layer, stifling in the warm night. I couldn't breathe. My knees locked. I was paralyzed, another column at the edge of the pit, turned to stone by her single glance.

"Hurry *up*!" Leiban shoved me into the glare of the floodlight. I lost sight of Troah, and started blundering in Hallie's general direction.

"What do you think this is, a vacation?" Althea grabbed my arm and pushed me next to Hallie. "Where's your medical scanner?"

I didn't have one, but I didn't have the spit to tell her. I didn't need a scanner anyway. Hallie's face was spattered with blood. The wounds in her side stank of bowel. Her eyes seemed unfocused, and she was holding her head at an unnatural angle. Her skull was fractured. She should have been unconscious, or at least on the verge of deep shock. Surgery. I was going to have to do surgery by my-self. I took her wrist in my shaky fingers for a pulse, but she shook me off.

"Give me a shot and let me wash," said Hallie. "Fuck. What a waste of time."

Althea pushed herself under the girl's arm. I slid under the other, not tall enough to be any real support. Hallie braced one sticky hand against the back of my neck and stood with a grunt. I staggered under her, hot in my throat. She was a slave, not even a proper human being. She would heal herself. A shot of the Virus was all she needed. I could do that. I swallowed the heat in my throat. Or tried to.

"This way," said Althea. The three of us blundered away from the office, into the indeterminate blackness of the breezeway.

"You were so unbelievably slow," said Althea. I thought she meant me, but she was talking to Hallie. "You were pathetic. I don't care if you did kill him. In competition, you would have gotten two points for skill, half a point for style."

Hallie spat into the sand.

I looked back once to see Rasha staring after me as Otis and the Inspector shook hands. I didn't see Troah, but I could feel her.

"Watch where you're going," snapped Althea.

In the dark wall ahead, I could see the backlit outline of a pair of tall wooden doors. Althea kicked one until it banged open. Yellow light seeped up from a downward flight of concrete stairs. The stairs were splattered brown, as though someone had spilled a bucket of paint. Except it wasn't paint. It was ages and ages worth of dried blood.

Althea and Hallie maneuvered their way down, leaning on each other. I followed, deeper into a pool of stifling humidity. The walls in the stairwell were slick with con-densation. The metal railings had corroded to black sticks, as though the constant rain outside the weather shields had found its way into the structure of the arena, and was slowly running through stone and concrete, to collect somewhere far below the ring.

The bottom of the stairwell intersected an arched hallway. Dim lights ran along the peak of the ceiling, illuminating complex water stains and patterns of mold. The suffocating humidity thickened in the locker-room stink of mildew and sweat.

"Here's the clinic." Althea kicked at the door opposite the bottom of the stairs, but it didn't budge. I twisted the loose handle, pushed the door open and lights came on.

A steel surgical table filled the middle of the small room, with no more than a body's width between it and the sink. White metal cabinets crowded along the wall next to the table, floor to ceiling. The only other entrance was a sturdy, metal-sheathed door in the opposite wall, marked TRAINING.

I tried to swing my door completely open and couldn't. There was a desk in the way. Piles of printout and holostills spilled off the desktop, an island of chaos in the otherwise spotless room. I squeezed past it until I was standing in the hip-wide space between the table and the cabinets.

Althea helped Hallie onto the table and scowled at the mess around the desk. "Where the hell's Troah?" said Althea. "I told her to get this place cleaned up."

Bare feet echoed off the low ceiling in the hallway.

Troah. On her way to the clinic.

Closing in on me.

She appeared in the doorway, her tattooed hand in a fist. She eyed me. I stared at the floor, my back against the cold white metal cabinets. I would see the mark if she unclenched her Hand. And if she did, then what? I could only imagine the worst things. Bursting into flames, somehow, if she touched me again. Or at the least, running from this room, screaming insanely about pheromones.

"You called, D'sha?" *D'sha* sounded wrong coming out of Troah's mouth. She spat the word, like bad food.

"This place is a wreck," said Althea. "I gave you a week, and this place is still—" She jabbed a finger at the desk.

"I thought Frei might come back," said Troah.

"He's never coming back," said Althea. "And even if he does, he's been replaced." She frowned at me. "What's the matter with you?"

My mouth felt like it was filled with arena sand. How could I answer? Did she really expect me to explain? "Tuh," I said, "Tuh. Tro-uh."

"Oh, *wonderful*," said Althea. "The medic's another one of Rasha's weak-kneed purebreds." She jerked a thumb at Troah. "Get out of here, witch. You can scare her to death some other time."

The Hand. The Hand stayed closed. Troah lifted her sharp chin, spun around, and stalked off.

"Stay away from her," Althea said to me, and pointed at the cabinets. "You'll find everything you need in there."

I fumbled with latches. Hypoderms by the case lined the top shelves. Disinfectant swabs—out of place here, where the patients were immune to infection—pressure bandages, suture kits, cartridges designed to snap into a standard hypoderm—-and a scanner. I grabbed it off the shelf and pointed it at Hallie.

"You don't need that," said Althea. "Just give her a shot." She pointed at the cartridges. "That's the stuff."

Boxes and boxes of the Virus in bright green cartridges. At least there was nothing new about this. I'd loaded a thousand needles for Olney. This dose would be a booster—augmenting Hallie's low levels. In a couple of hours, she should be fine. I snugged a cartridge into the hypoderm, twisted the plunger and cracked the seal.

"How nice," said Althea. "You've done this before."

Hallie smoothed the inside of her arm, still gritty with sand. Raised needle scars pocked her brown skin. I hovered over the side of the steel table and thumbed her arm past wiry tendons for the faint blue line underneath. Hallie clenched her fist. The vein bulged up. She shut her eyes. I emptied the needle and pulled it out. Tender skin closed around a tiny prick of red.

"Incredible," said Althea. "Rasha gave us something we can use."

Hallie sighed and rubbed her arm.

I turned on the scanner.

Red for life signs, green for the Virus. Just like Martine, except Hallie's graph showed an upward jag where I'd given her the injection. There was no indication of how badly she'd been hurt, only that she was recovering. I flipped to the more specific displays, which showed her abdominal wound. Still raw, but not oozing. Her skull fracture was healing. She was going to be fine. I was going to be fine.

"Well?" said Althea.

I nodded. "Okay," I said. "She's okay."

Hallie shrugged.

Leiban leaned into the doorway, ghastly pale under the yellow light and the dense blue lines of his tattoo. "Still alive, Hallie?" He winked at me.

"For now," said Hallie.

Althea pointed at her boy. "This is Leiban. He's going to give you the grand tour of our little pit, and find a place for you to sleep."

"There aren't any open cells, D'Althea," said Leiban.

"Put her in Frei's room," said Althea.

"*Frei's* room?" Hallie gave Althea an incredulous look. "In his *bed*? Why can't she sleep in here, like the rest of the clinic assistants?"

"Tony slept in Frei's room," said Leiban.

"That was different," said Hallie. "She's just another one of Rasha's rejects. Why should she get his room?"

Leiban shook his head. "You've got to be the only one who wishes Frei was still around."

"He was a good man," said Hallie. "He knew how to treat people."

"Which is why he let Tony Fail for five days," said Althea. "Very fucking merciful. Otis should never have hired him in the first place. Anyone could see that the guy had crazy ideas."

Leiban's expression tightened into bitter conviction. "I'm glad he's gone."

"Your loss," said Hallie.

"Get out, Hallie," said Althea. "Get cleaned up. Get some sleep. And shut up."

Hallie slid off the steel table. She rubbed at the caked blood on her side. "You could have at least hired a fan, D'Althea."

"Get *out*," said Althea.

When Hallie was gone, Leiban gave me a bright, artificial smile. "She can be real friendly. She's just hard to get to know."

"You're not here to make friends," said Althea. "You're here to do your job. You're damn lucky to have one." Althea slapped me on the back. "Welcome to the goddamn arena, medic," she said, and walked out.

SIX

Leiban watched Althea go, waiting until the sound of her boots had faded. When he turned around, the deference was gone from his face. He seemed thinner, and his pallid skin had gone sickly gray. He cleared an armload of paper off the chair by the desk and sat. "You're a lucky thing," he said. "You get a real bed."

"Thanks," I said.

"Don't thank me. Thank Althea." He gestured at the clinic itself. "Thank Frei for leaving. Or thank Tony for dying, finally." He picked up one of the holostills and tossed it onto the steel table. A light-skinned man with wispy white hair and brown, almond-shaped eyes stood with his arm around a rangy blond boy, presumably Tony. I studied the man's creased face for any sign of malice. I looked harder for anything that might put him in the same league as Renee. I couldn't find either.

"This is Frei?" I asked. "He doesn't look like a murderer."

Leiban's face twitched. "What happened to Tony wasn't Frei's fault. He did it because of Troah."

"What do you mean?"

Leiban peered into the corridor, reached over and pushed the door shut. He leaned forward in the chair, fists between his knees. "Troah has her own little cult down here. The fighters work for Althea because they have to, but they won't set foot in the ring until Troah tells them whether they'll win or lose. She's the one who sets the odds."

"What?"

"Troah tells Otis how to make the most money on the fights," said Leiban. "Usually he'll bet for us, but when Troah gets mad, or has a bad day, or wants to get back at someone, she sets up enough of the fighters to make the whole team lose. She fixes a couple of fights, and then she tells Otis to bet against us." Leiban knotted his fingers together. "You saw how he is. He doesn't care what happens to anyone, as long as he gets a little cash out of it."

"What does she do to the fighters?"

He let out a skeptical snort. "How can you ask that kind of question? All she did was smack you, and you were ready to fall apart."

"Doesn't Althea have something to say about it?"

"Of course," said Leiban. "But this is Otis' place. Everyone here belongs to him. Except for me. As long as Troah's happy, we're all fine. But when things go wrong . . ." He shrugged. "Frei used to keep Troah in line. He'd talk to her. Now Troah thinks she can do anything. She has friends on the outside. Accomplices. Or disciples. She wants them hired on." He nodded at the white metal cabinets, the small room in general. "In the clinic."

"Why?"

"I'll tell you," said Leiban, "but you won't believe it." He got up and came over to the other side of the steel table. From the center of his chest, Rexidi stared out in horror. Demons with snarling faces dove under his sternum into thick undergrowth of trailing vines and exotic flowers. Leiban leaned closer. His chain collar shifted on his neck, revealing permanent, tattooed links underneath. "Troah has this story she tells the fighters. She says that they don't have to die when they Fail. She says there's a way to survive Failure. She tells them that they can be free."

I looked down at my distorted reflection in the steel tabletop, and the pale blur of Leiban's face.

Troah. The Fateful Hand. Rasha's sister and Renee's unnamed cohorts. . . . *and our slaves would go free . . .* Were they all here, in the bottom of this pit, pounding out the truth of their own prophesies?

Whatever was going on, or not going on, Leiban was obviously not part of it. Althea would hear about it if I said anything to make him suspicious. He already thought I was an ignorant purebred. It was best to stay that way.

"She means life after death," I said. "Like heaven."

"She means life after Failure," whispered Leiban.

"Althea said something about that upstairs," I started.

Leiban grabbed my arms. "It's a lie," he hissed, too close, too hot, his brown eyes wide. "It's a fairy tale, it's *shit.* You understand? What she's saying is a *lie.*" His face was pinched with fear, a mirror of the prince, tattooed on his chest.

He let go, and leaned on the cool steel, his palms flat on the tabletop. "Frei was a smart guy, but when Troah starts talking, she has a way of making you believe the things she says. Frei believed her. I think even Tony believed her."

"What about Althea?"

His gray face flushed. He shoved his hands under his armpits. On the surface of the steel table, two hot prints of condensation slowly evaporated. "Troah doesn't want you," he said in an uneven voice. "The hospital tech was her idea, and she's still working on getting him hired. She'll try to make you look bad. She'll try to scare you off. You have to tell me when she does, so I can tell Althea. This is the best chance I'll ever have to get rid of her."

Troah fixed bets. Troah had friends outside the ring. Troah and Hallie had plans for someone else to be Frei's replacement. The two of them might know what Renee knew, and Leiban wanted me to be their enemy.

"Get rid of her?" I said.

"The sooner she's gone, the sooner this place can get back to normal." Leiban let his hands drop to his sides. "Come on," he said. "I'm supposed to be showing you around."

In the corridor, the medicinal smells of the clinic were replaced by damp and sweat and an undercurrent of mingled spices.

"The ring is divided in two halves," said Leiban. "Home side"—he gestured at the ceiling, the moldy walls—"and visitors. Both're identical. Both have three entrances. The clinic access—" He pointed up the stairs Hallie and Althea and I had come down. "And two residential accesses. So, Althea's rooms have a set of stairs—" He pointed behind us, then forward. "And so do Frei's." We passed a doorless arch to the right of the blotchy clinic access stairs. "That's the kitchen. Are you hungry?"

I peered into the empty room. A long counter divided it in half. Woven straw mats covered the floor on the near side. Steel pots hung from hooks in the low ceiling on the other. Ancient ovens hunkered in the gloom, low and grimy. There were no tables or chairs. It was a room where slaves were supposed to eat on the ground like animals.

"We've got plenty of leftovers," said Leiban.

"No, thank you."

Across from the kitchen, a pair of wooden doors were barred shut with a long steel hasp. One door had a window cut into it, sheathed on the edges with more metal, and screened with wire. Leiban had to stoop to see through it. I had to stretch up on my toes. Beyond the wire and locks, the dim room was deserted. Mirrors covered the opposite wall, reflecting the inside of the double doors and a row of black metal-mesh lockers. At the far end was another door, marked CLINIC.

"This is the training room." Leiban tapped the screen, indicating something in one corner.

I squinted into the gloom. A long staff leaned against the mirror. Flat steel crescents were attached at either end. At the top, one blade curved inwards like a phased moon. At the bottom, the other curved outwards, sharp points planted on the floor.

"That's a soga." Leiban touched long, raised scars along his side. "You know what a plume is?" I shook my head and he held up one hand, fingers fanned out. "The blades are razor steel strips at the end of a pole." He slashed the air, his wrist stiff. "Hallie says it gives her better reach. It's visual, and it's good for her scores, but it's more for maiming. Sogas are for a real kill, not just a kill-for-points."

"It's better to kill?" I asked.

"The referees won't deduct style points if the kill is real," said Leiban. "Kill-for-points can bring your average down if you get sloppy. Last year we missed the Championships by three marks because of Hallie's fight."

"She lost?"

"No," said Leiban. "Hallie's partner was killed. Hallie was upset." He shrugged. "Althea was furious."

"Hallie had a partner?"

"Partner. Girlfriend. Lover. Her name was Naritte." He shrugged again. "Althea always says it's stupid to get too attached to anyone around here. Like Tony and Frei."

He turned away. On his back, the scene on his chest and arms continued. Rexidi burst from a dense thicket, four-legged now, with hooves, antlers, and a blue-striped hide, human only in his face and neck. The pursuing demons reached up from under the waist of Leiban's green pants, with hooked claws and long teeth. The horror in the prince's face had turned to an almost religious expression of ecstatic fear.

A little further around the curve of the corridor, Leiban stopped. He pointed to a small door, like a storage closet, on the left.

"That's Troah's room," he said. "Just so you know."

There were three other doors further ahead, each marked with a stenciled slat of green plastic: *The Rock, Striker,* and *Rexidi.* Each had a window with a wire covering, the same as the entrance to the training room.

The Rock was Hallie. "Who's *Striker?*" I asked.

"That was Naritte," said Leiban. "It's a sort of memorial."

Rexidi. That had to be his. He glanced at me, the cell, me again. "I stay with Althea," he said, with the faintest hint of conceit.

Ahead, a barred gate blocked another, darker section of hallway, which curved into uninhabited blackness—the visitors' section, I assumed. On our side of the gate, a flight of stairs broke the left-hand wall, disappearing upwards. On the right, there was one last door.

Leiban rattled the handle, half wrenched out of its socket. "This was Frei's room."

Inside, dirty clothes draped open boxes of medical supplies in the middle of a scuffed green rug. A ragged sofa sat against one wall at an angle. Papers and pictures spilled over the only table in the room. In the far corner, the bed was rumpled and unmade, thin pillows crushed up against the wooden headboard. Beside the bed, a green dresser tilted on three legs instead of four.

Leiban stood in the hallway, as though he couldn't stand to set foot inside.

"What happened in here?" I asked.

"Tony's Failure." He picked at the splintered jamb. "We tried to get in. We tried to make him stop. The whole thing was a nightmare." Leiban let his breath out in a hiss.

"If you need me—" He pointed down the corridor, the way we'd come. "I'm on the other side." He smiled thinly. "Pleasant dreams."

I pulled the door shut as he walked off. The handle nearly came off in my hand.

Inside Frei's abandoned room, the cool stone floor was gritty with sand. The miserable rug was thick with it. There was a leftover tension, easy to feel. Part of it was the door that wasn't going to lock. Even the air had the deep stink of unfinished business, manifesting in sweaty, unwashed blankets, dirty socks, and the sour tang of old semen.

When I sat down on the couch, I found more sand between the cushions. The bed seemed to be a long way off, and a dangerous place besides, filled with the invisible detritus of Tony's death. The quiet and relative coolness of the room made me realize how tired I was. I lay down on the couch and stared at the cracks in the ceiling.

Five days of Failure.

My suspicions about Renee's *others* being here were starting to feel wrong. If any of the arena slaves knew how to survive Failure, neither Otis nor Althea would have survived their euphoria. No one—not even Troah, or a supposedly loved and respected doctor like Frei—could have held them back once they knew that there was more to their lives than being "killed for points" in the arena.

What if the arena was only what Rasha used it for: a warehouse for his troublemakers—Troah, and now me? Troah might be exactly as warped, deranged and sadistic as Leiban said she was. So what if she had friends outside the gates? So what if she and Hallie thought some free technician was preferable to Otis' choice of replacements for their team doctor? What did it prove if Troah told the fighters a fairy tale about lasting longer than the Virus and surviving Failure? Didn't Tony's five-day Failure prove that whatever she and Frei were doing was wrong?

And if they were, did that mean I was at my starting

point again? I had three slapneedle packs of Virevir, and I was light-years closer to Renee. All I had to do was find her, and Olney's Extension Service call-codes would work as well here on Traja as they had on Naya.

I sat up. It was time to set my own wheels in motion.

I got off the couch, turned—and saw Troah standing just inside the door.

The cool room went hot. All the feeling went out of my legs.

She'd been here all along. She was waiting for me.

"Jatahn."

Her voice was ice, slivers of ice, sharp as razors.

She came closer, her marked hand out, casual, like a greeting. My bones turned fragile. If she touched me, I would shatter.

"Kneel, my girl," she whispered.

I fell, knees and knuckles to the filthy rug, crouching at her unwashed feet. Her predatory smile settled over me.

She sat on the couch, and put her other hand—the unmarked hand—on my shoulder. Instead of ice, her touch was reassuringly warm. In my chest was the same bizarre rush of belonging I'd felt, days ago on Naya, when I'd first realized what Rasha was.

"My brother left you to spy on me," she said. "He should have known better." She slid her fingers under my chin and tilted my head up. "Are you some kind of peace offering?" She bent closer. Her hair brushed my cheek. She smelled of curry and bread, yeasty as fresh dough. Her hair fell around me like a net. She was smothering, reassuring, her closeness an equal substitute for breathing. "Does he think I'll stay quiet while he fights his stupid war?" she murmured. "Is that why you're here? To keep me occupied?"

Her mouth touched mine, just long enough to burn the tip of my tongue. I wanted to push her away before she scorched me, but even more, I wanted to roll in her flames.

I wanted scars from her, the kind that people would recognize. *Troah*, they'd say, *I see where she touched you.*

She pulled away from me. She stood up and tugged my hair. "Come with me, Jatahn."

In the corridor, she led me past the empty cells with their plastic name-slats, toward the kitchen and the training room. The stink of mildew faded near the kitchen, changing to dense, familiar aromas. Kimarra with pepper. Reshie fried in oil, thickened with curry. New bread baked with cinnamon.

She took my arm and led me past the clinic, around the curve in the water-stained wall.

Ahead, the corridor cut between two large cells. On the right, a couple of male fighters peered out to see what was coming down the hall, but most were asleep on the floor. On the left, the girl-fighters were crowded into their own cage, elbows and fingers and dirty bare feet sticking through the bars.

Between the cells, the corridor was wide enough so that the opposite sexes couldn't touch each other, but here in the hallway, Troah and I were well within reach.

Troah pulled me to a stop in front of a bristling red-headed boy, taller than Leiban and twice as heavy. Half a dozen other fighters got to their feet behind him.

"It's late, Ransom," Troah said to the redheaded boy. "You should be resting. It's better for your odds."

Ransom pressed his bulk against the bars, eyes bright and mindless. "A pass," he barked. "You brought us a pass."

Heads turned. Sleeping fighters rolled over on thin mats, awake now, and alert.

"She's not a pass," said Troah.

A blond boy with ragged scars across his belly studied me, avoiding Troah's eyes. "She's the hospital tech?"

In the other cell, a husky girl with coal-blue skin, her hair twisted into short coils, shook her head. "The new doc's a guy. A free guy."

A light-skinned boy peered at me. "Is she yours, D'Troah?"

D'Troah. So this was her cult. If Leiban was wrong about everything else, at least he was right about that. Any one of these slaves would have stood in the heat of Troah's fire and scorched themselves, just like me.

Troah squeezed my arm. "Tell them what you are, Jatahn."

Her malice numbed my jaw, my teeth, my tongue. She waited to see if I was going to sputter something. "This is supposed to be Frei's replacement," she said. "She's a gift, from Rasha."

The dark-skinned girl turned her head to spit on the blotchy concrete floor.

"She doesn't look much like a doctor," said one of the boys.

Ransom brushed his fingers along my hip. "Doesn't feel like a doctor."

Troah put her poisonous lips next to my ear, and said, in a loud, stagy whisper, "I think she's Rasha's spy."

The dark-skinned girl snorted. "What does Rasha expect her to find out? Tony's dead. Frei's abandoned us. All we've got now are your prophesies, and your promises." She draped her arms through the bars, patently unafraid. "If we want to survive, we should believe in something that works." She glanced at her cellmates. "Not some lie about life-after."

Eyes turned away. Bare feet shuffled uneasily at this heresy. Ransom gave the girl a glare of angry distrust, but I could see other heads nodding in agreement.

Troah saw them too. Her body heat went frosty cold.

I took a mouthful of stale air. I could save myself with one sentence. She had promised Tony's freedom—life-after—to these slaves, not his death. She, and Frei and their friends outside the ring, had some idea that it was possible to survive Failure, but none of them knew exactly how.

117

Now I could see my place.

"It's not a lie!" I blurted. "It's not a lie!"

Troah's Hand closed over my wrist. "Of course it's not a lie, Jatahn." As though she appreciated my support.

"But I *know*," I said. "I've seen it done. *I* can do it. I *know*!"

Blank, unbreathing silence filled the grimy corridor.

Troah's Hand ground my wristbones together. She shoved me down the hall, away from the fighters.

The dark-skinned girl grabbed at me. "Wait a second," she shouted after us. "Wait—what else does she know?"

Troah ignored her, her Hand tight and sharp as a bunch of sticks. When we were around the next curve, out of earshot, she stopped.

"That was a stupid thing to say," she hissed.

"It's true," I whispered.

"What else did Rasha tell you about me?"

"Nothing," I said. "He doesn't know anything. *I* know."

"*What* do you think you know?"

"On Naya," I stammered. "On Naya, I helped my friend. They left. They left me. I ran. That's why I ran."

"Helped your friend do *what*?"

"We freed her," I whispered.

She laughed, right in my face. "*Freed* her? And how did you do that?"

"With—with—" If I hadn't been so scared of her, I might have blurted out everything. I scrabbled at my leg, where the Virevir was taped on. I wanted to show her. I needed to prove myself to her. She stared at me, scratching and stammering, like I was out of my mind.

"Come with me, Jatahn," she said, "and meet the last Assassin."

Just ahead, on the right side of the hallway, was a single cell door. It was same as the others—wooden with a mesh screen over the window, except this door bulged. Thick boards strained against each other, held together with a web of iron straps. For a naïve moment, I thought the warpage might have something to do with the humidity. It didn't. The door had been torn open, once upon a time, by whoever had been inside.

Troah stopped in front of the cell. "Rasse?"

Something rustled. The stink of human shit wafted out through the wire mesh, too high for me, or Troah, to see through.

"Have a look," said Troah. She pushed me against the splintered wood.

All I could see was the dark curve of the ceiling.

Troah grabbed my collar and shoved me up higher, on my toes, half choking me. "Have a look, Jatahn."

Rasse filled the cell, huge as a bull. His black eyes glittered in a white, shit-smeared face. He was naked, filthy, shaved bald on his head and privates. He gazed up at me, one hand wrapped around his penis. His tongue darted over crooked, broken teeth. He scrambled to his feet and rushed at me.

I twisted out of Troah's grip, and flung myself across the corridor, into the far wall. Rasse's fingers and animal face pressed against the wire mesh, his tongue poking through, tasting the air.

Troah gave me a thin smile. "Sometimes he gets to have a whore. We think he prefers girls, but he's not picky. He takes the heads off all of them. Sometimes he eats the brains." She tapped on the broken wood, and Rasse wedged his pale face around to see her. "Remember me?" she said to him.

Rasse chewed at the metal screen. "D'Athee," he lisped through the mesh.

"Not Althea," said Troah, and she held her tattooed palm where he could see it.

The boy let out a terrified yelp and vanished into the cell, thumping against the putrid walls. "D'Athee! D'Athee!"

"Quiet, Rasse," said Troah.

"D'A*theeeee* . . ."

"Quiet," she whispered.

I heard him let out a shaky sob. Then, except for his rough breathing, he was silent.

Troah turned to me. "He's drugged right now. That's why he's so cooperative. When his dose wears off, we put him in the ring and stand back." She pointed to a small, oil-soaked leather bag that hung on a hook next to the door. "Can you guess what's in the bag?"

My tongue stuck in my mouth. "Enhancers."

"Clever girl." She took a step closer to me. "Now, how can I convince you to spend the night with Rasse?"

If she took out a fistful of Enhancers, and cracked their yellow casings barehanded, she would only 'hance herself. I knew that, but I also knew that somehow, Troah had made herself immune to anything she should have been afraid of. She could 'hance herself, or stick herself with knives, go head to head with Althea, or Rasha, or Otis, and only come out stronger. Her defenses were better than mine. I might be the sword, but her armor was thicker.

I made myself look away from her eyes, but it didn't help. She leaned over to touch me, and my knees turned to water. The rest of my body went numb, then hot, then freezing cold. She laid her palm on my chest. Underneath, I felt my heart shudder, and balk and then it stopped. *Really* stopped.

She pushed me down until I crumpled on the floor, on my face. She leaned over me, the way animals do, to see if their prey has died.

I shut my eyes tight, expecting her fingers around my throat, her nails in my flesh. Instead, her feet went *pat-pat-pat* on damp concrete, back to retrieve the bag by Rasse's cell.

Troah, Troah, Troah, in my chest. I lay where I was, too terrified to move, grateful for the frantic pounding. I opened one eye and saw her slipping her Hand into a plastic surgical glove. To protect herself from the Enhancers? Maybe not so immune after all. I shoved my knees under me. If I didn't look at her, I could get away.

"Jatahn!"

I got onto my hands and knees, my back to her, shoulders hunched around my ears so I wouldn't hear, awkward as hell. Althea's room and Leiban's meager support were somewhere further ahead. I crawled around the next curve of corridor. Doorless, blank, moldering concrete walls.

I made it onto my feet and ran, shambling, off-balance until I found one last door at the bottom of another set of stairs. All I could do was pound.

"Who the fuck is it?" yelled Althea.

She wasn't going to help me. She couldn't be bothered. I didn't care. I pounded harder.

Locks clicked from inside the room, and Leiban leaned out, stark naked except for the details of the story of Rexidi. "What do you want?"

"Troah," I gasped, and pointed down the hall. "She wanted to give me to R-r-r-r . . ."

"To Rasse?" said Leiban. "She's not keyed for his cell."

Althea sat up on the rumpled bed, swinging a shiny pair of manacles around one finger. "Go to bed, girl," she said. "Can't you see I'm busy?"

"But," I panted at Leiban, "you said I should tell you if she did something *wrong*. . . ."

Leiban shrugged. "Remind me tomorrow." He shut the door.

I listened for Troah, but all I heard was the terrified throb of my own innards. She was coming, though. I could feel her. The stairs were the only exit, and at the top, I knew I would find Rasha.

Upstairs, the night sky was a florid oval, trapped in the red haze over the pit. I crawled to the edge of the ring, defeated and terrified, put my head in my arms, and let the hot tears leak out.

It was an empty threat, locking me in with Rasse. How many hysterical newcomers did Althea get? Probably hundreds. How many died within the first few days? Was anyone likely to care? Even Leiban, who acted as though he had something to gain by keeping me in one piece? I wiped my face with gritty hands and pushed myself up on my knees. Life with Olney seemed like a walk in the park right now.

Sand crunched somewhere out in the ring.

Troah? No.

A slicker fluttered in the reddish dark.

Rasha. Heading for the front gate.

I shot to my feet. "D'Rasha!"

He didn't seem to hear.

I bolted into the ring, slogging ankle-deep in sand.

"D'Rasha!" I thought I saw him pause.

The gate groaned as he pulled it open. I saw him check the distance between us, and slide through the narrow opening. I lunged forward as the lock clicked shut.

I grabbed the bars with slick, sweaty hands. "Don't leave me," I panted. "Please don't. Please!"

"I told you," said Rasha, "I don't have a choice."

"Troah," I panted. "She'll kill me." Tears washed down my face, trailing through sand.

He shook his head. "Otis needs you."

I slid down the warm bars and wound my fingers into the hem of his slicker. "Let me go with you, D'sha, let me go . . ." The next word would have been *home*. I couldn't say it. It wouldn't have meant Ahmedi-Jatah to him, it would have meant his ship, and the taste of that was sickening.

He pulled away, and I let go.

"Have a little faith, Jatahn," he said. I didn't have to look at his face to see the false encouragement, or listen very hard to hear the disappointment in his voice. Despite everything, it cut to the bone. "Good luck, Yaeylie," he said softly.

I crouched on the other side of the bars as he vanished into the rain. His thin whistle pierced the night, and I recognized the tune.

> *See there, the wayward prince in white,*
> *bare of foot and bare of head.*
> *Threw off the hunting dogs tonight,*
> *but run to ground where demons tread.*

SEVEN

Back in Frei's apartment, I dragged the three-legged dresser all the way across the room to blockade the unlockable front door. The bed was too big and so was the couch, but if I'd had a mountain of furniture, I wouldn't have felt any more secure. Troah was under my skin, filling space like a tumor. A few heavy objects would never be enough to keep her away.

Frei's bathroom was a shabby, closet-sized space carved into the far corner of the bedroom. It was cluttered with a sink, toilet and a tub with a shower attachment. The flimsy door had a flimsy hook-in-loop assembly and might stay shut in a private moment, but that was all. I latched it anyway and retreated into the dirty tub, hidden behind a drapery of mildewing towels, a torn curtain, and an assortment of stiff-dried men's underwear.

The tub was gritty with flaking, crusted filth, clammy instead of cold. The blunt faucet pressed my spine, between my shoulderblades. I thought I was too uncomfortable to sleep, but the day had been too long.

The faucet propped me up instead of keeping me awake. The curve of the tub turned soft.

In my dream, Leiban acted as though he'd been waiting.

"I'll tell you the story," he said.

He slid out of his shirt and pants and spread his arms out wide. Tattoos blazed with a turquoise heat, coiling over his body until they rose away from the limits of his skin.

A cool spring breeze replaced the damp, thick air of the bathroom. Prince Rexidi stood at the edge of Leiban's tattoo-blue forest, his white clothes blowing gently. The crown on his head was an intricate ripple of gold wire. I looked down to see if his feet were really bare. They were. Around his neck was a chain, the same as any other slave. He was as tall as Leiban, but his face was blue, like calm water.

Behind him, at the top of the next hill, his castle pierced the sky—a dream version of Mosteph's Faraqui mansion. Men on horseback milled at the gates, surrounded by a pack of dogs. Someone blew a horn, and the sound came out as words.

See there, the wayward prince in white . . .

Rexidi's eyes rolled like eggs in a blue cup.

"You should go now," I said, but it sounded like bad advice.

He pushed up the sleeves of his white slave shirt. He turned away from his castle and began to run. His crown blew off and rolled into the tall blue grass at my feet, vanishing as he disappeared into the thickest part of the tattoo forest.

I followed, flying, tethered to him by the rest of the rhyme. Trees and bushes and flowers shot past me, blue to violet to deepest indigo. Rexidi dropped to all fours. His hands became hooves. Antlers emerged from his head in a new kind of crown and he fled through the darkening forest, half man, half animal. The rhythm of his running brought words out of the wind.

> *See there, the wayward prince in white,*
> *bare of foot and bare of head . . .*

The rest blurred with the thunder of distant horses and the cries of hunting dogs.

A man on a blue horse urged his mount over deadfall while his blue dogs snuffed for the trail. He wore an identical crown and collar, as alike to the prince as Troah was to Rasha. Nearby, his companions cast around in a trackless clearing, throwing their hands in the air, one by one.

"Have you seen him?" the hunter with the crown asked me.

"No," I lied.

"Favored One," said the man, "if we can't find him, our masters will. No matter what he looks like, he can never be free."

"I think you might be wrong," I said.

"Listen to the words," said the man, "and tell me what you really believe."

The wind came down, tossing the tree branches, frightening the horse. The dogs threw their heads up and bayed as a single creature. When I looked again, they had changed into blue-faced demons. They raked the dark air with their claws, and plunged into the woods.

I *knew* how this ended, I thought. Why had I bothered to argue?

I was high above everything now, part of the flat blue sky. The forest spread below me, motionless except for the roiling pack of horses and demons. The distance between

Rexidi's antlered head and his pursuers was only a few meters now. I didn't see them pull him to the ground, but I could see the flash of claws and teeth and bloody blue knives. The killing became a banging and pounding.

I jerked awake in the cold tub.

"Open up!" From a long way off, it was Hallie's voice.

The unlockable front door groaned against the meager stack of furniture. Hinges creaked. I heard the three-legged dresser crash down on the floor.

Hallie's bare footsteps came closer and stopped in front of the bathroom. The hook jiggled and popped out of its loop. I squeezed into the far end of the tub, still thick with the dream. The door opened, and Hallie pushed the towels aside with the end of a loaf of bread.

She took a long look at me. For a second, I thought she was going to laugh. "Better than the bed, Jatahn?" She tossed the loaf into my lap. "Eat something," she said.

The bread was still warm. It might have been comforting if I hadn't been absolutely sure Troah had made it, maybe just for me. Dire warnings in the soft crust.

Hallie settled herself on the edge of the tub and crossed her arms over her knees. Despite her size and her raw, bony intensity, she was nowhere near as frightening as Troah. Her face was thinner, more mature, with wide cheekbones that gave her a reserved, almost calculating, expression.

"The Meeds told me Troah brought you by for a visit last night," she said.

"Meeds?" I stammered.

"The middle set fighters," said Hallie. "The Meeds. What did you say to them?"

Hallie's alliances were with Troah. Troah wanted me quiet. Or silenced. I tore off a piece of bread and stuffed it in my mouth.

She watched me chew. "You won't last long if you don't start talking to me. I don't care if Rasha dropped you off with cake and cookies. Troah doesn't want you here, and that's a bad position to be in. For anybody."

I swallowed. "You're with her," I said, and took another bite.

Her calculating expression flattened into something less readable. "You don't follow the fights."

I shook my head.

"You've never heard of Striker."

The name on the empty cell across the hall. Hallie's dead partner. Girlfriend. Lover. It felt safer not to know anything. "No," I said, muffled, dry-mouthed.

"Her real name was Naritte," said Hallie, so softly I looked up in surprise. Her fingers were knotted between her knees, pale across the knuckles. "Naritte was my partner for six years. She got cut last season and she lost her fight. She was only in her fifteenth year. No one thought she was hurt enough to Fail, but she did." She looked away and the tendons in her neck stood out. "Althea wouldn't stop Naritte's fight, even when it was obvious that something was wrong. We were favored to win the Championships, but when Naritte lost, the odds went against us. Everything went against us. Otis made his money. That was the important thing." She turned to me, her face hard again. "It's never an accident when someone loses," she said. "Have you at least figured that out?"

I nodded.

Hallie frowned at her hands. "Frei tried to save Naritte. Althea told him to give her a shot of Thanas and get it over with. But Troah . . ." She took a breath. "Troah was the one who made her die."

"She touched her," I said. "With that . . . that Hand."

"Oh no," said Hallie. "Naritte wasn't a purebred, like you, or Rasse. She was tough. Troah had to use Enhancers." She hunched her shoulders, and her big body seemed to shrink in on itself. "Just like we used them on Arbitt, last night. Troah gave Naritte a pat on the back and told her to lose her match that night. By the time I figured out what was going on, it was too late."

I was squeezing the bread, throttling the loaf until it tore into two soft pieces. Hallie's alliances didn't seem quite so clear anymore. Still, this was no time to get careless, or desperate for friends.

"I'll tell you the real reason Frei left," said Hallie.

"He was grief-stricken." I said. "After the way he killed his boy."

"No," she said. "Frei left because Troah drove him out."

"She didn't like him?"

Her eyes narrowed, and I could see that playing dumb with her wasn't going to work as well as it had for Leiban. "When Tony died," said Hallie, "the Meeds didn't take it well. Troah'd gotten their hopes up. She'd gotten them to believe Frei could do . . . certain things . . . by stretching Tony's Failure." She cocked her head and waited for me to give myself away by filling in the blanks.

"You mean," I said carefully. "They thought Tony would be free afterwards?"

"Something like that."

I wondered if I had more to lose by telling everything, or holding back. Anything I said could easily find its way to Althea. "Did he try that with Naritte, too?" I said.

She nodded, slowly, stiff-necked.

"Did she die the same way?"

"Yes," said Hallie, flat and emotionless.

"Why did he think it would work on Tony?"

"Tony didn't fight in the ring. He'd never been cut." Hallie touched the long, raised scars under her ribs. "He had twenty years in collar without any physical trauma, and he died anyway." She raised an eyebrow at me. "If you're Rasha's spy, you can tell him he doesn't have anything to worry about. No slaves are going free. Troah's prophecies are crap. He can go ahead and fight his war. Maybe he'll even win." She leaned forward on the edge of the tub.

"I've told you all our dirty little secrets. Now it's your turn."

She watched me hesitate. I watched her expectations fade into dark, dangerous doubts.

"Maybe you don't know a thing," she said, tonelessly threatening. "Maybe Rasha gave you some words to use, and told you to see what kind of reaction you could get. Well. Now you know. The Beryl Arena is full of rebels and anarchists, all listening to Troah and her fucking prophecies." She started to get up.

"No," I whispered. "I have the cure."

"I think you're full of shit," she said.

I knew how this would end. The same as my dream. The way the story always ended for runaways. Run to ground. "You're wrong," I said. "You're wrong. I have the cure. I've seen it work. I—I have it with me."

She sat down. "Show me."

Laying out the Virevir like a bargaining chip was the wrong way to go. "I can't," I said, "but I can tell you how it works."

Her face didn't change. "Please," she said. "Do."

How had Renee explained it to me? I'd hardly been listening, focused on what I'd thought were the last seconds of Martine's life. "It's a cancer," I said. "It replaces the Virus after Failure."

"What do you mean, it 'replaces' the Virus?"

"You have to use something that can repair the damage," I said. "I mean—you know—the Drug isn't a drug, it's a—"

"I'm not an idiot," she snapped. "It's a virus that mutates itself to death over twenty years. So you replace a virus with a cancer. You're already dead from Failing. That doesn't make sense."

"Failure doesn't kill you," I said. "It's the cell damage that's fatal. If you can repair that fast enough, you can survive."

I expected complete disbelief in her face, but the calculating expression was back. "Now you sound like Frei," she said. "Why use a cancer? Why not just reinfect with the Virus?"

"What?"

"A fresh dose should kill off the mutations and fix everything. Right?"

The two damp halves of bread fell out of my hands, into the bottom of the filthy tub. "*That's* what your doctor was trying to do? That's how he killed his boy? And your partner?"

She nodded.

"But he was going to make you slaves for another twenty years!"

She shrugged. "Call it whatever you like. It doesn't matter what's left in your body. The only thing that matters is being alive."

"But—that's not—what if someone did a blood test? What if someone found *out*? They'd put you in collar again. They'd send you to the Mines, or send you to a place like—"

"Like this?" She almost smiled. "If Frei's ideas sound that bad to you, maybe your cure is better than his." From out in the corridor, an alarm gave a couple of sharp blasts and Hallie got up. "Come over to Rasse's cell when you finish eating. I'll take you to Practice afterwards. But in the meantime, take some advice."

"What?"

"Stay away from the Meeds," said Hallie. "Troah's been telling them what a jinx you are ever since you opened your mouth last night."

"I don't understand that," I said. "I tried to tell her I have what she needs. She laughed at me and then she said she was going to throw me in with Rasse."

"Don't get between Troah and her Meeds," said Hallie. "They're terrified of her and she's worked hard to make sure they stay that way. They'd turn on her like *that*"—Hallie snapped her fingers—"if they thought your cure would give them better odds than hers when they Failed."

"She'd kill me before they could figure that out."

"Right again," said Hallie.

"But how can I stay away from the Meeds?" I said. "I'm locked in with them."

She hesitated. "I'll keep an eye on you." She shrugged, as though the idea of protecting me made her immensely uncomfortable. "At least until you can show me what's in your bag of tricks."

She walked out. In a moment, the front door rattled shut. I crouched in the tub, not sure how much of a friend Hallie might turn out to be. Proving myself to her would mean freeing a fatally wounded fighter—but the fights weren't until tomorrow. In the meantime, Troah was lining the Meeds up against me. I might not even make it to the fights. All I was armed with was a little advice, and Hallie's grudging goodwill.

I got out of the tub and ducked through the hanging towels. I picked my way through Frei's room, over the carcass of the dresser, and peered into the hallway. It was empty, but I could hear voices coming from the direction of the kitchen.

Going around the lower corridor was a mistake. But I could get to Rasse's cell by crossing the ring and coming down by Althea's room—the way I'd tried to leave last night.

I hurried across the hall and up the stairs, expecting some kind of barrier at the top, but there wasn't one.

Out in the ring, the sand had turned a foreboding bloody rust color under the mauve canopy of the weather shields. A long way off, outside the front gate, rain battered the black paved plaza. Wide pools had formed inside the front gate, but the sand was bone dry. I started walking, keeping to the shadows in the breezeway.

In daylight, the bleachers up above were white stripes of benching over dark stone. The box seats were closer, and more precariously attached to overlook the ring. Under the box seats, a narrow, horizontal groove circled the inside wall of the pit. White shapes dotted the black gash, an uneven inlay in the sunless glare.

In a little while, I realized that the white shapes were human skulls.

They went all the way around, some dark ivory with age, a few the stripped-white color of new bone. Colored marks smeared every fleshless forehead—blue, yellow, faded red and gray lined one side of the ring. Green-marked skulls lined the other. Visiting team casualties, and home team casualties. No arms or legs or spines. And no way to know which one was Naritte.

I followed the shadowy breezeway until I got to the clinic access. In daylight, the double wooden doors seemed sunken into the black arena wall, sagging in the heat and humidity. The heavy wood was pocked and scratched. As I got closer, the texture became words—names.

TONY was cut into the wood in small, meticulous letters. **BREAKER BOY**, and **CUTTER**. Just above, in a different, deeper hand, **NARITTE**. There were hundreds and hundreds, carved up to the edge of the high lintel, into the jambs, around the steel hinges, gouged over each other, obliterating and marring the older ones, but still outnumbering the number of skulls around the pit.

I pushed the door open a crack and looked down the stairs.

The corridor below was filled with Meeds sitting on the bloodstained steps, three or four deep, plates of bread and kimarra balanced on their knees. They squatted on the floor of the hallway, concentrating on their food, so close together, I could feel their heat, and smell their smell.

I let the door shut and headed past the deserted office to the stairs that led to Althea's room.

At the bottom of her stairs, voices boomed in the low passage—from the kitchen, I thought, until something close by let out a huge, angry bellow.

Not the Meeds, I thought, probably *not* the Meeds.

When I got to Rasse's cell, it was wide open, and empty. The floor and walls were dark with water, washed down like a kennel or a stall. The bag of Enhancers on the hook by the door was gone.

Chains rattled from the clinic end of the corridor. I heard Althea shouting, and Leiban's voice, both incomprehensible, both irritated.

Rasse—and now I knew it was Rasse—roared again.

Metal scraped stone and Hallie backed into view from the direction of the training room, hauling on one end of a long chain, bracing herself against Rasse's jerks and lunges. Bare, wet feet smacked the floor and Rasse flung himself forward.

He was dripping wet, tall enough to scrape the ceiling with his shaved white head. When he shook himself, water sprayed as though the damp air in the hall had finally become rain. His feet were manacled and his hands were chained behind his back. Hallie's long shackle was locked onto his collar, and she held it taut as he squatted, naked in the dim light, sniffing and tonguing the air.

Two more chains led from his manacled hands to Leiban at the far end of the hallway. Althea was right behind him, slapping the butt of a whip against her palm.

"Well, goddamn," said Althea when she saw me. "Just in time to earn your keep."

I had a paralyzingly clear vision of being thrown into Rasse's cell, but Althea pulled the oily leather bag of Enhancers out of her pocket and tossed it at me instead. I didn't try to catch it, afraid to touch the outside. It hit the floor with a liquid thump. Althea snorted and flung a pair of surgical gloves after it. They landed short, next to Rasse's worm-white feet.

I didn't move. Althea glared at me.

"Put on the gloves, girl," she said, "and give the boy his dose."

Rasse swayed and twisted his head, watching me like a huge, bizarre bird. His eyes were a weak, watery blue, bulging out of his sallow face. He was bent almost double under the low ceiling. If he'd been able to stand up straight, my head might have reached the middle of his chest. Thin white stripes from dozens of beatings sheared down his body. When he shifted, I saw the hieroglyphic Faraqui eye, burned into his shoulder, just under his ID number.

Which meant he was pure-blooded, Faraqui-bred, like Mosteph's slaves, and my own ancestors. Had he been genetically designed, tailored specifically, for *this*?

"We don't have all day, medic," said Althea.

I snapped my damp hands into the gloves and spilled a palmful of yellow capsules out of the bag. Above me, Rasse grunted and swayed faster, tongue out, eyes rolled up into his head. I squeezed the Enhancers in both fists until the casings began to pop.

Rasse heard the sound, threw his head back and shrieked. He lunged at me and Leiban hauled on his manacled wrists, twisting backwards. Rasse flailed in the too-small corridor, losing his balance as Hallie wrenched him the other way. I shoved myself against the wall. Rasse toppled past me, scraped the wall, and hit the floor. The chains went tight as he thrashed, yelping in a high, wordless voice, blue eyes bulging, tongue all the way out. I slid oily gloves over his bare skin, and he screamed like he'd been burned.

"Quiet, Rasse!" bellowed Althea. The boy's wail thinned into a helpless wheeze. His eyes glazed over, and his tongue caught between his teeth. The rest of his body went slowly limp.

Hallie let her end of the chain go slack. "You can't hesitate," she said to me. "He sees it. He knows enough to see when you're afraid."

Althea leaned over and unlocked the manacles. "Get up, Rasse," said Althea. "Go to bed."

The boy lumbered to his hands and knees and crawled through the cell door, docile from the drugs, or exhausted. He curled up on the wet floor of his cell, one hand in his crotch, the other stuck in his mouth.

Althea shut him in and checked the locks. Then she turned to me. "We do this every day, Jatahn, and we do it a lot faster." She jerked a thumb at Hallie. "Put away the chains, and make sure the medic doesn't get lost on the way to Practice."

Althea walked off, trailed by Leiban. Hallie started coiling the chains on the floor. I peeled out of the gloves, shaking so hard that droplets of yellow oil pattered onto the stained concrete floor, next to the bag of Enhancers.

I knotted the gloves and bent to pick up the bag. Hallie's reassurances back in Frei's bathroom were starting to feel dangerously thin. I needed some kind of protection, no matter how small. If Enhancers were Troah's weapon of choice, they would certainly be good enough for me.

Hallie wasn't watching. I opened the bag, took a handful of the capsules, and stood up, trying not to look guilty or frightened as she turned around.

"Did he scare you?" said Hallie.

I nodded.

"At least you have the sense to tell the truth."

"I haven't lied to you yet."

"Better give me the Enhancers, then."

I hesitated. "The what?"

She gave me look of real sympathy. "I know you're scared. Anyone with good sense would be. But those things won't help you."

136

"You don't think so?" I asked. "What if my bag of tricks isn't good enough?"

She almost smiled. "It might be more than enough."

Which was probably as encouraging as she could bring herself to be. She held out her hands, and I gave her what I had.

EIGHT

"Practice is this way." Hallie guided me away from Rasse's cell, past the empty middle set cages, past the clinic, to the training room. She pushed the door open and the stink of perspiration and weeping concrete walls roiled out. Underneath, there was a taste too strong to savor, hot enough to make me break into a sweat.

Troah.

The fighters were clustered around a low set of bleachers along the side wall. Their naked backs reflected under a film of condensation over the long mirror, a dapple of different color skins. Troah stood on one of the bleacher benches, taller than any of them. When I looked for her in the mirror, I saw us both: her fine hair tied in a wispy knot, her eyes full of conviction, her mouth a seductive dark flower, and my own image, white clothes against the black metal mesh lockers.

"There's your new blood," said Troah, as gracious as a viper.

The fighters turned to stare in my direction, their faces pulled into a unanimous kind of dread. I looked around the wide room for Leiban, but neither he nor Althea were anywhere in sight.

Hallie gave me a stony glance and let the door swing shut. "What're you telling them, Troah?" she asked. "That she's a jinx on the fights? That she'll kill them if they get wounded enough to Fail?"

"Does it make a difference to you?" asked Troah.

"Not at the moment," said Hallie, "but it might later on."

The door banged open, and Leiban shouldered through, shaved down to the shine on his head. A heavy leather belt with a pattern of small, steel plates was slung over his arm, the buckles gleaming against his tattoos. He frowned at the silent clump of fighters and looked around until his flat brown eyes found me. His expression didn't change. It was impossible to know if he had any idea what he'd interrupted.

"Places!" he barked.

Troah's army scattered, thinning into a single, tense rank, kneeling with their backs to the long mirror, heads down, eyes down.

Hallie shambled to the end of the line. On the bleachers, Troah sat and smoothed her hair.

Bootheels rapped on stone in the corridor. The air in the room went from thick to dense. Leiban jerked the door open and dropped to his knees. I pressed against the wall as Althea surged in.

Her black hair was wet and plastered down, even more severe against her paper-white skin, and she left a wake in the sweaty stink that smelled of soap. She stalked down the line of kneeling fighters, slapping the handle of her whip against her palm, counting heads.

She stopped in front of Hallie. "What'd you do with the medic?"

Hallie nodded across the wide room to where I was, still frozen by the lockers.

Althea pointed at the bleachers where Troah was, sitting now, serene and guileless. "Get off my floor," snapped Althea. "You're in the way."

Troah beckoned, and I slunk along the wall, past the mesh lockers until I came to the edge of the worn, fiberboard benches. Three big steel pots lined the bench at Troah's feet. One was filled to the brim with unpeeled red kimarra, the next with mizpah pods, bristling with inedible green seeds. The third was half-filled with water.

"Sit down," said Troah, and patted the empty space to her left. "You can help with dinner."

I sat, awkward and sweating. Troah slapped a wet kimarra into my hand and a flimsy plastic peeler.

On the training floor, Hallie distributed the sogas and razor-edged plumes from one of the lockers. Leiban opened a rack of long, curved knives. The fighters took their weapons and sat on their haunches, carefully wrapping the blades in filthy gray padding. One spared me a sidelong sneer, but that was all. The rest seemed intent on muffling their weapons.

Althea circled the room, the studded belt fastened around her waist. Her intensity was a physical thing, a disturbance in the air. It was more than an impression. The atmosphere around her actually flickered. I squinted, not sure what I was seeing.

"Force armor," said Troah.

Her voice made me jump. "What?"

"Force armor," she said. "The belt Leiban brought in. It's military surplus force-field armor. Nothing can cut it except plasma guns, and we don't have any of those." She dropped a naked kimarra into the pot of water and held out her Hand for mine. The tattoo on her palm was a damp, glistening shape. I gave her my hot, half-peeled fruit and reached numbly for another.

Just in front of the bleachers, the fighters were collecting into a loose semicircle around Hallie and Leiban, who faced each other with gleaming, bare-bladed sogas. Althea stepped between her two Assassins and turned to face the Meeds.

"When you fight those Silver sons-of-bitches tomorrow," she shouted, "you keep in mind what the odds are on your round. I don't care how many times you've been in the ring, I don't care how hot the sports news says you are. The boss wants to keep his bets favorable, and by God, you'll accommodate him." She moved to one side, and made a wide gesture at Hallie and Leiban. "And since you've all been fucking up on strikes and angles, we're going to run through the basics today, until *I* think you can win on points for style." She glowered, almost theatrically disgusted, and waved the whip at Hallie and Leiban.

Hallie swung her soga in a low, fast arc. Leiban blocked with his own soga, and the blades made a dull clang in the close air.

My peeler stopped halfway across my kimarra, a strip of skin dangling. Watching arena matches on the holo over Olney's shoulder hadn't prepared me for this. Fights on the holo looked fake and rehearsed. Here, the ring would be a killing floor, with real blood for the sake of real blood. In a real fight, I would never have time to help one of these slaves through an injury-induced Failure. Even if I did, I could hardly picture myself trying to explain to Althea why a mortally wounded fighter who had "died on the sidelines" was somehow still alive.

I stared down at my kimarra, one white slice of flesh showing through the pink skin. Suppose I succeeded? Suppose I could prove myself to Hallie, to the Meeds—to Troah—and actually bring the dead back to life. What would I do with the slave I'd freed?

I couldn't dash off, like Renee with Martine. Frei could have walked his boy through the front gate and hidden him anywhere in the city. What was I supposed to do? Save myself by freeing one of them, then commit a murder to cover my tracks?

Troah eyed me as I sat, not working. "Is something wrong?"

I shook my head and peeled. My incomplete plans dropped away in a thin curl of skin.

Out on the floor, Leiban jabbed, then switched to the slicing end of his soga and swung, crouching for momentum and impact. Hallie leaped over the half-moon blade, balancing her height and weight with the airborne twist of her own weapon, landing on her toes. The two of them froze in position, a textbook tableau.

Althea turned to the rest of the fighters. "Pair up, you lazy bastards, pair up!" She cracked her whip and the fighters jumped to their feet. They fled around the room, pushing and jostling each other until each seemed to find their required partner and began flailing at each other, while Althea prowled the room for slackers.

"I want flawless strikes," Althea shouted. "*Flawless.*"

The kimarra had taken on a heat of its own from being held so long, pulpy from being squeezed. I made a couple of crooked stripes with the peeler, watching the muffled weapon blunder against bare arms and legs.

"You don't have to worry about Meeds getting hurt in practice," said Troah. "Althea wants you here because Frei was always here." She dropped a peeled fruit into the water pot. "Frei only hung around practice so he could tell Althea how to do her job, but she's used to having a doctor in shouting distance." Pink skin sliced off white flesh. "I'll have to remember to mention that to your replacement."

"Faster, dammit, faster—" Althea beat the air with the handle of the whip as one of the girls swung at her male partner. The boy made a wild lunge, and cracked the haft under the girl's jaw. The girl let go of her soga and dropped to the floor, hands over her face.

"Some Silver Meed'll take off your head if you do that

in the ring tomorrow." Althea fastened the whip to her coverall and snatched the girl's plume. She parried with the boy, complicated twists and slices that would've disemboweled him if the blades had been exposed. The boy backed off. Althea threw the plume to the girl and stalked over to the black mesh lockers.

She motioned across the room to Hallie. "Find that redhead and bring him to me." Under the curve of low ceiling, her voice carried clearly to the bleachers.

Hallie glanced around the room and pointed at the redheaded boy who'd made a grab at me from the cell last night. "You mean Ransom? What's going on?"

Althea opened one of the lockers and pulled a handful of leather straps off a hook. "Otis is promoting him. As of today, Ransom is an Assassin." Althea dangled the straps, untangling them into a sort of harness. There was a small plastic patch on the harness, at waist-level. She thumbed it until the color changed from milk-white to green.

Hallie frowned at the straps. "That's Naritte's projector."

"It's a projector," said Althea. "And I need it."

Hallie's face darkened. "It was Naritte's, Althea."

Althea gave her an impatient look. "What're you going to do, Hallie? Bring her back to life so she can fill up my empty roster?"

Hot color came up under Hallie's cheeks. "Give him a different one."

Althea tapped the plastic plate and the air around the harness glimmered into the faint outline of an enormous, green-scaled reptile. "Naritte's been dead for more than a season, and I need another Striker." Althea switched the holo off and held the harness out to Hallie. "You want to recharge it? Or would you rather get your new teammate?"

Hallie stiffened. "I'll get him."

I couldn't see her expression until she passed the bleachers. When she looked up at Troah, her face had gone from ruddy anger to ashen fury. Troah made a microscopic shrug.

Hallie's eyes went dark with rage, and she plunged into the crowd of sparring fighters to grab Ransom by his collar. She dragged him toward the lockers, past the bleachers, past Troah, who leaned over and hissed at him.

"How's it feel to be one of us, Red?"

He gave her a look of bewildered fear.

Althea shook the harness in the boy's face. "You know what this is?"

"Holo projector," muttered Ransom.

Althea plucked at his sweaty shirt. "Strip down, boy, and let's see how it fits."

Around the rest of the hot room, the thud of muffled weapons became perfunctory. Fighters craned their necks to see what was happening by the lockers. Leiban's shaved head was motionless at the far end of the room. His pairs had stopped what they were doing and had bunched up behind him, watching Althea.

Ransom fumbled with his clothes. His shirt stuck to his arms and wadded into a wet ball. He peeled out of his pants and stood in front of Althea, naked and pallid, streaked down his legs with sweat.

Althea reached into the locker for a second harness. She tossed it to Hallie, who snatched it out of the air, her face carefully vacant.

"What do you want me to do, D'sha?" There was something odd about the way she asked the question, and I realized that it was the first time I'd heard Hallie address her trainer with any kind of formality.

"Put the damn thing on," said Althea.

Hallie angled her arms through the straps, then her legs. The harness fastened around her wrists and ankles, fitting close against her knees and elbows, hips, and flanks. She fastened the last strap across her bare chest, high over her breasts. At her waist, the plastic plate glowed bright green.

Ransom tangled in the leather, trying to fit himself inside the shape of it. As big as he was, the harness was obviously sized for someone even larger. He struggled with the fittings for wrists and ankles, and Althea snapped her fingers at Hallie. "Help him."

The muscles under Hallie's wide cheekbones went rigid. "The harness doesn't fit him," she said. "We've got some smaller ones in storage."

"The ones in storage haven't worked for years," said Althea. "This one does, and this one can be adjusted." She put her fists on her hips. "Am I making myself clear?"

The tendons in Hallie's neck went wire-tight. She took a step closer to the boy and wrenched the straps until they more or less fit the contours of his body. Ransom flinched every time she touched him. Sweat dripped down the middle of his back, and his face had turned pasty. The plastic projector plate lay against his bare hip, glowing a dull, sickly green.

Hallie moved away and wiped her hands.

Althea reached into the locker again and brought out a pair of tall plumes. The feathery strip-steel blades barely moved in the viscous air. Althea shoved one of the weapons at Ransom, who hung onto the long haft with both hands. She started to give the other one to Hallie, hesitated, and rubbed her side.

From the bleachers, I saw her make an adjustment to the small metal plates on her belt. The force armor gleamed around her with a new intensity, dense as ice.

Beside me, Troah let out a breathy laugh.

Hallie took the plume, shoulders tense, her pyrite-blond hair spiked with perspiration. Althea slapped the green plastic at Ransom's hip. This time, the reptile projection was stronger, more distinct, a deep, metallic emerald. Its long tail coiled through the lockers, winding around Althea's legs, distorting through her armor. Its hindquarters hid Ransom inside an opaque, scaly tent while the rest of the creature vanished in the ceiling, too tall for the training room.

"Size it," snapped Althea.

Ransom, almost invisible inside the holo, fumbled with the plastic patch until the image shrank to fit the room. He peered up to see where the top was, and the projection mimicked his motion. It was a sinuous thing, narrow-headed, with flared nostrils and gilt armor plate arranged in overlapping layers from its horns to its haunches—a long-necked dragon with foreclaws the length of my arm. The boy waved his weapon experimentally, and the creature slashed the air, teeth bared, following the path of the strip-steel blades. In the training room, the effect was weirdly surreal. In the ring upstairs, at ten times the size, two or three projections in the ring at a time . . . I was starting to understand why people came to the fights.

"Light up, Hallie," said Althea.

Hallie dropped into a crouch, clenching the plume half-way up its haft. She hit the plastic patch on her own harness with the inside of her elbow, never taking her eyes off Ransom. Her projection burst into the moist dimness of the training room, obscuring Hallie in glossy black plumage, talons, and a hooked beak. Her ebony hawk glittered with its own internal light, artificial and huge under the low ceiling, just as solidly bizarre as Ransom's dragon.

Black wings shot over my head and through the wall behind the bleachers. Hallie lunged, a shadow inside the shadow, slicing into Ransom's scaly flank as her plume cut the air, one lunge a beak, the next a claw. Metal clashed on metal and the dragon twisted like a wingless insect, outsized and outmatched. Hallie's talons sank into the rep-tile's shoulder and I heard Ransom shriek.

"Enough!" roared Althea.

Hallie's image vanished into the girl herself. She threw the plume on the floor in transparent disgust, well away from the thrashing green mass of scales and the gouts of projected blood. The dragon flailed and abruptly disappeared. Ransom dropped to his knees, one hand clutching his scored shoulder.

"Frei!" bellowed Althea.

Troah put her awful Hand on my leg. "She means you."

I leaped out of the bleachers, hit the stone floor, and covered the short distance between Troah and Ransom in one long wobbly stride. The wound was nothing. Althea knew it, Hallie knew it. Probably in a few seconds Ransom would figure it out for himself. I slid to my knees next to him, close enough to Althea to feel the static from her armor.

"For the love of fucking *God*," Althea bellowed at Hallie. "You don't have to go for his fucking throat!"

"You owe me more that this, *D'sha*," Hallie yelled back.

"*Owe* you?" shouted Althea. "No one owes *you* a damn thing, Hallie. Your *job* is not to get in my *way*."

Hallie quivered with fury. She jabbed a finger at Ransom. "What difference does it make what he's called in the ring, or what his holo is?"

"Why don't you ask Otis?" demanded Althea. "He wants another Striker. He likes the projection and he likes the name. I need another player out there tomorrow, and as far as I'm concerned, it all works out."

Hallie gathered herself, dark beet-red. Her hands clenched into knuckled hammers, and she seemed to get bigger and hotter in the smoldering room.

Althea took a step past me and stood right in front of her. She was shorter than Hallie, but not by much, wiry where Hallie was thick with muscle. Althea flicked the armor off, crossed her arms and cocked her head at her seething fighter. It would have been a laughable standoff, except for the cold aura of authority that surrounded Althea, even without the armor.

"You don't like the rules, Hallie-girl?" said Althea, icy calm.

"To hell with the rules," hissed Hallie.

Althea slapped the whip, coiled at her waist. "Say it again," she said. "Say it louder."

Hallie's brown eyes flickered at the whip, past Althea to me, and back again. "I've been in this pit with you for six years," she whispered. "Doesn't that count for something?"

"No," said Althea, in a tone that carried across the room. "I don't think it does."

Hallie's face went tight, but she didn't say anything else. Althea glowered at Ransom. "Anything broken on him, medic?"

"No, D'sha."

"Then get out of here."

I made my way back to the bleachers, ducking between streaming bodies, through the rush of muffled weapons. Troah was eyeing me through the murky air, judging, I was sure, the simplest way to twist my head off. I stood by the edge of the bench instead of sitting on it, watching the fighters, concentrating on my beating heart, and every rhythmic vital sign, which meant that Troah hadn't willed me dead, not just yet.

Hallie and Ransom circled each other in a wide, empty space on the floor. They both had padded plumes now, but Hallie seemed less than interested. Her parries were terse and repetitive, the same four moves, over and over. Ransom tried mimicking her, then rushing her, swinging down, cutting across at throat-level, then parrying low, with an upward thrust. Hallie jumped, dodged, stayed just out of range, smacked the haft of his weapon with hers once in a while, but never came close to touching him. In fact, she didn't seem to be paying much attention to him at all.

After a while, I realized what she was concentrating on was me.

Every time she turned and swung, her unreadable eyes were on me. Her expression never changed, but the tension around her was plainly visible—a threat—or a warning?

Or a plan I was supposed to understand?

Her inattentiveness pricked Ransom's ego. He slashed at her, tired of being ignored, and caught her under the ribs. Hallie staggered and the electric tension around her changed. She turned and swung, and tangled the swaddled end of her weapon with the swaddled end of his. He wrenched loose. A strip of cloth tore off of her plume, fluttering to the ground. Strip-steel gleamed inside Hallie's muffle as the two of them sidled around the other, searching for the best angle to strike.

Swing, cut low, cut high and block. She banged his staff away, letting him shag the padding on her weapon again. Blades buzzed the air as she swung, faster this time, as though she'd found her rhythm. Ransom blocked, parried and snagged more of the muffle. Half of Hallie's plume was visible now, but no one seemed to have noticed. The whir of Hallie's exposed blades seemed far louder than the clank and crash of twenty other fighters. I looked for Althea, thinking that of course she could hear it, but she was at the far end of the floor, shaking a fistful of coiled whip at some luckless Meed, oblivious to what was going on right in front of me and Troah.

I looked back at Hallie and Ransom—slow as a dream— and watched Hallie's razor-steel slash into Ransom's arm, flaying it from shoulder to wrist. The boy opened his mouth wide. His scream flooded out, spilling into the room, filling the dank air, drowning out every other sound.

The swarming mix of fighters came to a halt, and Althea charged across the floor. She spun the boy around and stared at the mess hanging from the left side of his body. She turned on Hallie, who was still holding the stripped plume, grabbed her by the throat and shook her until the girl's head wobbled back and forth.

"Get off my floor!" Althea screamed at her. *"Get off my floor!"*

Hallie let her weapon fall with a deafening clang and

turned away, nothing in her face—no pain, no anger . . . and no fear. She shoved her way through the gaggle of shocked Meeds, and walked out.

Althea dragged the quivering boy toward the bleachers and shoved him at me. He dropped at my feet, his arm bleeding puddles on the stone floor, so shredded that it was almost unrecognizable as a human limb. Sweat popped out in gleaming beads over his face and neck. His pale skin had gone gray as ash, and I could feel the feverish heat coming off his body. He choked in a breath and coughed it out.

Althea's face darkened. "Goddamnit. One little cut and he's Failing." She looked around for Leiban who was standing right behind her. "Get that sloppy bastard to the clinic." She glared at me. "Take care of him, and make it fast. I don't want any screaming. We've had enough of that."

Leiban hoisted Ransom off the floor. Silent fighters stepped aside as I pushed through them to get to the clinic's training room entry. Knowing looks passed over me.

"Jinx," I heard them say.

One last waft of thick air from the training room dissipated into the cool scent of disinfectant. Leiban draped the wounded boy over the surgical table, and Ransom curled on his side gasping, gray in his face from loss of blood. His mangled arm smeared over the clean steel, sliced down to tendon and bone.

Leiban wiped his hands in long brown streaks over his green pants. "I know what you've been saying to the Meeds," he said to me in a low, uneven voice. "Troah's gotten to you already." He made a jerky motion at Ransom. "I'll come back to see if he's dead. Understand? We don't want another crazy doctor. We want to die in peace."

He didn't wait for me to answer, just bolted into the training room and slammed the door.

Ransom's harsh breathing had changed to painful sobs. His pale throat strained under his chain collar. I flung open the white cabinet with bloody hands, grabbed a scanner and switched it on.

Ransom's levels were plunging downwards on the tiny screen, red and green lines coiled like fighting snakes. He squirmed onto his back, shaking hard enough to make the steel table rattle. I groped in the cabinet for a fistful of green Virus cartridges and a hypoderm. If I used the Virevir now he might survive Failure, but he would die from blood loss and shock—a dead free man. He had to be healed first. I could bring his levels up like I had with Hallie last night, but the damage inside Ransom from the mutating Virus was already well under way. No amount of the Drug would keep him alive for long.

I pressed a cartridge into one of the hypos, and heard the door open. When I looked up, Hallie and Troah were standing in the hallway entrance.

"Get the Thanas, Hallie," said Troah, deadly calm. "Kill him. I'll take care of her."

If Hallie was really going to help me, now was the only time. I made myself look away, concentrating on the needle and Ransom's gory lacerations.

The desk creaked as Hallie sat on it. "I don't think you should kill her just yet, Troah."

A second of surprised silence. "What?"

"I want to see what she's going to do."

"She's going to stall until Leiban comes in to see what's taking so long," said Troah. "It's time to get *rid* of her."

"We can do it later," said Hallie.

"Don't be stupid, Hallie."

Troah started toward me, her marked Hand as wide as a coffin. I backed against the cabinets, and Hallie's dirty brown fingers clamped around Troah's wrist.

Troah tried to wrench away and couldn't. Her predatory expression changed to disbelief. "What the hell is wrong with you?"

Hallie gave her a tight smile. "I'm curious, Troah. We're

all curious what might happen if someone else was supervising the deaths around here."

"She's not one of us," Troah hissed. "She belongs to Rasha."

"Maybe," said Hallie, but she didn't let go. She nodded at me. "I think you'd better hurry up," she said.

Ransom shuddered on the table, shaking almost as hard as I was. His life signs had plummeted, and the bottom of the graph was plainly in view. Spasms rippled through his body. In seconds he would break into full-scale convulsions.

I slotted a cartridge into the hypoderm and cracked the seal. The boy's arm was too splattered to find a vein or intact artery. There was no obvious place to inject. I squirted the contents of the cartridge into the wounds, emptying a wash of green fluid into the ripped layers of muscle. Blood sloughed away, thinner and grayer, not the deep arterial red. Underneath clots and soft scabs, torn membranes crept together, wrapping exposed bone.

I thumbed the spent cartridge out and shoved in the next one, slathering Ransom's arm with the Virus in its purest form. I got a clean rag from the sink and gently wiped away the gore. His wrist was already covered with raw new skin. Along his upper arm, cut muscle had sheathed over membranes, braced with sinew and tendons. I loaded another cartridge and pricked him under a sticky layer of healing bicep. The regeneration was so fast, it looked like magic, but in minutes it would suck him dry. I glanced at the scanner. Ransom's indicators were rising, red and green together, one notch at a time, toward their last apogee.

The boy let out a shaky sigh and opened his eyes. Blood stiffened in his eyebrows and his red hair.

"You saved me," he whispered. "You saved me."

Of course I hadn't. If anything, I might be about to make his life even worse. Martine had anticipated her freedom for two years, and planned for it. Ransom had no concept of what was about to happen to him. I glanced across the room at Troah and Hallie. Hallie's face was impassive. Troah's was full of restless contempt—but her arm was still locked in Hallie's grip.

"Frei boosted Tony's levels too," said Troah. She glared at Hallie. "And Naritte's. Jatahn hasn't done anything new. For all we know, she found Frei's notes. She's just faking it." Troah eyed the exit to the training room. "Leiban'll be here any second, Hallie. The boy's got to be dead by then."

"He's not going to live," Hallie said to me. "None of them do when they're redosed like that."

"I know," I said.

Ransom gasped. His newly healed arm jerked and twitched. His nervous smile became a grimace. He squeezed his eyes shut and trembled.

On the scanner, the green Viral indicator had already fallen away, and the red line was beginning to jag downwards.

I shoved a hand inside the waistband of my pants, groping for the edge of the tape on my thigh. The tape was gummy with body heat, frayed at the corners. I scrabbed at it with too-short nails until I could tear off one of the three sealed slapneedles. The packet came away along with tiny hairs and tender skin.

In the bright light of the clinic, the slapneedle looked so much like Olney's standard medical supplies that my heart balled up with doubt. It was far too late to wonder if Renee had left the real thing for me, days and days ago on Naya. I stuck the needle packet onto the metal cabinet with its gray wad of tape, and turned to Ransom again.

Troah's suspicions thickened in the air. "What's that?"

"It's—" Naming the cancer wouldn't mean anything to her. Describing the Virevir would take too long. But those weren't the things I needed to tell her. "It's the cure," I said.

Ransom let out a gulping cry as his Failure surged over him. Red and green lines rushed together on the scanner and dove toward the bottom of the graph. A shudder pummeled him against the table, and he grabbed the steel edges with both blood-sticky hands, gaping at me, as though this was the last thing he'd expected. The next spasm caught him and crawled down his body, shaking him until he was flailing wide with arms and legs. He avalanched off the table headfirst, thrashing like a landed fish. I grabbed for his shoulders. He banged into the cabinets and slammed me under the chin with an elbow, knocking me down and landing half on top of me. The next spasm shoved him in the other direction, wrapping him around the table's steel brace. I squirmed out from under him as he convulsed on the floor. I was too light to hold him down. Even Martine, at half his size, had needed two people to keep her from hurting herself.

Across the room, Hallie had gone sickly pale, Troah dark with vindication.

"Kill him," said Hallie in a low, ugly tone. "Or cure him, but don't let him die like that."

"Help me," I panted. "I can't hold him."

Hallie hesitated. Maybe she thought I should prove myself, by myself. Or maybe she knew she'd never have Troah under such tight control, ever again. She let go of Troah's wrist, leaving deep red marks in the white skin, and took one long stride across the small room. She pressed herself between the cabinet and the table and pushed me out of the way.

She caught Ransom's arms, his shoulders, pinning him down, centimeter by centimeter. She shoved him onto his back, one knee against the boy's hip, her palms on his chest, settling her weight onto him. He bucked underneath, eyes rolled up to the whites, not conscious anymore, a kicking puppet of bones and flesh.

Now I was squeezed into the corner where the cabinet met the sink. I fumbled for the scanner on the tabletop and squatted on the floor with it, terrified that I would miss the correct moment for the injection. The green line wavered at the bottom of the screen, while the red life line drifted just above. Ransom's death was minutes away. I reached up to peel my slapneedle off the white cabinet, and found myself staring into Troah's face.

She leaned across the table, staring down, the slapneedle packet in her Hand. She ballooned into the tiny space, displacing everything—the light and the air and the smell of disinfectant. I froze in position, one hand out for the needle, one clutching the scanner, mouth open, eyeballs drying, unable to blink.

Hallie craned around to see what I was staring at, still holding onto Ransom. "Leave her alone, goddamnit," she snarled at Troah. "Can't you leave her alone long enough to see what she's going to do?"

"She's wasting time," Troah snapped back, "and so are you. The sooner she's gone, the sooner Otis has to replace her."

"He doesn't want the goddamn hospital tech!" Hallie's voice rose to a shout. "Weren't you listening last night? We'll end up with nothing if you kill her, Troah. All we'll have is you and your goddamn Hand."

Ransom gurgled and moaned, sweat sliding down his neck. He gave a huge heave. Hallie braced herself, but he shoved her so high, her shoulder brushed past Troah's face. Troah broke eye contact, and I mashed myself further into the corner with the scanner.

"Is that what you want, Troah?" Hallie pinned her knees to Ransom's heaving sides, riding him. She forced him down, her face dark red, her hair spiked up straight, every vein throbbing in her forehead. "You want us all down here on the floor, killing ourselves until you're the only one left who remembers what Frei was trying to do?"

"You're fooling yourself, Hallie," said Troah, the essence of icy calm. "Rasha didn't send his pure-blooded garbage to do us any favors."

"Then give her that goddamn packet." Hallie twisted sideways to glare at her. "Unless you're afraid it might work."

Troah gave her a thin smile. She held the slapneedle between her thumb and forefinger, examining it. "Whatever it is, this'll kill him. We both know that, but you're ready to believe anything. You're panicking, Hallie." She shook her head in mock sympathy. "It's not good in the ring, and it's not good now."

Ransom heaved, tongue out, eyes rolled back. On the scanner, the red and green had merged at the bottom of the graph, flickering in and out as his Failure squeezed him, cell by cell, organ by organ. I looked up. Troah's Hand was the threatening shadow on the white metal cabinets. In the corner of my eye, the packet was a gray square against the clinic's bright ceiling.

"I don't know what's wrong with you," Troah said to Hallie. "At least Naritte had some intelligence. All this one's got is a pretty face and a story Rasha invented for her."

I reached up. Troah wasn't expecting me to reach up. I swung, open-handed, knowing I would solidify if I met her eyes. My shadow on the cabinet arced toward hers. The edge of the packet brushed my palm. I closed my fingers around the packet and felt her jerk. Heard her take a surprised breath. Her palm touched mine, jarring as an electric shock, sharp as blades. I shrieked and yanked my hand away, blazing from the ends of my fingers to my wrist, and had to look to see if I was actually holding the packet. It was there, crumpled between unscathed fingers.

"Do whatever you're going to do, Jatahn," said Troah in a low voice. "When you're done, Hallie can have the honor of tearing you to pieces. Because I can tell you right now, nothing you do to poor Ransom is going to help him."

She was right. Every nerve told me she was right. Every carefully bred Faraqui gene agreed. Ransom shuddered on the floor, rattling toward death. I ripped the packet open and stuck the needle's adhesive patch to my palm.

Hallie's face clenched. "Do it," she hissed. "*Do* it."

I leaned into the heat between her and Ransom, too far from the scanner to see the screen. I wrapped my hand around the boy's slick throat and pressed the needle into his carotid.

His pulse galloped under my fingers, stuttered—and stopped. One last warm puff of breath came out of his mouth. His big body slumped under Hallie, limp, wet, heavy.

I pressed my fingers into Ransom's neck. Martine had "died" too. Hallie, still straddling the boy's chest, picked up his wrist and searched for a pulse. Nothing. All traces of hope disappeared from Hallie's face, submerging under her brown skin, vanishing behind her calculating mask.

Troah shifted lazily above us. "What did I tell you, Hallie?"

Hallie held his wrist a little longer and let it drop. She wiped sweat off her neck.

Troah picked up the scanner. "Why did Rasha make you do this, Jatahn?"

"None of this is his idea," I whispered.

Troah coughed a laugh. "Tell the truth, Favored One. He can't help you anymore."

Ransom's damp skin was cooling. His lips were taking on a faintly blue tint. I wanted to push Hallie away so I could pound on his chest, breathe into his mouth, and drag him back to life, however unwilling or doomed he might be. But Renee hadn't done that to Martine, and if I tried to shove Hallie away, one deadly glance from Troah would pierce me to my soul. All I could do was watch the sweat bead on his upper lip.

New sweat.

"Take Jatahn upstairs," said Troah. "I'll take care of this mess."

Hallie looked at me, nostrils wide, eyes flat. "I'll kill her," she said to Troah, "but you'll have to explain it to Althea."

"Don't worry," said Troah.

"Wait," I whispered. Still no pulse. "Wait."

"There's nothing to wait for," snapped Hallie.

Ransom's breathing was so shallow I could hardly see his chest move. Under my cold fingers, finally, a pulse. Feathery. Thin.

"He's alive," I said. "Give me the scanner."

Troah laughed. "Take her upstairs, Hallie. I've had enough."

I looked up at Hallie and saw my expression reflected in hers. "Give me the scanner," I said.

"No." Her big hands wrapped into my hair, took hold of my ears like handles.

I grabbed Ransom. I might be able to hang on until he showed some larger sign of life—if he wasn't killed in the struggle.

Ransom sighed and frowned with the effort. "Thirsty . . ." he mumbled, eyes squeezed shut. His head lolled to one side.

Hallie's hold on me went rigid. "What the *hell*?" She jerked away from me and jumped onto her feet. "He's alive, *fuck,* Troah, he's alive!"

I got a grip on the edge of the table and pulled myself up. Troah was watching the scanner where it lay on the bloody steel table. The readings were familiar. Low blood pressure, weak pulse, the overall symptoms of shock. The cancer was there too, *Virasi lymphoma*, metastasizing through Ransom's body, invading his lymphatic system.

Troah looked up, her cold face hot in the cheeks. "Where did you learn to do this?"

"A friend." My voice shook. My body felt as though it might drift apart into tiny, transparent pieces. "On Bellea-Naya."

"Out in the fucking Frontier?" said Hallie. "This is what's going on out there?"

Troah reached across the table and cupped my face in both hands. "Who's your friend?" she demanded. "Where is she? Did she tell you about us?"

I shut my eyes. Her touch was different now—a reassuring heat. She ran gentle fingers through my hair, down my neck. For a minute I was sure she was going to put her arms around me and kiss me again. The idea made me shake with anticipation, or fear, or relief.

"Stop it, Troah," whispered Hallie. "We don't have time for you to play with her."

The door to the training room swung open with a squeak. I opened my eyes. Troah turned around. It was Leiban.

"You're not supposed to be in here," Leiban said to Troah. He eyed me, and Hallie, and Ransom under the table. "Well?"

"Well what?" said Troah.

Leiban's face tightened. "He's dead. Right? He's dead."

Ransom let out another sigh. "Water?"

Troah pushed the scanner toward Leiban, her face gleaming with malice. "Have a look," she said. "See how dead he really is."

Leiban didn't move. "He's Failing," he said.

"If that's what you're going to tell Althea," said Troah, "you'd better make sure." She gave the scanner another nudge.

"What're you doing, Troah?" whispered Hallie.

"Rexidi." Troah smiled at him. "Come have a look at your demons."

He stiffened. He took a couple of short, tense steps across the room and snatched the scanner off the table. He aimed it at Ransom and his face emptied, bit by bit as he watched the screen, until the only thing moving was a muscle that shuddered under one eye. Leiban put the scanner down, carefully, on the table. He didn't say anything.

"There's no Drug sign," said Troah. "Don't you think that's interesting?"

He stared past her, at me, pale and sweating in the cool air.

"You should be happy," said Troah. "You're in your nineteenth year. You're slowing down. You don't heal so fast any more. The Gods forbid that you might die in the ring tomorrow." She made a shooing motion. "Tell Althea to come and see the cure for Failure. Tell her there's a way for her to keep you forever."

Leiban blinked, eyes a trace wider, full of dread.

"Don't you love her?" chided Troah. "We all know how much she loves you."

Cold sweat puckered his naked torso, making the tattoo of the fleeing prince seem grayish, distorted. He turned around and went into the training room, letting the clinic door bang shut behind him.

"So you scared him," said Hallie. "Now what? He won't stay scared for long."

"He'll be dead by tomorrow night," said Troah. "He'll win his match, but he's just lost everything else." She gave me a sharp, evaluating look. "You have a name, Jatahn."

"Frenna," I whispered.

"Frenna." She nodded. "Come with us."

Troah hooked her arm in mine, hurrying me down the deserted corridor. Hallie followed, Ransom slung over her shoulders. Swallowing a mouthful of water had exhausted him. His chin bounced against Hallie's hip as he slept through his first moments of being a free man.

Behind the closed training room doors, Leiban's voice rang out, counting through moves. Bare feet slapped on stone. Weapons thudded in an uneven rhythm. Althea's shrill objections cut through the muggy air and thinned to nothing.

Past the kitchen and around the curve of the hallway. We were heading in the direction of Frei's apartment, but Troah stopped in front of the narrow closet that Leiban had told me to stay away from—her room. Hallie came up behind me, swaying under Ransom's weight, and Troah pushed the door open.

Dim light from the hallway fell on the rickety wooden shelves that lined the walls. Troah touched a light panel, and the murky dark changed to harsh white.

Bones and human skulls cluttered the space at the head of her thin sleeping pallet, piled together in a sort of pyramid. Some were the same raw-white as the ones circling the ring upstairs. Some were blackened, sooty, as though they'd been thrown in a fire. At the other end of the pallet, dull chains—slave collars—were heaped around a dozen short, handmade candles. There was hardly enough space to spread your arms, and the air seemed almost thick enough to gulp. But what made the tiny room so close wasn't the lack of space or air, or even the bones and candles. It was what Troah had nailed to the shelving and stretched out tight. Her tapestry.

Not Rexidi this time. Three wide-eyed women—flat, painted images on graying fabric—glared down, their right hands flat against the stylized folds of their black robes, their left hands up, palm outwards. On the right, the first showed a hieroglyphic Faraqui eye, the same as Rasse's brand. The figure on the left had a wavering, water-blue line across her palm. In the middle was the *troah,* with her black Hand in the center of a white palm, her face a furious mask. They were painted on odd shapes of cloth, meticulously sewn together. I looked more closely and saw sleeves and necklines. Shirts. White slave shirts. Splayed shapes, patched together like human hides.

Troah turned to me. "Move the bed."

I took one unsteady step into the room and knelt by the mattress. The furies on the wall stared me down, as vivid as a nightmare. No matter how wet the air, the sewn-together shirts seemed remarkably dry—another act of Troah's resistance. If anything, there seemed to be more water right here than anywhere else in the seeping ring, dripping behind the wooden shelves, down the black stones, leaving chalky white streaks. I could hear it roaring below the floor, as though all the rain that sluiced off the red shields above the ring, had finally found a place to collect, a long way underground.

I folded the thin mattress over the pillow and blanket. Underneath, flat stones were interrupted by a square wooden hatch with a ring in the center.

"Open it," said Troah.

I pulled hard on the cold metal, and the trap opened.

Below, in the distant, rippling surface, my reflection was a pair of spidery arms outstretched on either side of one tiny square of light. The rank smell of water drifted up, gritty from running through street grates and gutters, oily from streaming down the arena's outside walls. Underneath the rush was the unaffected tone of the Emirate Report. I heard a soft splash, and the sound of the news faded into the echo of water.

"Do you know what a cistern is?" asked Troah.

I did know. It was a holding place for water—and for whoever was down there, listening to the progress of Rasha's war, not escaping from the arena. Waiting.

"It's a capture for rainwater," said Hallie. "Every building in this city has one." She nodded at the hole in the floor. "This is the service access for ours. It's the way out of this pit."

"How?" I whispered. The sound breathed into the space below me, a wide, empty space.

"The drainage grates in the street outside are loose," said Hallie.

I stared at her. My heart had gone liquid, gorged with hope and disbelief. "You could leave," I whispered. "Why don't you leave?"

"Sometimes we do." Troah pushed me away and closed the trap. She straightened the pallet over it, and Hallie eased Ransom down. "You can ask questions later."

Hallie tugged a blanket over the sleeping boy and looked sideways at me, not really meeting my eyes. "Do we need to tell you what'll happen if you say anything about this? To anyone?"

I shook my head.

Troah put her Hand over Ransom's eyes. "Stay put," she said to him. "And stay quiet. We'll be back for you tonight." She picked up one of the skulls and hefted it. "I think this one's about his size." She gave me the skull and scooped up an armload of femur and split ribs from the pile at the head of her bed. Hallie held out another thin blanket, and Troah let the bones tumble in. She picked one of the collar-chains out of the dull heap and warmed it between her hands.

"Now," she said to me. "We'll see how good a liar you are."

The skull lolled in the clinic sink, staring blindly at the ceiling, waiting for its next incarnation as Ransom's false corpse. The blanket of bones lay on the floor, in the middle of a confusion of bare, brownish footprints that led into the hall, where Hallie mopped at them with a stained rag. Behind the door to the training room, Althea's voice lectured in an incomprehensible monotone.

Hallie straightened, listening. "We've got about five minutes before she comes in, Troah."

Troah pulled a long, zippered plastic bag out of one of the bottom cabinets, and hung it over the steel table, not rushing, hardly concerned, as far as I could tell. "If all Althea sees are bones, that's fine," she said to me. "Frei only ever gave her bones." She took a small yellow bottle out of the cabinet and tossed it to me. "Some arenas have incinerators, but Otis is too cheap to put one in. Frei used enzymes to decompose the corpses. They leave a skeleton, and not much else. All you have to do is put in the bones and empty the bottle so it smells right." She pointed at the skull. "Don't forget that."

They were going to leave me to explain everything. I crouched by the blanket, my stomach winding itself into a knot.

"There's no pelvis," I said. "There's hardly any spine."

Hallie leaned in the doorway and tossed the bloody rag into the sink. "Althea doesn't care about anatomy. All she wants to see is the head on the plate."

"What if she doesn't believe me?"

"She will," said Hallie. "There's nothing else she *can* believe." She motioned impatiently to Troah. "Let's go."

Troah followed her into the hallway, and gave me a dangerous smile from under the weak yellow lights. "Be convincing, Jatahn," she said, and closed the door.

I stood in the cool room with the yellow bottle in one hand and a femur in the other, feeling as if I'd just woken up from a long, frightening dream. The sounds from the training room turned into relieved laughter and slamming lockers. I gathered up the blanket and opened one end of the body bag. Stale, sour air puffed out. I dumped the scramble of bones in and concentrated on arranging them.

A dozen toes, one patella for the knee, and two ulnae. They made a thin, unconvincing arrangement in the lower half of the bag. I found eight and a half ribs, a broken scapula, and twelve vertebrae. Three of the vertebrae were the same. The other nine should have been scattered at uneven intervals, but I pushed them all together at the top of the bag in an awkward semi-spine. The leftovers were from an animal of some kind, but I threw them in too. The collar-chain and the anonymous skull went in last, face up, jaws open, looking as scared as I was. I squirted the contents of the yellow bottle into the bag and yanked the zipper up as the training room door banged open.

Althea blew in, her lank black hair stuck to her pale skin. Leiban loomed behind her, tall and close as a shadow.

Althea surveyed the blood drying on the floor, the walls and the cabinet. "What a goddamn mess. You'll have this place cleaned up before dinner."

"Yes, D'sha."

Leiban had no interest in the leftover carnage. He chewed his lips, scrutinizing the body bag.

Althea came over to the steel table, and I stepped out of easy reach. She patted the bag, up and down. "You know how to do that thing with the enzymes?"

"Yes, D'sha."

She unzipped the bag far enough to expose the eyeless skull, reached in and felt around. Vertebrae clinked against metal, and Althea pulled the collar out. "Too damn bad," she said. "That one could have gone for at least another month or two." She toed under the table and a spent hypoderm rolled out. "Thanas?" she asked.

I nodded, dry-mouthed.

Althea kicked the second hypo out from under the table. And the third. If she looked, she would be able to see that the residue was Viral green. "Took that much?" she said, sounding surprised. "You should have saved him."

I held my tongue between my teeth and stared at the floor, determined not to say anything more than yes or no. Out of the corner of my eye, I saw Leiban nudge her, and Althea frowned up from the bag.

"What the hell was going on with you last night?" She crossed her arms, focused on me now, not the ersatz Ransom.

Through the wall, through stone and mortar and flaking concrete, Troah's presence was hot as needles. "Nothing, D'sha," I mumbled. "I—I got lost."

"Otis told me you tried to leave with Rasha," said Althea. "No one leaves this ring without my permission, girl."

Leiban scowled. "Just tell the truth," he said. "Tell her about Troah."

The truth was that I had seen the way out. The price of escape was silence. "I don't know what you mean," I said.

Leiban turned to Althea, flushed with frustration. "Troah threatened to lock her in with Rasse." He jerked a thumb at me. "She was in hysterics last night. That's why she was trying to leave."

"Is that true?" asked Althea.

I shook my head, not at Althea, but at the bloody floor.

"It *is* true," insisted Leiban.

Althea wiped damp hair away from her forehead. "Give it a rest, Leiban."

"But it's not just *her*," said Leiban. "Troah's got the entire middle set in the palm of her hand. D'Althea, you *know* it's true."

"Troah could cut every throat in the ring," said Althea. "As long as Otis likes her point spreads, Otis doesn't care what she does."

"This is different," said Leiban, and this time his voice trembled.

Althea frowned at him. "Troah's killed half a dozen of my best fighters, Leiban. Otis knows it, and he could give a shit. Why the hell would he care what she does to Rasha's medic?"

Leiban shot me an angry, desperate look. If Althea noticed, she didn't show it. She shrugged. "When Troah stops being golden, you can do whatever you want. In the meantime, ignore her. You've ignored her for years." She slapped his rear. "Get washed up. Medic," she said to me, and waved vaguely at the bloodstains, "get busy."

"Yes, D'sha."

Althea opened the hallway door and walked out, expecting Leiban to follow.

He didn't.

He reached across the short space between us and grabbed my shirt. He shoved me into the steel table, and hit me in the face. He was so fast, I didn't have time to yell, so hard against the side of my head that the room went dark and bright and dark again. My shoulder hit the edge of the table, then my chin. The floor knocked the rest of my breath away. Olney would have kicked me. I curled on the floor, eyes squeezed shut. Leiban's heels scuffed concrete and stalked away, following Althea down the hall. I swallowed blood and opened my eyes.

Bare feet shuffled in the doorway to the training room. Meeds, clustered gawking, while Hallie towered over them all.

"Don't just stand there," said Hallie. "Help her up."

"Help her?" said one of the boys. "Troah said she was a jinx."

"Troah was wrong," said Hallie. "She's no jinx. She's the one we've been waiting for."

NINE

My jaw felt like Leiban's knuckles had left permanent dents. I leaned against Frei's thin, ratty pillows, tracing the tender places under my left eye, along my jaw.

Hallie brought a damp rag from the bathroom and sat on the edge of the bed, squeezing it, forgetting to give it to me. She'd helped me off the clinic floor, walked me down the hallway to Frei's room and sat me on the bed. Now her voice was too high, too tight in her throat.

"How many of those needle things do you have?" she said.

"Two more."

Her calculating self-confidence, so obvious this morning, was gone. She looked young, weary and scared. "One for you," she said, "and one for Troah."

"How many years do you have in?"

"Eighteen."

"I can get more," I said, but I wasn't sure how true that was.

"Can you?" Hallie twisted the rag in her big hands. "I'm sorry I scared you in the clinic."

She would have killed me. Now things were substantially different. I liked her better when she was sturdy and self-assured. "Who's down in the cistern?"

"Can't you guess?" she said. "They're runaways."

"Why do they come to the ring?" I asked. "Because of Frei? Or because of Troah?"

She stared at the rag and finally gave it to me. "It's a long story."

"Tell me."

"About five or six years ago, the cops caught a dozen runaways, just outside the gates." Hallie made a slashing motion with one hand. "Me and Naritte were in the ring doing a High Set Pairs match. We were drawing blood . . . but those cops . . ." She made a squeamish shrug. "They were out of control. You could see them from the pit—hell, the fans could see them from the bleachers. Althea was complaining about the distraction, and Frei went out to stop them. Maybe he paid the cops to leave or told them some kind of story—anyway they left, and Frei disappeared with the runaways. He showed up after the fights were over, but I thought Althea was going to pop a vein in the meantime."

I dabbed at my face. The cool water felt good. "He hid them in the cistern?"

"We didn't know what he was up to back then," said Hallie, "but I guess he'd been doing it for years. He'd give them his own clothes and his own money, and get them passage off Traja. Of course Otis didn't pay him hardly anything, so he couldn't keep doing that. Which is why Troah got involved." Hallie ground her palms together. "Because of the money."

"She was fixing the fights for Otis," I said. "And Otis and Frei would bet against their own team."

Hallie nodded. "Troah'd only been here for a couple of years, and she was supposed to be a pass-girl. Instead of sleeping with the Meeds, she'd tell them how they were going to lose, down to the fractions on style points."

"She was always right?"

"Close enough for the Meeds. Althea didn't know about it until one of them lost—badly—and told her it wasn't his fault. It was Troah's prophecy. Althea was ready to cut Troah in half, except Frei objected. By that time, Otis was pretty invested in Troah's predictions. He liked the idea of solid odds, and that saved her neck."

"And Frei started betting with Otis."

"Frei saved a lot of lives," said Hallie.

"How did Troah find out about the runaways?" I asked. "Frei wasn't taking them through her room, was he?"

Hallie shook her head. "Troah was sleeping in the clinic. Frei was the only one who knew how to get into the cistern. Troah probably found out about them the same way me and Naritte did."

"How?"

Hallie shifted on the bed. "The acoustics down here are strange. On quiet nights, when there isn't a lot rain, you can hear the purifiers rattling in the cistern. If you don't know what you're listening to, you'd swear someone was running machinery up in the breezeway. You can hear the walls settling if the humidity's right. If it's a little drier, it sounds like the whole place is ready to collapse. So, when we started hearing these horrible screams, we thought it was just the walls. Troah told the Meeds the ring was haunted, and the screams were coming from the skulls, upstairs." She smiled. "Naritte didn't buy that, and one night, a couple of months after Troah moved into the storage closet, we went snooping around. We checked her room, and saw how the bed wasn't lying quite flat, and found the trapdoor underneath it. When we opened it, we could hear Troah and Frei down below."

"And?"

"She was giving him statistics. About how many of the runaways she'd kept alive through their Failure. Something like one in a hundred. And he was talking about Tony, and how Tony only had two years left, and how he thought he'd come up with a medical treatment that was more consistent." Hallie knotted her fingers. "You can't imagine how it felt for us, lying on Troah's floor, listening to that. We risked our lives every weekend in the ring, but we weren't supposed to know anything about what they'd been doing for—for years."

I leaned forward on the bed. "How was Troah freeing them?"

"With her big power," said Hallie. "That tattoo." She raised an eyebrow at my expression. "The first night you were here, she used it on you. You know it works."

I rubbed the middle of my chest where Troah had touched me. "It's not the tattoo."

"No?"

I shook my head. "Do you know what pheromones are?"

"Sure," said Hallie, and nodded, as though she really did. She saw my doubts and tilted her head to one side. "I do know a little biology, Frenna. They're markers, or sexual lures. When a dog pisses on a tree, that's a pheromone."

Now she was being patronizing. "That's what Troah's big power is," I said. "They're not usually that strong in humans, but Troah has a gland that produces them. Anyone with the same physiology has to respond."

"Oh?" said Hallie. "Who told you this?"

"Rasha."

"Rasha's just a lying son of a bitch."

"I know she has it," I said. "Rasha has it. I do too." I touched my throat and Hallie's eyes followed my fingers.

"What do you mean?" she said. "It's something extra? Like a mutation?"

"That might have been how it started."

"I don't understand," said Hallie. "It's something they bred into your people? But why would Troah and Rasha have one?"

"They didn't breed it into us," I said. "It's a Jatahn mutation that's spread into them."

"A contagious mutation? Like a disease? But how . . . ?"

"It's not a disease," I said. "Troah's people and my people are blood relations."

Hallie stared at me. "Who told you that?"

"Rasha."

She blinked. "Goddamn. You're Troah's goddamn cousin?"

I shrugged.

Hallie rubbed her chin. "So Troah—or Rasha—lets off a whiff of pheromones, and what happens to you? You feel sexually attracted to them?"

I could feel heat behind my face. I was afraid she was going to ask unanswerable questions. How did it feel to be overwhelmed by scents I couldn't even smell? How could I let myself be seduced by that? Didn't I have more self-control? "You know what it does," I said. "You've seen what she puts the Meeds through."

"So it isn't just a sex pheromone?" She chewed her lip. "A control pheromone? But I don't feel it. And Naritte didn't. Wouldn't that mean that anyone who responded to Troah—or Rasha—was genetically linked with the Faraqui? Shouldn't it work on everybody?"

"I think it only works on pure-blood Faraqui slaves."

"You're not pure-blood. Are you? After a hundred years of Emirate goons on your planet?"

"A lot of things skip generations," I said. "I look more like a Favored One than either of my parents. Or my grandmother."

"Lucky thing," said Hallie, and smiled. "How does it feel?"

"How does what feel?" I said evasively.

"To be—I don't know—pheronomed by Troah. Does it make her seem desirable? Or just more scary?"

"It's hard to describe." I shrugged, overly wide, wanting her to know how uncomfortable the question made me. "It's like being absorbed. Or becoming part of someone else's body."

"Is it like sex?"

"Not with Troah," I said. "I thought I was going to die."

Hallie leaned forward, suddenly more intense. "Do you think she could keep you alive if you were Failing?"

"Yes," I said. "Yes."

Hallie sat back. "So, there's a percentage of runaways with the right receptors, and when they Fail, they're too scared of her to drop dead." She rubbed her ankles. "Frei must have known. That's why he decided to use Enhancers."

"Enhancers?"

Hallie nodded. "You saw what happened to Arbitt in the ring. If I could tell him to die, and he did, why shouldn't I be able to keep him alive?" She looked away. "Or Naritte?"

"Did Otis know Troah's odds were against Naritte?"

"Sure," said Hallie. "It was fine with him."

"But wasn't she winning?"

"Of course," said Hallie, "but when Naritte found out Troah and Frei were freeing runaways, she got scared. She was afraid she was going to get so badly wounded, Frei wouldn't be able to put her back together. She stopped feeling . . . invulnerable. She'd win, but her point spreads got too predictable. Troah waited until Otis was really fed up with the low bets. Then she nailed Naritte."

"And she was so badly hurt, Frei couldn't help her."

"That's right."

"Did the Enhancers ever work?" I asked.

Hallie nodded. "Frei freed eight people. Troah freed ten. She says she did, anyway."

"Those are her friends on the outside?" I said. "Leiban called them her disciples."

"They're Frei's friends," said Hallie. "I've only met a few of them. They're runaways he's helped, or sympathizers. You'll be meeting them tonight."

"I am? They're coming here?"

Hallie shook her head. "Troah's taking you to see them."

"I'm—I'm leaving?" I stared at her. "I'm getting out? I can get away? But what about—"

"Don't get too excited," said Hallie. "You'll be back by morning."

"No," I said.

"Yes," said Hallie. "But if everything goes right in the ring tomorrow, we'll all be leaving."

"Through the cisterns?" I said. "Then you could have gotten out. Why didn't you and Naritte leave if you knew about the cisterns?"

"Because people knew us, Frenna. Fans have our pictures. We're on posters, we're on the holo. Naritte and I were famous."

"Then why did Frei try to free her?"

"He was doing it for me," said Hallie.

"Even though it might have given everything away?"

"The fans would have known she'd Failed," said Hallie. "No one would have asked, 'Hey, lady, aren't you that dead arena girl?' It would have been a stupid question."

"What about you?" I asked. "Did you stop taking chances?"

Hallie looked up. "I'll do whatever I can to get out of this place in one piece," she said. "And if that means fighting for Althea until the day I Fail, that's what I'll do."

Across the room, the door swung open. Troah came in, trailed by two of the Meeds—a pale boy shaved to dirty stubble, and a red-haired girl. He carried a tray of steaming food. She had a holoree.

"Put the 'ree over there." Troah pointed to the nightstand. The girl set it down carefully, not looking at me, but watching from the corners of her eyes. The boy put the tray down on the rumpled covers at the end of the bed. Troah made a dismissive gesture and the two of them left, practically stepping on each other, staring at me instead of watching where they were going.

"You're a celebrity, Jatahn," said Troah, unimpressed. She sat on the bed, and turned on the 'ree.

The Emirate Report announcer's bland, raceless face blinked into the stale air.

"*. . . the hour's lead story . . . news from the Emirate Frontier . . . unconfirmed reports that two Emirate battleships were attacked and destroyed by Faraqui weapons yesterday have been invalidated by both military and diplomatic officials. The following was recorded earlier today at Diplomatic Headquarters, on Lowry-Ethira.*"

He faded into a projection of a small, elaborately decorated room. A brown-skinned woman with graying hair stood on a raised podium, arms crossed over her uniform. Three reporters sat stiffly in three hard chairs. Two wore beige Emirate Report jackets. The third was dressed in a gray business suit—probably a reporter from an independent network.

One of the Emirate Reporters stood up. "Ambassador Trent, can you give us any details on the alleged attack?"

The woman gave him a sharp nod. "This unconfirmed report was called in by a shipper who refused to identify herself. When we tracked her signal to investigate the time and place of the alleged event, we discovered that she had transmitted the information at least twelve hours before she said this action occurred." She glared at the Independent in the business suit. "Although all information is available to the public, the Emir resents the lack of responsible reporting from the private media pools. The public doesn't want hysterics." She turned to face the camera. "Citizens are advised to remain skeptical of all information received through unofficial channels. The Emirate Report is accurate, dependable, and up-to-the-minute."

"What about the evacuations of Emirate personnel from the Frontier?" asked the Independent.

Her artificial patience evaporated. "If you'd bother to listen, you'd know these so-called evacuations are actually cost-cutting measures which were approved months ago. There is no evacuation. There is no invasion. No ships have been destroyed. I don't know how to make it any clearer to you people."

Troah switched the 'ree off. "She's lying, of course." She turned to me. "Have you heard anything about this?"

"I heard a lot of rumors before I left," I said.

"If any of that's true," said Hallie, "it won't be safe to stay here much longer."

Troah raised an eyebrow. "Don't count on going anywhere before the bets are paid off from tomorrow's fights. How many of those veterinary hypos do you have?"

"Two more," I said.

"The woman who gave them to you—where is she now?"

"On Newhall," I said.

"She has more?"

I glanced at Hallie and nodded.

"Can you make them yourself?" asked Troah.

"The Virevir?" I had to think. Could it be cultured like any other cancer? I didn't have enough to experiment with, but Ransom was infested with it. I could do a biopsy. "I don't know."

"Think about it," said Troah, "and get some rest. You're coming outside. With me. Tonight."

*　　*　　*

"Wake up, Jatahn."

I hadn't meant to fall asleep. Troah leaned over me, her hair dark with water, her shirt open to the crease between her breasts. The air around her was lush with sweat and curry. Heat rippled off of her.

She put her Hand on my chest, and my heart thundered against her palm. She took it away and I was freezing cold.

I pushed myself up against the headboard. Lights were on, but the room seemed darker than it had before.

"Where's Hallie?" I mumbled.

"Sleeping," said Troah. "Big day tomorrow. Remember?"

She put a bundle of dark green cloth on the bed and spread it out. An embroidered shirt and pants—not slave clothes. A pair of green slippers fell onto the blanket. "These should fit you," she said.

"Shoes?" I said stupidly. "We're not supposed to wear shoes."

"Put them on."

I pushed one slipper on. It felt tight.

She held the shirt up to my shoulders, touched bare skin, and the contact took the breath out of me. "That's fine." She took the slipper and rolled the pair of them into the clothes again. "Come with me, Frenna."

In her room, except for the bones and the three painted furies, Troah and I were alone. She slid her thin pallet away from the trapdoor, and pulled the hatch open. There was no rush and roar of water below, just soft, lapping sounds. Outside the ring, I thought, the rain had stopped.

"Put up the ladder," Troah whispered into the dark.

The ladder was wet, softening wood, slippery with mold and moss. I went first, Troah's heavy shadow above me, blocking the dim square of light from the trapdoor until she pulled it shut. I hesitated on the wobbling ladder, thinking I was in total darkness, but I wasn't.

Magenta light fell in hazy stripes below me, glinting across the surface of the water. The light was from the street, coming through the drainage grates, grimy and thick as rain.

Someone coughed—a hacking, liquid cough. I glanced around and saw shadows in the shadows. A sliver of white cloth. The gleam of an eye. The shadows solidified into people. The people became too many runaways to count, pressed together on narrow ledges and recessed shelves carved into the cistern's scummed walls. The cough came again. Ransom, I thought.

Troah poked her toes into my shoulder. "What's wrong?"

"Nothing." I edged down the ladder, hanging onto slimy rungs. Below, dim, writhing waves of light played over a rectangular concrete block in the middle of the shadowed lake—a wide, algae-covered island at the bottom of the ladder. My feet touched slick concrete, and a slender girl caught my elbow.

"Careful. It's slippery."

She was soaking wet, pasty-faced, hollow under the eyes. Her shirt was a free woman's blouse, but her pants were standard slave clothing, and she had no shoes. I thought of Rexidi, half changed from man to animal, easy to spot, no matter how thick the forest.

She peered past me, up at Troah. "Have you heard the news?" she whispered. "They say the Faraqui attacked an Emirate battleship. They say it's been destroyed."

Troah stepped gingerly onto the slick concrete. "Everyone's heard that."

"Is it true?" asked the girl.

Troah turned to her, all cool condescension. "Do you

think they tell me their plans?" She nodded into the darkness. "Get Ransom."

The girl crouched at the edge of the concrete island, slipped into the black water, and swam off into the gloom. Troah pushed the bundle of clothes at me and slid in after her. She turned in the dark, rank soup of the pool, arms out, hair floating around her white face. "Hurry up," she said to me. "We don't have all night."

I angled in, awkward, one foot at a time, keeping the clothes up, dry, over my head. The water was gritty and warm. More slime, and swirls of sand around my ankles. I was up to my neck before I found the bottom.

"There's another ladder under that grate." Troah pointed into the shadows. "Come on." She swam off.

I heard a splash by the far wall, and more coughing. The girl muttered cautions over the slap of water. Ransom hacked out an incomprehensible reply.

"Hurry up." Troah's voice was already a long way off, echoing along the ceiling.

I half swam, half walked across the pool until I found Troah at the bottom of the lightless wall. Ransom's face bobbed next to her, watery-eyed, hair twisted into lank strands. I touched his cheek and jerked my fingers away from the unexpected heat.

"He's sick," I said. "He needs a doctor."

"Of course he's sick," Troah hissed. "Feel here. . . ." She grabbed my hand and guided it along the wall to one rough, carved-in handhold, and then another. They led straight up, to the magenta-lit stripes of a drainage grate in the street above us.

"Where are we going?" I asked.

"Underground," she whispered, and started climbing.

Outside, the rain had changed to warm fog, condensing into sweat. Troah pushed the grate back into place while I stripped off my wet clothes, naked against the oil-colored stone. Ransom leaned against the wall, pale and hot. I pulled on the embroidered green pants, the shirt, and the shoes. Troah came close to fasten the collar of the shirt over the chain around my neck.

"Shouldn't you should be wearing these?" I breathed, almost in her ear.

"People know me." She slipped her arm into mine, and the heat of her made the sweat start under my breasts. "Now, Jatahn," she whispered. "Who belongs to who?" She beckoned to Ransom, and he stumbled after us into the dense night.

We headed away from the ground station and the slave markets. Ahead, a bank of garish halogens—pinks and purples, a flash of red—cut the fog in wide blades of color. Drunken laughter drifted through the humid air.

"Those are the brothels," said Troah. "If Rasha hadn't been so pleased with you, that's where you'd be right now."

The whores were leggy shadows against scarlet walls, their naked bodies striped with luminescent blue spirals, white handprints, or graphic drawings. The paint distinguished them from their customers—dull blurs on their slow, appraising patrols. Troah pulled me around the next corner, down a half-lit avenue, banked on either side by high black walls.

I glanced over my shoulder for Ransom, plodding along, weaving a little. To anyone who happened to look, I was a free woman with my two slaves—a girl on my arm and my drunken boy lagging behind. It was a solid illusion, even to me.

"Can't we get a skimmer?" I said. "Is there a doctor where we're going?"

"Do you have any money for skim fare?" asked Troah. She tilted her head, mocking my concern. "Aren't you the doctor?"

"He could die," I whispered.

"Not before we leave."

Footsteps echoed on the wet stones just ahead. Troah snugged my arm, pulling me tight against her. A man with an umbrella emerged from the pink-white fog. A skinny, shirtless girl trotted along behind him, hugging an over-stuffed satchel.

He nodded at me. "Evening."

Troah's chin bumped my shoulder and I nodded stiffly back.

The girl passed without appearing to notice us at all.

Ransom managed to wait until they were out of earshot before he started coughing.

"You seem nervous," said Troah. "Haven't you ever run away before?"

"Yes," I said.

"You probably didn't even change clothes," she said. "It's easier like this, you know. No one seems to think we'd have the bad manners to disguise ourselves."

"I did," I said.

"A rebel," she said. "I didn't notice."

"But I did," I said.

She laughed. "Tell me how you ran into Rasha."

Her arm was like a vise on mine, squeezing hard enough to cut off the flow of blood. She seemed more tense than she acted, and it occurred to me that she thought I might try to break away from her and run off into the envel-oping fog.

"I met him—he found me—on Naya," I said.

"Where was your woman-friend with her magic potion?"

"She'd already left. I wanted to go with her, but—" I shrugged. Troah's arm kinked tight, like a reflex.

Did she really think I would run? Didn't she trust the gene-deep hold she had on me? And if she didn't, why should I?

She released me and slid her arm around my waist. Her

palm was a warm island on my hip, fingers sliding along the thin green cloth. I licked water off my upper lip and tasted sweat.

Not far ahead, bare feet splashed in standing water. Two slave boys emerged from the fog, carrying an impact-crate between them. Behind them, four more slaves lurched along, loaded down with boxes, covered birdcages, and suitcases. One staggered under a pair of ornate endtables.

Two free men, one with a tiny dog on a long leash, brought up the rear. "I still think we should have called a skimmer," said one.

"And I keep telling you, that's the way to start a panic," said the other. "If the pilots find out people are leaving, then the pilots leave. When the pilots leave, everyone knows there's trouble, and there's a run on offworld tickets. If we have to wait for tickets, we'll be stuck with the rest of these—" He saw me and Troah and bit off whatever he'd planned to say. "What're you staring at, lady?" he said to me.

Troah watched the two men and their household belongings vanish into the night. "You know the story of Rexidi, Jatahn?"

"Yes."

"Do you know the moral?"

"Don't run," I said.

"Run if you like, but there's no escape." She held up her tattooed palm, ran her thumb over the tips of her fingers. "Rexidi was supposed to be a slave with excellent bloodlines, but when he ran away, it was an indication that something was wrong in the gene pool." She squeezed me. "What happens to him in the story?"

"He's hunted down and killed," I said.

"Suppose Rexidi was spared because of some sentimental reason," said Troah. "Suppose he was allowed to breed? What happens to the bloodline then?"

"More runaways?"

"Exactly," said Troah. "The wrong gene, and the story of a successful escape gets passed down the generations. You see what the real moral of that story is?"

"No," I said.

"The moral is, test the infants," said Troah. "If you find an anomaly, destroy it before it grows into something you can't control. If Rexidi had been killed when he was born, there would have been no trouble, no story." She glanced at me, her face tinged magenta on one side, shadowed black on the other. Her eyes glittered. "Don't you see what I am, Frenna?"

"You're not Rexidi," I said. "You're no runaway slave."

"No," she said. "I'm what happens when the Faraqui don't follow their own rules. I'm their *Troah*, the Hand of Fate, the great change."

The street narrowed abruptly, winding between huge houses with every window lit. At first it seemed festive, but the houses were empty.

"The Faraqui are the last thing these people should have worried about," said Troah. "You and I are far more dangerous. Compared to us, Rasha's war is insignificant."

"You talk like there's a revolution ready to start," I said. "We can't free anyone until they Fail."

"Failure doesn't matter anymore," said Troah. "We can survive it, and if you can survive, you can change your clothes, and cut off your collar and walk away from what you hate. You can't do that if you're counting down the years, waiting to die."

I tried to imagine Jamilla cutting her chains and wrapping herself in Rasha's robes. It was easier to picture the boys we'd just passed, weighted down with furniture and boxes, dropping their loads and running laughing into the night. I tried to imagine myself walking away from Troah, alone, or with Hallie. For a minute the vision was clear, and urgent. Troah's Hand slid under my shirt, a finger at time, and the image faded, against my will.

Overhead, skimmers murmured through the hazy dark. I counted one, two, four, each passing low enough to move the fog in wide, lazy spirals. The houses became further and further apart, separated by extravagant shrubbery, and sheer walls of whitewashed black stone. The scent of aging flowers saturated the air.

We followed one high wall until it ended in a blue-tinted security field. Beyond the field, another immense mansion was lit by a scattering of pearl-white globes on the lawn. Troah put her palm on the entry screen.

"Runaway slaves live *here*?" I asked.

"When Otis wins, we all win. Everyone at the Beryl is a collaborator, whether they know it or not."

"Not Leiban," I said, "and not Althea."

Troah smiled. "I suppose you're right."

A slave girl hurried out of the shadows, frowned at me, and then saw Troah. Behind us, Ransom hacked and spat on the ground. The girl's eyes widened. "We weren't expecting you."

"You should stay in touch," snapped Troah.

The girl tapped a switch on the other side of the gate and the security field shredded into air. "When we call, we get Otis Tarda, or your trainer, or her dog-boy," she said. "We can't just leave a message."

"You could come to the fights, like everyone else," said Troah.

"We've been busy." The girl eyed Ransom and stood aside for me. "D'sha," she said, and I remembered to turn. "I'll get something dry for you to wear."

"That's all right," I mumbled.

"It's nothing." She reached up to switch on the security field and her sleeve fell back to her elbow. I saw a long, ragged mark on her arm. A shadow, I thought.

It wasn't. It was a scabbed-over cut.

A wound like that should have healed in seconds on a slave, gone back to skin within minutes. But she wasn't a slave.

The slave girl . . . the young free woman *dressed* as a slave girl, glanced at me and fastened her cuff tight around her wrist.

"This way," she said, and started across the lawn.

"Why is she dressed like that?" I hissed to Troah.

"Because," said Troah in a normal tone, "the slavers won't touch her. She's safe until she's too old for the Virus."

Such a simple solution might have done me some good, three long years ago, home on Jatah. Now I found myself peering around the shadowy yard, searching for the police, or the soldiers, or even Rexidi's demons, who might have noticed that unhealed cut.

Troah walked toward the house, looming in its decorative lights. I took Ransom's feverish hand and followed. There would be a hundred runaways inside this clandestine mansion, a thousand more who'd been and gone, and millions waiting to arrive.

Not one of them would be Jatahn.

The woman in the blue dress stared at me as I sat on the sofa.

Troah had called her Cheska, but hadn't bothered to introduce us. Cheska was slender, with graying hair cut into a silver brush on top, trailing down in a long thin braid. I didn't have to be told that she was a freed slave, like Renee. And like Renee, it was difficult to picture her in a collar and slave whites.

Troah lounged in a deep armchair across from me. Ransom sprawled, sweating, on the divan on the other side of the cool room, asleep almost as soon as he lay down.

Troah took a tall glass of cold tea from the free-slave girl and waved her away. All of Troah's resemblance to Rasha showed in that motion, every ounce of her arrogance. I was embarrassed for her until the girl bent toward Cheska with the tray of refreshments. There was no sign of outrage in her face, just compliance. She looked the same as any other house slave, and then I was embarrassed for her.

Cheska took two glasses and gave one to me. Condensation cooled my palms. I toed out of the too-small shoes. The tile floor felt good under my cramped, hot feet.

"You're Jatahn," said Cheska. "Troah said you're a runaway. I didn't think that was possible for your kind."

They had already discussed me? I tried to decide if she was being insulting. For her, Jatahn was probably synonymous with blind allegiance to the Faraqui. If she was part of a freed underground, wasn't she entitled to a few doubts?

"I did run away," I said, but the words felt awkward. I took a mouthful of the freezing tea and swallowed it. "Where are the others?"

"Others?" Cheska frowned at Troah as though she needed a translator.

"The rest of your—" Troah made little circles with her fingers. "Your houseguests. The ones Frei brought before he left. I've been wondering that myself."

"They've been gone for two weeks," said Cheska. She made it sound as though Troah should have known.

Troah sat up straight. "You had a ship? Why didn't you say something? Our pool's more than full."

"You'll have to wait for the next freighter," said Cheska. "There should be plenty on their way out of the Frontier, what with the news the way it is." She turned away from Troah—I would have said dismissively—and frowned at me. "Tell me about this drug you have."

I'd been wondering how long she'd been out of collar. Long enough to become a little too full of herself, I decided, and that made me feel strangely protective of Troah. "Who freed you?" I asked.

Her face tightened. "You don't ask that kind of question, girl."

"Was it Frei?" I persisted.

"I did it myself," she said stiffly. "With two friends. We didn't have any miracles, or Enhancers. I decided to survive, and I did."

"Did your friends survive?" I asked.

Her expression went cold. "No," she said. "This cure. Tell me what it is."

I ran my thumb around the edge of the glass. Her tone made me feel like I should be on my knees, on the floor at her feet, answering, "Yes, D'sha, no, D'sha." Troah had laid me out like a bolt of cloth, and in a minute, I thought Cheska might actually offer money for me.

"It's a cancer," I said unwillingly.

Cheska gave me a disbelieving smile. "Trading one fatal disease for another isn't my idea of a cure."

"Cancer cells are the only things that can grow fast enough to repair the damage from Failure," I said. "After that you have to find a doctor you can trust."

Cheska hesitated, then twisted in her chair to look at Ransom. I couldn't tell how convinced she was. "He's sick."

"Free," I said. Now I was starting to understand that we were here to prove something. Maybe this woman trusted Frei, but she had doubts about Troah. And Troah didn't like that.

Troah let out an impatient snort. "He's the proof," she said, "and think about this. What if he was reinjected with the Virus, right now?"

"He'd be a slave again," said Cheska.

Troah shook her head. "He'd be cured of his cancer, and no doctors would be involved. Without the collar and the clothes, nothing makes us any different than free people." She nodded after the free-slave girl. "Like her. Who would think to check?"

Cheska rubbed her left shoulder. "His brands . . ."

"They can be grafted over, just like yours."

"What if someone found out?" said Cheska. "What if he was scanned for some reason? What happens to him? Back to the arena?"

"Of course he'd have to be cautious," said Troah, "but half of any disguise is attitude. Some of us might never be convincing as free people. Right, Jatahn?"

I felt myself flush. I took another sip of tea and swallowed those protective Jatahn feelings. Let Troah fend for herself.

Troah leaned forward in her chair. "Even if a slave—a person—built up an immunity to the Virus, or died from Failure after six or seven doses—that's over a hundred years of not aging. All the advantages of being in collar, and none of the—" She made an uncomfortable motion with her shoulders.

Cheska twisted her thin gray braid. "Free people wouldn't let us keep that for ourselves."

"They'll rewrite history to get rid of the stigma of being infected," said Troah. "The shame would be in getting old, not in being collared."

Cheska turned to me again. "Let's see your medicine, Jatahn."

What would she do with my tiny germ of knowledge? Thank us kindly and kick us out? What did I have to protect me from Troah if I gave it up? Not a thing. "I don't have it with me," I said.

Troah looked up in surprise.

"I don't," I said to her. "I didn't think it was safe to bring it."

Troah gave me a curious, searching look, knowing none of this was true. She stood up abruptly and nodded at Cheska. "We'll see you at the ring tomorrow."

Cheska frowned. "I expected more than this," she said. "You told me you had a sure thing."

"I do." Troah made a motion toward Ransom. "There's your proof. And if you want more, you should call your doctor. Sooner than later. Like she said, it's a cancer, and he's very sick."

CH**A**PTER

TEN

When we left the house, it was raining hard. I'd forgotten my shoes, but it didn't matter. Water filled the street, up to my ankles, warm as a bath. The downpour soaked my clothes, still cool from being inside.

"You insulted her," said Troah.

"I don't trust her," I said.

"Is that why you lied to her?"

"What makes you think I lied?"

Her Hand slid against my thigh and brushed over the tape. The contact was like fire. "I need those," I said. "For the fights."

"You won't be freeing anyone tomorrow," said Troah. "If Althea finds out what you have, she'll destroy it, and then she'll get rid of you." Troah slid her arm through mine, not friendly, not even seductive, just a different kind of chain. "When the war's over, you and I and Cheska should all be on the same side, Jatahn."

It almost sounded like she cared. "She's not on your side," I said. "She has Ransom. Any doctor can culture the cancer. He's an endless supply until he's cured, and you just handed him to her. What makes you think she'll be at the ring tomorrow?"

"Money," said Troah. "She can't leave without us."

A surge of pragmatism told me she was dead wrong. Maybe Frei'd had other connections outside the Beryl, but Troah was limited to Cheska and Cheska's agenda had nothing to do with us. Whether or not she showed up at the fights, in a few days we'd all be running for our lives, caught in a flood of refugees. Outside the arena, no disguise could hide Troah's iron will and nasty attitude—the things that had served her so well in the ring would only get her in trouble elsewhere. For a disorienting moment I understood my murky breeding and what it was really for. Troah was the one who needed guidance and protection, not me. I was the armor. Not the sword.

Troah stopped and pulled me around so that we were facing each other. Water streamed down her face, her neck. Her white shirt clung to her body, half transparent. Her eyes were as deep and black as cistern pools. "You think I'm naïve," she said. "Or crazy."

"No."

"Then what do you think?" She put her arms around my waist and kissed my throat, low, warm and soft under my collar. Her hands slipped beneath my soaking shirt, the mark on her palm burning as she touched me, here, then there, sliding down my spine.

"Stop," I whispered, positive that she wouldn't, but she did. Even that was a hot assault, her fingers and tongue leaving fiery trails behind.

"You think I want to steal your miracle," hissed Troah. "But I don't need it." She smoothed her marked palm. "Two little needles are nothing compared to this."

Not true. What she had couldn't be cultured. It couldn't be passed around in slapneedles. And she couldn't use her Hand on herself when her time came to Fail. I could imagine her Failing, and the images made my throat go tight around the place she'd kissed me.

"Tomorrow night we'll be free women," said Troah. "But you'll leave me, I think, once we're offworld." She crossed her arms. "Where will you go? To find your friends from Naya?"

"Probably," I said.

She turned and started to walk again.

Her intensity fell on me with the rain, soaking into my shirt, trickling down my sides. I started after her. "What about you?"

"It shouldn't matter to you, Jatahn."

I fell in step next to her. "You want me to come with you." Saying it made me angry, and the edge came out in my voice. "You want me to drop everything and keep you company, and—and wait on you." I rapped my thumb over the tape and the needles. "You want *these*. You'll take them, and then you'll leave me, for Rasha, or the Meeds . . . or Rasse."

She stopped in the middle of the street. "I wouldn't leave you."

I almost laughed.

"Jatahn . . ." She took a breath and let it out through her teeth. "Why do you think Rasha brought you to the arena?"

"Because I wouldn't sleep with him."

"Punishment," said Troah, "would have been to put you in a whorehouse. He left you here as an act of mercy."

"Mercy?"

"He left you in a safe place because of what you are, and because of what he is." She came a little closer. "None of us can get away from what we were born to be."

She touched her own throat with the fingers of her Hand, and I tasted her, curry under my tongue. The phantom sensation of her fingers on my neck, in my hair, was vivid, and reassuringly warm, like being next to a fire on a cold, cold night. My mouth opened, and I knew what would come out—my voice with her words—agreeing to lie down, here in the street, in the gutter, anywhere, wet or dry.

Troah let her Hand drop. Her heat and comfort left me, replaced by fog and chill and damp air.

"Rasha must have been very disappointed when you turned him down," she said.

I didn't answer. Couldn't.

She moved closer. "Did it feel the same as Rasha, just now?"

I shook my head.

"Did you like it better?"

"No," I whispered, without conviction.

Troah smoothed her hair, lingering in her own damp curls. "I see," she said, and started down the dark street again.

I trailed after her, through what must have been a virtual fog of pheromones. I knew where this was going. Sex would be a victory for her, but not necessarily a loss for me. I knew how she would taste—metal, then salt, then silky flesh. Did it matter what she won, when I knew how she would make me feel? Rasha had forced me to take my first plunge of this weird, mingling pleasure, but this time it could be my choice. I could walk away, I told myself. I'd done it before.

"Troah?" I stumbled after her, past the ancient buildings where her ancestors had made love to mine, hundreds and hundreds of years ago. She stopped. Behind her, the Beryl's weather shield showed over the top of the black stone wall, full and red as a rising moon.

"Wait," I said. "Wait."

*   *   *

Up the ladder in her room, we stripped off each other's clothes. Yellow light from the ceiling made her naked body lustrous, like polished metal. Her weight was sudden, sultry, pressing me down on the thin pallet. The iron ring of the trapdoor dug into my spine as her teeth and tongue came across my throat. Her hips pressed between my thighs, and the rough brush of her pubic hair took the strength out of me. I clung underneath her, drenched in heat, from belly to knees.

Her mouth covered me, her tongue carrying the taste of her will. She was heavy, spicy warm, soft. I squirmed under her, wanting to seduce her, to suck her cold nipples, but she moved lower, nuzzling my belly. She rubbed her teeth over my hip, and her fingers crept between my legs, through tight curls into hot folds of flesh. She explored me, tracing back and forth. She stopped, and I felt her thumb press inside.

Her cheek was a cool place against my thigh. Her tongue slicked a path along the tendon there, until the pressure of her thumb and the texture of her mouth came together, moving in close, tense rhythms. I grabbed the edges of the pallet in my fists, holding her with my legs, breathing harder, waiting for the other hand, the left one, the one with the Mark. It moved slowly, charring a trail that started at my breasts. When she pushed those fingers into me, we would scorch each other, so hot, the humid air would catch. She was too slow, too slow. I couldn't feel her tongue and thumb under the slow immolation of her Hand, moving across my leg, searing flesh, stinging—like tape torn across my skin.

The needles.

I yelled and she jerked, and I shoved away from her, grabbing at my leg. The tape was still there, the needle packs underneath. All she'd managed was to smother me with so much need and desire that I could have just given them to her, right there, if she would just go on.

I crawled backwards and she pushed herself up on one elbow, catlike. She opened her lips over teeth—a demand, not a seduction.

"Give them to me."

I was afraid she would touch me. She would put all her ire and revenge into the palm of that Hand and lay it on my crotch. I got up, quivering from the half-sex. My clothes were tangled with hers in a soggy pile, and I didn't have the nerve to grope around for them. I had to get out. Naked in the hallway? I thought of the Meeds. And Rasse.

She rose up on her knees, the painted furies on their human hide of shirts flanking her, ready to burst from the dirty cloth and pull me down.

I backed up to the door and opened it.

"Don't leave." She said it so gently that my throat began to hurt. She turned her Hand so I could see the Mark on her palm, then ran her fingers across the tip of her tongue.

I stumbled into the hallway, her eyes on my back, two points of dull heat.

The empty corridor was dense with consequences. Troah would come after me. She'd find me alone in Frei's dirty bed and finish what she'd started. The image of her, descending on me, nightmare or succubus, was terrifying and enticing at the same time.

I stopped by Hallie's door, midway to Frei's room, and knocked.

"Hallie?"

I heard her grunt.

"Hallie!"

"Whuh?"

I pushed the door open. She sat up in the dim shaft of light, scrubbing her eyes with the heels of her hands.

"S'matter?" she asked, all gravely.

I crouched by her thin pallet, struggling for the shortest

explanation. Her face was patterned with wrinkles from the pillow. She was shirtless, as usual, and I didn't think she was wearing pants either.

"Where're your clothes?" she asked. "Oh. I know. You were out. But you shouldn't walk around like that." She reached over and pushed the door shut. The room went dark and close.

I listened to her fumbling with something near the wall. Her bed smelled of light sweat, a little musky when she moved between the sheets. I wound my fingers together. There was a lot left over from what Troah had started with me. The adrenaline rush was ebbing, leaving the taste of unfinished sex.

Hallie snapped on a small light. Our shadows loomed across dozens of holo posters, plastered in peeling layers on her walls. *Sticks and Stones*, shouted one, where Hallie and a much bigger girl brandished their sogas, arms locked together. Another showed Naritte inside the projection of her scaly green dragon. When I turned my head, she swung, clean and graceful, making the dragon lunge, teeth bared, wings outspread.

Hallie rubbed her eyes. "You went to see Cheska?"

I nodded.

"How did it go?"

"She wanted my needles," I whispered. "And then Troah tried to take them."

Hallie frowned. "Troah? I'll bet she did. What happened?"

"She tried to . . ." Talking about it made my heart speed up. The line between fear and desire was too blurred for me to decide which it was. "Her Hand, you know. She tried to . . ."

"Oh." Hallie scratched her head. "That's what happened to your clothes." She pulled a blanket off her bed and pushed it at me.

I balled it in my lap, winding my fists into the corners. "I'm afraid to go to my room. I think she's waiting."

Hallie glanced at the closed door. "So. Stay here."

"Thanks."

She untangled the sheet from her knees and ankles, but she didn't move over. "Did you walk out on her? Just like that?"

"It wasn't that easy," I said, and shivered.

She didn't say anything for a while, and then she looked over at the wall. "What if I want a needle? Would you walk out on me?"

I sat, clumsily, cross-legged, and scratched at the tape, picking at the filthy gray edge. A night of safe haven was all I wanted. Let Troah cure herself of Failure. Hallie was dependable, and my own choice. If I slept with her, it would be for the right reasons.

"What're you doing?" whispered Hallie.

"I'm giving them to you," I said. "Troah doesn't affect you. They're probably safer with you anyway." The tape curled under my nails, soggy, barely sticky anymore.

Hallie took a breath. "Don't."

I kept peeling. "Why not? If Troah comes near you, you can knock her down. All I do is think about how she'll taste."

Hallie reached over and took my hands. "That goes away after a while." She squeezed my fingers. "When she first came here, I felt the same way. Give yourself some time. A couple of months. You can learn to block her out."

"I don't think I have a couple of months. I made her mad. Tomorrow she could—the fights, you know, she might—"

Hallie pulled me onto the thin pallet and put her arms around me, surprisingly tight. "She won't touch you."

I leaned against her, enveloped in her dry warmth. She was wrong, I thought. And if anyone was vulnerable, now

197

it was Hallie. All Troah had to do was walk down the hall to Frei's room and see how empty it was. She would feel me behind this door, in this bed, and tomorrow, Hallie's odds would plummet.

"She can hurt you," I said.

She shook her head against my hair. "Later, maybe, but not tomorrow. If I lose, the big bets won't pay. If the bets don't pay, no one gets out of here. We're all stuck, waiting for Rasha, or the Emir, or whoever happens to win." She put her hand over my cheek. "Don't worry about me. Yet."

Nervous flutters filled my stomach—different from Troah's unwelcome intrusions. I put my arms around her neck and kissed her. Her mouth was a warm, honest pressure.

She took a deep breath, glanced at her poster-covered walls again, and back at me. "Can we go," she whispered, "somewhere else? Where Naritte won't . . . watch?"

"You mean Frei's room? What if Troah's there?"

"It's your room now," said Hallie.

Someone had cleaned the bathroom while I was gone. The sour smell of mildew was at least masked by soap and scouring powder. Clean towels were folded on the back of the toilet. Hallie sat on the edge of the tub, naked, waiting for hot water to dribble down from the showerhead.

I sat in the lid of the john, staring at the white scars that striped her belly, her sides. I looked for any mark from Arbitt's wild stabbing, but if it was there, it was lost in the tangle of weals and knots.

The plumbing groaned. Hallie leaned over the tub to thump the wall, and ducked as steaming, rusty water gushed out of the shower. There was hardly room for two people in the small room, and her knees bumped mine.

She turned around and saw me looking at the marks on her body.

She blushed—a rush of color under brown skin. My heart speeded up. Her armor had a crack in it, and that made me more afraid for her. Or more attracted.

"Is there soap?" I asked.

Hallie angled her head at the near corner of the tub. A broken gray bar lay on a torn piece of towel.

"Would you wash my back?" I said.

Hallie nodded slowly, her face guarded again, except for her eyes, and they glittered with relief.

I stepped past her, over the side of the tub, into the stream of the shower. She got in behind me.

The water was almost scalding. I let it wash over my face and neck while she lathered the rag with soap. She pushed my hair away and moved the rag between my shoulderblades, side to side, too light to scrub.

"You've never been cut," she whispered, breathy in my ear.

Her body pressed against me, hot as the water. She touched my face with callused fingers and thumb. Her other hand came up to cover my hair, my ear. She turned me around, and we were gripping each other, my face against her damp breast. She had to bend to kiss my neck, and I turned to find her mouth. Her tongue was rough and cool and reserved. Her fingers slipped along my belly, underneath my breasts and stopped. I put my hand over her knuckles, wanting her to go on, and she wrapped her arms around me, silent, soaked. Her knees seemed to give way. She slid down until she was sitting on the side of the tub, and pulled me into her lap, so my arms were around her neck, my legs were straddling hers. Her left hand came down my back, sliding through hot creases until she found my vagina from behind. Her right hand explored in front, careful and slow, searching, until her fingers touched each other.

She leaned forward and her small breasts pressed against

199

me. I gripped her shoulders, twisting a little sideways as she opened her legs, and mine. Her fingers traced slow, wet designs on my clitoris, hot from the water, blunt with sleep. I could feel every whorl in her skin, distinct ridges, her short nails and wet knuckles, back and forth. Every time our nipples brushed, my heart would slam. I pressed my mouth on hers. She moved her fingers faster, in unbearable combinations, in, out, and around. She pulled me a little wider and the surge of sex came out in animal sounds, my mouth to hers, moans and words she swallowed and tongued and bit off.

She held my hips while I panted against her neck. Her thighs were warm, slick pillars, and I throbbed against them until she turned the shower off, picked me up and carried me to the bed.

Our wet skins smacked together, dripping, and wadding the sheets. When she moved, it was tendon and muscle and scars. Her belly was a map of every round she'd fought, and below that, whatever Naritte had left for a successor like me. Damp and hot and closed as a fist.

I played with her until she spread herself a little wider, and then showed her what Martine had showed me. Two fingers inside and the knuckle of my thumb against her clit. I moved inside her and she sucked in her breath. She rocked, slow, then faster. I matched her rhythm, the tempo of her need, twitching and twiddling. She grabbed my head, hair, arms, clamped her fists around my arm, and gasped. She dragged me up across her chest and wrapped me tight, breathing hard, then slower, her mouth on my neck.

"Naritte," she mumbled.

I lay on her chest, listening to her heart pound.

"Sorry," she said after a while. She rubbed my back, and that was all I needed to sleep.

She was there when I woke up.

As far as I could tell neither of us had moved. I was still

lying across her, fitting exactly against her ribs, her breasts. The rhythm of our breathing was the same. She smelled warm, comforting, like someone I'd known for a long time. Or someone I'd waited for, for a long time.

She ran her fingers over my ear. "We have to get up," she said, sounding wide awake. "It's noon."

"How do you know?"

She pushed herself up against the battered headboard, her short hair stiff as a bristle. She kissed me on the mouth and swung her legs over the side of the bed. "It's a fight day," she said. "I always know what time it is on fight days."

My stomach made a nervous lurch. "Oh," I said.

"Rasse's probably off his dose by now." She ruffed my hair, stood up and stretched. "You can bring him something from the kitchen and we'll 'hance him for the afternoon. I'll clean his cell, and then I'll show you how to put Frei's triage kit together." She scratched absently at her scars. "The FC Officer'll be here in about an hour. You'll have to be upstairs for that."

Not ready, I thought, and sat up, wrapping my knees in the warm sheets. Not ready for the things I'd seen over Olney's shoulder, which I'd always been convinced were fake. Fake blood, and phony kills. Not ready. "What's an FC Officer?"

"Fairness in Competition." Hallie grinned. "He's a government goon who's supposed to make sure we're all healthy enough not to Fail in the middle of a fight. But . . ." She gave a doubtful shrug.

"But what?"

"It's a volunteer position. The more fighters he thinks are in questionable health, the more money he makes." She rubbed her thumb over her fingers—an old sign for cash money. "Understand? He comes to pick up his bribe. That's how he makes his living. Your job is to make sure whatever he decides to tell Otis is actually true."

"He's going to lie?" I said. "And I'm supposed to argue with him?"

She nodded. "You'll have to. There were times I thought Frei was going to sock him, but in the end, Otis would just pay up so we could field a full team."

I looked up at her. "How many is a full team?"

She smiled, half disbelieving. "Don't you know?"

I shook my head.

Her smile disappeared. "You're scared."

"Yeah," I said.

"You don't have to worry. You don't have to fight." She dropped onto the bed next to me. "All you have to do is read a scanner and give shots. As long as you have a couple dozen hypos of the Virus, and enough Thanas for emergencies, you've got all anyone could ask for."

"What if someone dies?" I said.

She shrugged. "Then Althea can't beat the hell out of them for losing their round."

"What if it's my fault?"

"I imagine she'd beat the hell out of you too," said Hallie lightly. "My advice is not to do anything wrong."

I wound my fingers together between my knees. "Hallie," I said. "What if she finds out I've never worked in a trauma clinic on Naya?"

She frowned. "You never worked in a . . . ? But Rasha said you'd . . ." She scratched her nose. "But you know how to read a scanner. You know how to give injections."

"I worked for a veterinarian."

"Oh." She got off the bed, paced around the bedroom and came back to stand in front of me. "You were fine with me when Arbitt—" She slashed the air vaguely. "You were fine."

"Just one person," I said, "not dozens."

She ran her hands over her pyrite brush. "I think you can manage. Just don't tell Althea."

"I think she'll figure it out."

Hallie shook her head. "If you screw up, she'll think you're scared shitless, and she'll be right. She saw you work on me. She's pretty sure you know what you're doing." She sat down again, pensive. "I'll help you as much as I can before I go in. High Set rounds are the last fights of the day."

"Thanks," I said.

"Just don't panic and run off screaming," said Hallie.

I tried to smile. "Does that happen?"

"You bet," said Hallie. "It's a fucking circus up there. That's why people come to see it."

Hallie'd cleaned the clinic. Everything, from the white cabinets, to the sink, to the steel surgical table, gleamed, spotless, not even a drop of blood left from Ransom the day before.

Hallie sat on the edge of the desk, watching me fill hypoderms, fitting them between their plastic spacers in Frei's leather satchel—the triage kit.

The triage kit was divided into three sections, opening like a book, leaving a central compartment standing vertically. The central compartment was stuffed with various bits of garbage—old needles, broken suture kits. I was too rushed and anxious to spend time emptying it. What I was going to need were in the two outer sections anyway. One opened onto packs of pressure bandages and anesthetic slap-needles. The other had a rack of slim plastic drawers. Each drawer had compartments for ten needles. The bottom was already stocked with Thanas.

Hallie pointed at the Thanas. "Don't use that without Althea's permission. Be sure she *tells* you to do it. When Tony first got here, Frei had him kill a Meed who was Failing—really messy. Loud. Terrible. But Althea wanted this Meed to suffer for being stupid enough to lose his round. I thought she was going to yank Tony's head right off."

I closed the drawer. "Do the Meeds know what Frei was trying to do?" I asked.

"Most of them have some idea," said Hallie. "Troah made it a fairy tale for them, though, because she was only saving something like one in ten or twenty. Surviving Failure was a sort of metaphor, like life after death."

"Does Althea know?"

"Althea knows Frei tried to save Tony and couldn't," said Hallie. "If he had, Leiban would have been next in line."

"Does Leiban know?"

Hallie let out a short cough of a laugh. "If he knew Althea had a way to free him, Leiban would die anyway, just so he could get away from her." She leaned forward, elbows on her knees. "Do you ever think about what you'd do if you were free?"

"Not really," I said.

"I know what I'm going to do," said Hallie. "I'm going to get a job. I don't care what it is. I'll sweep streets, as long as I can get paid for it."

"After you Fail?" I said.

"Hell no," said Hallie. "Why wait? After we're out of here, why should we stay in collar? If one of us is free, why shouldn't we all be free?"

I'd had this conversation before, what seemed like years ago, with Martine. I tugged at my own collar. "What did you do before . . . ?"

"I was in school." She smiled. "I was studying XenoBotany."

"Would you go back?"

"I might," said Hallie. "What do you want to do?"

I filled another needle, dropped it into its slot, and closed the drawer. "What do you think Troah would do if she was free?"

Hallie laughed. "Isn't it obvious? She'll set herself up in the biggest house she can find, get herself a couple of Favored Ones, and live like a fucking queen for the rest of her life." Her grin froze for a second. "You're not thinking of staying with her. Are you?"

It was hard to imagine Troah on her own, even harder to imagine her set up in a fine house with all the comforts she'd been denied. Out of the ring, she was out of her element. No matter how the war went, whether her family won or lost, when it was over, her prophecies would be spent. It was strangely easy to imagine her as directionless.

Hallie slid off the desk and came closer. "You don't owe her anything," she said, with too much intensity. "All Troah's going to teach you is how to be a better slave. Of all people, you should be the one practicing to be a free woman." She squeezed my arm. "It's not your job to belong to her, or your fate. Not now."

To hear her say that, to listen and feel the truth of it, was like letting go of a huge burden. She put her arms around me. "I can take care of you," she whispered.

"I know," I said.

The kitchen was even hotter than the corridor, thicker in the air, heavy with burnt curry and the copper taste of boiled water. Piles of dirty dishes and empty serving platters covered the countertop, heaped in the sinks. A holoree blared from one corner, its projection scattered with static.

"Still no word from the battleship, Proviso, missing since yesterday in the Faraque. Statements from the Emir and the Diplomatic Corps continue to assert that the ship was required to keep radio silence, and urge citizens to remain calm."

Troah glanced up from one of the sinks, up to her elbows in soap and steaming water. Perspiration ran down the side of her face, plastering hair against her cheek. "There you are."

205

Maybe she knew I'd slept with Hallie, maybe she didn't. Not caring what she thought made me almost lightheaded.

"I'm supposed to feed Rasse."

Troah dried her hands on her pants and turned off the 'ree. "He gets two full plates," she said. "I'll go down there with you." She made a motion at the mess on the counter—either generosity or indifference. "Eat something."

I found a clean spoon and enough cold kimarra in the bottom of one huge steel pot to feed half a dozen people. I sat on the counter, shoveling into the sweating pot. The kimarra was gritty and bland and, at the bottom, watery. It didn't matter. I was starving.

"Did Hallie give you the schedule for the day?" Troah was watching me from one of the cutting tables now, bent over a piece of paper.

I nodded, my mouth full.

"There may be some changes," said Troah. She made a mark on the paper with a bright green stylus. "I think we'll be starting earlier than usual."

She was setting up the odds. Hallie's too?

I swallowed. "Earlier? Why?"

She shrugged and made a few more marks. "Just a feeling."

"Do you set everyone's odds?" I asked, trying to sound casual.

"Even Leiban's." Another green mark.

"How's he going to do?"

"Leiban always wins," said Troah. "He can't avoid it." She straightened, and I could see the forest of numbers and names covering the paper.

"Are you ever wrong?" I asked.

"Sometimes." She looked up at me. "Would you like to hear your odds, Jatahn?"

She let the question ooze out. Her tone made my stomach cold and the taste of kimarra sour in my mouth. No forgiveness for walking out on her last night. But then, I hadn't expected any.

Her eyes flickered past me and the expression on her face changed. I turned to see Otis in the doorway, fanning himself. His silk jacket was rumpled, as though it was sticking to his clothes, which were in turn sticking to his skin. Even his jewelry seemed filmed over with sweat.

"Good afternoon, D'sha," said Troah.

"Hot as hell down here," he said.

"Yes, D'sha," agreed Troah.

"Are you finished?" he asked.

"Yes, D'sha."

"Show me."

Troah capped the stylus and rolled the paper up in a lazy motion. She came over to the counter, leaned past me and held the odds sheet out like bait.

Otis came across the room to the other side of the counter, kicking worn straw floor mats out of his way. He turned the paper around so he could read it, which gave me a clear view of what Troah had written down.

The Meeds were divided into different teams: Double-on-Triple, Single-on-Pair, Single-on-Single. None of their odds seemed extreme. A realistic number might win, or lose, or tie. Below that, a list of numbers and names—High Set—Althea's *Assassins*, and the Silver's *Elite*. I found Hallie's odds. Four to two, in her favor, against someone called Rampage. No vengeful retribution from Troah—not in the numbers anyway.

"The Meeds get fifty-fifty." Otis nodded. "That's reasonable."

"I'm glad you think so, D'sha."

"The Assassins have a clean sweep—and Rasse's odds are thirty to one?" Otis frowned. "Who's he fighting?"

"Silver's Butcherboy," said Troah.

"Thirty to one?" Otis rubbed his thumb over the figures.

"That makes Butch look like an amateur. What were his odds last time he was here?"

"Three to one," said Troah.

"He's been injured recently?"

"No, D'sha."

Otis studied the sheet in silence. In the neat, handwritten rows of numbers and names, Troah had doomed Rasse, the same way she'd doomed Naritte. The rationale was easy. Cheska would bet against Rasse. The payoff on the Silver's Butcherboy would cover offworld passage for every slave in the ring, and more.

"The only way these odds make sense is to presume that Rasse will lose," said Otis.

"Yes, D'sha," said Troah.

"Rasse is the best money-maker this ring has ever had," said Otis, and now he was being careful, picking his words. "The boy's nowhere near Failure."

"I'll certainly change the odds, D'sha," said Troah. "If that's what you want me to do."

Otis hesitated. "The payoff against Rasse would be a small fortune. If he loses. And if he loses, he'd be hard to replace."

"The Faraqui breed a hundred Rasses every year," said Troah. "All you have to do is ask Rasha for a replacement. I'm sure, once the war is over, he'll be glad to give you whatever you want."

"Only if the Faraqui win," said Otis. He dabbed sweat from under his lip. "Is that your prediction for the war, my girl?"

"Call it what you like, D'sha."

Otis put the sheet of paper on the counter and spread it flat, still weighing the advantages of Rasse's defeat. "Yes," he said finally, "I think this will do." He walked out of the kitchen, wiping at his forehead with a silk sleeve.

When he was gone, Troah turned to me. "You understand, Jatahn?"

"Yes," I said.

"Good."

Troah went over to the sink and rinsed two plates. She tossed a hunk of bread on each, and carved out two huge portions of cold kimarra. She pushed the plates at me and wiped her neck.

"Let's get out of here."

As we came out into the hallway, an avalanche of noise thundered down from the ring. Upstairs, chain rattled against metal and someone yelled a warning. A tremendous, deafening bang echoed in the corridor.

"They're lowering the dropgates," said Troah. She started up the stairs. "Come on. It's cooler up there."

It wasn't. Across the ring, outside the main gate, rain fell in sheets over the plaza. Inside, heat shimmered off the arena's high black walls. The air was as stiflingly thick as it had been in the kitchen. Cooking in that kind of swelter was bad enough. I couldn't imagine fighting in it.

Most of the Meeds were in the center of the ring, slogging through their calisthenics, trampling the hot sand. Althea marched around them, barking out the count, keeping time by slapping the handle of her whip against her palm. Leiban leaped and twisted in front, grimly setting the pace.

Three more Meeds, two girls and a boy, conferred with each other by one of the black stone columns. Behind them, the empty space between the last half-dozen pillars was filled with sections of barred fence—dropgates—which caged the breezeway off from the pit. One of the girls jabbed at a panel in the back of the column, and the entire breezeway began to shake. Chains rumbled under stone. Another iron gate shrieked down from a recess in the vaulted ceiling, picking up speed to slam into place between the next two columns.

The boy saw Troah and he and the two girls waded toward us through shallow black puddles.

"D'sha," said the boy to Troah, "when are you giving odds on the fights?"

"When I usually give odds," said Troah. "After the other team gets here."

"But we need to know now," said one of the girls. She nodded in Althea's direction. "She ignores us during practice. She stuck us with this job." She rolled her eyes upwards to indicate the barriers still waiting to drop from the breezeway's pitchy ceiling. "We're all supposed to fight in a Pair-on-Triple today." Her voice faltered and she clamped her teeth over her lower lip.

"Can't you give us some idea?" asked the other girl.

"We just want to know what'll happen," said the boy.

Troah reached for the boy's hand, turned it over to examine his knuckles, then his palm. "You'll be fine," she said without any particular sympathy.

The muscles along his jaw quivered. "We'll be free afterwards," he whispered. "Like Ransom."

Troah looked at him as though he'd lost his mind. "Don't be ridiculous."

"But," said the first girl, "that's what happened to him. Isn't he free?" She turned to me. "Isn't it true, D'Jatahn?"

D'Jatahn? It caught me up short. I didn't dare meet Troah's eyes. I was supposed to say, *Don't be ridiculous*.

"There isn't enough of the—" I started, but Troah broke in.

"Whatever it says on the odds sheet," said Troah, "that's what you'll do. Is that very clear?" She glared at them, but her anger pricked me, like shards of thin glass. "If one of you goes down, you all go down." She tapped my arm and stalked off.

When we were out of earshot, she glanced back at me. "Did I tell you your odds, Frenna?"

I adjusted my grip on Rasse's plates. "I'm not fighting," I said.

"You are, Jatahn," said Troah. "You're fighting right now. But you don't know how to win."

She started down the stairs and I followed, into the suffocating dungeon below.

Rasse's door was wide open.

Troah stopped when she saw that. "Hallie?"

Hallie leaned out of the cell, holding a mop and a metal bucket. "I hope you brought him something to eat."

Troah waved me ahead. I peered inside. Rasse, naked as ever, squatted at the far end of the small space. Two long chains ran up from manacles on his wrists to a pair of steel eyelets sunk into the wall. Another chain from his collar fastened him to the floor.

Rasse sniffed the air and shot out his tongue. "Kimmah," he said.

"Yes, lovely kimarra." Hallie put the bucket down and took both plates. She set them on the wet cell floor where Rasse could reach them. The boy sat cross-legged and began stuffing the food into his mouth by the handful.

Troah stood in the doorway, just out of reach. "Why's it so wet in there?"

"Rain must be worse than usual," said Hallie. "Leiban said Althea's rugs are soaked, and the breezeway's turning into a moat." She squinted at the ceiling where rivulets trickled over stone. "This whole place is going to sink into the ground one day."

"Is that a prediction?" said Troah.

Hallie wiped her hands on her pants and cocked her head at Troah. "Figured out my odds yet, Hand?"

Troah gave her a suspicious look. "Since when do you care?"

"Just feeling lucky." Hallie smiled at me. "If you dose Rasse while he's eating, he doesn't mind so much."

"Thanks," I said.

Hallie picked her bucket up and left, whistling.

Troah took the bag of Enhancers off its hook and gave it to me with the oily wad of plastic gloves. "A quarter dose," she said. "It has to wear off by the time he gets into the ring."

I angled gingerly into the sticky gloves and poured out a small handful of Enhancers . . . what I thought might be a quarter of what I'd grabbed in my panic yesterday. Troah nodded at the gooey clump of yellow capsules, and I edged within an arm's length of Rasse's doughy white shoulders.

His skin shuddered like a horse bitten by flies as the oil dripped onto him, but he didn't stop eating. He licked the first plate clean and started on the second. I brushed at the oil until it was more or less evenly spread. I backed out of the cell and realized I'd been holding my breath.

"You're a good boy, Rasse," said Troah.

"Good boy," I echoed, stripping off the gloves. Rasse chewed, blank-faced, smeared from chin to ears with ki-marra and bread crumbs.

Troah moved into the cell until she was close enough to touch him. She crouched down and ran a finger over his shaved scalp.

The boy shivered but didn't budge.

"Rasse, love," said Troah, "listen carefully."

"Yah, D'zah."

"You'll lose tonight, Rasse."

"Looz?"

"Don't tell anyone," she said. "And don't forget."

"Yah, D'zah."

"You're a good boy, Rasse." She kissed his forehead, and came out of the cell.

"He'll be killed," I whispered.

"If you say another word," said Troah, "so will you."

Bare feet slapped damp concrete and Leiban came around the curve of the hallway carrying a scanner. Sweat ran off his sides, his neck, his legs. He wiped his face when he saw us, but more sweat dribbled from his forehead. He was like a rag being squeezed dry. A free man in his condition would have been on the verge of heat stroke, but Leiban was on the near edge of Failure.

He wiped his face again and handed me the scanner. "Althea wants you upstairs. The FC Officer's here." He swung around and ran back down the hallway.

"Go ahead, Frenna," said Troah. "I'm right behind you."

By now, all the barriers had been lowered around the ring, changing the breezeway from an open passage to a caged-in corridor, barred off entirely from the pit. In the office, the Meeds were lined up along the black wall, drenched and sallow, panting from the heat. Hallie and Leiban were at the far end of the line and Hallie winked at me. I smiled back until I saw Leiban staring.

Someone bumped me from behind, and I turned to see the FC Officer.

He was a short man in a dressy, heavy uniform, dabbing at his chin with a dark blue handkerchief. His long, thin hair hung in damp strands over bruised purple bite marks on the side of his neck.

Otis Tarda sat by the desk, fanned by a slave girl I hadn't seen before—a steely blond, buxom to the point of surgical enhancement, either deeply tanned or golden-skinned. Her brands were hidden under her white shirt, but I suspected she was another gift from Rasha.

The FC Officer eyed me. "New pass?"

"New medic," said Otis. "I'm sure I mentioned that Frei left?"

"I always thought of him as a career man," said the FC Officer. "He was a fixture. Hard to believe he's gone."

Otis patted the girl's behind. "He was too sensitive for this kind of work."

"Too sensitive?" The Fairness in Competition Officer didn't look satisfied with the explanation, but I suspected he was too hot to care. He held his handkerchief against his flushed forehead and waved me over.

"Let's get started," he said.

I switched the scanner on, and pointed it at the first girl, a redhead with ghostly pale skin. On the screen, her life signs were high on the graph, a steady red pulse next to the green Viral indicator.

"Pass," said the FC Officer. "Next?"

He hadn't even looked at the readout. I followed him to the next fighter. This was the boy who'd just gotten his dubious odds from Troah. According to the scanner, he was in his sixteenth or seventeenth year. His life signs were low, as though he'd been injured recently and hadn't healed well. A serious wound might push him into early Failure.

I turned the scanner to show the FC Officer, but he'd already moved on to the next Meed. He wiped his neck impatiently. "Your medic's a slow one," he said to Otis.

"Don't you want a reading, D'sha?" I asked.

The FC Officer's expression tightened. Sweat squeezed out from under his lower lip. "Just do your job, girl, and I'll ask the questions."

I started to turn away from the boy and heard him whisper something. I looked back to see his mouth pulled into a straight line that didn't match the uncertainty in the rest of his face.

"D'Jatahn . . ." He said it so softly, he was only mouthing the word.

I frowned, not sure I'd understood him.

"D'Jatahn," hissed the red-haired girl I'd just scanned.

"Hurry it up, medic," said Althea.

"Next?" said the FC Officer.

Next was the girl with the coal-blue skin, her hair in sweaty twists. Her readings were fine, and I angled the scanner so she could see. She nodded ever so slightly, and when she let her breath out, it was the same word. "D'Jatahn."

The prickle at the back of my neck was Troah, watching from somewhere, keeping track of loyalties—mine included.

When we got to Hallie, the FC Officer leaned over to squint at the readout for the first time.

"How many years are you, Hallie-girl?"

"Eighteen, D'sha."

The FC Officer turned to Althea. "She's looking kind of low these days. How long before you retire her?"

In fact, Hallie's levels were better than a lot of the Meeds'. I glanced up from the screen into Althea's demanding green eyes, and shrugged.

"She's fine," snapped Althea. "Pass her."

The FC Officer gave her a damp, smarmy smile. "Where're the rest of your Assassins?"

"Rasse's downstairs in his cell," said Althea.

The FC Officer dabbed at the hickeys on his neck. "Hot down there, I suppose."

"Like a fucking swamp," said Althea. "And you might remember from last time, the heat puts Rasse in a hell of a mood."

"I remember." The FC Officer beckoned to Leiban. "Come out here, Rexidi."

Leiban shook his head. Water and perspiration covered his body, glittering like jewels.

"He's fine." Althea crossed her arms over her green coverall, gripping her own elbows. "Pass him."

"He hasn't been scanned," said the FC Officer.

"Pass him anyway." Althea gave Otis a terse, angry look.

"I can't let him fight unless he's passed a health check," said the FC Officer. "Rules are rules."

Otis shifted in his chair, studying Leiban. He turned back to the FC Officer and pushed the steel-blond slave girl at him. "Pass him," said Otis, "with my compliments."

The FC Officer twisted a finger in the girl's hair. She smiled at him, blank and pliant, purebred to the marrow.

"A clean bill of health, Mister Tarda," he said to Otis. "Good luck tonight." He leered at Althea and led the girl down the caged breezeway, toward the front gate.

When he was gone, Otis turned in his chair. "Your boy's Failing, Althea."

"He'll fight," said Althea. "He'll win."

"I'm sure he will," said Otis.

ELEVEN

Troah stepped out of the darkest place in the breezeway, appearing from absolutely nowhere. She ducked her head at Otis, hands clasped at her waist, a cynical imitation of Faraqui-bred manners. "D'Tarda," she said. "The Silver team's here."

"Already?" Althea frowned across the ring at the main gate, opened a panel in the closest column and palmed the lock. Across the ring, the gate squealed on its hinges. "Leiban—Hallie—" She jerked a thumb at the Meeds. "Get them out of here."

"Let's go!" Hallie barked. "Downstairs! Weapons! Final practice! Get moving!"

I started to follow, but Troah caught my arm. "Stay," she whispered, "and watch."

Out in the ring, the Silver team streamed into the pit, strung ankle to ankle with a length of cord, all dressed in gray clothes with a cheap silver sheening.

"Why are they coffled?" Althea muttered to herself. "Where're their flags and horns and the damn marching band they usually bring along?"

Two free men in silvery rain jackets brought up the rear of the Silver coffle. They shut the main gate and hurried across the sand, toward the office. One was tall, rangy, probably in his forties, with a deep tan over weathered skin. The other was in his early twenties. He moved with straight-backed assurance, and carried a medical bag.

Althea met them at the entrance to the caged breezeway. "Strix Aluka and Doctor Nacke." She grabbed the tall man's hand, and shook it with exaggerated friendliness. "Strix, you look like hell."

Strix gave her a tired salute. The doctor held out his hand, but Althea slapped it away, still grinning. "Keep your whorehouse diseases to yourself, Doc." She turned to Otis. "You remember these two lying, cheating sons of bitches?"

"Gentlemen." Otis nodded politely. "Better luck this time."

"Yeah, yeah." Strix, the trainer, I assumed, glanced around the office. "So. Frei got out before the shooting started."

"Frei ditched us," said Althea, "but he did it for personal reasons."

"Whatever," said Nacke. "He was smart enough to get his ticket before everybody and their uncle got in line." He waved in the direction of the ground station. "I'm surprised you're still here, Otis. You've got the money to cash in and take off. Why don't you?"

Otis folded his hands in his lap. "I don't jump when I hear an irresponsible rumor."

"Rumors?" Strix gave him an incredulous look. "Haven't you seen the news on the Independents lately? People are running out of the Frontier like it was a house on fire."

"Now the government's talking about sending in a fleet

of warships to occupy the Faraque," said Nacke. "Except they're not really saying that." He tapped the side of his head. "You have to know how to listen."

"Some people will believe anything they think they hear," said Otis.

"If you're so worried, why the hell'd you bother to show up?" asked Althea.

Nacke gave an uncomfortable shrug.

"We're not staying long," said Strix. "Our captain said he'd leave us if we weren't on board by midnight."

"Midnight?" Althea's head jerked. "That means we'll have to start early. People won't come early. They come after dinner."

Strix wiped his forehead. "Looked to me like all your fans were doing their best to get out of town."

"Because of some stupid rumors on the news?" said Althea. "If we were being invaded, don't you think they'd be a little more straightforward about reporting it?"

"No," said Nacke.

"You're paranoid," said Althea.

"Think so?" said Nacke. "Have you seen a sports report lately?"

"I've been busy," said Althea.

Strix raised an eyebrow. "We haven't had any coverage for the last eight days. The Sports Bureau at the Emirate Report won't return our calls, and the last live fight they carried was two weeks ago. If you watch long enough, you'll see stats and scores, but that's all."

"If the Sports Bureau shows up tonight, I'll be awfully surprised," said Nacke.

"So there's no coverage?" Althea swung around to Otis. "You better call your friends at the Emirate Report and tell them we've got sponsors—hell, we've paid for the publicity."

"Of course we have," said Otis. "I'll do whatever I can."

"Don't waste your time," said Nacke. "Do yourselves a favor and get out of town."

"And get paranoid," said Strix.

"You're overreacting, gentlemen," said Otis.

"You think you'll still be in business when the dust settles, Otis?" asked Nacke. "Maybe you can give your Faraqui pals a discount on season tickets."

"Are you making an accusation?" asked Otis mildly.

Nacke eyed him, and then Althea. "Not me, Mister Tarda."

Althea rubbed her head in agitation. "No coverage?"

"See you in the pit, Althea," said Strix. He and Nacke ducked through the opening in the dropgate, and made their way to the opposite side of the ring, where their team was waiting.

Althea glared at Otis. "You'd better make some calls, boss."

"I'll see what I can do," Otis said. He nodded toward the main gate. "In the meantime, perhaps you should go out and encourage the fans, so the bets don't fall too low."

"I don't have time to shake hands and give out door prizes."

"Then get someone else to do it," said Otis. He got up and brushed off his jacket. "Someone with more name recognition."

Althea watched him walk off, turned and beckoned sharply to Troah. "Get out there and open the betting windows." Her face twisted. "I'll get the door prizes."

Outside the ring, the rain had stopped for the moment. The early afternoon air had turned breathless and cottony, flattening distant black buildings against the lead-white sky.

Except for the pressing heat, the Beryl's wide plaza was starting to look like what I'd left behind on Naya—piles of luggage and huddled families collecting at the corners, nervous slaves in their white clothes moving cautiously, unaccompanied, toward the wide avenue that led to the ground station. There were a few fans as well, in green slickers and rain hats, but they seemed less than enthusiastic.

I stood in the open gateway, up to my ankles in water while Troah punched combinations into a wall panel behind me. Something buzzed briefly to my right, and a holographic portion of the oil-black outer wall fizzled away, revealing fifteen or twenty old-style digital betting screens, lined up at eye level.

Troah kicked at the water. "You'll catch your death," she said.

Concern or a different kind of threat—I couldn't decide.

She adjusted something else, and above me, a huge old speaker began to squeal.

Troah came over and peered up at it. "Volume high," she said to it, and the squeal turned deafening.

" . . . the Emirate Report urges citizens to remain calm, but what are the authorities on Traja planning to do in the face of an actual invasion? Demand answers, citizens!"

The noise echoed, deafening, across the plaza. Every single person within earshot stopped where they were and stared toward the gate.

Troah grinned at me. "Independent station," she shouted in my ear. "They're jamming everything." She made an adjustment in the wall panel and cut off the noise. For a moment, there was empty silence. Then music—loud marching music, and a shouting chorus of male voices.

> "Greens, Greens, Greens
> are winning every day!
> Greens, Greens, Greens,
> will blow your team away!
> Greens, Greens, Greens,
> are big and mean and green
> Assassins, Assassins, Hooray!"

All I could think of was Olney, glued to the 'ree, and a hundred long, alcohol-soaked weekends in the Extension Commons on Naya.

Troah shook her fist in time with the beat, teeth bared in a carnivorous grin.

Althea came over with a box of green hats with blinking holo projectors. *Assassins!* and *Go Greens!* floated as disembodied phrases in the air, filmy, laying over each other in shades of emerald and chartreuse. Periodically, the lettering would vanish, and a tiny holo of some important match would run in graphic double-time, fast and bloody. The hats themselves were the color of dead grass, with a long waterproof flap down the back to cover the neck. A broad brim sloped over the front, like the bow of an overturned boat.

Althea set the box down by the wall, in the only dry place. "What're you running the news for?" she demanded over the noise. "No one wants to hear the damn news."

"Sorry," said Troah, the soul of indifference.

Althea gave me a push toward the box. "Grab some hats and get out there, and don't get out of my sight." She pointed at the blaring speaker. "And don't forget to sing."

I grabbed an armful of the projector hats and stepped into the plaza. I couldn't believe anyone would interrupt their escape from the Faraqui to see the fights, but a crowd was starting to collect by the betting windows. Althea motioned me toward them. I stuck a hat on my head and started for the line.

"Greens, Greens, Greens . . ."

I couldn't bring myself to sing along. I made myself smile, but no one was watching. My blinking hats and I belonged in this slow-motion frenzy. I was part of the scenery, part of the event. I started at the end of the line, holding out hats like offerings. A woman took one absently, handing it to the man she was with.

"I figure we need two thousand more to cover passage for Keldy and Rey," she said to him in a low, nervous voice. "Rasse is rated at thirty to one, so it's got to be a setup. Bet against him and it's a sure thing. We'll all be on a ship by tomorrow morning."

"You're the big fan," said the man. "You should know." He ran a thumb along the edge of a plastic voucher card, and the two of them took a step closer to the betting screens.

Which explained why they would stand here when they could be running for their lives. I went to the next line.

> ". . . big and mean and green
> Assassins, Assassins, Hooray!"

"Hat, D'sha?" I asked a thin, terrified-looking man. He snatched one and ground it onto his head. I started to move on, but he grabbed me.

"They lock the gates during the fights, right?" he said. "No one can get in, right?" His eyes fixed on mine. "I mean, is the place secure?"

"Right." I pulled away.

The line moved and he took a step forward. "Are these odds legit?" he asked. "I mean, this isn't some crooked joint, right?"

It wasn't just money these people wanted, it was a fortress. What if the gates didn't lock? What if the bets didn't pay? They were probably scared enough to turn on each other given the slightest excuse—or on people like me.

"Right," I said.

In a few minutes, I'd given out all my hats, except for the one I was wearing. There was a little boy in a bright red slicker just in front of me, clinging to his mother. I dropped my hat on his head, turned around and headed for the main gate.

By now Althea herself had collected a crowd, waving and shaking hands, trying not to look tense. Troah was giving out hats from under the black arch, and I reached into the box for another load.

"Do you know why these people are here?" I whispered to Troah.

She nodded. "They think the bets are going to pay their way offworld."

"They think they can hide from the Faraqui in the ring," I hissed.

Troah laughed. "Don't they know Rasha walks in and out of this dump like he owns it?" She tossed a hat to a woman in a green slicker with a cartoon of Hallie's face drawn on the front—THE ROCK lettered underneath. "Go Greens!" Troah shouted, and bent for another armful.

A man in an emerald slicker shoved a gangly slave boy into the crush of fans around Althea.

"Hey, D'Orso!" he shouted. "What'll you pay for this one?"

The boy, whose stringy blond hair was tied into a pony-tail, wasn't watching where he was going. He saw us and stumbled. His man pushed him, and he almost fell into Althea.

"I think he's uncoordinated," said Althea. "Good height, though." She slapped the boy's nonexistent biceps. "Muscle him up," she said. "Bring him back when he can take a punch."

"He can," insisted the man. "See—?" He made a fist, but his boy dodged away. The boy slipped into the thick of the crowd, ducking under elbows, between legs, stepping on feet, heading in our direction. He broke out of the crush and dropped to his knees in front of Troah.

"Tell me if it's true," panted the boy. "Tell me if it's true."

"Be more specific," said Troah.

The boy glanced over his shoulder as his master struggled after him. "They say we can be *free*," he hissed.

"I can't imagine what you're talking about," said Troah.

The man thundered up behind him and yanked him to his feet. The boy shot Troah a helpless look as he was dragged off.

Troah studied my face. "You don't approve."

"No," I said.

"Then advise me, Jatahn."

"You could have said 'yes,' " I said. "That's all he wanted to hear. No one would have known what you were talking about."

Troah shrugged. "We can't save everyone."

Althea broke away from her admirers, flushed red down her neck. She came over and shook a slip of paper in Troah's face—bright green, with silvery lettering. "What the hell is this?"

"It's the odds sheet," said Troah.

"Otis didn't approve this," snapped Althea. "Rasse's odds can't be that—"

"Hey, D'Orso! How 'bout an autograph?" Another fan pushed in close and held up a corner of his green slicker. "Go Greens!" he shouted, almost in her ear.

"Sure," said Althea. "Sure." She let go of Troah, reluctantly, and shoved the crumpled odds sheets at me.

It was no different from the one Otis had agreed to. The Meeds' fifty-fifty odds took up a single line near the top. Below, in big, glittering letters, were the Assassins.

BERYL'S <u>ASSASSINS</u> VS. SILVER'S <u>ELITE</u>
Beryl's Rock vs. Silver's Rampage 4:1/Beryl
Beryl's Rasse vs. Silver's Butcherboy 30:1/Beryl
Beryl's Rexidi vs. Silver's Demon 4:1/Beryl

"What's the deal with Rasse's point spread?" asked the

fan as Althea scribbled over his slicker. "Hey, that Butcherboy's no amateur. He catches up in points for style, and last year, I remember, his odds against Rasse were more like three to one, right?"

Althea gave him an unfriendly grin. "Yeah," she said, and practically flung the corner of the slicker at him. "Enjoy the fights, all right?"

He had more to say, but she turned her back on him to glare at Troah, and then at me.

"Whatever you're up to," she hissed, "I'll find out about it. You understand me, Troah?" Troah didn't bat an eye. Althea turned to me. "*You* understand," as though I had some kind of influence.

I shrugged, not wanting to be an accessory to Troah's plans for the afternoon. Althea gave me a look of deep, frustrated fury and stalked off.

I started into the plaza again, swimming against the crowd with another armload. I pushed past two elderly women, each lugging a heavy suitcase. It was starting to rain again, and I stood still for a minute, almost too far from the gate, almost out of sight of Althea and Troah. In the distance, darker clouds were gathering in the afternoon sky. The first cool breeze I'd felt in days lifted my hair off my neck. I shifted my souvenir hats, wanting to throw them to the ground and run until all of this was well behind me.

Someone touched my arm and I turned, expecting Troah, but it was Cheska.

She was wearing a green slicker, her gray hair tied with a green band, her thin braid done up in green ribbon.

"I thought it was you," she said, and took a hat.

"I didn't know you were a fan," I said.

"I'm not," she said, "I think the whole concept is barbaric." She peered over heads, toward the gate. I peered into the crowd. I wanted to see her companions—I guess I expected them to have the same guarded, seasoned expression as she did, but no one in the crowd resembled her, at least not like that. All I could see were tired refugees and impatient fans.

"You're alone?" I asked. "Where's Ransom?"

She gave me a hostile look. "That's really none of your business, Jatahn."

"I freed him," I said. "I treated him. Why isn't it my business?"

"Because it isn't," she said, as though I was a child.

I hesitated. "He's dead," I said, knowing she would never have let that happen.

"That's right," she said.

Ransom was gone. Some freed doctor was culturing Renee's secret cancer from his infected blood. He might even be offworld. Cheska was here for the money, not for us.

Now I was expendable. And so was Troah. And so was Hallie.

"That's a shame," I said, wanting to hit her.

"Isn't it, though," she said, and turned, stiff-backed, toward the betting windows.

"I've been expendable before," said Hallie. "Haven't you?"

"Not like this." I set Frei's triage kit on the stone floor of the breezeway. Further down the caged-in passage, the Meeds knelt in a single line, chained together in the order they would fight. Their weapons leaned against the drop-gates, out of easy reach, bristling in the damp, hot air. The stands were jammed, but here, near the clinic stairs, the breezeway seemed ominously empty. "Where's Troah?"

"She's not allowed upstairs during matches," said Hallie. "It's the only time Althea gets superstitious."

She squatted next to me in the wavering afternoon glare, watching the stands fill. "That's a hell of a crowd for this time of day."

Through the bars, in the open air above the ring, a hol[ ]of Otis Tarda's face—hundreds of times larger, and year[s] younger—flickered under the red weather shields. Th[e] holo-Otis flashed a wide smile, jewels glittering in his ear[s] white teeth gleaming.

"Welcome to the Beryl Arena," said his recording[.] "Health and long life to the Emir!"

"Health and long life!" echoed the fans.

Bootheels clicked on the damp stone, and Althe[a] marched around the curve of the breezeway, an audio fee[d] clipped into her ear, and a wire microphone lying again[st] her cheek like a long black whisker.

"All right, all right," Althea said into the mike. "Ru[n] the Emir, and we'll get started." She scowled into empt[y] air, listening. "Otis, we don't have time to wait for th[e] bets to come up. Silver's out of here by midnight, and if [I] stall, Nacke might just walk." She rolled her head sideway[s] and massaged her left shoulder. "No, goddamnit, I can[']t talk him out of it. You know what he said about his god[ ]damn ship. Yeah, Otis, yeah, I hear you." She slapped a[t] the wire and turned to Hallie.

"You and Leiban and Rasse're going to have to figh[t] early," said Althea. "I don't like that."

"We'll manage," said Hallie.

Althea crossed her arms and glanced around the curv[e] of the breezeway at the Meeds. "What the hell's wron[g] with them?"

Hallie eyed the line of kneeling fighters. "They look fin[e] to me."

"They aren't," she said. "They're scared shitless."

"Just nerves," said Hallie. "They don't usually fight th[is] early." She gave Althea an unconvincing grin. "I'm a litt[le] nervous myself."

"Don't bullshit me," said Althea. "Something's bee[n] wrong with them ever since Frei left. But it's worse now[.] They act like they're afraid of getting hurt. Or dying."

This was remarkable insight for Althea, I thought, as I unfastened the snaps and catches of the triage kit.

"And what's this crap about Butcherboy getting one-in-thirty against Rasse?" Althea demanded. "When Butch loses, all thirty-to-one does is make us sound overconfident."

"You're right about that," agreed Hallie

"How can Otis go along with this shit from Troah?" said Althea. "All he wants is money off the top, but he doesn't understand the kind of investment he's got in here. He's never understood that."

"Never," said Hallie.

Althea rubbed the back of her neck. "Thirty-to-one. You know somebody out there's going to bet against Rasse. But he can't lose. He's a fighting machine

"He's never lost," said Hallie.

"That's right." Althea scowled at the Meeds again. "But they could." She made a frustrated motion. "Their scores and stats are fine. Silver's ranked two steps below us. They should be fired up."

"They're set at fifty-fifty," said Hallie "Only half of them should be fired up."

"Troah's odds," Althea snapped. "And Otis'."

"It's his ring," said Hallie. "That's what you always say. If he has a preference, that's how we go

"Yeah. That's what I always say." Althea turned to me. "You tell me. What'd Troah say to the Meeds?"

"Nothing," I said, too quickly, too defensive.

Althea took a step closer. I tensed, ready to duck, but Hallie moved between us.

"It's just the heat, Althea," said Hallie "They're nervous because they're off their routine. It's nothing. The odds are good. The Meeds are fine."

"It's Troah," said Althea. "She's put her damn Hand on every single one of them. She's put it on Rasse, and you, and—" She took a gulp of air, not saying *and Leiban*. She clapped her palm over the feed in her ear and turned away from Hallie. "What? That's right, run the damn Emir!" She lunged down the breezeway. "Places!" she barked at the Meeds. "Places, you bastards, on your feet!"

Hallie leaned over to kiss me. "It's going to be a long day," she said, and followed Althea to the front of the line.

The fight song started up again—*Greens, Greens, Greens, are winning every day*—and a huge holo of the Emir replaced Otis over the ring. It was a cheap projection that had lost its coherence long ago. Red weather shields glowed eerily through the old man's eyes and thinning hair. The effect was a long way from inspiring—more like some kind of scavenger, poised to descend at the first hint of blood.

The Emir dissolved as the Silver's fight song filled the air—

> *"Tikki, tikki too-va,*
> *Silver's gonna do ya!"*

Across the sand, the Silver team jogged into the ring, coffled ankle to ankle in a long, gleaming, faux-silvery column of grim-faced slaves. Each of them held a long chrome streamer, including Nacke. If there had been any kind of breeze, the streamers would have whipped around, gleaming and glittering, but there was no breeze, so the streamers dragged, limp as worms on the hot sand.

"Everybody out!" Althea bellowed over the music. "Meeds first, Assassins follow! Smile and wave, dammit!" She smacked her whip against the bars, and drove the Meeds into the ring. Behind her, Hallie caught Leiban's elbow as he stumbled. Rasse was nowhere in sight—too dangerous to be put on display.

Troah appeared at the top of the clinic stairs. She shaded her eyes at the two teams, converging in the pit.

"Althea should just let them loose right now," she said.

"It'd be more interesting than the fights, and it d take less time."

It did look like the fighters were about to rush out bare-handed and fall on each other in one long melee, but instead they lined up in two straight columns, marching in place.

I glanced up at the scattering of colored flags in the stands. The Silver fight song blared as loud as ever, but only a few people seemed to be clapping or singing along. All the enthusiasm was in the recordings, and most of the spectators might have agreed with Troah: Get it over with and pay off the bets so they could catch their ships and leave.

Still, when the fans saw Althea, they erupted, shouting, applauding and waving. Althea saluted them, turning in a stiff circle, her face set, while an announcer's voice echoed around the walls.

> *"Silver's Elite against the Beryl's Assassins!*
> *Consult your scorecards for the odds on the following matches—*
> *Beryl's Rock versus . . . Silver's Rampage!*

Hallie turned to the boy across from her, half again her height, half again her weight. She leaned toward him in the quivering, stifling air, and made an obscene gesture with both hands. He lunged at her, but Nacke grabbed his collar and pulled him back in line.

"Theatric," said Troah, "isn't it?"

> *"Beryl's Rexidi versus . . . Silver's Demon!*

The volume went way up over the speakers—

> *". . . are winning every day!*
> *Greens, Greens, Greens,*
> *will blow your team away!"*

231

A pale boy from the Silver team, huge across the shoulders, his short hair streaked blue and chrome, raised his arms and shook his fists, but when Leiban stepped forward, the yells from the stands weren't from impatient outworlders, hungry for a payoff. Entire sections were on their feet, refugees, fans, probably disguised runaways as well.

Troah breathed in my ear. "Different when it's real, wouldn't you say?"

I nodded, throat tight. What I'd seen on the holo had always been a useless, bloody exercise for people who would only feel the loss in their bank accounts. Now, with the deafening fight song pounding in my chest, my cynicism squeezed out in beads of sweat. I was part of this, win or lose, I was enveloped in it. On the sidelines, or in the torpid water of the cisterns, for the first time in my life I was dangerous—invisible and potent—like a cancer.

TWELVE

Back in the breezeway, the Meeds were silent, already dusted to their knees with sand. Hallie pushed through them and came over to crouch on the floor next to me and the triage kit.

"If I was going to lay odds on anything," she said in a low voice, "I'd bet on whether Althea lets Leiban into the ring when it's his turn."

At the other end of the breezeway, Leiban waited until Althea wasn't looking, then bent down to lave his face with water from a puddle. Sweat glittered over his body, like a net of jewels. He saw Hallie and me watching, turned and disappeared into the line of Meeds.

"Pair-on-Triple—" Althea opened the shackles on the first two Meeds, separating out the teams. This Pair consisted of a lanky boy and short, muscular girl. The girl was sweating so much, her green shirt had turned almost black. She took her soga out of the bristle of plumes and blades like she'd never seen one before. The boy balked until Althea shoved his into his hands.

Across the ring, three of the Silver's Meeds emerged from their own gateway, sogas glinting in the dull light.

"Three against two?" I said to Hallie. "Is that fair?"

"This has nothing to do with fair," said Hallie. "It's a betting handicap."

The Beryl's Pair hesitated at our edge of the ring. Up in the stands, scattered cheers and catcalls settled over the high walls. Heat shimmered off the sand, distorting the Silver fighters across the pit into a mirage of wavering, long-legged creatures. I waited for the holographic images to break the thick air, but the opposing Meeds circled each other, plain and tiny, unadorned.

"They don't fight with holo projectors?" I said.

Hallie shook her head. "Only High Sets do. Gives the crowd something to look forward to when they get bored with this."

I'd been crouching next to the triage kit for so long, my knees were numb. I stood up, watching the Beryl's Pair shuffle warily around the Silver's Triple. When I looked away, I found the Meeds in the breezeway staring across the dark, damp space between us, scrutinizing every move I made.

Althea stopped in front of Hallie. "What're you doing over here?" she said. "Giving medical advice?"

Hallie got to her feet. "No, D'sha," she said, and went over to the Meeds.

In the ring, the Beryl's girl swung frantically at one of the Silver fighters while her teammate tried to fend off the rest of the Triple. Someone's shriek drifted in from the hot sand, a thin, helpless sound. Inside the breezeway, the rest of the Meeds shifted. Althea leaned on the barred gate, with Leiban at her side in exactly the same position.

In the ring, the action moved closer as the Silver's Triple

pressed the Beryl fighters toward our side of the ring. All five of them were drenched with sweat and streaked with blood from minor cuts. The girl from the Beryl backed up until she was against the bars, close enough for me to hear her panting. One of the Silver boys jabbed at her with the prong end of his soga. She ducked, and his blades caught briefly in the dropgate. She bobbed up before he could twist away, and gouged her blade deep in his belly. It was so fast, no one in the stands seemed to notice. The wounded boy dropped his weapon, grabbing at the gorge of ripped intestine spilling out of his abdomen. He collapsed with a horrified yelp, but it wasn't until he began flopping around, Failing in the sand, that the audience cheered.

"Took you long enough," Althea yelled as the knot of fighters battered their way past her for another gory circuit. She cupped her hands around her mouth and shouted across the pit. "First blood on your side, Strix!"

The Pair and the abbreviated Triple had fought their way into the middle of the ring, hacking at each other. The biggest of the surviving Silver fighters was focused on maiming the Beryl girl, while his partner held hers at bay. The girl dodged and ducked under his swings, losing speed, tiring under the weight of her weapon and the cuts across her arms. His sweeps and stabs were rhythmic, like a fast dance. Her parries dropped lower, until she was crouched on the sand. He had a clear strike across her chest and swung. She folded and fell over, cut almost in half. The other Silver Meed sank his blades into the Beryl boy's side, and shook his soga over his head gleefully.

Up in the stands, the refugees applauded or booed.

A buzzer sounded in the unbreathable heat, and the round was over.

"Decision, Silver!" shouted the announcer. Static cut his voice, other voices underneath.

". . . *demand answers, citizens . . . what does the local government plan to do if the rumors of attack . . .*"

235

"Shut that thing off!" Althea yelled into her headset, and the static went dead. "Frei!" She pointed at me. "You! Out there!"

She dashed into the ring, with me and a couple of Meeds behind her in a dogged run. From the other side of the pit, Strix and Nacke rushed out with two slaves and a stretcher. I ran past their boy, dead in the sand. I kept running, and passed the Beryl girl who'd killed him. Her eyes were still open, staring dully at the red, red sky. Her chest lay wide open. Her spine was visible through the wreckage of her heart and lungs and the cut ends of her ribs. I lost my footing in the sliding sand, nauseated to the core. High walls loomed like the inside of an obsidian bowl. The oppressive air stuck in my throat. Althea grabbed my arm as I started to fall, and half dragged me to where the Silver Meeds were still prancing in a victorious circle around the surviving Beryl boy.

He writhed in the sand, two big gashes on his left side, between the top of his hip and the bottom of his ribs. I crouched next to him, so dizzy I wasn't sure I could stand up again.

"One for our side." Strix Aluka appeared in the shimmering heat and gave Althea a sneering thumbs-up. "Good start for the day, right, Althea?"

"Get him on his feet," Althea snapped at me, and hauled us both up. The boy wheezed in my ear, almost sobbing.

"Will I Fail?" he gasped. "I'm Failing. Am I Failing?"

He couldn't stop asking, and I couldn't give him an answer. He was shaking hard enough to throw me off balance, and my hand kept slipping in his blood when I tried to brace him against my hip. We managed to stumble after Althea and the other two Meeds as they collected the girl's body. They dragged her into the breezeway, and deposited her in a heap, away from the rest of her teammates.

"*Round Two—*" started the announcer, "*—lies and deceptions from the Emirate Report won't help the government—*"

"Otis!" shouted Althea into the whisker-mike, "can't you do anything about that? Yeah? Well, everyone can hear it down here." She pointed into the line of Meeds, three quick jabs. "Triple-on-Triple, move it, *move* it!"

I squeezed by them with the wounded boy half collapsed across my shoulders, still babbling and crying. I got him to the open space by the clinic doors, and eased him down on the wet stones.

The next three Meeds, two boys and a girl, armed with plumes this time instead of sogas, took a few halting steps toward the gate.

"I said, let's *go!*" bellowed Althea. Her whip cracked, and the Triple blundered into the pit, feet scraping in the sand, weapons banging the bars.

I grabbed the scanner and cleared it. On the screen, the boy's life signs and the green Viral indicator pulsed side by side with only a minor downward dip. He was going to be fine, but I was panicking. I yanked the triage kit open, bloody up to my elbows, and uncapped the first hypoderm. I angled the needle into his body, emptied it, uncapped another, emptied it, got through a total of five before I felt the gash began to close—a weird creeping of ruined skin, like toothless gums around my fingers. I looked up to see Hallie nodding.

"You don't need to use so much," she said. "Save some for later."

"Okay," I said. "Okay." I tried to brush hair away and smeared my cheek with cool, sticky blood.

She licked her thumb and wiped my face. "You're doing fine," she said, and left again.

Down by the open gate, Althea had one ear covered against the jeers from the stands, listening to Otis in her earpiece as the Beryl team fled from one side of the ring to the other. "They're going to call time on this one?" she shouted to the invisible Otis. "That's crazy! They haven't been out there long enough." She glared at the Meeds. "They're not scared, boss, they're just off their usual schedule. Makes them nervous. Yes, I know it's a big, goddamn crowd." She glared up at the stands. "I'm handling it, Otis." She twisted the wire away from her mouth and shouted at the Meeds in the pit. "Engage, dammit, before I come out there and show you how it's done!"

One of the Meeds from the Beryl Triple edged along the perimeter of ring. His teammates backed up along with him until they were all just across from me. The girl and one boy held off the Silver Meeds while he peered between the bars. Plumes buzzed behind him, like bristling metal feathers. His mouth moved in a question I could hardly hear.

"How is he?" whispered the Meed.

"He's fine," I hissed.

"He's free?" whispered the boy, still wondering, but in the rush and crunch of sand, his teammates turned in surprise, as though they had heard me say, *yes.*

The Silver Meeds descended on them. Althea's furious howl of dismay went up with their shrieks as the Silver Triple cut into the Beryl Meeds, right in front of me, slicing faces, stomachs, legs. My patient, the Meed from the first round, flung his arms around me and shoved me into the corner by the door, as though the murder might make its way through the bars. His shoulder and sandy throat covered my face. He huddled me down to the soaking wet stone, so close and tight, I could hardly breathe. When the screaming gave way to half-enthused cheers, he let go, hunched on his knees, hands over his face, his own blood under his fingernails. Behind him, in the ring other Meeds dragged off what was left of the Triple.

One was dead by the time they got to me. The other two were so badly cut, I couldn't decide where to start. The girl's readings showed red and green lines plunging steadily downwards, no matter how much of the Virus I pumped into her. The boy's life signs would jump every time I gave him an injection, but his Viral indicator didn't respond. The girl heaved and shuddered and sucked a lungful of air, on the verge of Failure. The boy lay still, leaking blood.

In the ring, someone screamed, and the crowd roared like thunder. Lights came on from the ceiling of the breezeway, and the dark floor was suddenly blinding bright. Above the pit, the sky had changed to a bruised, brackish purple. The rumble of cheers came again.

It was thunder, not the crowd.

Lightning cracked, and the speakers blasted static. Althea yanked her headset off with a yelp of pain.

". . . *confirmed fact. Faraqui warships have been sighted near the Point Seven border station. Not an entourage, as the Emirate Report maintains, but an armada—*"

"Turn that thing *off*," bellowed Althea.

The girl's hand was lying against my leg, and it trembled. I emptied another hypo into her side, where the wounds seemed worst, but on the scanner, her life signs only hesitated on their way down. The boy from the first round sat against the wall, arms wrapped around his knees, waiting for me to do something miraculous.

"I can't do anything unless they're healed," I told him, and stopped when I heard my own voice, all high and shaky and rasping with uncertainty. He gave me an accusing stare and the girl began to convulse.

Althea's shadow blocked the bright lights. "Why're you wasting that stuff on them?" she shouted as I opened another hypo. "Thanas! Both of them! Hurry up!"

She shot down the breezeway, and I smeared handprints all over the triage kit, trying to open the other side.

"Let me," said Troah, descending out of the dark, weightless, deadly and poisonous. She pulled out the bottom drawer, picked out two hypoderms and uncapped one.

Black liquid welled out of the tip, and she sank the needle into the girl's wrist.

The girl's body shuddered and relaxed. Her face went slack, exhausted. It was nothing. It was a mercy. I felt tears spill down my face and Troah gave me a long, appraising look. "This is the wrong place for you, Jatahn," she said in an incredibly gentle voice. Then she leaned over the boy and killed him too.

"Decision, Beryl. Score is now two to one, Silver . . ."

Lightning flashed. Down by the gate, two Meeds wobbled in from the ring, one with her soga chopped in half.

"Next . . . Quad-on-Pair . . ."

Althea grabbed the next Meed by her shirt and pulled the girl to her feet. "Quad-on-Pair," she shouted over the blaring speakers, but the girl, ashen, shoved her away.

"No!" she shrieked at the top of her lungs. *"No!"*

Althea wasn't even fazed. She pushed the girl into the open gate the way a big man might shove balky cattle. The girl was taller than Althea, and a good bit heavier. She stopped in the gateway, raised both fists above her head and took aim at Althea's skull.

A soga blade flashed in the bright lights and caught her in the neck. The girl fell backwards, decapitated. Leiban stepped into the space where she had been, white as paste. He aimed the pronged end of his soga, belly-level, at the next set of Meeds.

"Anyone else want to argue?" he shouted.

The three surviving Meeds in the Quad shouldered their weapons and shuffled past Althea, into the ring, keeping whatever distance they could from Leiban.

I slid down to sit against the seeping wall, out of breath, cold in every joint, aching under my teeth, freezing sweat under my arms. Even without their teammate, the Beryl fighters outnumbered the Silver three-to-two. They swarmed around the Silver Meeds, falling on them, cutting and piercing. The sound of steel on steel came in waves, a second or two after the actual strike, making the action seem silent, safe, and removed from where I was.

Someone bent into the corner of my vision—Hallie directing a couple of Meeds, who gathered my corpses and dragged them away.

Hallie leaned closer. "You all right?"

I wasn't exactly sure who she was talking to. The boy from the first round was still crouched in the corner by the door, and Troah was still behind it, watching everything.

"*. . . decision, Beryl . . . score is now tied, two to two.*"

In the ring, the Beryl Meeds flung their arms up, and danced around in victory. I looked around for Hallie, but I couldn't see her.

"Ransom was alive after he Failed," said the boy from the first round, abruptly, as though he'd been having this conversation with himself for some time. "He was Failing when you took him into the clinic, but the bones in the bag were someone else's."

Althea was too far away to hear anything. "That's right," I said.

"You can save us," said the boy. "You can free us. There's a life after, like D'Troah says."

The Meeds trooped past Althea, into the breezeway, while she stood in the hot sand and thunder, bowing to the adulation from the stands.

"It's different than what she told you," I said.

"What have I told you?" said Troah, behind the door.

The boy hesitated. "Survival is in belief, D'sha."

"Belief in what?" prompted Troah.

"In you, D'sha," replied the boy.

"This Jatahn girl is mine," said Troah. "But she has no faith in me. That's why she can't save you."

The boy covered his face. "She can't save us?"

"I can," I whispered.

"Then why don't you do it?"

I looked up to see a broad-shouldered girl, just in from

the ring, splattered with gore and sand. A huge cut across her stomach bled freely down her legs.

"Why *don't* you?" she said again.

Troah moved out into the breezeway, silent, intent on her own victories. The girl dropped to her knees, and Troah bent over her. She put her marked palm over the girl's deep wound, and moved so I could see.

"Heal," said Troah.

The girl took a quick breath, her head turned to one side. The muscles in her abdomen convulsed, crawling in a fleshy wave. Her shoulders stiffened, and she coughed. Troah took her Hand away and cleaned it on the tail of her shirt.

I stared at the girl's stomach. The bleeding had stopped. The wound was still hurtfully raw, and a slathering of the Virus would have quickened the scabbing, but it was closed. The girl touched the slash in her belly with shaking fingers, sat down heavily, and wiped her eyes.

Troah squatted next to me and touched my thigh, tracing the outline of the tape under my pants. "You have two needles left?" she said.

I nodded.

"Give them to me."

"No," I said.

Down the breezeway, Althea shoved a lone Meed into the ring with a plume. Three Silver fighters emerged from the other side and started running toward him. The sky got even darker. The point seemed quick, inevitable.

"There's nothing you can do without me," said Troah.

In the ring, the darkness wasn't just the storm overhead. Smoke descended in thin veils through the still air. The fighters noticed it, coiling in the wakes of their blades.

"Single on Triple . . . ladies and gentlemen, check the scoreboards for adjusted odds . . . confirmed eyewitness reports of Faraqui ships heading unopposed for Emirate targets. Government resistance has fallen at the border of the Faraque, leaving a clear

path to Frontier ports such as Bellea-Naya, Bey-Perkenji, Bey-Cassadagga, and near-Frontier planets including Traja. . . .''

"Otis, will you cut the *goddamn* speakers!"

". . . contingency plans for Emirate civilians trapped on these target worlds? No! Nonstop propaganda has left hundreds of thousands . . .''

Althea's voice broke in. "What's burning? Where? By the ground station?"

A burst of static—dead air—and then the familiar baritone of the Emirate Report announcer.

"Attention citizens . . .''

"Otis!" bellowed Althea, not noticing that the Independent had been stifled.

". . . are urged to remain calm . . .''

Another crack of lightning and the speakers went dead. The government rebuttal choked into silence. In the breezeway, the lights blinked out, on again, and off. The lights over the ring went out too, leaving the fighters in a ruddy twilight.

The match, such as it was, came to an unorganized halt. The Meeds milled around in the half-dark, and shuffled away from each other. The lone fighter from our side ran over to the main gate, and shaded his eyes at something in the distance. I squinted to see what he was staring at, but all I could see was the black sky through the black opening in the black wall. That was when I noticed the rain, pattering on the dry sand. Up in the sky, the clouds were gray, not the writhing red of the weather shields. Rain fell harder. I looked toward the main gate again and saw the Meed racing for our side of the ring.

"They're here!" he shrieked across the sand. "Faraqui! At the ground station! The smoke! They're burning it down!"

Inside the breezeway, the sweaty aura of fear surrounding the rest of the Meeds became electric. The ones who hadn't fought were still shackled, and the chains hissed over stones like escaping steam.

"You can't keep us here, Althea!" shouted one of the girls. Her voice rang off the breezeway's vaulted ceiling, high and thin.

"She'll get out by herself!" yelled one of the boys. "She'll leave us!"

The line of Meeds heaved to its feet. Leiban jumped in front of them, brandishing his soga, a slender blue figure in an ocean of arms and fists and shouting mouths.

Althea grabbed the bars and pulled herself up above their heads. She waved the whip, cracked it, and snapped it in their faces until the noise died down. "What you're hearing," she said, low and furious, "is some goddamn amateur hacker out there with a bunch of stupid stories he thinks you should hear." She emphasized *stupid stories* with the butt of the whip against her leg. "Now look up there—" She pointed to the roiling surge of people in the stands. "They're not leaving." She tapped her earpiece. "The boss says they're coming in. The betting pools are doubling every fifteen minutes, and *no* one gets out of *that.*"

She let herself down from the bars. Leiban took his position next to her, soga up, as nervous as Althea should have been.

Behind me, on the other side of the door, hard soles clattered on the concrete stairs. Strix Aluka burst out of the stairwell, his pants soaked with water to his knees. He waved Althea over, and leaned close to her ear.

"We've got another ship lined up. We're out of here in an hour."

"An hour?"" she said. "Didn't Otis talk to you? The bets are outrageous! You can't leave now."

"I don't care about the bets. If you want your High Set to fight, you'd better get them up now."

She snorted. "Just because you're losing—"

Strix grabbed her shoulders. "Get a little reality in there, Althea," he hissed. "There's a war on. The fucking Faraqui are on their way. If you stick around too long, you'll end up putting on your show for *them*. You want that?"

She knocked his hands away. "You believe everything you hear on the 'ree?"

He swallowed and the motion in his throat made his taut face even tighter. "Not everything," he said. "Just the stuff that scares me the most.'

"Then you'd better send out your High Set," said Althea. "And pack your bags."

He turned and bolted down the stairs. Below, in the corridor, his footsteps were echoing splashes.

Althea turned her attention to Troah. "Where're you supposed to be, witch?'

"It's flooded downstairs," said Troah.

"Flooded?" Althea frowned down the stairs.

"The weather shields are off," said Troah. "There's a power interruption, or something. Water's coming in everywhere. Rasse's up to his shins."

Althea shot a glance into the ring and beckoned to Leiban. "Strix is getting ready to run out on us," she said to him. "Take the Meeds down and lock them in. Get Hallie to help you. And bring Rasse up. You're all going in ahead of schedule."

Leiban nodded and spun on his heel. Althea turned her back to us, covering one ear, murmuring to Otis in the whisker-mike.

Troah watched her, cataloguing every move, then turned and went down the stairs.

I stood in the doorway, listening to her splash toward Rasse's cell. In a moment, the sound faded under the steady drip of water.

"Don't make an announcement for anything," Althea yelled into her mike. "I don't want to hear anymore of that Independent crap Just put it on the scoreboard. Meeds are done for the day High Sets run early. That's what everybody came for—" She stuck a finger in her other ear. "What? It's on the betting sheet, Otis. Rock and Rampage. Then Rasse fights Butch, and then Leiban takes out that sandbag they call Demon. Yes, that's the order they go in." She listened for a minute, her face more and more tense. "Leiban always fights last. Why? Because it's—dramatic. He'll make it. Otis—you may own this place, but he's my . . . Otis? I can't hear you, Otis." She pulled the headset off and draped it around her neck.

The weather shields were back on, and the rain had stopped falling into the ring, for the moment. High above the center of the pit, a holo scoreboard solidified into flat planes of green and chrome and began a slow spin. A timer blinked underneath, flashing green lights at the top and red at the bottom. Words filled the empty boards, haltingly, as though someone was writing them in by hand.

> *Middle Sets Now Final*
> *(50:50 return on all bets)*
> *Next:*
> *Assassins vs. Elite*

The order of the fights appeared underneath. Hallie first, then Rasse, and Leiban at the end, as though Otis had acquiesced on this point.

Althea nodded to herself, pushed her straight black bangs off her forehead and held them on top of her head with both hands, elbows out.

A bellow echoed up the stairs. Leiban appeared first, backing into the breezeway with a fistful of chain and Althea's whip, hauling on Rasse and fending him off at the same time. Rasse bulged through the doorway, hunched in wrist-to-ankle shackles that kept him from exploding to his full height. He blundered into the breezeway, doubled over almost to a crawl and still animal-huge, his face crammed into a grimace of undrugged pain and raw fury. He rolled his watery blue eyes in my direction, and I caught my first and only glimpse of how completely he understood his life, this humiliation, and what he was expected to do in the ring. He saw Althea and his comprehension vanished. His body shook, with excitement or rage, or fear.

Hallie emerged from the stairwell with the other end of Rasse's chain. She held it taut while Leiban looped his end into a steel ring set into the wall. Hallie clipped hers into another loop so that Rasse was cross-tied, like an unpredictable horse. Rasse dropped to his hands and knees on the wet stone floor, unable to free himself, hardly able to move.

Althea peered at the timer on the revolving scoreboard. "Get yourself ready, Hallie."

Hallie unknotted her harness from around her waist. She pulled her pants off and kicked them away, naked now, except for a pair of shiny green briefs. She slid into the projector harness like it was a shirt. It fit snug across her hips, across her chest, covering only the interruptions in her scars, where, during one fight or another, the leather had protected her. The plastic patch at her hip glowed emerald.

Althea came over and checked the harness, tugging on it. "Watch this guy," said Althea. "Watch him every second. Remember, he leads on the left, and throws in a feint from the right when he thinks you're not paying attention. So pay attention."

Hallie kept her eyes on the ground, not answering.

Althea tightened a strap. "You're not listening."

I got to my feet, wanting to put my arms around her before she went out, wanting to promise her anything.

"You're going to get killed if you don't listen," said Althea. "What the hell is wrong with you people today?"

At the other end of the breezeway, Leiban watched the scoreboard. The green light flashed over the timer and he shouted past Rasse, "Time, Hallie!"

Hallie shook Althea off, shook herself inside the harness. "I'll see you," she said to Althea, but it was me she was looking at. She jogged past Leiban to the open dropgate. I hung on the bars wanting to see, not wanting to see.

On the other side of the ring, Rampage stepped into the pit, sheathed in silver from head to foot. At first I thought the costume was part of his projection, but it was real. He raised his fists to the crowd and exposed tarnish-colored stains under his arms and along his sides.

Leiban came over to stand next to Althea as Rampage marched around the ring, waving at the crowd. His face had a fine-boned look that didn't match his bulky body. The closer he came, the more positive I was that he was another Faraqui-bred fighting machine, like Rasse. More self-aware than Rasse, but easily as dangerous.

"He must be burning up in that suit," said Leiban.

Althea nodded. "Strix thinks it makes him look superhuman, but I think it's cheap." She eyed the timer.

The red light flashed at the bottom of the clock and a buzzer went off. A shadow rushed across the corner of my vision—Hallie—enveloped in the black plumage of her green-eyed bird. She spread her arms and the holo wings shot out.

Across the ring, Rampage raised his weapon. His projection bloomed up to swallow him, solidifying into a bulky, black-striped silver creature, earless as a fighting tom, with huge paws and rough spines instead of fur.

"That's new," said Leiban. "What *is* that?"

"Who cares?" said Althea. "Same old Rampage underneath."

"Go Greens, Go Greens!"

Chanting echoed off the walls, drifting with thin wisps of smoke from the fires downtown.

"Tikki tikki too-vah!
Silver's gonna do ya!"

Hallie flung herself across the ring, all wings and talons and emerald eyes. The cat bristled its spines, arching its back clear to the top of the wall. Inside the projection, in his silver suit, Rampage swung his plume down and ran at Hallie with long, loping strides. The cat mimicked him, bounding, mouth gaping over chrome teeth.

Chanting from the stands changed to approving yells. Hallie made first contact, talons to a foreleg, wings out wide enough to reach the side walls. Her plume raked the air where the two projections met and mixed, light to dark, spines over feathers. Metal rang on metal as beak and claws made contact. I saw Hallie dive under Rampage's swing, recover and bang the blunt end of her staff into the boy's abdomen.

He danced sideways, plume low, ready to rake the blades up and down her body. She closed in on him, fast, without theatrics, cutting underneath his sweeps, blocking so close that the holos merged into one unidentifiable creature.

Althea turned to Leiban. "What does she think she's doing?"

"She's going to take him down in the first two minutes," said Leiban.

"That's not what people pay to see," said Althea.

"It's not her style, either." Leiban wound his arms through the bars. "She'll tire herself."

Rampage plunged forward, a thrust from the right, a feint, a block to Hallie's blade, a parry from the left. She blocked, banged at his blades, slashed, and left slices over his face and neck. He tried to break, but she pressed him. Black wings were a canopy, obscuring the real blood, the real pain with jabs and strikes from beak to eyes, talons to flanks.

Rampage broke away, galloping sideways until he had some distance. He angled his cat, shoulder-on to Hallie's bird, one foot raised, claws spread. Inside, he held his plume like a pitchfork, both hands around the haft. She moved closer, feinted. He slashed, and the bird shot back, head low, wings high, stained crimson in black breastfeathers.

My hands slipped, sweaty on the bars.

"That's a fight, now that's a fight," muttered Althea.

Go Greens! Go Greens!

"Go Greens," breathed Troah, right behind me. She glanced at Althea, too absorbed to notice her, and pointed into the stands. "We've got company."

At first I had no idea what she was talking about. She was too close, too sticky-warm in the heat, and I could almost bring myself to elbow her away. Then I realized she was pointing to Cheska, high in the bleachers, just visible over the edge of the wall. On either side of her, refugees shook their fists and waved their flags, but Cheska was impassive, waiting for her money.

The crowd bellowed, and I looked down in time to see Hallie roll to her feet, bloody to the waist, cut in red stripes down one side of her chest from Rampage's chrome claws. She grabbed her weapon out of the sand, panting, staggering.

The spiny cat charged after her, swung, and she swung wild, catching air, ducking, awkward and off balance, stumbling until she fell.

Troah's hip touched mine. The sensation was like being burned. "She's got herself scared," said Troah.

Althea checked the clock. "She can hold him off until they call time on her. She can at least do that."

"It's like watching Naritte, all over again," said Leiban.

They were closer now, Rampage bullying Hallie around the perimeter of the ring, their blades ringing along the bars of the dropgates. The projections became foggy haze as the distance closed between them and us, giving a clearer view under the holos. Hallie was breathing hard, cut all over her sides, sand sticking in sweaty patterns along her legs and arms. Rampage's silver suit was black with perspiration, torn to strips across his shoulder where she'd marked him, but he was winning, and he knew it, and Hallie knew it too.

And I knew it, and that was a hotter, harder pain than Troah's Hand on the small of my back.

"You hold him till they call time on you, Hallie," Althea yelled through the bars.

Rampage slashed, fast and hard, with no intention of letting Hallie wait that long. She blocked, parried, but not fast enough. The next strike cut her. She jumped back, too far, slamming into the bars, almost lost her footing, and dodged as he swung again.

Rampage's blades raked the bars where she'd been, where Althea and Leiban and I and Troah were. I jerked away. Leiban leaped sideways. Althea moved out of range, but Troah didn't budge.

Rampage and Hallie circled each other, just on the other side of the dropgate, slow and deliberate. She panted, blood running down her legs, and made him circle once more until his back was to the bars again.

Hallie paused, facing him, and us. Rampage made a half-step to the left, testing her guard. She blocked him. He feinted right. She swept the air with a rush of razor steel. He stopped, his back against the bars, boxed in for the moment, but not sure why.

Hallie shook sweat out of her eyes and looked past him.

Not at me, but at Troah.

Over the ring, lighting fluoresced the weather shields, turning them an electric scarlet. The weird light shot through the breezeway, freezing the moment for me in needle-fine detail: Leiban holding off his Failure, excruciatingly casual, as it engulfed him, cell by cell—Althea's stark disbelief that Hallie was about to lose—and Hallie's naked plea for help.

The only motion was Troah. In the strobe of lightning-red, her eyes met mine.

I knew what she was asking.

I knew what I would say.

And there was no question what her interference would cost me.

Across a vast space, I nodded.

"Dammit!" shouted Althea. "Pay *attention!*"

Hallie swung and Rampage ducked. He braced himself against the iron dropgate, plume up for the next slash.

Before he could move, Troah was behind him. She put her Hand through the bars. She slid her arm around his waist, and she touched him with the fire her race had bred into his.

He let out a yell, dropped his weapon. Troah yanked back and Hallie shoved her blades into Rampage's belly without hesitation, grinding his guts and silver fabric.

Applause mixed with jeers filled the thick air as Rampage fell, soundlessly twisting and clutching at his wound. Across the ring, Strix and Nacke shot out of their gate and raced across the sand.

Althea yelled at Otis through the whisker-mike. "I know, I *know*, no points for *style*."

Hallie wobbled into the breezeway, sweat dripping down her nose, her sides heaving. Althea grabbed her harness. "You can't ask for *help*," she shouted.

"I needed help," panted Hallie. "I won. What else do you want?"

Althea shoved her away as Strix and Nacke ran up on the other side of the gate. I looked around for Troah, but she'd vanished.

"Whaddaya call that, D'Orso?" shouted Strix, red-faced. "Is it interference in your book, or only in mine?"

"Prove it," Althea shouted back. "Prove whatever you think you saw, and I'll give you the goddamn point!"

Strix wasn't listening. He and Nacke slung Rampage between them and hobbled back to the other side.

When they were gone, Hallie dropped to her knees beside me, still gasping for breath, bloody knuckles pressed against gritty black stone. Her head hung down, and I couldn't see her face. Her body quivered. Her shoulders heaved. I steadied myself on the bars, watching her silent tears drip down. I didn't have the strength to comfort her.

Behind us, in the breezeway, Rasse gnawed the air, bowed over in his shackles. A big-shouldered boy emerged from the Silver's side and shook his soga at the crowd. Spotlights crossed the sand, glinting off the black and silver paint that striped across his ribs and hips. His holo glittered formlessly huge, not quite solid enough to be distinct.

Althea pushed Rasse into the open dropgate. She thumbed the manacles off his ankles and reached for the ones on his wrists. Rasse wove his head from side to side, eyes fixed on the Silver's fighter. His fists clenched and unclenched. He shuffled, straightening as his chains loosened, until he towered over Althea. She slapped the plastic projector on his harness, and Rasse's holo burst into the breezeway. Ragged claws on black legs formed two columns. Steel spikes radiated from the ceiling. The rest disappeared into dark stone, too big to make sense of.

Althea took a long step back from the boy and uncoiled her whip. "Where's his chopper, Leiban?"

Leiban passed her an ax with a blade like a paving stone. Althea held it out with an effort, left-handed, toward Rasse, her right arm cocked, the whip uncoiled. She slid the ax handle into Rasse's palm. Rasse, utterly focused on the other fighter, closed his fist around it, a reflex, not a thought.

"Rasse-boy, you know what to do." Althea moved the whip over the stone floor. Rasse licked his lips, half shadowed by his own projection. Sweat ran down his sides, glistening and beading over a faint smear of yellow oil under his harness, just above his buttocks.

A hand-shaped smear.

Althea raised the whip.

"Get out there, Rasse!"

Rasse bolted as she swung, and the whip snagged empty air behind him.

In the open space of the ring, Rasse's holo became a wolfish black dog with a spiked collar and red eyes, tall enough for the top of its head to be level with the first row of seats. There was no art to the image. The head was too big, and the legs too long. Every time Rasse waved his ax, the jaws opened and shut, like a mechanical toy, showing fangs as long as I was tall.

The glittering air around Butcherboy, the Silver's fighter, coalesced into a chromed mantis, matching the dog for height, gleaming silver from its pincers to the ranks of spurs on its back legs.

Hallie slid closer to the bars, her face blotchy from crying, her cheeks crusted with sand.

Fans threw green flares over the edge of the pit, where they fell into the sand and sputtered out. Silver flares smoked on the other side of the ring. Their white-chrome haze drifted over the sand in clots in the dim red evening and spotlights.

Rasse lunged around the ring, a pale ghost between the black forelegs of his dog-form, nowhere near his opponent. Above the ring, the timer was already running.

Butch crouched over his own long-ax, his black-and-silver stripes running with sweat, dribbling gray down his legs. He pivoted in the middle of the ring as the dog jogged in and out of shadows along the edge of the breezeway.

Rasse rushed by our end of the ring, his face a sweaty mask of terror.

Althea leaned out to peer after him. "What the hell's wrong with him?"

"He's got one minute to engage," said Leiban.

"I'll be goddamned if he loses by default," said Althea. She sounded amazed. "Not at thirty to one."

Out in the middle of the ring, Butch's mantis waved bladed forelegs, scuttling in a circle, watching the scoreboard, counting seconds.

"Fifty seconds to default," said Leiban.

Boos and catcalls drifted down from the stands. Silver flares arced over the pit in clouds of silver smoke. Rasse fled around the ring as though he could outrun Troah's intentions and Althea's requirements.

"Twenty seconds." Leiban peered into the ring.

Althea pushed past him and stepped into Rasse's path. The huge dog slowed, jaws hanging open, Rasse panting between the forelegs.

"You son of a bitch," shouted Althea. "You *will* fight, and you *will* win!"

Rasse swayed. He looked around for Butch, saw him in the middle of the ring and tore toward him.

Hallie turned to me with her hands over her mouth. "Oh my God," she whispered. "He's 'hanced."

Butch braced himself, mantis squatting, silver arms up. He raised his ax inside the image, blades gleaming brass. Rasse's dog pulled cartoon lips off white teeth and ran at him.

The two projections grappled, Butch's slicing and clawing. The dog chewed empty air, black feet churning as Rasse struggled underneath. Butch hacked at Rasse like he was taking down a tree. Rasse swung and missed, swung and missed. Butch landed two deep blows on Rasse's left side. Rasse howled and flung himself away, rolling in the sand, bloody from shoulder to hip.

Althea stood at the edge of the pit, hands wound into her short hair. Rasse's dog scrambled to its feet, limping out of the spotlight, streaked with scarlet, tongue hanging out like a long piece of red carpet. Some of the projection was missing now, from the back of the dog's head to its right shoulder. When Rasse turned, I could see part of his harness dragging in the sand.

Up in the stands, people jammed together at the top of the wall, shoving each other for a better look. Green and silver smoke billowed down, drifting into the breezeway.

Butch's mantis darted forward, forelegs extended, every blade exposed. Rasse swung the heavy ax over his wounded right shoulder and couldn't hold it. Butch rushed in, slashed, backed off, charged and slashed again, making contact every time. The black dog bled ruby-colored fluid from under its throat. Rasse's wail was lost in the roar from the stands. The dog listed, stumbled, and rolled on its side.

"Goddamnit Rasse!" Althea shrieked into the ring. "You get on your feet and win this goddamn match, or I'll break your goddamn neck!"

The Enhancers were the only thing that made him care. Rasse shoved himself up, ax clutched in his left hand. Butch danced back and forth, snapping pincers, flashing his blades, ready to pounce as soon as Rasse cleared the ground, but Rasse lunged low, too wounded to stand. He caught Butch under the knees, slicing skin, shaving down to white bone and gristle. The chrome mantis projection dropped, legless, writhing in the sand. The dog slashed again, all teeth and artificial tongue. Inside the holo, Rasse's heavy ax landed in Butch's abdomen. Chrome turned scarlet. White teeth went red. Mantis pincers stabbed past ribs into Rasse's lungs. Rasse grunted and kept chopping as his wolfish black hindquarters vanished. Underneath the cheers from the stands, Butch squealed in agony. Even when he stopped, Rasse kept going.

Butch's projection quivered into silver static, thin as snow. Then it was gone.

Rasse hewed the corpse for the silent crowd.

Gore splashed his face.

Ax up. Ax down. Ax up. Ax down.

Someone was running across the sand—Althea, with Leiban brandishing a soga, close behind her. From the other side of the ring, Nacke and Strix were shadows between the white flash of a spotlight.

On the scoreboard, green letters flashed over the timer:

Decision: Beryl—30:1

Rasse had won. In spite of Troah, in spite of everything.

Hallie turned her face upwards and so did I. High above us, Cheska peered down. There was no pity or compassion in her face, and no sign of contingency plans. She made a small, blameless gesture, either for us, or for herself, and turned away. The space was immediately filled with gaping fans.

Althea and Leiban dragged what was left of Rasse out of the ring and laid him in front of me.

Hallie smoothed his shaved scalp while I emptied half a dozen hypos uselessly into his belly wounds. I could have soaked him in the Virus, filled him with it. I couldn't fill the bleeding hole that had been the side of his face, or bring back the shreds of him still lying in the sand. The Virus would heal what could be healed and thin to nothing. His Failure would be a kindness. I reached for the triage kit—and found Althea behind me with the scanner.

She squatted next to Rasse, studying the readout with icy calm as his life signs dropped in a long, slow twist of red and green.

"How would you find Enhancers in his system?" she said.

My mouth went dry. Hallie's eyes widened.

"I'd have to run a diagnosis, D'sha," I said.

She handed me the scanner. "Do it."

I changed the settings while the scoreboard flashed the next match.

Silver's Demon vs. Beryl's Rexidi

Althea got to her feet. "I want to see everything that comes up on that scanner. And I don't want any unauthorized acts of mercy." She pulled out the triage kit's bottom drawer. "This is all the Thanas you've got?"

I nodded.

She scooped up the hypoderms and dropped them in her pocket. She ran her finger around the edge of the drawer to make sure she had them all and snapped the bag closed. She put her knuckles against my cheek, like she was taking aim for later. "He stays alive."

"Yes, D'sha."

When she was out of earshot, Hallie leaned close. "Where's Troah?"

"She disappeared after your fight."

Hallie peered up at the stands. "She's gone with Cheska," she whispered. "Bitch." She got to her feet, unfastened her projector harness and let it drop. "I'll find her," said Hallie, and disappeared down the stairs.

I turned back to the triage kit. Troah was long gone. Hallie could search the entire arena, but in my gut, I wanted her to come back empty-handed. Once Leiban stepped into the pit, Hallie and I could just walk away.

At the edge of the ring, Althea took Leiban's arm and pulled him out of the shadows. Sweat ran down the side of his face and dripped off his chin. He was so feverish, his body was actually steaming, even in the heat of the breezeway.

Althea caught Leiban's harness and yanked him around. She took a harsh breath, as though it hurt to inhale. "We'll lose the point," she said. "You don't have to fight."

He shook his head. Behind him, one huge blue demon flashed into solidity, knuckles in the sand, tongue lolling. It threw its head back and bellowed. Silver flares haloed the scoreboard. The default timer began counting down.

Leiban started into the gate and I thought Althea might actually throw herself at him and drag him to the ground, wrestling him down until time ran out. Instead, her narrow body tightened and she hugged herself with bony arms.

The spotlight caught Leiban and the crowd roared. A volley of green flares sailed over the pit. Green smoke washed around Leiban's ankles. He tapped his projector, and Rexidi—not the prince in his human form, but the escaping, antlered half-man—shimmered under the wash of white lights, blue as his demon and twice as tall.

Althea moved, stiff-legged, to the side of the ring and stood there, shoulders hunched up to her ears. Leiban and the Silver fighter circled each other with theatric patience, not wildly like Rasse and Butch, or with Hallie's murderous determination.

I crouched next to Rasse, watching his life signs drop on the scanner, listening to him choke on his own blood. I switched screens until the diagnostic showed. Under the analysis of his pulmonary wounds was a tiny graph showing a level for transdermal augmentors—Enhancers—dropping as the Drug sign fell. In seconds, Rasse would be down to nothing.

I touched his sticky throat, feeling for his pulse. For a while it banged hard and optimistic. Then it fluttered under my fingers. Then it stopped.

Out in the ring, Rexidi sliced through the demon's blue arm, and the mob in the stands howled. Althea was a silhouette against the sweep of spotlights. She never moved as I crept through the wooden door and down the blood-stained concrete stairs. There would be no Rasha to trap me at the ground station this time. I would find Hallie, and we would wash off this blood and bile in the cistern pool.

This time, I would be free.

In the yellow-lit dark of the hallway below, the water was up to my shins.

The noise down the hall was the Meeds, tearing out the bars of their cell. Metal sheared away from rotting concrete with a human-sounding groan. I peered around the curve of the wall, not close enough for them to see me. The Meeds—no longer divided by gender, but jammed into a single cell—heaved against the bars, one mass of bodies. They pulled back and regrouped. Parts of the ceiling fell in chunks, splashing into the water on the floor.

"Try it again," said one of the girls. "Before we all drown."

I turned down the hall in the opposite direction, past the clinic and the kitchen, leaving brown, brackish swirls of Rasse's blood.

I came around the curve to Troah's closet temple and found the door wide open.

The trap under her mattress was the plug in the drain for the entire ring. Water sucked downward, through the cracks in the wood, making a slow whirlpool in the middle of the floor. Her mattress spun in it, bumping her pile of skulls up to their eye sockets in the flood.

Hallie was below somewhere, or out in the street on Troah's trail. I pushed the mattress against the wall and pulled on the trap's iron ring. The weight of the water was like a load of stones. I hauled, and made a crack of space under the trap. Water rushed past my legs, picking up speed as I pulled. It sluiced against the backs of my legs, gushing in, half throwing me into the hole. I braced myself and pulled until I could see the flimsy, slimy ladder, shaking under the force of the falling water. I let the trap fall open on the floor and slid down, scrabbling for footing on the first slick rungs. Water rushed past my waist and legs and then my shoulders, into my clothes and my mouth. Hallie had closed the trap behind her. How? I tried to yank the door shut again, lost my grip and slid down fast, grabbing at fungus and soft splinters, choking and spitting until I managed to hook an elbow. I got a foothold and climbed down shakily until the angle of the ladder let the spillage fall past me.

I hung in the blackness for a minute, suspended somewhere between the surface of the water and the ceiling. Drainage from the grates in the street gushed down the cistern walls, murky orange. Below, the surface of the cistern pool was much higher.

"Hallie?"

No answer.

"Anybody here?"

Even the runaways were gone.

Above me, the waterfall from Troah's room stuttered. The square of light from the open trap went dark and light, and dark again. The ladder shuddered as someone started down.

I froze. Not Althea. Not yet.

"This is it." A female voice, trying to be loud without shouting. "There's got to be a way up to the plaza from here."

The Meeds.

I slid down the ladder until I was up to my neck in the water and swam into the shadows by the cistern wall. If anyone was fated to be caught in the open, it would be this gang of escaping arena slaves. If they saw me, they would take me along—to grill me about my version of life-after—or to punish me for my uselessness during the fights. Either way, their agenda had nothing to do with mine.

The Meeds swarmed down, splashing and coughing, clustering around the columns of water that fell from the drainage grates, searching for a way up. One of them found the handholds in the wall, clambered up and wrestled with the grate in the street. They crawled out one by one, until their noisy escape was complete. I listened for the scrape of the grate on stone, but they left it open.

I kicked in the bottomless, bathwater pool, treading water, waiting for them to get a long head start before I followed. By now Althea would have discovered Rasse's corpse and the fact that I wasn't where she'd left me. All she had to do was walk downstairs to see that the Meeds were gone. Their trail was wide enough for the blind to follow and it looked like I was the last one out. Troah might abandon everyone, but I was sure Hallie would come back. I wanted to wait, but this was the wrong place.

I swam under the open grate, and the cascade from the street poured past me in a long arc. I ducked into the spray and started climbing, clinging to the moldy wall with toes and fingernails as the flood roared against my face and chest. I scrambled out of the hole on my belly, crawling in the flooded gutter, in the downpour, in the free air.

Half a dozen skimmers shot past me, so loaded their antigravs scraped and sparked against the paving stones. Three men and a woman ran by in green slickers and flashing hats—*Assassins!*—rushing across the plaza in the direction of the ground station. Police lights strobed the sides of windowless houses, freezing a hundred fleeing fans in a shaft of blinding white light, their slickers flapping like reptile wings.

A stumbling, uncertain fire burned along the rooftops, clawing the night sky. Smoke boiled into air too dense to lift it, not quite wet enough for the flame to smother. More lights cut through the low violet haze, knifing sharp edges in the rain, throwing everything into purple relief.

I got to my feet, close against the arena wall.

Troah. She was at the center of this. I mouthed her name, and tasted the cilantro tang of her. All I had to do was lean into the current of her will, and any sudden wind would blow me to her. I knew where she was—at the ground station, arguing with Cheska, or haggling with some freighter captain, already overloaded. She would be back, and I knew that, because I owed her for saving Hallie.

But where was Hallie? It was too dangerous to stay put.

The Meeds were out of sight, but the next person to come through the grate would be Althea. Was Leiban still fighting? I started toward the main gate, past elbows and wet slickers, making my way along the wall.

Ahead, the arch of the main gate was a smoky opening beyond the betting screens. It was as good as a free show, but no one was watching. The betting screens were deserted as well, and it seemed to me that the bleachers were nearly empty. Rasse's fight was the one everyone had depended on. Leiban was too predictable to stick around for.

I leaned on the bars of the main gate, my cheek against the winding filigree. The power was off again, and the rain made a thin curtain over the haze and projected light. Green smoke drifted in the hot air, choking thick, almost too dense to see through.

Leiban and the Silver's demon grappled, sogas ringing across the sand. Rexidi seemed unhurt. The demon was missing a leg, but the fighter inside was still standing, half-visible in his pall of projected light. Leiban's holo mirrored his moves, graceful instead of clumsily adapted, like Rasse's dog. He danced in and out of range, fast, efficient, smooth, playing out the fable the way it never ended for the real prince. He was winning, and winning beautifully. I looked for Althea in the distant shadows. Her skinny silhouette could have been one more weapon leaning against the bars.

Rain slapped at my clothes, soaked and filthy from the cistern. Leiban swung with consummate grace and speed, holding his opponent, and his Failure at bay. For a second I could pretend it might never happen to him.

His soga cut through blue hands, slashed left, right and down. The demon flung its arms out, chromed claws vanishing as his soga dropped. Leiban swung again and the boy inside the holo folded over his belly, falling into a drift of white smoke.

Rexidi raised his antlered head, but there was no one left to cheer.

Someone coughed and I wheeled around. Troah. Black under her eyes, streaked with grit. Hallie was with her, nervously hunched into herself, wearing a shirt for once, arms crossed over her chest.

"You idiot," said Troah. "Who told you to leave the ring?"

"I thought you were gone. I thought—"

"You thought the underground might take me along for free?" She shook her head. "Not a chance in hell." For the first time, she looked tired.

"You can't go back," I said. "The power's out. The place is flooding. The Meeds tore their cage down and ran away. And Althea knows Rasse was 'hanced."

Hallie's eyes widened at the news about the Meeds, but Troah was hardly listening. "You told her about Rasse?"

"No," I said. "She figured it out."

"And," prompted Troah, "you said . . . ?"

I stared at her. "I didn't say anything about you."

Troah shrugged, as though I should have taken full responsibility.

"Rasse's dead?" said Hallie.

I nodded and she wiped rain off her face. "Poor bastard."

Troah hooked her arm in mine. "Let's go."

"Where?" I said.

"To the ring, of course," said Troah.

"What?"

"We have to," said Hallie grimly. "No slaves are getting off this planet without a free person to run them through the ground station."

Troah nodded. "They're scanning everyone. When they found runaways dressed in free clothes, the police just grabbed them, no questions asked." She squeezed my arm. "Think, Jatahn. Who's the last free person we can get our hands on?"

"Althea?" I said. "But she won't go. She doesn't even think there's a war."

"It doesn't matter what that woman thinks," said Troah. "All she needs to know is that you can keep Leiban alive when he Fails."

I swallowed. "She won't buy it."

"She will," said Troah. "He's the only thing she really wants."

THIRTEEN

Althea was waiting at the top of the ladder. She didn't say a word until the three of us stood in front of her, dripping on the floor in the unsteady ceiling light.

She kicked the trap shut. The noise banged around the small room, through the open door, into the hallway where Leiban steadied himself against the wall.

Water trickled from the ceiling onto the back of my neck. I shivered. Althea eyed me. And then Hallie.

"You," she said to Hallie, low and hoarse. "I can't believe you're part of this."

Hallie gave her a tight shrug. She looked genuinely scared.

Althea turned to Troah. "The Meeds are gone," she said. "Nice of you to take them with you, Troah. I never knew you were such a humanitarian."

"They should have waited," said Troah. "There's nowhere for them to go."

"You 'hanced Rasse," said Althea. "You told him to lose."

Troah nodded.

"For thirty-to-one odds?" Althea's voice was far too calm. "What were you planning to do with the money? Buy yourself something nice to wear?" She pointed at a wet pile of embroidered green cloth—the clothes I'd worn outside the ring last night. "If you wanted to get out, you should have told me. I would have sent you home to Rasha."

"Rasha's going to be here by tomorrow morning," said Troah. "Along with the rest of my family. If you had any brains at all, Althea, you'd leave right now."

I expected Althea to yank her off the ground and beat her until there was nothing left, but even Althea could see she was missing some important detail. "You were trying to get a place on a ship," she said, "but you couldn't do it yourself. Who did you think was going to help you?"

"Frei's friends," said Troah.

"Frei's friends?" Althea studied her and her face clouded with comprehension. "That's why you set Rasse up? So they could win their bets and leave town? But Rasse won. They lost their money. And now you're stuck. You're all stuck."

Troah cocked her head at Leiban. "How're you feeling, Rexidi?"

"He's fine," said Althea.

"He's dying," said Troah.

Althea flushed from her neck to her forehead. She caught Troah by the front of her shirt, lifted her onto her toes and shook her. Her self-control boiled off, like steam. Her mouth twisted with threats she couldn't quite make into complete words.

Troah hung in the air, not bothering to struggle. "I should tell you something, D'sha . . ."

"You don't tell me *anything*," said Althea.

"Leiban doesn't have to die," said Troah. "None of us do. Frei was right. There's a way—"

Althea punched her in the face, slamming her into the wall. Troah dropped on the floor, holding her jaw. Blood leaked out of the corner of her mouth. She sat there for a minute and then wiped her hands on her knees and got up. "So," she said, breathless and shaky. "Let him die. Who cares? You can find another boy."

Althea balled her fists and swung. Troah ducked under the first punch, but the second caught her in the throat. She fell on her knees, gasping.

"Stop it," said Hallie.

Althea whirled around. "You," she panted, "have done *enough*. You want to stay, and fight, you *shut* up."

"I don't want to stay," said Hallie. "And I won't fight anymore."

"Because Frei was right?" Althea's voice cracked over the taunt. "Because you'll be a free woman?"

"Why do you think Frei put Tony through that kind of hell?" asked Hallie. "You think it was just a theory? Or an impulse?"

"Frei was out of his *mind*."

"He freed eight slaves," said Hallie. "He saved their lives."

Althea squeezed her eyes shut. "You're part of this. I can't *believe* you're part of this."

She turned to Troah again, but Hallie caught her shoulder. "You want Leiban tomorrow? Or for another month? Or for a year? Or twenty more? You can have him. You understand? There's a way he can *survive*."

Althea shook her off, but coming from Hallie, the idea seemed to carry some tiny amount of weight.

"It doesn't take long," said Hallie. "It won't hurt him. We just need one thing."

"You want me to pay," said Althea, in a low, ugly tone.

"We can't stay here," said Hallie.

"You want me to get you offworld," said Althea. "And then you want me to give you whatever you need to pass for free people."

Out in the hallway, Leiban took one sideways step, and another. Three or four paces would put him out of sight. He was the pawn in all of this, and anyone could see Althea wavering. With enough clothing, Hallie might not be recognized outside the ring, but Leiban was tattooed to the ears, permanently marked. No matter how he carried himself, no matter how he dressed, surviving Failure would make no difference in his life.

Another step and Althea saw him out of the corner of her eye. "Where're you going?"

Under the blue lines, his skin was colorless. His flesh seemed to have shrunk around his bones. He didn't have the strength to answer. He leaned against the seeping wall and collapsed slowly onto the wet floor.

Althea stumbled across the hall and crouched next to him. "Tell me how you do it," she said.

Hallie and I glanced at each other.

"We need the money first," I said.

"Call the ground station," said Hallie. "Tell them we're coming."

"Not yet," said Althea. "Not until I see this work. Then you can have whatever you want." Leiban quivered and she cradled his head.

Troah pushed herself to her feet, one hand over her throat. "Get a scanner," she rasped to Hallie. She nodded at me. "Do it."

Hallie bolted off in the direction of the clinic. I turned my back to Althea and peeled the next to last needle off my leg. Even if Althea had the time and imagination for some ulterior plan when Leiban was free, it wouldn't matter. I would still have one needle left, and it wouldn't take

Troah long to find some other way to use Leiban as a lever. Or she would kill him.

Althea gave me a suspicious look as I crouched beside her boy. "Troah taught you what to do? Already?"

"Frenna came with her own skills." Troah, uninvited, settled next to Althea the way she'd settled next to the Failing Meeds in the breezeway. "Her methods are different from Frei's. More dependable."

Althea's jaw tightened. "Did the Meeds know that?"

"Oh, yes," said Troah. "That's why they were too scared to fight."

Hallie came around the curve of the hallway, wet to her knees. She handed me a scanner and dropped Frei's triage kit next to me. "Is there another drain on your end of the ring, Althea?"

Althea shook her head, not knowing, or not caring.

"There's water coming down the stairs," said Hallie. "The clinic and the kitchen are flooding."

"So get a bucket," said Althea.

Hallie stiffened, but she didn't leave.

On the scanner, Leiban's readings were right where I knew they'd be. Green Viral indicators hovered along the bottom of the graph, just a hair lower than his life signs. I touched his damp, hot arm, and felt the tension under his skin. He was hardly letting himself breathe, holding every muscle tight, determined not to shake and scream like a wounded Meed.

Althea peered at the screen and chewed her lips.

I palmed the slapneedle in my other hand. It felt strategically wrong to let Althea see it, though even if she tried to grab it, Hallie could grab it right back. If Althea did anything out of line, she would doom Leiban. But there was something about the way she held herself that bothered me. She was tense, but not with a lover's—or a mistress'—concern. She was ready to spring up on her feet and fight.

Leiban's cold fingers slid into my hand. He felt the packaged needle and turned his eyes up at me. His face was a gray crumple of exhaustion and betrayed dignity. "Don't," he whispered.

"Don't what?" Althea bent too close and the readings on the scanner scrambled. She sat back. "Don't what?"

Leiban rolled his eyes at me, too weak to fight me off.

I put down the scanner and stripped open the slapneedle. The adhesive snugged on my palm, warm and tight. Althea stared at the screen in tight-lipped horror, watching Leiban's levels drop. She flinched as I put my hand on his throat, covering tattooed birds and flowers, and permanent blue chain links. I felt his pulse, thready under hot skin, knowing what I was about to do was wrong. Nothing could have been more wrong. This was Rexidi's fairy tale— only one possible ending—and it occurred to me that if I wasn't the prince's master, or a trusted companion, the best I could be was one of those lurking demons. I slid my knuckles under his collar for better pressure. His carotid shuddered against my palm, and I felt it stop. On the screen, the Viral indicator touched bottom. I pressed the needle in.

Leiban went limp. The scanner blanked. Althea took a breath. And another. She looked up from the screen, eyes sharp.

"You've killed him," she said to me.

"No—" I started, but Troah interrupted.

"He would have appreciated that," she said. "But then, we're doing this for you, Althea, not him."

"He'll be all right," I said. "It takes a few minutes." I kept the needle against his throat, making sure the injection was complete, holding his wrist with my other hand, waiting for a pulse.

Althea shifted her crouch, her arms at strange angles. "What're you trying to say, Troah?"

"Think about it," said Troah. "What does he have now? Freedom?"

"That's not what he wants," said Althea.

Troah raised her eyebrows in artificial surprise. "It's not?"

Althea rubbed her knees with wet hands, leaving dark stains on her green jumpsuit. "He wants things to go on," she said. "Things should stay the same. That's all anyone wants."

"That might be true for you," said Troah.

"Troah . . ." Hallie gave her a warning look.

I felt a quiver in Leiban's throat. "I've got a pulse," I said.

Althea took his wrist, feeling under the wiry tendons. Hallie let out a relieved hiss, but we all knew this was a long way from over.

Troah leaned over Leiban. "You still haven't told me," she said to Althea. "What does he have to live for?"

"I don't have to justify this to you, witch," said Althea.

"You have to justify it to him," said Troah. "What is he now? A free man with his life's story all over his body? Or were you planning to put him in the ring again?"

"He's mine," said Althea, but she sounded defensive now, and almost frightened. "We'll stay together."

Leiban trembled, breaking out in gooseflesh. He lay against my arm, lighter and less substantial than he should have been, wasted with the effort of trying to die.

Troah cocked her head, poised for the kill. "I see," she said. "You'll marry him."

"What?" Althea stared at her.

"You can make him do that," said Troah. "And if he doesn't love you, it doesn't matter. You've made him do everything else you wanted."

Althea's body tightened. "You don't know how he feels about me."

"No?" said Troah, and she put her hands over her heart, eyes wide and pathetic. "Don't," she whispered, mocking Leiban. "Don't."

Hallie got to her feet. "Troah, that's enough."

Althea flushed dark, dark red. "He didn't want to *die!*" she shouted. "No one *wants* to die."

Troah laughed and held her Hand out to Leiban, letting it hover palm-down over his chest. "Take it," she said to him. "My gift. There's nothing she can do to you now."

Leiban swallowed, and I felt his weak pulse pound. His free hand fluttered, a fractional motion.

"No!" Althea shot to her feet, one fist clamped around Troah's Hand, the other in her pocket, scrabbling at something. She pulled out a hypoderm and the cap fell off. Oily black liquid dripped out.

Thanas.

I had time to yell. Hallie shoved past me, stepping over Leiban. Althea sank the needle into Troah's arm, fast and deliberate as a soga strike. Hallie pushed Troah to one side, grabbed Althea and slammed her against the seeping wall, holding her by her neck.

I yanked myself up from Leiban, who slid sideways, limp and cheated.

"She has more, Hallie," I shouted, "she's got—" She had all the Thanas needles she'd taken from me, to make sure I didn't kill Rasse. Hallie wound her fingers into the hem of Althea's pocket and ripped it open. A dozen hypos spilled out onto the floor.

"Frenna?"

I turned around. Troah was standing under the dank yellow lights, swaying a little. Her legs gave way and she sat heavily. She steadied herself on the floor, taking short breaths. She looked around until she found me, crouched right in front of her with the scanner. Her graph was a weird stasis—Viral signs and life signs suspended on the graph, frozen solid.

"Troah—" I touched her shoulder, and she lay down on

the wet concrete. Black Thanas smeared over her arm. A black welt was forming under her skin.

"Is she dead?" said Hallie.

"You should be glad if she is," Althea choked. "She's a menace. She's always been bad fucking luck. Good ridda—" Hallie's grip tightened. Althea kicked her in the ribs.

"*Is* she dead?" demanded Hallie.

"Not yet." Still no motion on the graph.

Hallie took her hands off Althea's throat, pushed me out of the way, picked up Troah and headed for Frei's room.

I grabbed the triage kit, started after her.

"Wait!" Althea's voice cracked through the close air.

I stopped. She was on the floor, next to Leiban, patting his cheeks. Leiban stared past her at the ceiling.

"At least tell me if he'll survive," said Althea.

"He might," I said. "It depends on what he believes."

Troah's body jerked each time Hallie pounded her chest, limp on the bed, bloodlessly pale.

"If I thought she could feel it," panted Hallie, "I might enjoy this more." She pounded again. "What's the scanner say?"

"Nothing." The readings were still motionless—she wasn't dead, but not exactly alive either. I dug in the triage kit for the last hypoderm of Virus, but when I pushed my thumb into Troah's arm, there was hardly enough pressure to bring up one blue vein.

Hallie pounded some more. Troah bobbed lifelessly. "Stupid," said Hallie. "*So* stupid. If she wanted to kill herself, why give Althea the satisfaction of doing it for her?"

I pawed in the triage kit for anything that might be useful, past everything that Frei had ever thrown in: used hypos and empty plastic casings—half-unraveled sterile gauze.

Hallie's fists on Troah's chest made hollow thuds in the

quiet room. I found a broken pair of scissors, bits of balled up paper and one sock.

Hallie wiped her face. "This is Troah's quick exit before her family wins the war and shows up tomorrow and finds out she's still alive. If I was their *troah*, I'd off myself too."

"It's not suicide," I said. "She's not scared of any of them."

"You've got a better explanation?" Hallie shook Troah by the shoulders. "You don't get out of this mess so easy, you hear?"

More junk at the bottom of the triage kit, and finally, something I could use.

Surgical gloves turned inside out and knotted so the yellow oil on the fingertips wouldn't seep—Enhancers.

I grabbed the gloves, found the scissors again, and poked holes in the plastic fingers. Yellow oil welled out.

"Move," I said to Hallie. She saw what I was doing and jerked back.

I smeared the stuff over Troah's neck, not much, just a thin layer of suggestion.

Hallie crouched over her. "Breathe, you contrary bitch," she hissed in Troah's ear. "You can drop dead some other time."

On the scanner, Troah's life signs wobbled into motion. Her mouth worked. Her fingers clawed the sheets. Her eyes opened, rolled back to the whites, and she took a strangled sob of a breath.

Hallie gave me a sharp grin. "She'll never forgive you, Favored One."

Troah's hand found mine. I looked down to see the tips of my fingers touching the dark tattoo in the middle of her palm . . . hot . . . but not burning. Her fingers wrapped tight around my knuckles, but it wasn't the familiar, overwhelming pressure of her will crowding into mine. This was communication, subtle as a nod across a room, and it took me a moment to understand.

On the scanner, her indicators fell like stones.

Hallie gave a yelp. "What the hell? *Now* she's Failing? What the *hell*?"

Troah's body heaved. Her arms shot straight down at her sides, feet together, her body stiff with concentration. Hallie pinned her against the twisted pillows. I grabbed her legs. Muscles jumped under my fingers. Troah wrenched from side to side, mouth wide open, eyes squeezed shut.

She shook and the bed shook, and it felt like the floor shook too.

"A 'hance shouldn't have started that," said Hallie.

"She's doing it herself," I panted. "She's pushing her own levels down."

"*She* is? How? What for? But you can use the Virevir—" Hallie glanced at me over Troah's flailing body. "How many needles do you have?"

"One."

"*That's* what this is about?" Hallie shoved Troah deeper into the mattress, shouting at her. "Nine years in collar and you *still* think you can snap your fingers and get whatever you want?"

The convulsion yanked Troah back and forth, tangling her legs in the sheets, her hair on the pillow. It waned and Hallie let go.

"How low is she?"

"Low," I said, and showed her the scanner. Troah's readings grazed the bottom.

Hallie sat on the edge of the bed, hunched over her knees. "We should walk out of here," she whispered. "We should leave her and take our chances."

"We can't," I whispered back.

"Why not?"

"If she's free, Troah can get us past the ground station," I said.

"With your very last needle?" said Hallie. "What about

when you Fail in—what—seventeen years?" She blinked instead of adding, *And what about me, in two?*

"There's more Virevir," I said. "I can culture it."

"Culture it?"

I pointed at Troah. "From her. It's a cancer. All it needs is a medium to grow in."

Hallie stared at Troah's pale face. "You know what's going on in her mind right now?"

"Are you kidding?"

"She's got a list in there," said Hallie. "All her revenges are charted out, and all she ever does is figure out how to get from point A to point B." She rubbed her arms. "She probably had this whole episode planned weeks ago—with Leiban Failing, and Althea losing control, and us sitting around, waiting for her to Fail. And now all we can do is wait for the next installment."

"She'll kill Rasha," I said.

"And Althea," said Hallie. "And probably Leiban. She'll take this whole place down."

Something rumbled, behind the walls.

Hallie sat up straight.

The rumble came again. I felt the floor tremble. It resonated in my teeth. It shook cold drops of water off the ceiling.

Hallie went to the door and opened it.

Water from the hallway surged past her, gushing up around her hips, soaking her to the chest. Hallie bullied the door shut and kicked at the water on the floor. She swished the water with her fingers. "It's full of sand." She stared at me. "Sand from the ring."

"The weather shields are off," I said. "It was raining inside during Leiban's match."

"There's no way for the pit to drain," said Hallie.

"Has the pit ever been open to the weather?"

Hallie shook her head, eyes wide. Outside, metal

squealed, and something splashed into the hallway. "We'll drown," she said, "if the damn Faraqui don't get here first."

"Block the door," I said.

She nodded and dragged the sofa across the filthy green carpet with no visible effort.

Troah wobbled, lips pulled back, dribbles of sweat down her neck. The next convulsion built inside her, shuddering into her hips and knees. Her breathing changed to short moans. On the scanner, red and green lines wound along the lowest end of the graph. I peeled the last bit of damp gray tape off my leg, and split the slapneedle's thin plastic envelope.

Hallie came over and sat beside me. "I can't believe this bitch is going to be our last resort."

"Think of her as a great change," I said.

Troah's skin quivered. The muscles in her neck spasmed. Her face convulsed, blind, horrible expressions flickering over her mouth and eyes as she sucked in gulps of air. The Viral indicator and life signs wound across the bottom of the scanner, working their way to their lowest, fatal point. I clamped one arm across her waist, and positioned the slapneedle in my palm, ready for the last, slewing wave.

For a moment, all I could hear was water in the hallway. Then Troah let out a wail of pain. Her body rocked and squirmed, fingers grabbing at nothing, toes spread, mouth wide open. On the scanner, her indicators flickered, blinked, and bobbled off the graph.

I pressed my last needle through the tender skin inside her elbow. Her pulse pounded under my palm. A warm dribble of blood welled between our skins.

And then the lights went off.

"Shit," said Hallie.

Pitchy, humid blackness. The scanner's yellow grid was the only prick of light in the blanket of dark. Water trickled across the floor.

Troah's pulse stopped. Her body went slack, a motionless island of heat in the bed.

We waited. The lights didn't even flicker.

"Isn't there some kind of backup?" I asked.

"Not exactly," said Hallie.

Somewhere down by the training room, muffled by thick walls, an alarm started, blaring in short bursts.

"What's that?"

"The security system." Hallie's weight came off the mattress. "Otis must have set it after the fights. If the power cuts off, it locks down all the cells and the front gate."

"What about the room where the cistern is?"

Hallie hesitated. "I don't know."

I fumbled for the scanner. "Does it turn the lights back on?"

"Only if it has enough power. First it's going to secure the ring and call the police."

"The *police*?"

"We have to get out," said Hallie. "Right now."

"The police're swamped," I said. "The whole city's on fire. Why would they bother to come here?"

"Because," said Hallie, "the Chief Inspector's a *very* committed fan."

Her feet slapped in pools of water. In a minute, the couch scraped across the floor. I heard the latch rattle and the door banged open. The alarm blared, louder, echoing off the walls, and the flood pushed into the room with a rank puff of mildew. Warm water, full of grit and sand, rushed over my feet and under the bed. It smacked the wall behind me. When the surface calmed, it was past my knees.

Hallie sloshed over to the bed. "Is she coming out of it?"

There was no pulse, no sign of life. "Not yet."

Hallie sucked air through her teeth. "We can't wait." She felt past me and lifted Troah off the bed. The soft splash was the scanner, falling into the water.

"Wait," I said, groping for it in the swirling, tepid grit. When I found it, the screen was blank.

"Leave it," said Hallie.

Outside Frei's room, water rushed down the stairs. The current was strong enough to grab my ankles, and I held onto Hallie's elbow in the smothering dark. We found the edge of the wall, and groped for the cell doors with their plastic name slats. *The Rock. Rexidi.* By the time we reached Naritte's, Troah should have been breathing.

"Is she doing anything?" I shouted over the rush of water and the alarm.

"No, dammit." Hallie's fingers slipped past mine, searching Troah's throat for a pulse. "She can't just *die.*"

"It's got to be a reaction to the drugs," I said. "It's the Thanas. Or the Enhancers. Or the Virevir."

"Make up your mind," said Hallie.

Up ahead, the alarm blasted in deafening bursts, close and loud enough to make my bones vibrate. I felt along the wet, moldy wall, trying to calculate where Althea might be. The stretch of corridor between the High Set cells and Troah's closet temple went on and on. I let go of Hallie, thinking frantically that I'd somehow missed Troah's door. The water was noticeably higher—up to my waist, and as far as I could tell, rising.

Troah's rough closet door scraped my hand. "Here!" I yelled to Hallie, and felt her bump against me. I twisted the handle. It didn't move. Twisted harder. It edged in its fittings, but it didn't turn.

"It's locked!" I yelled over the alarm.

Hallie shoved Troah into my arms, heavy and lifeless. In the blackness, the alarm blasted a rhythm as Hallie wrestled with the door, shoving and wrenching. Nothing.

"Let's try the main gate," panted Hallie. "Maybe Althea's gone. Maybe she left it open for us."

Incredibly unlikely. But better than standing under the

alarm in the rising water. Hallie splashed toward the next set of stairs, leaving me to wrestle Troah's limp weight.

"Wait!" She couldn't hear me. I followed, almost swimming, Troah's head lolling on my shoulder. Something brushed the side of my face. Powdery, and dry. Something else hit my face, not big, but sharp. More of it fell in the water. Under the alarm, between the blasts, I could hear the stones groaning in the walls.

More powder from the ceiling. "Hallie!" I yelled. "Hallie, wait! *Hallie!*"

My shout echoed in abrupt silence.

The alarms were off.

Which meant the police were here? More of the ceiling pattered in the dark water around me. I listened for Hallie but couldn't hear anything over the ringing in my ears.

Troah moved in my arms. Her mouth brushed my ear. Her lips were deathly cold. "Rasha . . ."

The floor quivered under my feet. I braced myself, expecting the entire ring to fall in—but there was a sharp tang of ozone in the air now. My skin prickled with static and every wet hair stood up on the back of my neck.

Skimmers. Close by. Landing.

In the *ring*?

"Put me down." Troah pushed loose from me and slid into the water. I couldn't see her. I tried to steady her. Her nearness was like ice.

"Are you . . ." What should I say? Was she all right? Free? In some way alive?

"Rasha," she whispered.

"I don't know," I said. "It might be the police."

"No." Her freezing hand found my wrist. "We'll leave," she said in a low voice, "but first tell me something."

"What?"

She pulled me close. She was as frail as burnt paper, as thin as feathers. I touched her shoulders, her spine, amazed at how fragile and hollow her bones were. If I squeezed, I was afraid they would snap.

She leaned her cold cheek against mine. "You must feel this." Her Hand came up over the nape of my neck. "Don't you feel it?"

Not heat this time, not lust or some reassuring illusion of comfort. This was silent, agonizing revelation—a wounding pain, like a nail being driven through my throat. My head jerked backwards. My mouth hung open, but she wouldn't let me scream. Her Hand traveled down my spine, along my ribs to the mortal spaces behind my heart. She pinned everything she wanted in suffocating crimson under my eyelids: power and submission, loyalty and betrayal, fierce love and boiling, bottomless, wordless hatred.

She released me and I staggered in the hip-deep flood. What she'd had before—what Rasha had granted her by letting her live—was stronger now. Maybe it was me. Maybe it was the arcane mixture of cancer and drugs. Maybe it was simply the right time.

She'd become what she'd always known she would be. *Troah.*

"Anybody down there?"

Rasha's voice echoed in the stairwell. A handheld light gleamed at the top of the training room stairs.

I leaned on the crumbling wall, out of breath, out of sight. Had she planned every part of this from the time I'd set foot inside the arena? I tried to catch a glimpse of her, because if I could see how she looked, I would know.

"He'll believe you," whispered Troah, "if you tell him I'm dead."

"Jatahn? Can you hear me?"

That was the voice of a doomed man.

"Jatahn?"

"Answer him."

I waded unsteadily to the bottom of the stairs. "D'Rasha?"

"There! Are you by yourself?" The light flashed around, glimmering off the wet walls. I looked for Troah, but all I could see was a faint blue haze in the dark over the water.

Rasha picked his way down to where the flood lapped at the stone stairs. He smiled at me and the stripe across his eyes creased in real pleasure.

"Come up, Jatahn," he said. "The fighting's over. I've come to take you home."

Upstairs, all the spotlights were on, white and glaring, flattening the black walls of the ring to shadowy cardboard. The weather shields were back on, and the sky loomed in its oval shape, florid and gaseous. Skimmers packed the ring, each hull marked with the blue-on-white Faraqui Eye.

Scurrying, immaculate, Faraqui-bred slaves were everywhere. Half a dozen boys cranked the dropgates up by hand. Girls with shovels dug a channel around the perimeter of the ring in an attempt to drain it. On the other side of the main gate, smoke drifted with ground fog, darker gray layered over lighter gray. The buildings across the plaza were charred silhouettes, and the street was deserted.

I didn't see Hallie.

Rasha stopped at the edge of the pit where too much rain had made sand into a gritty soup. Ten or twelve meters in, the soup turned to half-solidified muck. Toward the middle, where the skimmers were, the surface was hard enough to stand on.

I smoothed my tangled hair and soaked clothes, half believing this was a bad dream. It felt like one.

Rasha bent next to my ear. "Where's Troah?"

I hesitated, wondering how much, as her brother, he could feel.

"She escaped?" he asked.

I shook my head.

"She's still here." As if this was the answer he'd been most afraid of.

"She's dead, D'sha."

The relief in his face was undisguised. "How?"

"Althea," I said, "it was Althea."

Rasha put his hand on my arm, gentle, almost grateful.

He led me around the breezeway to where an elderly Faraqui man stood, surrounded by other slavers, all draped in white. Sand coated the hems of their robes. Their sweat, dense with curry, filled the humid air, and breathing it made my chest hurt. This was no deep genetic memory, or sentimental longing. It was simple fear.

The older man nodded as one of the slavers ticked off points, finger by finger.

". . . some isolated resistance from the police. The runaways, of course, and here"—the slaver gestured at the black walls—"structural problems due to the flooding. We're opening the drain into the cisterns, and that should prevent the—"

Rasha cleared his throat. "Kassim?"

The older man turned. "Ah. Rasha. Yes?"

Rasha pushed me forward. "Kassim, this is the Jatahn girl I told you about."

"The old bloodline?" He frowned at me. "She's filthy."

"She cleans up well," said Rasha. "Quite authentic."

Kassim came closer and wrapped his damp hand under my chin, examining my face. I held my breath, waiting for the stab of pheromonic desire that would grab me by the throat and shove me to my knees. I stared past his white head wrap at the black ceiling, listening to my heart pound. I didn't feel anything. Neither did he.

I pulled away and Kassim blinked, insulted, or vindicated.

"She has the look, more or less," he said. "But she can't possibly be pure. Her hair isn't . . ." He made brushing motions with his fingers. "Her body's not . . ." He squinted and shook his head. "Besides, she's trouble. You can see it in her face." He wiped his hands. "And she's filthy."

Rasha stood next to me, wordless for a moment. "She's as close as we're going to get," he said.

"To what?" Kassim asked blandly.

"To a renewal of the Jatahn gene pool," said Rasha.

Kassim shrugged. "If you want to run a cloning program, and you think she's a good genetic source, that's fine. But frankly, we've done without the Jatahn for a hundred years. I'm not sure how much we need them now."

"It's a matter of tradition," said Rasha.

"As you say," said Kassim, "but at the moment, tradition is a low priority." He made a small, conciliatory gesture. "Join us for the Blessing, Rasha. And bring her, if she's what you say she is."

A crowd of slavers was collecting on the far side of the office, and Kassim's group shuffled off to join them. Rasha trailed along.

I stayed where I was, hoping none of them would look back, but Rasha did.

He stopped and turned around, his face pinched with anger. For a second he looked exactly like Troah. He beckoned to me. I didn't move. He made a sharper motion. I stayed where I was. He held up a finger and pointed it at the ground.

Sit, he meant. *Stay.*

He stalked away, and when he was out of sight, I spat where he'd been standing.

I headed for the stairs. Whatever Troah had in mind, time was running out. If Hallie knew the cistern was accessible, she might already be outside. I started down the bloodstained clinic access. Three steps into the darkness, instead of Troah, I found Althea.

Her sharp, narrow face was white with exhaustion, bruised-looking under her eyes. She stared at me.

"You look like hell," she said.

"So do you," I said, "D'sha."

She ran her hands over her face, pushed her hair behind her ears. Dried tears patterned her cheeks.

"He's dead?" I whispered.

She shook her head, almost a shudder. "He's sleeping. I had to see what the noise was." She stepped into the light and saw the crowd of skimmers in the ring. "God," she said. "We're infested." She glanced across the sand where white-robed backs clustered on the other side of the office. The muffled cadence of men's voices drifted in the heavy air. "What're they doing?"

"Blessing themselves," I said.

Althea's eyes flickered around the edges of the ring, where the level of the sand was now distinctly lower than the breezeway. "They'll need more than a blessing when my pit collapses. It's not a goddamn landing pad."

I started down the stairs, but she caught my arm and pulled me into the shadows of the breezeway. "We need to talk." The corners of her mouth pulled tight. "Tell me about the slaves you freed."

Her fingers were wrapped over my wrist like steel wires. I winced and was amazed when she let go. "What do you want to know?" I said.

"What happened to them afterwards?"

"They just—lived their lives." I hoped.

"Were any of them . . . lovers?" The word seemed to catch in her throat.

I nodded, wondering if grief could really touch this woman. "They were all lovers," I said. "That's why they tried to save each other."

Althea stared through the front gate at the charred ruins outside. Morning light sifted through the smoke and low fog. "I can't take him to any other arena," she said. "Everyone knows him. Even if we went to some buttfuck amateur ring out in the Frontier, someone'd recognize him from his tattoos. I can't take him anywhere. We can't stay here." She let her breath out through her teeth in a ragged hiss.

"I did the wrong thing," she whispered. "I should have let him go. I did the wrong goddamn thing."

It would have been suicidal to point out that Leiban was a free man, and by rights, should be making his own decisions about his life. I kept my mouth shut, waiting for the end of this conversation.

She took a breath. "What happens if he's reinjected?"

"Reinjected?"

"With the Virus, girl."

Strategic lies were beyond me. "I don't know."

"Could he go for another twenty years?"

"I don't know."

She wiped her face. "You think it might kill him?"

Voices echoed under the breezeway's vaulted ceiling, mixing with the moist air, the old Faraqui language, the same familiar sounds and intonations as the insidious lullabies from my childhood. There were no particular words I understood, except one.

Troah.

They paused and said it together.

Troah.

Althea turned to me. "Tell me where Troah is."

"You killed her," I said. "Remember?"

"You'd be gone by now if she was dead." She glanced around. "And where's Hallie?"

"I don't know."

"Find her," said Althea. She clenched her teeth, as though she was forcing out the words. "I owe her. And you. For what you did. As soon as I find Otis, we're leaving. Both of you are coming with me and Leiban."

I didn't bother to hide my skepticism. "We are?"

"Leiban needs a medic," said Althea, "and whatever happens, I'll need a lead fighter. You'll both stay with me. You'll do your jobs. And if you work hard, when you hit your twentieth year . . ." She let her breath out.

"What about Troah?" I said.

Althea's face went wire-tight.

"Althea?"

Otis's voice drifted through the breezeway. He beckoned at Althea from the office. She took a step toward him and stopped. She turned back to me, her concern for Leiban now a dread fear of what I might do to him once I was out of her sight.

She clamped her hand on my neck and steered me down the breezeway, toward the office and the Faraqui Blessing.

Otis sat at his desk, watching a holo of a thin brown-skinned man. The sound was off, and the man beat his fleshless fists in the air, noiselessly.

Althea dropped into a chair next to him and stared at the holo. "Don't you know who that is?" she said.

"The Emir, of course," said Otis.

"Turn him up—" She reached for the volume but he blocked her. Althea spread her hands on the table, like she was trying not to punch Otis in the mouth. "They dug the damn Emir out of his mausoleum for this stupid war, and you don't want to know what he has to say?"

"I know what he's saying," said Otis. "His side is losing, but he won't admit it. It's just more propaganda from the Emirate Report."

The thin brown man—the Emir himself—raised his aged fist and shook it. Behind him, a map showed the Frontier as a bright red welt between Faraqui blue and Emirate green. As I watched, shades of green flitted over the red Frontier, obliterating it. Another sliver of green edged over the blue border of the Faraque. And another.

Otis shut the holo off. "Wishful thinking," he said.

Althea leaned over the table. "How much do you get for being Rasha's friend, Otis?"

Otis ignored her, focused on the Blessing, elbows on his desk, chin balanced on steepled fingers.

"I just wanted to let you know," said Althea. "I'm out of here. I want my pay, plus bonus, and I want it now."

"There's no reason for you to leave," said Otis. "And there's nowhere for you to go." He gestured at the smoky ruins outside the main gate. "At least Traja's secure."

"Is it?" Althea pointed at the Faraqui skimmers in the ring. "If Traja's so secure, why'd these clowns land in a place where they could lock themselves in?" She pointed at the front gate. "Why didn't they use the ground station?"

"It was destroyed in the riots last night," said Otis.

"No one's stupid enough to burn the only bridge out of town," said Althea. "And these idiots need it too much to blow it up." She shook her head. "I know strategy, and I know *that*—" She curled her lip. "*That's* wishful thinking."

Neither of them was paying any attention to me. I edged toward the far end of the office.

Troah.

The word wavered in the air, a different tone to it now, as though the Blessing was about over. I stepped across the wet breezeway, behind a black column, ankle-deep in warm water. Beyond the clutter of Faraqui skimmers, someone in white moved into the shadows of the breezeway. Hallie, I thought, waiting for me by the stairs that led to Frei's room. If I went the long way around, Althea wouldn't see me. I started away from the column, but another motion across the ring caught me short.

It was just a flicker, as though someone had lit a match, then moved to block the flare. I squinted past the skimmers and the pools of water.

A gust of wind blew against my face. Dry wind.

Abruptly it was silent—no shovels in sand, no chanting. The slavers came out of their huddle to look at the sky. Grinding gray clouds blew apart, congealed again, and thinned. Blue morning sky showed through.

Rasha lifted his robes and stepped to the edge of the muddy pit, smiling. "It's a good sign," he said. "An excellent sign."

No one was listening. One by one, the Faraqui turned, like a flock of white birds, to stare at the woman at the top of Frei's stairs.

Troah.

Her forced Failure had mauled her, sucked her dry of everything but a husk of flesh. Hair fell across her face in gaunt white strands. She was so frail, the wind was enough to pick her up and blow her across the quicksand pit. She drifted toward the Faraqui like some nightmare spirit.

They stared at her, transfixed by her.

I took a step forward to the edge of the pit, heart pounding.

Once her kin figured out who she was, they would *shred* her.

I stepped into the soupy muck at the edge of the breezeway, and sank in past my knees. Protecting Troah from her bloodthirsty family had nothing to do with some long-ago-sullied breeding program. No nagging questions about loyalty or belief. This was my survival. And Hallie's.

Across the pit, through the crowd of skimmers and gawking slaves, Troah held up one thin arm. The tattoo in the center of her palm was a black hole, blacker than the ebony walls.

"You know who I am." Her voice had changed. Adamant. Shrill. It echoed around the ring. "*Troah*. There has been a great change."

No one said anything.

I wallowed closer. Half-solid sand became chunks under my feet. A few heads turned accusingly toward Rasha.

"You shunned me when I could have given you guidance," said Troah. "I've raised myself from the dead to bring you the news of your annihilation."

"What's this, Rasha?" A voice I recognized—Kassim—cut through the silence. "You said you'd killed her."

Solid sand. I started to run, dodging between surprised

purebreds. Now I was close enough to see what had happened to her face.

Skin hung in folds, papery thin, wrinkled and raw. Her eyes gleamed, pearl white cataracts sheathing blank cornea. Her heat was tangible, and her smell hung in the air, thick and blunt as sex. All her revenges had boiled into a dense concentration washing one familiar taste after another under my tongue, all of them tinctures of Faraqui lies. In my mind I knew I was *not* her armor, *or* her sword, but my gut told me otherwise.

Rasha stepped out of the pack, into the quicksand mix. He floundered in it, trying to hold his robes above the muck and mud. He waded into more solid sand, but left his boots behind.

I stood between him and Troah, breathless, surrounded by her heat, sweating in it, protected by it.

He stopped, an arm's length away, and I saw the plain fear in his eyes. His expression was mirrored in every blue-striped face.

Rasha glanced at his tribe, and made a tentative gesture at his transformed sister. "Look at her," he said. "She's harmless. Her prophesies are wrong. Surely we can make a place for her now?"

He moved closer, barefoot, inside her circle.

I thought he might actually have the nerve to touch her.

Troah's voice hissed behind me. "How do we survive, brother?"

It was the tone she used with the slaves in the ring. He looked at her with disbelieving eyes, something between innocence and unforgivable naïveté. He had tried to save her and instead condemned her. There would be no mercy for him.

That understanding crept slowly over his face.

"Troah?" Less than a whisper.

"Rasha." Like a swear word.

Her metal taste was under my tongue. Her Hand pressed

into me, stabbing under my heart, through my shoulders and arms.

My palm burned, a scorching pain, radiating to each finger. I looked down and saw *her* tattoo, puddled and dark in the middle of my hand—as dangerous as any weapon.

Rasha stared at it too. His robe flapped in the dry wind. One corner touched my fingers. I caught it and pulled. The robe slipped off his shoulders. His hood fell away from his face. Blond hair spilled down his back.

Troah raised my arm without touching me and pushed my scalding Hand against his chest.

He didn't move, didn't push me away, just stood there, eyes wide, head and feet bare, as defenseless as any one of the fighters she'd killed. He blinked once. He took a breath, as though he had one more thing to say before she murdered him—but she'd run out of patience.

Her fury fell on him and her justification was ravenous. Rasha's last act of faith was to *believe* that he would die, not by her touch, but by mine. His heat rushed up my arm and across my eyes, like a blur of tears. The taste of him was strong spice. He went stiff, his face red, then ash-gray, and then airlessly blue. He fell away from me, onto his knees. He put his hands over his heart and collapsed in a heap of white clothes and long, light-colored hair.

I looked down at my hand. Her Mark was gone.

I looked up. The black walls spun around me and I realized I hadn't been breathing. I sank down next to Rasha's corpse, gasping over metal and curry.

Troah stepped out from behind me. She faced the rest of her family with blind white eyes and her voice rang off the walls.

"Your forces along the border of the Faraque are surrounded by Emirate warships. Your faith, your future, your history and heritage are gone. Your children will be hunted until the last one is killed. *Troah*. The Hand of Death has come."

From the clear blue sky, rain pattered into the ring, soft at first, then harder. It hammered at the skimmers, banging on the hulls. And then the pit began to tremble.

A handful of slaves broke and ran for their masters' skimmers. One by one, the Faraqui dashed after them.

Antigravs spat sand and water. Skimmers shot out of the ring, blundering upwards at dangerous angles. Otis shoved past a gaggle of purebred boys, struggled across the wet sand, and into a skimmer, seconds before the slave inside could shut him out.

Rain beat down on Troah, surrounded by the rush of escaping slavers. Her heat and fire had vanished. Her body loosened and her legs gave way. She slid to her knees, a heap of dirty clothing in the mud beside her brother's corpse. I stayed where I was, shivering, rubbing my unmarked palm.

When the last skimmer was gone, I saw Hallie splashing toward us through the pudding sand.

"Are you okay?" She peered at me and pulled on my hair. "Great show," she said. "Did you rehearse?"

The ring trembled again. "I think," I said, "the cistern's open. I think we can get out."

Hallie picked up Troah and tried to stand. The sand sucked her down, halfway to her knees. Troah hung in her arms, head lolled to one side, white hair straggling. Hallie shoved through the mire. I half walked, half swam, until we got to the crumbling edge of the breezeway.

I pushed hair out of my eyes and saw Althea.

She stared at Troah for a long incredulous second, and then she turned on me.

"Where's Leiban?" she demanded. "Did Otis take him? Have you seen him?" Her worry was so raw, so unpracticed, the expression seemed glued onto her face. "I left him downstairs. He was too sick to move. He couldn't get very far." She yanked at my shirt. "You look in the cisterns.

You"—she pointed at Hallie—"check the other side of the breezeway." She waited, panting, expectant.

Hallie and I glanced at each other. Behind us, sand shifted in the ring, slithering over itself, poised to drop into the very bowels of the arena.

Althea let out an awful cry and ran for the nearest stairs. Her footsteps faded into hollow echoes.

Hallie stared after her. "Who the hell does she think she is? The fucking queen of the universe?"

"The cisterns," I said. "Let's *go*."

Down in the corridor, only a few of the overhead lights were on. They gleamed off the dark surface of hip-deep water at uneven intervals, giving the hall a claustrophobic, tunnelish look. Althea's door was open, and we plunged past her flooded apartment. Her bed foundered in the middle of the dim room, half submerged, rocking gently in a flotsam of green shirts and underwear. There was no sign of Leiban.

We passed Rasse's empty cell, pushing our way deeper, past the Meeds' vacant cages.

Troah curled against Hallie's chest, even smaller and more frail, her feet trailing in the murky water. Her eyes were half open, but I didn't think she was conscious. I tried to judge her breathing as we sloshed along, one hand clamped over her wrist and the thready pulse under paper-thin skin.

"She feels cold," said Hallie. "She feels like a bag of ice."

"I need a scanner," I said. "And medicine. Antibiotics. Whatever Frei left here."

Hallie stopped under one weak yellow light while I shouldered the door inward. It moved in sluggish ripples, and bumped something in the dark room—the desk, I thought, wallowing freely instead of in its corner.

"Frenna," said Hallie. "Look."

Down the flooded hallway, the water was motionless.

"There's no current," said Hallie. "If the trap's open there should be some kind of current."

"The cistern's overflowing?" I said. "There won't be any air."

Hallie gnawed her lip. She pushed Troah into my arms. Soaking wet, she weighed nothing. "Stay here." She plowed away.

Water curled around my legs, brown and stinking, as I backed into the clinic with Troah. Behind me, someone coughed.

I jumped and the lights came on.

Leiban sat naked on the steel table, water up to his ankles. His skin was sickly transparent. His breathing rucked over mucus, deep in his lungs. All of the white metal cabinets were open, ransacked, as though he'd been trying to find something. Empty hypoderms were scattered over the steel table, still in their plastic sleeves.

I stood by the door, clutching Troah. "What're you doing?"

He coughed. "Looking for Thanas. Do you have any?"

I shook my head. "Althea's trying to find you."

"I know."

Something creaked behind the other door, the one that opened into the training room. I felt the air condense, a change in pressure inside my ears. The creak became a long, wailing groan.

"It's the ceiling in the training room," said Leiban. "It's been falling for a while, now."

Troah stirred in my arms. She unfolded herself like a spider and slid her thin legs into the water. I tried to steady her, but she shrugged me off.

Leiban took a shaky breath. The rest of the color went out of his face. Sweat filmed his throat, his forehead. "Troah?" he whispered.

She waded over to him, blind, her thin arms out, her

white hair lank against her dirty clothes. She stopped in front of him, not touching him.

Wet concrete spattered on my shoulders. I lurched toward the white cabinets. Troah would kill him, and he would let her—that was the hammering certainty in my chest—I didn't want to know how. I didn't want to watch.

I found a scanner in the first cabinet and a green plastic satchel. I shoved the scanner in and began stuffing the bag with antibiotics and loose packs of hypos—Frei's agenda as a packing list. Medicine for freed slaves.

"Leiban?"

Althea's voice cut through the groans of waterlogged concrete. I heard Leiban make a tiny gasp, and turned to see him cover his chest. Troah backed away from him and slid behind the open door, out of sight.

Althea splashed into the clinic, her dark hair stringing across her neck. She saw me and Leiban, but not Troah, and slogged over to drag him off the table. "Let's go! Let's go! Where's Hallie?" Her hands hovered around his face. "What's the matter with you?"

Wet, white muck showered down from the ceiling and into her hair. I edged around the table with the satchel. Troah stood silently behind the open door, oblivious to everything but Leiban's final moments.

Leiban gasped again. A single bead of red trickled out from under his palm, down his ribs. It dribbled over the coiling branches of blue trees, past the frightened, animal face of Rexidi.

Althea pushed his hand away.

A bloody five-fingered print covered the left side of his chest, just above his nipple. Tiny wounds, pinpricks from a hypoderm, seeped where Troah had plunged the needle between his ribs, a dozen pierces, through his heart.

Althea's disbelieving green eyes found me, pinned me in midstep. "You did this—"

"No," said Leiban. "I did."

Althea's mouth worked noiselessly. She finally saw Troah out of the corner of her eye and swung toward her.

Leiban grabbed her sleeve. "*I* did it, Althea."

She stared at him. Her hands flew over his bleeding chest. She caged his face with hard fingers, thumbs against his cheekbones. "You wouldn't. Not if you had any feeling— after fifteen years? You've got to have *some* feeling."

"I don't." He coughed. "I don't feel a thing." He rolled his eyes, glassy and fearless. "I never have. I never will."

Dust from the ceiling sifted into the water. I sidled away from the table, caught Troah around the waist and started pulling her toward the door. The splashing in the hallway was Hallie coming back.

A chunk of concrete cracked off the ceiling. It fell next to the steel table. Water sprayed over Leiban, into Althea's face.

It snapped her out of her unrequited stupor.

She saw Troah. And lunged.

I hauled Troah around the open door. One big step put us on the other side. I tried to shove her out ahead of me, but Althea was faster. She twisted one hand into Troah's white hair, wound the other in her shirt and slammed her against the wall.

Troah grunted out a lungful of air. Althea pushed her under the water and held her down.

The satchel was heavy where the scanner was, and I swung it at Althea as hard as I could. Its plastic weight cracked across the back of her skull. She let out a roar of amazement and reeled sideways, holding her head. Leiban slid off the steel table and hung onto her, arms locked around her waist, his bloodless face straining.

Troah came up spitting grit. I grabbed her, spun in the filthy wash and plowed into the hallway. Hallie was there. She plucked Troah out of the water and threw her over her shoulder.

Water heaved around us. I turned in time to see the shower of wet concrete inside the clinic. Bigger chunks pelted the steel table, the desk, the cabinets while Leiban and Althea spun in the center of the room. They were locked together, his face pressed into the hollow of her neck like a terrified child. She pummeled his back, eyes squeezed shut, mouth stretched in a futile, silent cry. A slab separated from the ceiling and tilted over the table. Hallie shoved me toward the training room stairs. I heard the clinic's ceiling split. I heard Althea's final, inarticulate bellow of denial.

The surge hurled us down the corridor to the backwash by the kitchen's wide doorway. Hallie crawled up the stairs, Troah over her shoulders. I paddled up after her, grabbing at the corroded handrail. There was a deep, bone-crushing *thoom*, and the concrete stairs shook like loose boards. The handrail sheared off the wall and I fell backwards, scrabbling at loose stone and gravel.

Hallie turned, her bulk framed against the light patch of daylight at the top of the stairs. Then even the light patch went dark. A wad of gray cloud, flecked with black, rushed across the open space. The water that was sucking me toward the clinic changed direction. Stones and sand and chunks of shattered concrete sloughed under me, shooting upwards, dragging me along, throwing me past Hallie and Troah, dropping me at the top of the stairs.

Hallie crawled up beside me, her blond hair slicked flat and dark, Troah clinging to her back. The middle of the ring was nothing more than a huge crater, bordered by a splatter of flaked concrete and viscous white mortar from far below. Black metal mesh lockers, twisted sogas and broken plumes disappeared slowly under caving runnels of sand.

Hallie gulped a couple of times. "There goes the training room."

The far side of the pit rumbled, and sand sloughed down

into the chasm. The sheer black wall was visible all the way down to what was left of the collapsed corridor. The door to Frei's room hung on its hinges. The couch and green dresser tumbled away, small as toys.

I got up, legs quivering. "The front gate's free-keyed. Isn't it?"

"It is," said Troah. "I can open it."

Across the disintegrating ring, metal wrenched in the breezeway. Chains shrieked through their channels as dropgates hurtled out of the dripping black ceiling and slammed against the floor. Flat black stones, careful, two-thousand-year-old Faraqui craftwork, jittered under me.

Hallie scrambled to her feet, jerky and pale. She hoisted Troah into her arms, wheeled and headed for the gate at a dead run.

I raced along behind her as broad sections of breezeway broke off and roared down. Water boiled up over sand and rock and broken concrete, foaming past Frei's room and the broken vault of the hallway ceiling.

The arch over the gate was battered and obviously unstable. Black mortar sifted out from between the uneven stones.

Hallie shoved Troah against the gate, and Troah groped for the palm lock.

"Got it—" She pressed. The mechanism clicked, but the lock didn't turn.

The rumble across the pit was part of the office. Desks and chairs tumbled down.

Hallie flinched. "Try again."

Troah tried the other hand, the marked one.

"The lock's not accepting," I said. "It thinks you're still . . ." I dug the scanner out of the satchel. The dark screen flickered into a dim yellow grid. I pointed it at Troah.

A red line for life signs. It was low, crawling along the bottom of the graph. "There's no . . ." I stopped. A green line surfaced next to it, the Viral indicator, parallel to her life signs, pulsing with them, exactly the same as last night.

"For God's sake, Frenna," panted Hallie. "Is she free, or not?"

"She should still be Failing—" I couldn't begin to explain it. Now there was a third line, a yellow one. I didn't need a diagnostic to know what it was. *Virasi Lymphoma*, woven into Troah's metabolism, keeping her alive, combining with the Virus in some weird new mix.

"She's not free?" demanded Hallie. "After all that, she's still like us?"

"I'm the Hand of Death," said Troah. "I've never been like you." She wrapped her fingers around the cold iron bars and shook the gate. Dark mortar hailed into the straggles of her white hair. Behind us, another section of the breezeway avalanched into the rubble below.

Troah rocked the gate, back and forth. Metal squealed on metal. A piece of the stone arch skittered down, breaking into pieces as it hit the ground.

I peered up at the dark arch. Stones ground together like teeth. Black mortar fell in clumps. Wet, gritty muck smacked my hair, my face.

Troah shoved blindly at the gate. The hinges groaned. I hung the scanner over my shoulder and wound my fingers into the ancient filigree. Troah wrenched the gate back, and I wrenched with her. Stones crumbled off the arch. A sharp piece hit me in the neck and bounced off my leg. I kept my eyes on the scorched plaza, the blackened skimmers, the wreck of the world outside, framed by iron bars. I could hear sections of the breezeway roaring into the canyon of rubble below. Some of it was very close. I wanted to look back, to see if Hallie had fallen silently away, but I didn't dare.

The hinges scraped in their stone fittings, loose, but then, the whole arena was loose. By the time we worked the hinges free, if we could manage that, the arch might be too weak to support itself. Troah grunted next to me. The gate swung forward with enough force to pull our feet off the ground. She hauled the other way and the gate moved faster, wider than it should have. The palm lock creaked. I looked past Troah and saw Hallie, fists locked around the bars. Her muscles knotted as she slewed the gate forward, swung it back, hauling on the iron until it bent. We hung on the gate, inside the breezeway, weightless at apogee for one long second. Then Hallie heaved forward, charging at the plaza, hands clamped on the bars, arms straight out. The gate swung outwards, squealing, bulging over the plaza's black paving stones. It stuttered in the dark air, and the palm lock snapped like dry bone. The gate sprung open, and we fell into the deserted city.

EPILOGUE

The boy held out the plastic card, trying to give it to me. It was a stolen cash voucher with altered identification. "We still don't know your name." His voice trembled with emotion, and exhaustion.

"It's not important." I got up off the floor. His girlfriend, free after a long struggle, dozed on the damp mattress, motionless except for her breathing.

Our fourth night since we'd left the ring, our third in this wet basement. I'd lost track of how many I'd freed.

Word had spread, fast, about me, and Hallie, and Troah, here on the outskirts of the city, where everything smelled of wet smoke. Now that the Faraqui had been driven away, the city was starting to grope its way back to normal. It wasn't safe for us to stay.

Hallie got up from the broken armchair, the only real piece of furniture in the cellar of this burned-out house.

She smoothed her long slicker over her new clothes—free clothes—and took the voucher. "All we have to do is designate an account?" she said to the boy. "You're sure it'll work?"

The boy nodded. He'd belonged to a banker, he'd said, and his clothes seemed to verify that. He was dressed like someone's overindulged son. Now he pushed his arms into his fancy suit jacket and brushed mud away from his stylish shoes.

I tucked a blanket around the girl's shoulders. "Take her home," I said to the boy. "Keep her warm. When she's better, you'll have to get her to a doctor and have the cancer taken care of."

"I'll bring her back to you," said the boy.

"Don't," said Hallie. "We're leaving. We'll be gone by tomorrow morning."

The boy's eyes widened. "I can't take her to anyone else," he whispered. "They'll know—they'll *know*."

"Cut her collar off," I said. "Make sure they don't see her brands. What she looks like is the only thing that matters. No one'll ask any questions."

"But—" said the boy.

"You have to believe me," I said. "The only way for either of you to survive is to believe me."

On the other side of the dark, damp cellar, Troah sat up on her own mattress and stretched. Her long blue dress coiled around her ankles. Her white hair writhed around her face and her blind white eyes. "You're done?"

I nodded. She couldn't see it. "Yes."

"We can get on a ship now?"

I glanced at Hallie. "Can we?"

"Yes." Hallie tucked the voucher into the breast pocket of her slicker with the rest of the money. She turned to the boy in his fancy suit. "Can you remember everything you've seen tonight?"

The boy nodded, trying again to decide if he recognized her.

Hallie pulled the slicker's hood up and jerked it over her hair, short as ever, but dyed black as of two nights ago.

I opened the box of slapneedles. What I'd milked out of Troah's lymph system was a thin gray liquid. Not exactly Virevir. Not exactly an inoculation against the Virus, but something her body had manufactured that acted like both. She was a virtual reservoir of curative fluids—as long as she would let me stick her with needles.

I gave the boy a hypoderm, sealed and sterile in a plastic sleeve. He took it, wrapped it in a satin handkerchief and carefully put it in his pocket.

I knelt next to the girl and checked the scanner one last time. Her life signs were framed by standard medical information, and of course, the cancer. There was no trace of the Virus left in her.

The boy held her hand, stroking her fingers. "There was something else I wanted to know. If you don't mind?"

They all asked the same thing. If I wore free clothes, or slave whites, they knew what I was, and every one of them had asked.

"I don't mind."

The boy flushed a little. "Aren't you Jatahn?"

Hallie stiffened, like she always did. "It's *really* none of your—"

"It's all right," I said. "I am."

"I thought . . . we were always told that . . . your people were different. I guess that's not true."

"It is true," I said. "It always has been."

In her long blue dress, Troah could pass for harmless, but the illusion didn't last long. The ship's steward had tried to be polite, holding her arm instead of letting her pick her blind way down the corridor to our cabin. He'd been nice, even when she snatched her arm away and shrieked at him. Hallie was too nervous to do anything about it, preoccupied with how her new clothes fit—a gray shirt with a gray vest, black linen pants and leather shoes. So, it was my job.

"Just me, D'sha," I said to Troah, and took her Hand. The steward, in slave whites, with the liner's blue insignia over his heart, dropped behind me with transparent relief. Hallie tipped him at the cabin door, since she was handling the money, and shut it before he had time to smile and thank her.

I sat Troah on one of the beds. The cabin was small, but not microscopic, like we'd thought third class would be. It was carpeted, with two beds, a cot and a john in the closet. There was no holoree, but that was fine. The war was over. The Faraqui who hadn't been captured were on the run. Emirate ships were all over the Faraque—what the Emirate was calling the New Frontier. Breeding populations on the slavers' isolated worlds were being liberated by the thousands. On the 'ree, they stood around their little huts, gaping at Emirate troopers. One day they would end up like me and mine.

Or maybe not.

Troah.

Hallie stood by the window, arms crossed. The white curtain was the only homey touch in the industrial beige cabin. Outside, Traja's gray, cloud-covered bulk filled half the sky.

"Last time I saw Traja from up here, we were off to fight at the Regionals," she said.

Troah turned her face toward the sound of Hallie's voice. "You miss the ring," she said. "You miss it so much, you'll be dreaming about it for the rest of your life."

"Shut up," said Hallie.

Watching Hallie as a free woman was like standing by while she struggled with the basics of swimming in the middle of a whirlpool. Nothing in the ring had trained her for the casual determination she needed to smile past a dozen disinterested emigration officials at Traja's ground station. Troah's bland arrogance was genuine enough. To anyone who cared to look, I was Troah's property. This escape seemed practically routine for me, but Hallie had been terrified. Almost speechless. Discovering how scared she was made her even more scared. Troah's handicap was nothing compared to Hallie's sudden plunge in courage.

I sat down on the cot. With enough time, I kept telling myself, Troah would become another harmless, crazy old lady. Hallie would mellow into one more tall, muscular woman in the crowd, smiling and holding my hand. With any luck, both of them would be used to their new lives by the time I Failed.

Until then, I had stopped trying to pretend that the three of us would live happily ever after.

When they were asleep, I put in a call to Renee. At the ground station on Traja, there had been a government kiosk set up to reunite refugees with their families—and their wayward property. They were brisk and efficient, and more than happy to tell me where Renee had ended up—on Newhall, deep in the safety of Emirate space. At some tiny morning hour, the ship's steward woke me up to say that the contact was complete, and would I take the connection.

I turned on the monitor and saw Martine. Her pale face was still thin from her Failure. She looked as exhausted as Hallie.

"Hello," I said, and didn't know what to say next.

Neither did she. "Frenna?" she said finally. "Where are you?"

"On a ship," I said, "coming from Traja."

She frowned at the dark cabin and lowered her voice. "With Olney?"

It felt as though I hadn't seen her in years. "I got away from him," I said, "I got away from all of that."

"You ran?" she whispered. "Are you all right?"

I nodded. I put my hand against the cool screen, along the side of her face. "I'm free, Martine," I said, and had to smile and say it again. "Martine, I believe I'm free."

Hugo Award-Winning Author

BEN BOVA

"Not only at the forefront of hard SF writers,
but one who can write a novel of character
with the best of them." —Orson Scott Card

SAM GUNN FOREVER
79726-7/$5.99 US/$7.99 Can

MOONRISE
78697-4/$6.99 US/$8.99 Can

MOONWAR
78698-2/$6.99 US/$8.99 Can

COLONY
79315-6/$6.99 US/$8.99 Can

Ray Bradbury

SOMETHING WICKED THIS WAY COMES
72940-7/$5.99 US/$7.99 Can

QUICKER THAN THE EYE
78959-0/$5.99 US/$7.99 Can

GOLDEN APPLES OF THE SUN
AND OTHER STORIES
73039-1/$10.00 US/$14.50 Can

A MEDICINE FOR MELANCHOLY
AND OTHER STORIES
73086-3/$10.00 US/$14.50 Can

I SING THE BODY ELECTRIC!
AND OTHER STORIES
78962-0/$10.00 US/$14.50 Can

And in Hardcover

THE MARTIAN CHRONICLES
97383-9/$15.00 US/$20.00 Can

THE ILLUSTRATED MAN
97384-7/$15.00 US/$20.00 Can